THUNDER
IN
HEAVEN

THUNDER
IN
HEAVEN

Armine von Tempski

OX BOW PRESS
WOODBRIDGE, CONNECTICUT

Cover painting by Cecelia Rodriquez

Copyright 1942, copyright renewed 1970

1990 reprint by
Ox Bow Press
P.O. Box 4045
Woodbridge, CT 06525

Library of Congress Cataloging-in-Publication Data
Von Tempski, Armine, 1892–1943.
Thunder in heaven / Armine von Tempski.
p. cm.
ISBN 0–918024–75–7. —ISBN 0–918024–74–9 (pbk.)
I. Title.
PS3543.O647T45   1990
813'.52—dc20   89–78472
                                                           CIP

The paper used in this book meets the guidelines for permanence
and durability of the Committee on Production Guidelines for Book
Longevity of the Council on Library Resources.

Printed in the United States of America

To my
beloved DAD, LOUIS VON TEMPSKY
and to my
beloved HUSBAND, ALFRED BALL

———

And to all those
whom the Gods have saluted with
THUNDER IN HEAVEN!

THUNDER
IN
HEAVEN

1

APRIL WILDE stood in the liner's prow, her fluent body straining forward, as though the flight of her spirit could pull the ship more swiftly through the warm purple sea. In spite of the expensive simplicity of her white silk sports dress, she was as airy as apple blossoms, simple as earth, and as exciting as wine. Hair like fire and honey waved back from her forehead, rain-gray eyes were wide open and candid, and there was a gallantry about her dainty and resolute chin.

A pale daffodil dawn was creeping into the east, retreating stars slowly withdrawing their light from the earth. Gunmetal and platinum clouds massed above the horizon ahead, givers of recent rain. At any instant now she might glimpse the shadowy shapes of the Islands soaring up from the sea.

Like a person satisfying a long hunger, she drew the air streaming against her face deep into her lungs. It held the loved scent of Hawaii: the fragrance of forests growing out of wet, wild earth, the tang of salt water breaking on clean beaches and lava headlands, the sweetness of ripe guavas blown over by wind, and the rich odor of sugar cane in tassel.

She was vaguely conscious of slanted funnels behind her, pouring out smoke, tiers and tiers of decks, hurrying sailors. In two hours at most they would dock. Her mind lingered briefly and fondly on the tree-smothered, colorful town of Honolulu, then soared like a homing bird to the proud green land of Kona, wedged in between monster volcanoes on the island of Hawaii.

During the two years at school just outside New York, she had felt without cessation the magnetic tug, the mysterious insistent beckoning of the land where she had been born and had spent the first sixteen years of her life.

Glossy coffee plantations, jade-green fields of cane, rain-soaked, luxuriant forests, the black scars of old lava flows, the awesome shapes of volcanoes thrusting at the sky were lodged in her bones, printed into the million cells of her body. The rumble of her father's sugar mill, the majestic dissonances of the Pacific, the shuffle of laborers' feet going out at dawn and coming in at dusk, landshells singing in the forests at night, the rustle of cattle sliding through brush on the rough, steep slopes of Hualalai, had never been extinguished by the louder, more insistent noises of civilization. Like any young person on tiptoe inside, she had flung herself into new ways of eating, living, and thinking, but behind the intriguing pattern of new days she had sensed some fundamental lack that nothing she saw, or did, could ever quite obliterate.

Already a wild free feeling was stealing along her bones and dusting her skin. Ahead, cloud masses were breaking up. A long spear of sunlight pierced them, flung across the sea, and day leaped out of the east, lacquering the deep cornflower blue of the ocean with copper and gold. The liner dipped her bow solemnly into the water, as if silently saluting the recurrent mystery of light being born out of darkness. Then a thrill, like a thin, hot silver wire, pierced her as she glimpsed the shapes of islands, secret, withdrawn, rising with splendid abruptness from the sea. Tears stung her eyes, her throat ached. Lovingly, her lips shaped the names of mountain summits visible above dispersing clouds.

"Mauna Kea . . . Mauna Loa . . . Haleakala."

Below the cloud line, extravagant slopes plunged down to meet the blue of the Pacific. Throwing back her head she held out her arms as if trying to sweep the towering blue shapes to her heart, then like a person under a spell softly chanted the names of each island as it rose to her view. Names like battle cries, names like songs.

"Hawaii . . . Maui . . . Oahu . . . Molokai."

"Are you—nuts?"

[4]

April wheeled. A dozen feet away, half concealed by a winch, a tall man with tightly folded arms leaned against stacked freight boxes. She got a swift impression of a lean torso, long legs, and broad shoulders. Fiery red hair was brushed back from a bold forehead, a chin thrust belligerently at the world, but the man's eyes, blue as Arctic ice, had a glassy, far-away expression.

"Why do you think I'm—nuts?" She chose his word deliberately. Resentment at being observed in a moment when she fancied she was alone surged through her.

"You were—making such strange sounds."

Fiery rose scorched her cheeks.

"You're rude!"

He gave a short mirthless laugh.

"What's funny?" April demanded hotly.

"Everything. Life. Living. Seeing a girl standing in the bow of a ship holding out her arms and—"

"I thought I was alone. I was sending my Aloha—my love, ahead of me to Hawaii, where I was born," April retorted, then wondered why she bothered to explain.

"You mean those bits of land sticking up out of water stir you to your—soul?" His voice mocked the last word.

"Yes, Hawaii—"

"The Hawaiian Islands are made of earth, rocks, and vegetation like any other land."

"I know, but they're put together differently. The Islands are alive. They have lava running in their veins. They *get* people. Wait, you'll see. In Hawaii you *live!*" She flung the words at him like a challenge.

"To use a slang phrase," the man said, "I'm not to be 'had' by anything, any more." Something about the way he held himself made April think of a proud thoroughbred harnessed to a garbage wagon. "As for living—to hell with it. Life lays traps for people—" He broke off.

April gazed into the glowing east, but even when she was not looking at him she was acutely and irritatingly aware of his presence. Although every word he had spoken was resentful, she liked the deep male quality of his voice.

"Have you been to Hawaii before?" she asked, without looking at him.

"No."

"Why are you going there?"

"God knows."

"Look." She turned her gray eyes toward him, the warm kindness of her nature stirred. "You're tearing to pieces inside over something, aren't you?"

"So what?"

"I'm so happy about getting home I'd like to give a *luau*—feast for the whole world, one that would never end. Is there anything . . . can't I—"

"Toss a crust to the beggar-in-the-street?" he inquired coldly.

April's face grew white. "You're horrid. Here, I begin to be sorry for you, want to help you, heaven knows why, because you're boorish. But even so one can't help wondering—"

"Take your mind off me!" His voice was rough.

April stared at him curiously. A man like this would stand out in any company but she could not recall seeing him once during the voyage.

"You've spoiled my beautiful first moments seeing Hawaii," she said, "broken something precious that—"

"Skip it, I'll clear out."

With elaborate deliberation he straightened up, then lurched slightly. April's eyes widened, her nostrils caught the faint, stale smell of whisky.

"You've been drinking," she accused.

"Yes, all I can hold. For days, weeks, months maybe."

"How hateful to watch day come *drunk!*" She stared off into the splendor filling the east. "Dawns are sacred to me, especially in Hawaii."

"They're vile to me. Anywhere!"

He started off, tacking a little. April watched him go, outraged. Then, resolutely she determined to put him out of her mind and

[6]

surrendered herself to the joy of returning to Hawaii. It was quiet, except for the usual sounds of the ship. Light poured out of the east, blue water flowed with pleasant rustlings against the hull of the liner.

By degrees her tranquillity returned. Beautiful to feel the Trade wind against her face, to gaze at familiar headlands whose dearness had been intensified by two years of absence. Holding out her left hand she admired a square-cut four-carat diamond on the third finger. A glow of youthful tenderness stole through her, thinking of her fiancé, Dale Hancock. Their engagement had been a last minute decision, outgrowth of a week-end party at his mother's home on Long Island. They weren't to be married for a year. Dale had to finish college. It was a relief to let her mind rest on him after her stormy encounter of a few minutes before.

When she met Dale she had been slated for six months in Europe, her parents' reward for a straight "A" record at school. The trip abroad was to have been followed by a brief visit to New England relatives, finished by a winter and spring in New York. And instead she was heading home. An elfish smile curved her lips. In a family such as hers, which moved through each day with mechanical precision, any upset of schedule savored of a bombshell. She wondered how her father and mother had received the radio which she had sent off two days previously. She hadn't informed them of her engagement, time enough for that later. She had merely stated that she was on the Pacific instead of the Atlantic. As yet there'd been no reply, but one would surely come before the boat docked.

She inspected her diamond thoughtfully. Dale had not understood her sudden impulse to go home, but had been finely considerate about it. His only protest had been, "But you'll be away from me a year, instead of six months." She had nodded, a far-away feeling in her heart, realizing the impossibility of conveying to Mainlanders the passionate love which white people who live there feel for Hawaii. Perhaps because of her slim fairness, Dale always treated her as if she were spun glass, but in reality she was tempered steel.

Dale was such an amusingly delightful product of civilization.

[7]

There were governors, generals, financiers, and statesmen perched in his family tree. He had a becoming, costly tan acquired from yachting and polo. He knew all the head waiters in the smart restaurants in New York by their first names. His dinner clothes always looked blacker and whiter than anyone else's. Newspapers ate up his activities. Hardly a Sunday rotogravure was without pictures of him charging down polo fields, being best man at ultra-ultra weddings, host at costly suppers, standing at the wheel of his sloop with scuppers in foam and white sails bulging overhead.

After her father and mother became adjusted to the thought of her living away from Hawaii they would be all for the match, so there was nothing to fear in that direction. The main bone of contention would be her unexpected return home when her parents had planned on Europe instead. In mid-flight as it were she had doubled on her course and was hurrying back to Kona, and the things of Kona which she would never have again permanently after she married Dale.

She looked at the morning walking with sparkling feet across the sea, allowing her mind to drift forward. Her mother wouldn't be down to meet her, for Mrs. Wilde fancied herself an invalid. Her father wouldn't come; it was grinding season and the sugar mill was running day and night. But they'd send someone, Ainslee the bookkeeper, probably.

"Miss Wilde."

She turned. A steward was approaching with a sealed envelope. "Radio for you," he said, smiling.

Swooping on it, April ripped it open.

ALOHA MY CHILD STOP WILL BE ON THE WHARF TO GREET YOU
STOP TOMORROW WE GO HOME TO KONA   KAUKA

Kauka! She might have known he would meet her. How Dale would chuckle, how her smart erstwhile schoolmates would titter if they knew her wholehearted worship for the old plantation doctor who had brought her into the world. A lovable, shabby part-Hawaiian, brown-eyed Kauka had never looked condemningly on

[8]

anyone. He was too sane to judge his fellow humans, and when he smiled the most abject heart was warm. His swift kindness, his flashes of fun, his understanding of motives that pushed people into seemingly unwise acts, gave stability and riches to days as they marched on.

The sprawling old house which the plantation provided him had been her real home. Mamo, his daughter, had been and still was her best friend. Loki, his sumptuous wife, had been her real mother. . . .

A pang of excitement jabbed through her. In forty-eight hours she would be back in Kona with these three people who had helped her to find the full flavor of living. And now in less than two hours she would see Kauka's smiling, fatherly face, hear him calling, "Aloha, April, Aloha, my child. I am glad you are home."

"Any answer, Miss Wilde?"

April started, realizing that the steward was still there.

"No," she smiled, "the answer will be—on the wharf."

She re-read the radiogram and sighed happily. To all practical purposes she was home. Her eyes caressed rugged, colorful headlands, forests of a thousand greens tapestrying the sides of steep valleys which seemed to guard secrets of the ancient earth. After the restrained, careful landscapes outside of New York, the tidy fields, the gentle contours of neatly folded hills to come back to— Hawaii. Her heart gave a wild throb, kicking her ribs like an exultant horse. Then, for some obscure reason, she wondered what Kauka would have thought of her red-headed companion who cherished a wholesale resentment for his fellow men and insulted the purity of dawn with insobriety.

2

AS quarantine inspection drew toward an end, invisible excitement injected itself into the atmosphere, intensifying the tempo of people's words and actions. Passengers who had been passed fell out of line, collecting in groups to re-pledge voyage friendships and make after-landing plans. Snatches of conversation, like brittle sparklers from Roman candles, whizzed away and sputtered into space.

"See you at the Nuuanu Country Club this afternoon. Tiptop golf course. . . . Dinner at Mokazuki's tonight. I'll lead you to lobster you'll never forget. . . . Remember, the Moana for dancing. We'll meet about ten-thirty. . . . We'll run you around the island Sunday. . . . Swell passage, wasn't it? Grand crowd. I could take another week of it."

Thord Graham grimaced. Jargon. Jabber. He held his red head at a defiant angle but was resentfully aware of curious stares directed at him. He didn't want peoples' minds fastened upon him. There had been enough of that during the months immediately behind.

Then his face went bleak as he saw the khaki-clad Federal doctor, wearing the insignia of Esculapius on each side of his collar, coming down the line with the Fort doctor, clad in tropic whites.

Passengers stared landwards impatiently. Stewards stacked smart hatboxes, golfclubs, valises, beside cabin doors. Officers walked by briskly. A girl took tremulous farewell of a voyage sweetheart. Two women, obviously schoolteachers fresh from the Mainland, began pointing out landmarks to each other which they had seen in tourist folders. A middle-aged couple had a brief, spicy spat.

The squat, beamy launch which had brought out the doctors, waited importantly below the gangway. Lazy swells, trailing long, gauzy manes, traveled past, to break in white curling splendor against the reef. Three surf-riders, diminished by distance to pygmy proportions, caught a wave and sped triumphantly landwards.

Diamond Head, with its fluted sides and sharply chiseled ridges, stretched out in the sun like a sphinx with its head sunk between its paws, keeping everlasting watch over the Pacific. Cocoanut groves moved rich, glittering foliage above the small crescent of Waikiki Beach. Flame trees flaunted vermilion umbrellas, sapphire-blue jacarandas, rosy coral trees, golden showers, made splotches of color against tangles of solid green. Beauty of sky and sea such as only islands know, lay upon everything and an almost audible symphony rose from smoking reefs, verdant soil, and high-piled clouds massed above the horizon.

April headed for a vacant spot at the rail, dodging among milling passengers. A gaunt woman with an authoritative chin halted her. "Remember me to your mother. I do hope that her health's better. It's tragic to be confined to the house as she's been these past years."

"I'll tell Mother you asked after her, Mrs. Hall," April replied, starting again for the side of the ship.

"Family meeting you?" asked a lanky youth, with washed-out blue eyes gazing down an adenoidal nose.

"No," April answered blithely.

"Then let me—"

"Kauka'll be there. He radioed," she retorted.

The youth shot his neck out of his collar like a gamecock on the defensive. "Kauka your beau?" he asked.

April's laughter chimed like bells. "Kauka's our plantation doctor," she explained. "I'll introduce you. He's tops!"

"Hi—April!" A lusty Islander, back from Yale for the summer, bounded up. "What are the chances of taking you dancing tonight?"

"Not one in a million, Hal," she laughed, indicating the diamond on her left hand.

"Phooey to that," Hal returned, brandishing a big arm at the long, green island basking contentedly in fiercely blue water. "After you've been home a week, Dale'll begin to dim. Why, already the chaps I week-ended with and played polo with are just— mist. *Hawaii no ka oe!*" And he made an extravagant gesture of flinging an arm around the island.

"When I think of seeing Mauna Loa, Kona—" April's voice went almost tremulous.

"And then you tell yourself you're going to marry a Mainlander and live in New York!" Hal jeered, giving her a playful, affectionate shove. "If I don't make the inter-island polo team this summer, I'll come and visit you in Kona. Till then—Aloha!" and he went barging off.

April leaned her elbows on the polished railing and turned her back determinedly on everyone. She wanted to be alone to soak in the full flavor of this homecoming. She realized that for two years she'd been starved for beauty that was splashed about in a wholesale way. She had hungered for violent colors, wide distances which seemed to hold eternity in their core. Here it was again, spaces of sea and sky, beauty reckless and extravagant, which went to a person's head like strong wine.

Something inside her which had been leashed was quickening, waking to life. She glanced down at her diamond in a youthful, satisfied way. What fun to come home, engaged! Then she wondered how, if Dale had been at her side, he would react to scenes that seemed to shake every atom of her body out of a drugged sleep.

Steaming onward, the ship turned majestically into the narrow passage of the harbor proper. Buildings and roofs soared out of massed tree tops. Ships, docks, and warehouses came into view. Liners and freighters from all over the world were discharging and taking on cargo. Blue sampans, manned by squat, knotty Japanese, chugged past to disgorge their loads at the fish-market pier.

As the vessel slid along the guiding arm of the breakwater,

flocks of diving boys sprang off the docks into the sea, their brown bodies flashing and turning in the sun. They struck out and swam toward the towering shape sliding through the water.

The liner began warping into the wharf. People on shore, their arms loaded with garlands of flowers, jammed forward. Passengers called over the railing to loved ones down to meet them. The band played joyously. Shouted orders from the ship, cries of greeting, of laughter, filled the air. Then sonorous voices, singing in Hawaiian, swelled up, as if the island was calling out welcome to those returning home, and to strangers landing on its warm, hospitable shores for the first time.

The rich, strong odor of bagged brown sugar stacked roof-high in sections of the dock, waiting for shipment to California, drifted up. The sharp, salty smell of *shoyu* in wooden kegs, mingled with the scents of tar, rope, sunshine, flowers, coffee, and copra.

April hung over the rail, like a horse snuffing its home pasture, while her eyes searched the faces below, brown faces, yellow faces, white faces, turned up like cups waiting to be filled. In spite of her smart attire, her short, indeterminate nose and her lips, dainty, loving and unfinished, branded her a child. Sunlight spun flecks and flames of gold in her hair. Her slight body threw out a gladness that was almost a tangible fragrance. Then suddenly she began waving the hat she held in her hand.

"Kauka!" she cried. "Kauka!"

Thord, a few yards and several persons away, glanced around like a person struck unexpectedly by a lash. The sheer joy in her high young voice laced across his mind. Folding his arms more tightly across his chest, and pressing them on the railing, he stared at the crowd below with unseeing eyes, as if he were trying to entomb himself within himself. But it was impossible to shut out her voice.

"Kauka! Kauka!"

She kept jumping up and down, hair flying, her face lighted.

Inarticulate anger tore Thord. Need she make such a confounded noise, such a spectacle of herself? Did she think that she was the only person aboard who had friends or families down to meet them? What right had she, had anyone, to splash joy over the landscape in such a wholesale way? Then, recalling their encounter in the bow at dawn, he felt ashamed. She had attempted to pass on to him, a stranger, something of what she felt and he . . . A flush burned along the roots of his flaming hair.

His eyes rested on her. Her fresh youngness made him feel more soiled. Her joy in life drove home the fact that for him life no longer held any joy. Then, through the shouts of sailors flinging mooring ropes to longshoremen on the wharf, through bursts of singing, cries of greeting from ship and land, came an answering hail.

"Aloha, April! Aloha, my child!"

The resonant quality of the voice penetrated to Thord's consciousness. Cadences were in it, like a sustained surf. Automatically, his eyes followed the beam of it until his eyes located its source.

A rather thick-set man of medium height, who obviously had Polynesian blood in his make-up, was waving a mass of garlands. Middle-aged and without physical distinction, he stood out from the crowd on the wharf in some arresting way. He had a wide, flexible, expressive mouth and winged eyebrows. His head thrust forward slightly from massive shoulders, yet about him there seemed to be the simplicity, the joyousness, the freshness of very young children.

Their eyes met and an incomprehensible thing happened. Something in Thord and something in the dark-skinned man standing on the crowded wharf below met and merged. It was over in an instant. For some reason which had no sound justification, Thord wanted that man of alien race for his friend.

He glanced away, but after an instant his eyes found their way back to the brown face below. Thord saw an obviously important American business man come up and clap him on the shoulder, pausing for a few words of talk. A thin Chinaman with a few straggling gray hairs on his chin stopped, chatted and moved on. A fragile Japanese woman, carrying a lump of a white child on her arm, halted to address him. He smiled, took the child off her arm, and tossed it on his shoulder. The Japanese wiped her warm face, then taking the child's hand began waving and gesturing at the long line of faces hanging over the rail. "Baby-san, Baby-san, there Mama-san, number three from post."

The gangway down, people began streaking for the wharf. Others swarmed onto the ship to greet and decorate returning loved ones with garlands. The band played exultantly. Tears, laughter, embraces, cries of delight filled the morning.

Although he did not look around, Thord was conscious that the man whose eyes had met his so strangely was hurrying aboard. The girl called April flew at the man and they embraced in the extravagant Island way.

"Oh, Kauka, Kauka, how dear of you to come!"

"I am happy you are home, April. You are almost, but not quite" —his voice went laughing off—"a young lady!"

"It's heavenly to see you, Kauka," she cried, her eyes spilling over.

He began loading her with leis of strange, heavily scented flowers. As though he had eyes in the back of his head, Thord got it all. Suddenly the ship was emptied of people except for the pair behind him. His steward came up.

"Shall I take your bags ashore, sir, and call a taxi?"

"Wait a bit."

"Expecting friends to meet you?" the steward asked.

"I've never been here before." Thord said, his voice rough and sore in his throat. "Hell, I may as well shove off." Turning, he came to a full stop.

Facing him was the man he had singled out on the wharf. Dark eyes looked into his bloodshot blue ones. "I overheard. This is your first landing in Honolulu," the man said simply. "Aloha—my love to you, and greetings from Hawaii."

Taking one of the three garlands still hanging over his arm, he lifted it. "Bend down," he ordered, smiling. Thord obeyed mechanically, and Kauka placed a garland about Thord's neck, then a smaller one around the crown of his hat. Thord went hot and then cold under the eyes gazing into his.

[15]

"Any idea where you'll be staying?" the man asked, as if they had known each other for years.

"I have no plans."

"I'd recommend the Young Hotel for a day or two. It's centrally located, accessible to everything. Later in the day, we'll drop by and drive you around to see some of the sights."

"That's kind of you, but—"

"I don't know your name," the man laughed.

"Thord Graham."

"Aloha, Graham. This is April Wilde—"

"We've met, after a fashion," April said, in remote tones.

The atmosphere crackled with hostility. Kauka did not seem aware of it.

"Well, my name is Stephen Kamuela Haines, but everybody calls me Kauka. I have to buy some supplies for my hospital this morning"—his face lighted—"but shall we pick you up this afternoon, around three?"

"You are—a doctor?" Thord exclaimed.

"I try to be. I work for April's father. He owns plantations and a ranch on the island of Hawaii. I need equipment, a new hospital, for that matter." His eyes caught April's and, from being aloof, the girl's grew soft.

Thord started at Kauka as if he were a specter, then slashed off. His steward, waiting near by, called after him, but Thord did not stop. It was clear he wanted to get away from Kauka, from everyone. Shaking his head, the steward snatched up Thord's bags and streaked after him.

"He's an odd one," Kauka remarked, removing his hat in an unhurried, thoughtful way, to run his fingers through his graying hair. "But he's stuff. I spotted him from the wharf."

April related their encounter in the bow. Kauka's eyes grew concerned. "He must be in trouble of some sort. I feel uneasy about him. Come." Tucking April's arm through his, he signed at her room-boy to follow with the luggage and charged down the gangway.

"What are you going to do?" April panted, burying her nose

rapturously in masses of gardenias, white jasmine, and glistening silvery ginger blossoms heaped about her neck.

"I'm not sure," Kauka murmured, his eyes fixed on Thord's head visible above shifting throngs of people. "When a man feels as that young fellow is feeling, he's prime to do something he'll regret afterwards."

"Why should you care, what does it matter to you?" April began, darting a look at Kauka's face. Then her lips closed. On it was an expression she knew well, the expression he wore when he came home to an always overflowing household with another ailing waif, which Loki must, largely, care for . . . half apologetic but, behind, an immense, unswerving sense of responsibility to the unfortunate.

Fellow passengers, Island friends called out, trying to detain them as they hurried toward the wide steps leading down to the street. Kauka brushed them aside, signaling warmly that they'd see them later. April kept pace beside him. Natural resentment for Thord's behavior that morning mingled with interest and curiosity at Kauka's reaction to Thord's personality.

Lei vendors of both sexes, swaying masses of beautiful garlands, surged forward as they emerged from the dock. Kauka spoke to them in Hawaiian and they fell back.

"There he is." Kauka gestured to Thord's tall figure on the far side of the street. His panting steward had just overtaken him and set his bags on the sidewalk. A taxi, driven by a lounging Hawaiian, drew up. In the clear air, above the sounds of dispersing cars and people, voices were plainly audible.

"Driver, take my bags to the nearest hotel," Thord ordered.

"Young Hotel most best and most near," the driver announced, getting deliberately out of his car.

"I don't want to go to the Young," Thord retorted, stressing the last word.

"Blaisdell not so high-style, but good place."

"That'll do. Take them to the Blaisdell and check them. I want to walk around for a while." Thord thrust a bill into the man's brown hand.

[17]

Kauka beckoned to a lei vendor. He sprinted over, swaying long red and white carnation leis temptingly.

"Trail that newcomer, Moku," Kauka instructed in Hawaiian. "When he checks in at the Blaisdell, phone me. I'll be at—" He gave the Nuuanu Valley address of April's aunt.

"*Maiki*—good," Moku replied. Thrusting his leis into his wife's already overflowing hands, he strolled across the street. Thord watched the taxi drive off, passed his hand across his eyes, saw the flowers dangling around his neck and with a sharp jerk, snapped the wreath and dropped it on the street. Then he struck off. Moku waited until a discreet distance was between them, signed at Kauka, and followed his man in a careless, leisurely fashion.

April's fingers dug into Kauka's arm. "He—broke the lei you gave him. How—how horrible! I feel like hitting him."

"You are young, you do not understand," Kauka said mildly. "That man is running away from something. He needs kindness, love—yours, mine, many people's—or he may be lost for good."

April directed a long, thoughtful gaze at him. "How do you know he's worth trying to help?" she enquired.

Kauka shrugged. "My *mana*—spirit essence—talked to his *mana* while I was on the wharf and he, on the ship. Now, my child, tell me about your two years in America. I want to know the worst." His laughter echoed off. It was an old joke, dating back to when she had been small and had rushed to him with youthful misdemeanors which he had had to smooth out with her parents.

"There isn't any worst, Kauka, believe it or not," she said brightly. "It's all best! Let's drive around for a bit before we go to Auntie's. I want to have you to myself for a bit."

"That is my wish too, April. Loki and Mamo send warm alohas. It is fine to have you home. Kona is not Kona without you. It waits for you, as we have waited, with a deep heart."

The resonance of his voice conjured up the slumbrous beauty of Kona. Her heart gave a little catch in her side. She had not realized, until she stood on Hawaiian soil again, what a wrench it would be leaving it forever.

In her purse were a dozen radiograms from Dale, on her finger his magnificent ring, but never-to-be-forgotten smells and sights surrounding her, made him seem far away and unreal. Her small face grew thoughtful. Could Dale's lips, his eyes, the demanding hold of his arms, compete forever with the long, slow shape of Mauna Loa when the great star of morning burned above it? Or fight the dawn wind bringing down the incense of forests and cool, winding trails? Or still the eternal whisper of the sea against lava headlands? Snatching Kauka's hand, she held it tightly.

"Something *pilikea*—wrong, April?" he asked, with quick concern.

"No," she caught her breath, "but I'm going to be married to a *haole*—who lives in New York." She displayed her ring, then opening her purse, drew out a wad of radiograms and handed them over.

While Kauka went through the sheaf of papers in an unhurried fashion, weighing the wording of them, she gazed about her. Along an open, turfed square, tall cocoanut trees moved their long fronds like mournful dancers posturing to an invisible audience. A native policeman, directing traffic with hula gestures, lent spice to the scene. Hawaiian women in flowing *holokus* moved along the pavements, laughing with one another. Hawaiian men in Sailor Moku pants lounged in doorways and on street corners. American men in smart suits, wearing leis about the crowns of their straw hats, dashed in and out of impressive business buildings. Japanese men, in store suits, followed by women in kimonos, went past. Chinese merchants in black alpaca suits, accompanied by wives or daughters in brocaded pantaloons, wearing jade in their sleek, pomaded hair, proceeded serenely on their way. Filipinos, in gaudy shirts and flaring breeches belted about impossibly small waists, jabbered and showed off while tiny-boned women, in narrow muslin gowns finished with huge transparent sleeves, trailed them meekly. A clanking street car rushed by; automobiles flashed to their destinations.

April's face grew thoughtful. A fine sweetheart she was, hardly fifteen minutes ashore, to begin wondering if she could tear herself from Hawaii and live in New York.

"Well, your *haole* knows how to make love across space," Kauka

[19]

remarked, smiling, as he handed the radiograms back. "How long have you known him, my child?"

"About four weeks," she spoke slowly. "We met at a dance a week before I was to sail for Europe, and I came home instead." She laughed, her volatile nature soaring again.

"From that diamond, he is rich, April."

"Yes." She told him details of his family.

"Well, we have you for a year, anyway," Kauka said.

"Yes, and a year's a long time! Maybe Dale will come out and we can be married in Kona. No, I guess that's out. His mother's like my mother, except Dale's mother fancies she has a bad heart, and that makes a long voyage to Hawaii impossible. She wants me to be married from their big house in New York. But it would be more fun to be married here. Maybe, after seeing the Islands—because I'm going to write to Dale and tell him he must come for at least a short visit—he'll want to live here."

"Maybe," Kauka agreed cheerily, as they started toward a sleek limousine waiting a short distance away.

"Were Mother and Father wild when they got my radiogram?"

"Yes, but I talked to them and—"

"Smoothed down their ruffled feathers?" April finished. Kauka nodded, a reminiscent smile on his lips.

3

IT seemed impossible that the seated pair could come from the
same stock. Pushing deeper into the cool wicker chair, Kauka
watched Laura Wilde talking to her niece. April faced the
garden adjoining the palm and fern-filled *lanai*. She was efferves-
cent as sparkling water, and lovely as a slim waterfall drifting into
a jungled valley. Laura Wilde sat with her back turned on the
colorful flower beds and sweeps of green lawn. She had the thin,
high nose, the tight mouth and bleak bone-structure of her New
England ancestry.

For thirty years, her days had ticked off with the regularity of a
metronome. She rose at seven-fifteen, and breakfasted in solitary
state at seven-forty-five. At ten-thirty, the Packard rolled up to the
front steps to take her to market where she, followed by a uni-
formed chauffeur, drove as shrewd bargains for fish, vegetables, and
fruit, as the poorest inhabitant of Palama or Aala Park districts.
Lunch was on the dot of one. From two to three, she rested, then
attended Welfare Committees and other benevolent societies.
Week-day evenings, she ate at six. Sundays a two-o'clock dinner
was served, with occasionally three or four Wildes, of the Honolulu
branch of the family, invited to share it. Only birth or death among
the Wilde clan altered the regularity of her days.

She sat erectly in her chair, her small, bony, well-bred hands
folded in her lap. "But I don't understand what on earth prompted
you to come home when Hiram and Elsbeth had planned on
Europe for you instead," she reiterated.

"Well, Auntie," April explained, "I simply had to or I'd have exploded. Haven't you ever felt as if everything inside you was going up in smoke which will burst into flame if you don't do something about it at once?"

"Most definitely I haven't. Self-control, my dear, is more important than self-expression."

"I know, Auntie, but"—April's eyes held back mischief—"it's such fun, sometimes, to letta-go-your-blouse, as the Hawaiians say, do the things you want to, *when you want to do them,* instead of waiting until the wanting's all—stale."

To conceal the amusement in his eyes, at what he knew Laura's reply would be, Kauka glanced at his watch. Five-twenty. Dinner would be on the dot of six, despite the fact that it necessitated going indoors and missing the most beautiful time of the evening. Already a perfumed island dusk was creeping into the garden. In the west a faint, fiery afterglow lingered above the horizon and the sea, dimmed to smoky purple, moved as if it were trying to rid itself of something that troubled it.

Kauka's flexible, expressive lips tightened imperceptibly about the half-smoked cigar thrusting from the corner of his mouth. His shoulders sagged slightly, weighted from a lifetime of activity, but his head thrust forward like a hound following a keen scent. While he had been listening with half his mind on the conversation, the other half had been focused on Thord Graham, to whom he had been so swiftly and strangely drawn. Surely by now, he must have walked himself to a standstill and checked in at the Blaisdell. But Moku could be relied upon to phone when he did.

Polynesian blood predominated in Kauka, and he accepted impulses and hunches without question. They were the inner nudgings of the soul, which went beyond mere brain wisdom. Instinct, plus an eternal urge to befriend those in distress, determined him at least to try to see Thord before sailing for Kona in the morning.

The telephone began ringing, and one of the houseboys appeared. "Terefone for you, Miss April," he said, smiling slightly.

"That's Hal, trying to high-pressure me into going dancing with him tonight," she laughed, getting out of her chair. "But I don't feel in the mood. Excuse me for a minute, Auntie."

Kauka watched her walking lightly among easy-chairs and potted plants. In a grass-green voile dress, crowned with her bright hair, she suggested a daffodil. He loved her as he loved his own daughter, Mamo, and felt a pang at the thought that she was destined to marry a New Yorker and live away from Hawaii. Her mother, after the spasms of a neurotic's emotions had been enjoyed, would be entirely for the match. Hiram would be coldly satisfied to know his only child was marrying wealth. But the fact that April had come scurrying home proved she was tied to the Islands with bonds deeper and stronger than she realized, and Kauka wondered if she would be content forever with the sort of life she would lead as Dale's wife.

Then, with Polynesian wisdom, he dismissed the problem. There were more immediate matters demanding his attention. Foremost the problem of talking Hiram into enlarging and remodeling the plantation hospital. It was shamefully inadequate and run down. But because it netted no tangible profits . . . He smiled a gentle smile. Men of Hiram's type were that way. Perhaps with April's already promised assistance, they could swing it.

Then he thought of Thord. Kauka hated to picture him thrashing around the colorful, enchanting streets of Honolulu, friendless, probably subconsciously aware of the beauty about him which would tend to make him feel still more bereft and divorced from normal living. Smiling as only Hawaiians can, making conversation superfluous, he glanced around at Laura Wilde. The desiccated woman felt the warmth of his allegiance to all things Wilde, and spoke as though Kauka had addressed her.

"I can't see that two years in the East have altered April in the slightest," she observed in chilled tones.

April's returning footsteps cut off the necessity of a reply. "It was Hal," she told them, sinking into her chair.

The telephone rang again. Kauka waited. Presently the houseboy came again. "Terefone for you," he said, bowing to Kauka.

Kauka rose. April flashed a look as he passed.

He walked swiftly down the lofty, formally furnished hall. Before he finished talking, the dinner gong sent silvery chimes floating through the house. "Keep an eye on him, Moku," Kauka instructed in Hawaiian. "He may dine out. I can't get away, now, until after we've eaten."

He hung up just as April and her aunt came down the hall.

"Was it the lei breaker?" April asked.

Kauka nodded.

"What are you going to do?"

"After dinner I shall try to see him."

"Why?"

Kauka looked faintly uncomfortable. "Maybe because I always feel heavy inside my heart when people are unhappy and others do nothing for them."

April slid her arm impulsively through his. "You're *pupule*— crazy," she announced. "But if you weren't that way, we all wouldn't love you as we do."

"To what, specifically, if I may enquire, are you both alluding?" Laura Wilde asked, leading the way toward the dining room.

Kauka told her briefly. The stringy woman gave a faint, ladylike sniff of disapproval.

"I suppose you'd like to drag this person to Kona and foist him off on Loki, the way you do sickly plantation children."

"I would be happy if I could persuade him to go with us tomorrow," Kauka said. "Kona is a good place for people who are in trouble, or have sorrows. In time, beauty heals everything."

"But you know nothing about him. He may be a criminal."

"No," Kauka said quickly. "I may be only a fat old plantation doctor, but in the long years I've worked I have learned to know men and women."

"No one is infallible. You have Mamo to consider. She's only sixteen. Impressionable. If he's six feet tall, red-headed, and personable—"

"Mamo is in love with Liholiho," Kauka interrupted, calm as a pool.

"It mightn't be a bad idea to drag Mr. Graham to Kona, after all," April broke in, watching her aunt. "There aren't many attractive young white men here. Even if he's done something off color,

[24]

he'll be fun to dance and ride with." She waited impishly for the explosion.

"April, upon my word—"

"Oh, Auntie, I was only having fun," she laughed. "Besides, I'm engaged to be married," and, with a rush, she told about Dale.

"Your young man seems to have sufficient credentials," Laura said approvingly. "I know of the Hancock family. They rank with—" she ran through half a dozen world-known New York names, and gave a satisfied little nod. "Hiram and Elsbeth should be pleased."

In the coldly lovely room where they dined, Kauka pulled out Laura's chair, the houseboy assisted April into hers. Overhead, unshaded lights glared down. A tight, small old-fashioned bouquet of flowers sat in the center of the table. Laura always arranged the flowers herself.

Heavily framed, oversized pictures of bearded men, with faces of granite, tightly buttoned into dour black coats, women with precisely shut mouths and small, watchful eyes, their bodies carefully concealed by voluminous dresses, stared down from stark white walls.

Courses came and went. Kauka ate with the large, leisurely pleasure of a Polynesian. As dessert was being served, the telephone rang again. The second houseboy, who only served if four or more were present, came to the door.

"Terefone for you," he said, indicating Kauka.

"*Mahalo*—thanks. Excuse me, Laura."

Laying his napkin beside his plate he went out. When he returned he looked regretfully at his dessert.

"That was Moku again," he explained. "Our young friend's left the Blaisdell and has gone to a saloon. I must see him before he gets so drunk he won't—"

"Stephen Kamuela Haines!" Laura bit off each word. "It's scandalous that you, a member of the Reverend Thisbe's church, should—"

Kauka's dark eyes met hers and held them. For an instant, Laura Wilde was unable to free her captured gaze, then she moved as if she were trying to rid her mind of a thought that Kauka's had put there. Silently. But the unspoken words hung in the room. "Even as ye do unto the least of Mine—"

"Very well," she said. "Go along. You're missing a good dessert. Guava whip with marshmallows in it."

"I know." Kauka sighed like a regretful boy.

Laura tasted hers, then said, without looking up, "Take the Packard. It'll be quicker than calling a taxi and waiting for it to get here."

"*Mahalo nui loa*—thanks a lot, Laura. You're a good woman." He patted her thin shoulder fondly.

"You're a fool," she remarked.

"Maybe," he replied, smiling, and the smile wiped out lines which the years had etched about his eyes. Walking around the table, he kissed the top of April's bright head. "Go to bed early," he ordered. "The boat sails for Kona at six."

When the long shining Packard slid up to a saloon in a badly lighted side-street in a shabby portion of Honolulu, a lank figure detached itself from the shadows and came forward.

"Moku?" Kauka asked, leaning out of the car.

"Yes, the man with hair as red as the paddles of a warrior's canoe is in there." The old lei vendor gestured at two swinging half-doors spilling twin wedges of light into the street.

"*Mahalo nui loa,* Moku." Kauka got out of the car deliberately, closed the door and said, "Come back in an hour, Valentine. Here's a dollar—"

"No need," the part-Hawaiian assured him blithely. "I go see my *aikanes*—friends, on Mauna Kea Street." And sliding in the gear, he drove off.

"How is he, Moku?" Kauka signed with his head at the saloon.

"I tink little *pupule*," Moku announced. "Walk all day, but no see enny kind. Some-few times he catch *ino*—drink, then walk some more. My old leg little more broke." He laughed. "Not till after five, when I phoning you, do he go to Blaisdell. Then only stop fifteen minutes and come out again. He sight me and ask, 'Where's the nearest saloon that isn't too high-priced?' And I bring here.

Then I phoning you from Ling's store, where I can look see spose the *haole* go while I talking you." He signed at a poor little shop on the opposite side of the street, where an old Chinaman waited hopefully for a possible late customer. Occasionally, the old man brushed away insects undulating about a solitary electric-light globe strung up in the doorway behind him, but for the greater part sat contemplating time.

"How long had he been in there when you phoned?" Kauka asked in lowered tones.

"Might-be five minutes."

"Good. Here, take this for your trouble." Opening a worn wallet, Kauka drew out three dollar bills.

"No need."

"You might have sold all your leis," Kauka said. "You have now five, six children?" His eyes were mischievous.

"Seven," Moku announced, looking embarrassed and proud.

"Not so bad," Kauka chuckled. "Name the next one after me, and take these to start its bank account. Give my warm alohas to Mele and the seven *keikis.*"

"Okay!" Moku sung out and, signaling gaily, swung off down the street.

Kauka paused briefly, looking at the down-at-the-heel houses lining the street. They seemed to hold unhappy grudges against the years that had passed over them. Then pushing through the swinging doors, he took a swift survey of the room with its iron tables and chairs, and headed slowly for the bar. At a table in a corner, Thord sat, an almost empty whisky glass before him. With his long body, ruddy hair and skin, he looked like a fallen Plantagenet staring with blank eyes at a lost kingdom. His hat was pulled over his eyes, but Kauka saw that the gardenias he had placed on it were still about the crown. Probably Thord had not removed it from his head and didn't realize that the flowers were still there.

Walking to the bar, he leaned his elbows on it and waited until the cockney behind it had finished serving two customers who had evidently had several rounds. One was a Norwegian sailor off some freighter in port, the other a Hawaiian longshoreman with the

[27]

shoulders of a blacksmith and forearms like thighs. Liquor had loosened his handsome features, but his eyes were filled with child-like delight for a night when someone he had spoken to casually, with saved money to spend, had elected him for the companion of his roisterings.

Kauka's eyes wandered about the dimly lighted room. King Kalakaua in uniform, and Queen Liliuokalani seated impressively in a chair, decorated one wall. Another flaunted a calendar of a large, voluptuous, nearly nude woman, reclining on a couch. Beside it, in absurd contrast hung a gilt-framed faded picture of Queen Victoria. Over the fly-specked mirror above the bar was a ship model, slightly atilt. The bartender came toward him.

"What'll it be?" he asked.

"*Kinni*," Kauka directed.

"Okay," and with a flourish and a soiled, sopped rag, the bartender mopped up the spillings of other drinks.

When he was handed his gin, Kauka headed for a table, one away from Thord's. Drawing a cigar from his breast pocket he lighted it, waved the flame off the match, and unhurriedly sampled his drink.

Thord was staring foggily at his glass. After a bit he straightened up, removed his hat and placed it on the table. Seeing the flowers he frowned. He fingered a gardenia, in a puzzled way, as if trying to comprehend the motive which had prompted a stranger to decorate another stranger with flowers. He started to remove the wreath, then, like a man under a spell, put it back. Batting his eyes, he looked around.

"Bring me another double Scotch," he called.

With feigned surprise, Kauka rose and walked over.

"Well, friend, well met," he said. "I was tired and dropped in for a gin to pick me up. Mind if I join you?"

Thord gathered himself together in an obviously dazed way.

"Of course not. Sit down. "You're the man who gave me these flowers, aren't you? Or are you?"

"I am," Kauka said simply, and drawing out a chair, sat down.

"Two drinks, bartender," Thord called, sagged onto his elbows, then stiffened his spine doggedly. Kauka noted the mysterious élan which distinguished some men from others, and smoked placidly. Thord stared at him.

"Why do I like you?" Thord asked, staring at him.

Kauka shrugged. "How should I know? A man's thoughts are his own business."

A fat Chinaman slid through the swinging doors and sidled up to the pair seated at the bar. "Aloha, Pili," he said.

The longshoreman blinked. "Aloha, Wing. Have *ino* with us. This my friend, Nils. Off Norwegian freighter. Nils hot-style fella. Come on."

"Is, yes. Drink with us," the Norwegian said heavily.

The portly Chinaman looked satisfied, as though he'd accomplished some secret goal. Heaving his bulk onto a stool, he settled down and waited.

"It happened when we looked," Thord said into the air.

Kauka's wise eyes lighted faintly. "Yes, it happened when we looked," he agreed.

"You're—you're a—" Thord halted, trying to size Kauka up.

"I'm a half-white, a *hapa-haole,* we call it here," Kauka told him.

"Can't figure out why I like you so damned much. It's beyond me. But I do."

"Let's shove to your hotel. We can order drinks sent up to your room," Kauka suggested.

"Yes, let's. This joint stinks." Lurching to his feet, Thord slapped down a dollar bill and started for the swinging doors. Kauka picked up Thord's hat and held it out.

"Just a minute. I must leave a message with the bartender to tell my driver where to find me."

Thord waited unsteadily. "I'm at the Blaisdell," he said. "Why in hell do you bother?"

"You don't know why?" Kauka asked, smiling a little with the outer corners of his eyes.

4

THORD struggled out of sleep. Faint gray showed outside the open windows, but the room was still dark. Shivering, he buried his head deeper into the pillow and lay like a person senseless and inert under a lash. Then he flung out his arm. Some heavy object thudded to the floor and rolled across it. Leaping up he switched on the bedside light just in time to see a partly emptied whisky bottle disappearing under the dresser, as though it were trying to hide itself. On the table were two glasses and beside them a coil of tinfoil, like a twisted gold and silver leaf.

He thrust his fingers through his hair. Shivers, like icy little breezes scurrying across a lake, chased over his body. In fragments the evening came back. He had been in a saloon where a Chinaman, a Hawaiian, and a Norwegian had sat drinking at the bar. Later he and some man had left the saloon together and come to the hotel. If only he hadn't been so damnably drunk. If only he could recall the man's features. He remembered his eyes. Friendly. Concerned. Uncondemning. The man had called himself by some odd-sounding name. Kauka? Yes, that was it. Kauka. Which signified he was a Hawaiian. He'd been drinking with a native. Christ!

Then some fragment of his brain shifted into action. Clamped down. Kauka had done no drinking to speak of. He'd sat quietly. Talked. As if they'd known each other a long time. Something began scratching feebly at the back of Thord's mind trying to get his attention. The scratching changed to a small whisper trying to speak to him through muffling curtains. He'd—had he committed himself to something?

Throwing back the covers he leaped out of bed, shook his head like a horse with an insect in its ear, and came to a quaking standstill. Then, in jerks, he remembered. He'd agreed to go by boat to some place on another island.

Then he saw the wilted garland about his hat and slumped down on the bed. It had been that man, Kauka, not just someone he'd picked up in a saloon. Like most men trained for some specific profession, Thord had acquired the ability subconsciously to classify and pigeon-hole people while he interviewed, or worked, with them. Class A. Class B. Class B-C. And so forth. But he realized that he had never met Kauka's exact counterpart. Yet this Hawaiian, or part-Hawaiian, for he recalled he had some English name as well, had managed to penetrate through the solitude surrounding his soul, as simply as water soaking into parched soil. Actually, Kauka was an ordinary man, loving ordinary beings, but at the same time he gave an impression of solemn, veiled happenings to come, which the future had entrusted to his keeping.

Thord realized he was practically sober, his mind going in a straight line. Maybe he hadn't drunk as much as he fancied he had. Going to the dresser he fished out the bottle and saw with relief that less than a third of the quart had been consumed. He had been accustomed to wake up fogged for so long that he expected to be that way. And this morning he wasn't. He was far from clear, but clearer than he had been for weeks.

Why in hell shouldn't he go with Kauka? He had no plans. No objective. Nothing could be lost. Something possibly might even be gained. And confound it, he liked the man.

A breath of wind, loaded with the fragrance of the earth, redolent with dawn, came through the open windows. Getting in the shower, Thord turned on the water. Hot first. Then cold. That would make his dulled body react. He watched steam pouring out and stepped into the tiled stall filled with the scent of rushing cleanness. After a bit he turned on the cold faucet, endured it for as long as he could, then switched to hot again. Cold once more. Hot.

He stepped out feeling lifted. Then suddenly it was as if he had been struck a dull blow on the back of his head. Probably with a drunk's garrulousness he'd told Kauka everything. No man, especially a doctor, would want him under his roof knowing . . . The only thing to do was to clear out as fast as possible, leaving no word. Hurrying to the chair beside the bed he began hauling into his clothes. Then he saw a note and snatched it up.

"I'll come for you at five-thirty. The Kona boat sails at six. I'll leave word at the desk to have you called at five-fifteen. Kauka."

Thord glanced at his watch. Five-three. He could check out, get a taxi, and be miles away in thirty minutes. But as he assembled his belongings, thoughts like bats in aimless flight crossed and recrossed his mind. Maybe he hadn't said anything. If he had and Kauka still wanted him to visit him, wasn't that Kauka's business?

"Blast everything," he thought. "My mind's like a squirrel spinning on a wheel in a cage. I'll fix it!"

Grabbing up the whisky bottle he jerked out the cork and took a long swallow. Then he snatched up the bedside phone. "Send a boy up for my bags. I'm ready to check out."

Taking up his hat, he dropped the yellowing wreath of gardenias into the waste basket, shrugged roughly into his topcoat, then glanced about to see if he'd forgotten anything. A tap sounded on the door and relief surged through him. The boy for his bags.

"Come in," he called.

A square, heavy figure in an overcoat, with a hat pulled over his eyes entered, signed in a pleased way with his head, and said, "Up already? Fine! I came early, as April and I were awake anyway."

Thord slumped. Kauka glanced at him and a hint of concern, or vague dismay, came into his eyes.

"You don't look well," he said in his slow way. "Sleep badly? I thought when I left that you were headed for a good seven hours' rest. That's why I left word at the desk to call you."

Thord beat about in his mind. How could he turn away this kindly man who took it for granted that he was going with him?

"Here, I'll take the handbag and the black suitcase. You take the others," Kauka suggested. Then he glanced over his shoulder and remarked in pleased tones, "Ah, here's the boy."

[32]

A bellboy hurried through the still open door.

"Aloha," Kauka said. "Our car is at the door."

The boy returned the salutation and began stacking bags under his arm.

"I'll take this one." Kauka picked up a satchel. "You no nuff big for carry all."

"Wait, you see." The young Chinese's almond eyes flashed a quick smile. "Me velly smart making this-kind now. Before not so smart."

They laughed together. Thord heard them as though they were speaking on the far side of an abyss which yawned between him and the homely comfort of everyday things, then the boy went triumphantly with three bags under one arm, and carrying the fourth in his right hand.

"Well, *aikane,* let's go. Tomorrow, this time we'll be landing in Kona." There was a ring in Kauka's voice, a wide gladness behind the last word that showed his love for his own particular corner of the earth. "After you've been in Kona for a while, all your troubles will be *pau,*" he added.

Thord rammed his fists into his overcoat pockets and clenched them until his forearms cramped. "Look here, I think after all I'd better not go with you."

The expression of surprise, of hurt unbelief in Kauka's eyes made Thord wince inwardly.

"You see, on second thoughts—" he began.

"Often second thoughts are not best," Kauka interrupted. "Because they are—only thoughts." He stressed the last two words slightly. "Man possesses a higher intelligence than mere brain power, to guide him under stress. Hawaiians call the force *mana* —spirit essence. My *mana* directed me to seek you out last night. Your *mana* told you to come with me."

There was a compelling quality to Kauka's voice, a compelling faith in his words.

"But I was drunk last night," Thord protested.

"Your brain was not functioning, so your *mana* took command,"

[33]

Kauka announced, holding Thord's eyes with his own. *"Aikane,* you've been through a distressing experience—"

"Did I—"

"You told me nothing, only that your life had been derailed. When people are unhappy they are never very smart. I know." He laughed a little. "Once, long ago, I too was young and—" He gestured, making whatever was past of no consequence.

"Come," Kauka urged, "if you don't like Kona you do not have to stay. I want you to see it, to feel it. It is my home. It was loved by the chiefs of old. It is known as the Land of Hang Rain, the Land of the Setting Sun."

Again that sense of loss, for something he had never known, swept through the American like the waves of an invisible ocean. This half-white knew things he did not.

"Okay, let's shove," he agreed.

"Fine." Kauka sounded like a delighted boy and though they walked side by side, Thord felt in some intangible way that he was being herded out of the room, firmly and gently, and herded out of the past, which Kauka had implied was of no consequence because it was finished with.

When they stepped out of the hotel, morning had come. The vibrations of violent colors in shrubs and flowering trees injected an added tempo into the atmosphere. Fresh wind pouring over damp, forested ranges behind the town smelled of adventure.

"Get in behind with April," Kauka directed. "I'll sit with Valentine. Okay, Val, Kona steamer. *Wikiwiki.* We don't want to miss the boat."

"Sure"—the driver chuckled—"always Kona fellas scare missing Kona boat. Kona swell place, maybe."

"Damn swell," Kauka said heartily.

Thord bent his tall body to enter the car. "Good morning," he murmured.

"Good morning," April replied, her face just visible above the collar of a big, loose coat. "It's sort of chilly, isn't it?"

"A bit," Thord agreed.

The car started down the empty street, gained the waterfront, majestic with ship's prows, and sped along the road paralleling the docks and wharves. The spicy fragrance of a tropic morning filled the air, and the excitement of departures and landings wrapped the waterfront, just awakening to activity. Thin-legged Chinamen in coolie hats, with baskets of vegetables slung from poles across their shoulders, were trotting to market. Japanese merchants hastened to their places of business. Hawaiian longshoremen strolled with leisurely dignity toward ships scheduled to depart. Groves of cocoanuts lifted their casual beauty to the sky. Between the towering shapes of ships, blue glimpses of sea showed.

"Are you glad you're going to Kona with us?" April asked from the depths of her coat collar.

Thord wondered. Actually he didn't know, actually he had had little choice in the matter.

"It's always interesting seeing new places."

"I bet Kauka browbeat you into coming," April laughed.

Kauka turned, raised an eyebrow, and smiled his disarming smile. "I did. Young people haven't much sense. Last night, yes. This morning, no. So I decided for him."

There was a royal beauty to the new day being born swiftly out of the morning. Color was everywhere and a sheathed strength crouched in earth, sky, and sea.

"Well, here we are. There's the good old *Kinau.*" Kauka indicated a fair-sized Inter-Island steamer, docked at one of the slips. Another smaller ship was moored in another slip, some distance away. About both vessels there was the bustle of pending departure.

Early as it was half a dozen lei vendors surged forward as the car stopped. Kauka got out, his overcoat flapping about his legs.

"Aloha, aloha, you like lei?" men and women chorused.

"*Malama, malama*—take it easy," Kauka laughed. "I can't buy from everybody. I got leis from you last time, Annie," he said to a stormy-looking woman in her middle thirties. "And the time before from you, Pili." He smiled at a stalwart lad. "This time is Tutu's turn." He beamed at an old woman with a seamed face, whose eyes spilled benevolence on the world.

[35]

Digging under his overcoat, he searched his trouser pocket for coins, while his eyes appraised the garlands dangling from the woman's dry, wrinkled hands.

"I'll take this for myself, Tutu." He selected a maroon carnation lei. "Ginger, and one gardenia lei for April. What flowers do you prefer?" He turned to Thord.

"I don't want any, I'm not an Islander," Thord said.

Kauka looked at him from under his eyebrows, grinned, and inspected the fragrant wreaths. Finally, he selected a small strand of white jasmine, like carved ivory and pearls.

"Fix it on his hat, April," he directed over his shoulder, while he paid the old woman.

April took the wreath and with a couple of deft turns twined and shaped it to the proper size. "Give me your hat," she said.

Thord took it off and she stared at his hair.

"It's very red, isn't it?" she remarked.

"Frightfully," he admitted.

They both laughed, and suddenly were friends, as the antagonism, generated in their meeting the morning before, was dissipated in their laughter.

"Go aboard you two," Kauka said. "Here are your tickets. I'm going to the Wharfinger's office to call the radio station and tell Loki I'm bringing a guest."

Thord took the tickets. "What do I owe you?" he asked.

"You're my guest *this* time," Kauka laughed, cutting him off and heading for his destination.

April led the way through a big dark door leading into the internals of the vast shed-like wharf. They walked down narrow aisles between brown bags of sugar, stacked almost to the roof, which filled the structure with a heavy, almost sickening odor. April inhaled it joyously.

"This smells like home," she exulted, noting stenciled letters stamped on the tight, round bags. "Those are from H. C. and S. Company on Maui." She gestured at one stack. "These are from Ewa plantation on Oahu." She indicated others, then her face lighted. "And these are from Daddy's plantation, K. S. C.—Kona Sugar Company." She almost sang the words.

Lei-bedecked Hawaiians were taking leave of each other at the foot of the gangway. Japanese families bowed and inhaled. Filipinos chattered excitedly. No other whites were sailing. April sprinted up the gangway and Thord followed.

"Aloha, April, Aloha!" the portly half-Hawaiian, half-Chinese head steward greeted.

"Aloha, Maikai," she cried, shaking both his hands.

"I think never you coming back from New York," he scolded.

"Pooh, New York!" she laughed.

"*Hawaii nei*—our Hawaii more good?" the jolly old fellow asked.

"Bet-you-my-life!" April cried. "Oh, I forgot to give our tickets to Kimmo." She glanced back down the gangway at the crowd on the wharf.

Maikai let out a fine boom of laughter. "Kimmo forgetting about tickets. He got new sweetheart. Lively young girl." He pointed down at a handsome young Hawaiian in an officer's cap, dark coat, and white breeches who was violently embracing a girl of about fifteen with a cloud of dark hair flying loose about her shoulders. "Give tickets to me. I have fun when Kimmo come aboard and make big boob on hims."

April handed them over. "Which number is the *haole's?*" she indicated Thord.

"Take enny, not many peoples this trip," Maikai gestured expansively. "Aloha, *haole*, swell you going to Kona."

"This is always my cabin, and this one is Kauka's," April announced airily. "You better take No. 3. If you're on this side of the boat you'll see all the islands as we pass them and be right to watch Hawaii loom up at dawn tomorrow."

"Whatever you say," Thord agreed.

Two stewards came up the gangway with their bags and April directed them into the correct staterooms. Thord looked on, like a person in a dream.

"I'm going to get out of this heavy coat and into a sweater. It's warmer now. See you in a few minutes."

Thord strolled slowly along the deck. There was elixir in the blue sky. The air was gay and buoyant with sunshine, wind pouring over the island was laden with the incense of valleys and forests, spiked with the strong smell of tar, ropes, ships, and sugar. A group of volunteer musicians was singing a hula. People were coming aboard, calling out to those left behind, listening to messages shouted back to carry to loved ones living on other islands.

"Okay, okay, I no forgetting to tell your Cousin-sister Annie to come down. . . . Sure, I give this mangoes to your old Mother—Yes, I tell to Lehua you getting new baby in July. . . . Aloha! Aloha! Us have jolly fun with you guys in Honolulu . . . you come quick and stop with us on Hawaii."

Thord studied the warm laughing faces, listened to rich mellow voices. There was no shoving and hurrying. Everyone seemed to have time to be kind, merry, and the thought came to him that human beings in Hawaii were more like the way God intended them to be when He created them. Kauka came swiftly up the gangway, glanced up, and, seeing Thord, waved.

"Well, we're about to cast off," he remarked when he joined Thord, glancing down to where brawny Hawaiians worked with heavy ropes looped about iron stanchions.

A burst of singing came from the dock, people waved, the gangway came up, and the ship began backing slowly out of her slip. Then from somewhere came a long-drawn-out dreadful wailing. Thord listened, then shook his head as if trying to get the sound out of his ears.

"I hear people crying," he exclaimed, "or am I crazy?"

A curious change came over Kauka. His slack, happy figure grew rigid. The long cry came again, chilling Thord's blood. It was the most heart-rending, God-forsaken sound he'd ever heard and gooseflesh prickled his skin.

"Great God," he exclaimed. "What on earth—"

Taking him by the arm, Kauka led him silently to the opposite side of the ship. Pointing at the steamer Thord had noticed when they arrived at the dock, he said heavily, "That is the Government boat, taking lepers to Molokai. They, and the friends and relatives down to see them off, will never meet again on this earth." His eyes narrowed. "The boat leaves Honolulu either very early in the morning, or about sundown, to spare people's feelings here."

Silence stretched between Thord and Kauka, broken only by the terrible wailing. Taking out his handkerchief, Thord mopped his forehead.

"Those are the living dead—in Paradise," Kauka said, his face haggard.

The long cry came from the ship again, was answered from the shore and blended into an eternal farewell. Kauka stared out across the blue sparkle of the Pacific, then, finding a cigar, he lighted it. The ship with its grim burden of awful despair waited to give the *Kinau* right of way to the open sea, but a sort of dreadful smothered moaning came from it that swelled and decreased as the wind freshened and fell.

5

THORD opened his eyes and blinked. The cabin light had been turned on. Kauka stood in the doorway, a benevolent figure in rumpled pajamas.

"Wake up. We'll drop anchor off Kailua in about thirty minutes."

"I'll be dressed in nothing flat," Thord said, swinging his long legs over the side of the narrow bunk.

Kauka closed the door and Thord began dressing. While he got into his garments, pictures of the previous day and night drifted through his mind. Island after majestic island, rising out of incredibly blue seas and vanishing into massed clouds. Rough channels where the ship bucked, rolled, and tossed spray like wet diamond bullets off her bows. Strange landings at ports where the steamer often anchored a mile off shore and passengers were taken to their destinations in great white whaleboats, manned by muscled Hawaiians who handled long heavy oars as if they were feathers. The sun dying in crimson and gold, stars coming out, a vast night descending on the ocean. The sonorous names of new ports: Lahaina, Mahukona, Lapahoehoe, Kawaihae.

Islanders were like a houseful of crazy children enjoying a perpetual Christmas. At each port Kauka had paddled about barefoot in his pajamas, April had flitted around in a colorful kimono, her hair blown by the wind. Native men and women in various stages of undress took farewell of departing friends and greeted arriving ones with a hearty abandon that rang true each time. Children played tag, and somewhere, hidden from sight, a young Hawaiian strummed a guitar throughout the night, softly chanting a plaintive, ancient air which seemed to hold lost secrets of the Pacific.

"Aren't you dressed yet?" April called impatiently through the door. "Dawn's come. We're passing Hualalai and Mauna Loa is just showing up. I want you to see it first with the morning star above it."

"I'm ready." Flinging the door open Thord stepped out.

Light from an overhead lamp fell on April's face, and Thord realized, all at once, that she was very young and immature. She seemed to have been sketched into the morning with a few swift, delicate strokes and left for life to finish.

"Come," she said, and linking her arm through his, headed for the rail. Against the pale lemon light in the east Thord saw the navy-blue mass of an island bulking against the sky.

"That's Hualalai." April pointed at a sinister-looking mountain slipping astern. Half a dozen sharply tilted cones showed on the summit. "Hualalai hasn't been active since 1801. But that"—catching her breath, she pointed ahead—"is Mauna Loa, the Great Dome of Fire."

The volcano rose with masterful simplicity from the sea, an awesome blue shape, touched with unearthly sublimity.

"Great God, what a mountain!" Thord exclaimed.

April's face lighted. "Yes," she agreed. "It's the biggest individual mountain mass in the world. It rises eighteen thousand feet from ocean bottom to sea-level, and goes almost fourteen thousand feet above that. It's a perfect dome, built up from layers and layers of lava. In full eruption all the words in the dictionary can't describe it. When it's still, it does things to you. If you live even for a while in its shadow you can never get the image of it out of your mind. All the time I was in New York—"

"You were in New York—recently?" Thord asked in guarded tones.

"Yes, Miss Briar's School, just outside the city. I was supposed to go—" Laughingly she related her impulsive homecoming.

There was a brief silence.

[41]

"The morning we landed, yesterday, I felt—" His eyes came to hers.

"I was angry because you broke the lei Kauka gave you; he was putting a circle of love and beauty around you—for Hawaii," April said.

"I'm sorry. I didn't know what the flowers signified."

"It's *pau*—finished with."

"Hi, *aikane*," Kauka joined them. "What do you think of our mountain, of our island?" He gestured fondly at long forested slopes growing more distinct with each passing minute.

"It knocks the wind out of you," Thord said.

"That's North Kona." Kauka indicated long green reaches swelling toward the summit of Hualalai. "That's Kona proper." He pointed toward vast stretches of forested country sloping off toward Mauna Loa. "Wait till you land. Maybe you think April and I are crazy, to—"

"On the contrary, I was thinking how lucky you both are to love anything so much."

"After you've been in Kona for a while it'll put its spell on you, too." Kauka promised. "There's Kailua, the port where we land." He indicated a straggle of houses along a curve of amber sand, bounded on one side by a black arm of lava, and on the other by cocoanut groves drooping glittering fronds. "Swell to be home, April, eh?" he asked, placing an arm along her shoulders.

"Gorgeous," she said, her eyes riveted on the island.

"Well, we'd better get our things together," Kauka suggested. "We'll drop anchor in ten minutes."

"I wish that you—" April began rather wistfully.

"Better for you to go with Hiram alone," Kauka broke in. "He'll see that"—he indicated the diamond on her left hand—"and you can tell him about Dale. It'll make him feel good to know you wanted to come home and be with us before you go to live in New York for good. Besides, I have plenty to do on the way home." Spreading his fingers, he began marking them off. "Kalani's wife has a bad leg and I must stop and see her. Old Kapohakimohewa had a fever when I left, four days ago, and Mary Ako is due to have a baby. When you get home phone Loki and tell her we'll"—his voice included Thord, making him one of them—"be home round lunchtime, maybe a little sooner."

"I won't forget," April promised, starting for her cabin.

"Well, here we are," Kauka said gaily, as the whaleboat bumped the wharf crowded with lusty Hawaiians, knotty Japanese, stringy Chinese, and chattering Filipinos. Everyone living in Kailau was down to see who had arrived from Honolulu and wayports.

An immoderately tall white man, with carefully brushed gray hair which exactly matched his dry, gray skin, was approaching, bystanders falling back to make way for him. His yellowish eyes, set above prominent cheek-bones, emphasized the unusual width of his face. His skin, despite the fact that he went hatless, had an unpleasant pallor, as though he'd been kept in the dark.

"Father!" April called, waving to attract his attention.

His eyes came down to the boat and found her.

"April!" Somehow, warmth was lacking in his voice.

"How's Mother?"

"The same."

Sailors were boosting giggling Hawaiian women ashore, tossing children into outstretched hands. Kauka placed a foot on the bulwark, waited until a wave lifted the boat level with the wharf, and sprang out. Thord bounded after him.

"Hi, *haole*—white man, you help. Nice young girl," a sailor shouted roguishly, tossing April to Thord.

"Thanks," she said, as Thord set her down, then hurried to her father. He deposited a cool kiss on her cheek.

"Let's be going," he said. Then, as if it were an afterthought, he added, "Hello, Kauka."

"Aloha, Hiram. I want you to meet my friend, Thord Graham. From New York."

Thord's skin scorched. He knew his eyes were still bloodshot, and hangover signs had not, as yet, been completely erased from his face.

[43]

"Pleased to meet you, Graham," Wilde said with eyes as cold as a halibut's. "Staying long?"

"I have no plans," Thord answered.

"I see. Come, April," and Wilde set off toward a long car parked at the end of the wharf.

Kauka's eyes lighted with amusement. "That's the King of all Kona." He gestured at the tall angular figure moving off among piled bags of sugar that formed an aisle down the middle of the wharf.

"I'd hate to be dependent on his mercy."

Kauka nodded. "It's odd how a person without actual violence can succeed in making others feel ill at ease. Everyone working for Hiram, except me, is scared of him, though he pays good wages." Then his face lighted. "Aloha, Carlos, Aloha!" he shouted, waving at a stocky Filipino hurrying toward them.

"Aloha, Kauka! Sorry I little late. Catch one flat tire." He mopped his brown face.

"No matter, Carlos. This *haole*"—Kauka indicated Thord— "come stop our house. Loki getting my radio?"

"Yes, very happy to meet you, Mr.—?"

"Thord," Kauka finished.

"Mr. Thord." Carlos began picking up valises. Thord seized two of his bags, Kauka took another pair.

"How's old Kapohakimohewa?" Kauka asked as they started toward a dilapidated Ford.

"I see yesterday. More good."

"And Kalani's wife?"

"Leg little more all heal up. I look yesterday."

"Has Mary Ako had her baby yet?"

"Not yet."

"Well, it looks as if we can drive right home," Kauka announced, turning to Thord. "Originally I hired Carlos for a gardener, but he's ended up being my driver and right-hand assistant. He can do about everything but operate and I bet he could do a creditable appendectomy if he had to."

[44]

The Filipino writhed his shoulders like a pleased boy and began jamming suitcases into the fenders of the shabby car.

"No falling off if no go too fast," he announced confidently when the last bag was in place.

"If they do we'll stop and put them on again," Kauka grinned. "I'll ride behind with you, Thord, so I can point out spots of interest."

Carlos settled himself behind the wheel and the car rattled off shaking itself like a hen after a vigorous dust bath. A solitary street, flanked on one side with little rundown stores and shabby houses followed the curving beach.

"That big building in the cocoanut grove is the old Palace." Kauka gestured ahead. "Kailua was the capital of Hawaii, until Honolulu supplanted it. This sleepy little town's seen stirring times, as Kona has."

The car began climbing a steep rise, through the drugged peace of the morning. To the left the summit of Hualalai, violently colored, scarred by fire, flaunted cones that looked like unsightly purple eruptions on the mountain's rough hide. To the right, and below, lay the sea, huge, serene, rimming the world with blue.

The day seemed breathless, awed by its own beauty, and a waiting stillness lay on everything. Mango trees, like green volcanic bombs, dotted hills and pastures and beyond the bulge of a ridge ahead, one long, sullen slope of Mauna Loa showed against the sky. The air was filled with the sweetness of fallen guavas, the faint elusive scent of coffee trees in bloom and the fragrance of fat stock browsing through the luxuriant growth of the land.

Occasionally little native houses showed, sitting back in careless gardens, enclosed by neat stone walls. Meditative fowls picked listlessly at flower beds, pale-eyed dogs dozed with crossed paws. People, moving unhurriedly about household tasks, waved and called out. A sense of release stole along Thord's limbs, and knots, which had been pulled tight inside him, began relaxing.

"I'm not going to think, I'm just going to be," he thought.

Twenty-four hours previously the promised magic of Kona had seemed a mirage. Now he was physically and mentally conscious

[45]

of its spell. It drugged his beaten body, poured through his mind, beckoned to his spirit.

The sturdy stone walls flanking the road were crowded with orange and amethyst air-plants. Plantations of glossy coffee, which seemed to be in berry and blossom at once, alternated with tangled trees and vines. Little careless paths led off across ancient lava flows and disappeared into straggly growths of *koa* and *lehua* trees.

The road made a swift turn and a Japanese boy of about eleven, waiting at the edge of the highway, dashed forward. Carlos brought the car to a stop. The boy leaped onto the running board. His eyebrows slanted downwards like arrows in his forehead, and his mouth was quivering.

"Kauka-san, plis come quick," he choked. "Us got bad trouble. Papa-san mill-hand. Sometime Papa-san berry tired and drink little *sake*. Three night before now might-be he drink too much to make berry strong for work. And he falling inside molasses vat. It cook him quick. Us put inside ground next day. Then Mama-san starting to have No. 11 baby, but he come wrong. I pull and pull. Big freshert coming last night so I no can go and ask kind Hawaiian people for help. And you gone to Honolulu—" his voice broke.

Kauka had got out of the car, his arm was about the boy's shaking shoulders. "You're a fine man, Takeshi," he said. "I'll come at once. Thord"—he turned—"Carlos and I may be gone quite a while. This sounds bad. Do you want to wait here or walk up through the coffee with us?"

"I'll come," Thord said. "Perhaps I can help—with the other children," he finished hastily.

Carlos fished a black doctor's bag from under the front seat, and Takeshi led the way manfully up a narrow, rocky trail winding through young coffee trees. Kauka panted a little, for the grade was steep. Carlos talked to the small boy in Japanese. Great green spiders swung hopefully on webs, jeweled with moisture, waiting for insects hovering along the white snow of blossoms, flanked by ruby berries, lying thickly along each branch of perfectly planted trees.

In about twenty minutes they emerged on a small, leveled strip

[46]

of ground, cut into the steep, rough hillside, where a small house of second-hand lumber snuggled among massed greens. In the lean-to at one end, neat rows of dippers hung on the wall and blue and white bowls were stacked on a narrow shelf. *Shoyu* kegs, filled with rain water stood in a line, waiting to be used. From the house came low moaning.

Takeshi's eyes flew to Kauka's. Nodding reassuringly, Kauka rolled up his sleeves and, reaching for a piece of soap, began washing his arms and hands in a small basin filled with water.

"Got hot water inside," Takeshi said. "Iku fix when I trying to help Oka-san—Mother."

"You're all right," Kauka said. "Where are your small brothers and sisters?"

"Inside. Some sleep. Some only cry."

"Tell them to come outside and stay with this *haole*"—he indicated Thord—"while us fellas work."

"Okay."

Carlos spoke to Kauka in Hawaiian, and he gave a slight, assenting nod. "Look, Thord, there's the stove." Kauka indicated a kerosene tin with a flap cut out of one side. "Stoke up the fire, will you? There's the rice pot. Iku'll show you where the rice is. Probably the children haven't eaten much while this birth's been in progress." And he and Carlos vanished through the poor little door.

Thord looked after them, started involuntarily to follow, then, squatting down, began stuffing ends of guava roots, stacked beside the stove, onto the coals. The door opened and Carlos gently herded out children of assorted ages, who, seeing a stranger, froze in their tracks.

Carlos spoke to them in undertones and the largest, a girl of about nine, with a sleeping baby strapped to her back, took a few steps forward; younger sisters and brothers crowded at her bare heels. Their smooth idol-faces, soft slanted eyes, and woebegone expressions touched Thord's heart.

"Come, we cook rice," he said.

The oldest sister slid forward and whispered in a tired voice, "Rice here." Taking the lid off a big wooden barrel she waited,

[47]

then began crying silently, hopelessly. Going to her, Thord put his arm about her and the baby bound to her slender little body.

"Don't cry," he begged. "Kauka's here, everything will be all right."

"Three days before Papa-san get cook in molasses, Mama-san no can *hemo*—get out baby." Iku's voice trailed off.

"Kauka will get it out, Mama-san will be okay." Thord promised. "You're the oldest sister, aren't you?"

"Yis."

"Show me how to cook rice for your little brothers and sisters."

"Okay, I helping."

She began moving about in a mother-like way. Measuring out a big bowl of rice she began washing it swiftly in repeated doses of cold water, pouring off solution after solution until the water ran clear. Selecting one of the dippers off the wall, she measured more water, with painstaking precision, and poured it into the heavy black pot filled with glistening rice. When the measurements were right she set it on the makeshift stove while the brood of brown babies watched hopefully.

"Hadn't you better take the baby off your back?" Thord suggested when she squatted down. "It's heavy."

Iku shook her head. "Japan peoples make this style," she told him.

Little breezes rustled the coffee, a bird whistled three shining notes overhead, spiders rocked on their webs. Little flames, like greedy red tongues, licked around the guava roots in the stove, children moved about in the sun, or slept suddenly. Thord was at a loss what to say, and listened to sounds coming from inside the house, voices, steps hurrying back and forth. Once he heard, or thought he heard, a cry, stifled quickly. The unbelievable agony that women endured! Rice bubbled in the pot.

After a little Iku rose and began busily rinsing and wiping bowls while the waiting children brightened. After what seemed hours, Takeshi emerged from the house, his face pale, his eyes feverish.

"Baby-san out," he announced, and sat down on a lava fragment.

[48]

"Swell," Thord said mechanically, thinking of all this eleven-year-old boy had endured as head of his suddenly bereft household.

"Now us eat," Iku announced.

The small children brightened. Takeshi went off into the coffee trees and Thord heard him being ill. Iku began filling bowls with steaming rice, setting them on a near-by table. Beside each bowl she laid a pair of yellow chopsticks, then began pouring a dark, strong-smelling fluid on the flaky white grains.

"You like *shoyu* on top rice, *haole*-san?" she asked, turning to Thord.

"I'll try it," he said, because her small figure threw off a faint, instinctive hospitality that even the pressure of tragedy could not quite kill.

Takeshi reappeared, wiping his mouth on his wrist, then, as master of the household, held out his hand to be served first. Iku presented him with a steaming bowl of rice. Sitting down he began busily shoveling white kernels into the scarlet cave of his mouth. Smaller children edged closer and squatted down. Iku went around the circle, serving them, hoisting the sleeping child on her back into position when it sagged. Presenting Thord with a blue and white bowl of rice, she curtsied slightly.

"Thank you, Iku," he said.

"Us fellas speak thank you, *arigato*," Takeshi said through a mouth filled with rice.

"*Arigato*," Thord echoed, carefully weighing the strange syllables.

The solemnly eating circle beamed.

Kauka came to the door, his face relieved. "The baby's delivered. Breech presentation. Our hands are full. The mother and the child must be taken to the hospital as fast as possible. The boy's breathing, but—" He looked around the busily eating group. "Takeshi"—he addressed the head of the household—"you and Iku and the five older children can making out here for tonight? I'll come back tomorrow."

"Can-do, Doctor-san."

"Fine. I'll take Mama-san and small new brother to hospital and

[49]

leave two boys and one girl with Momi. Others I take my house. Have you plenty food?"

"Yis. Papa-san get pay before he get cook." Takeshi dashed an unmanly tear away with an impatient flick of his wrist. "Got tea, rice and *curis*—cucumbers," he said proudly. "Plis tell to *Haole Hao* for give me some small jobs on plantation. Me Papa-san now."

"I fix," Kauka promised.

Thord moved restlessly. For the first time in months he found himself unable to disassociate himself from his surroundings and fellow humans. He noted stone walls flanking the narrow trail winding up from the highway to the small clearing. About him were faint, delicate tickings of chopsticks against china. Taking firmer hold of his rice bowl he waited, like a person listening for a summons.

"The first problem," Kauka said, "is, how we're all to get into the car. Mama-san, new baby, four small children, and our three selves. But we'll manage."

"Let me carry the mother, I'm huskiest," Thord said, straightening up.

Kauka smiled, then said regretfully, "The house is a shambles, it may upset you. I'll have to send up a nurse to clean and sterilize the place and get it fit for—" He tilted his head at the children who were to remain.

"I can take it," Thord said. "My grandfather and my dad were both doctors. As a kid, and in my teens I knocked around with Dad when he made calls."

"Handle her gently," Kauka cautioned.

6

LOKI rocked back and forth, her eyes fastened expectantly on the curved driveway leading to the road. Occasionally she glanced in a satisfied fashion at the wide verandas surrounding the old house, a house that breathed contentment. Grouped palms and enormous baskets of drooping ferns linked it to the bright, colorful garden sloping seaward. Sunlight rained downward. Secret splendor wrapped everything.

Loki's heavily lashed, curiously young eyes rested fondly on her garden. Proud breadfruit trees, tall Norfolk Island pines, groups of bronze and green bananas, solid green and purple mangoes, the vermilion umbrellas of flame trees mingled carelessly together. Hibiscus bushes with blossoms like gaudy butterflies splashed color about. Snapdragons, begonias, jasmine, Chinese violets, Japanese musk, and Bird of Paradise lilies grew above prim English daisies bordering the flower beds. Cup-of-gold slumbered into trees, fighting with crude magenta-colored bougainvillias for supremacy. Yellow almanders, sapphire-hued Pride of Kona blossoms blazed together. Gardenias, frangipani, and banks of blossoming yellow and white ginger poured out assorted fragrances.

Loki brushed a fly off her plump, beautifully boned wrist, crossed her bare feet and felt her breadth spreading pleasantly against the weave of the big wicker chair. Despite her bulk, a sumptuous grace enveloped her, and the loose *holoku* she wore disclosed the noble curves of her body.

Hearing footsteps indoors, she called out. A Chinaman with a wrinkled face and wise, narrow eyes, appeared.

[51]

"Keep lunch hot, Ching. Enny time now, Kauka coming."

"Mebbe yes, mebbe-so no!" Ching retorted crossly. "Cook swell breakfast and no come. Now, lunch stop on top stove two hours!"

"Might-be Kauka having to stop to see many sick peoples," Loki observed serenely.

"Gar-damn, this month *pau* I go Honolulu work in a restaurant. Humbugger cook for doctor. Food always spoil!"

Loki's eyelashes quivered mischievously. It was an old threat. Ching eyed her crossly, then a slow grin cracked his face and he went off with the air of a privileged personage who has lived long in a household where service was one of love rather than a mere livelihood, and grumbling was quite in order.

A Japanese woman in a neat cotton kimono came out, her sandals slapping soothingly on the floor. "Small Filipino boy like go play inside garden," she said. "More better today."

"*Maikai!*" Loki beamed. "That make Kauka happy when he come. Pedro eat good?"

"Yes, milk, egg, and rice," the woman said contentedly.

"Okay, take out little whiles. Maybe better put on sweater so he no take cold."

"Yes, Loki-san." And the woman went off.

A tall girl in a vermilion kimono came down the veranda. Long dark hair, lighted with bronze and curling at the ends, spilled over her shoulders as she moved like a bright flame through the afternoon.

"Ah, Mamo," Loki said.

"Papa hasn't come—*yet?*" Mamo asked, seating herself on the steps at her mother's feet with a single swift movement.

"No, but come soon, I think."

Clasping her knee in her long arms, Mamo tilted back her head. She was almost six feet tall but delicately boned as a gazelle. Her skin had the quality of a gardenia. Richness enveloped her as though she'd been born at high noon in golden sunlight. Her eyes were enormous and fringed with outrageously long up-curling lashes. A mouth like a scarlet blossom completed the restful beauty of her face. After a few moments she got up, went indoors, and reappeared with a half-finished lei of gardenias and a bowl heaped with flowers. Seating herself, she began busily weaving them together with long fingers, finished with rosy tips and glowing nails.

"Liholiho coming down tonight?" Loki asked roguishly.

"Not till Saturday, tomorrow," Mamo replied, a faint flush tinging her cheeks. "This is for Papa."

Loki nodded in a lazy, happy way. "Better make one, too, for the *haole* Papa is bringing," she suggested.

"Sure, if I have time," Mamo replied. Then she added into the air, "Papa never thinks how much it costs to keep so many people."

"The happy of others is Papa's life," Loki replied. "What matter if us always short? The more faces at table the more big glad in the heart. That Hawaiian styles."

"I was just teasing," Mamo laughed.

"Might-be good ideas if us go look again and see if everything nice in the *haole's* room," Loki suggested.

Mamo laid her garland on a damp towel, tossed back an armful of black hair and rose. Loki got up, swept the train of her *holoku* about her and moved off on big bare feet with the sure grace of a cat. Mamo walked beside her into the cool, lofty hall covered with tapa cloth and lined with long, polished *koa* spears and beautifully finished paddles, tacked to the walls.

"Did you put flowers in Papa's office?" Loki asked.

"Plenty," Mamo replied.

The telephone rang.

"Better you get, Mamo, might-be that Liholiho," Loki gestured. Mamo ran down the hall.

"Hello?" she said rather breathlessly, then paused and cried in delightful tones, "April!" Her lustrous eyes filled with affection. "Come down, quick! I wanted to go to your house and see you but thought maybe your mother and *Haole Hao* might want you to themselves. No, Papa and the *haole* haven't come yet. Okay, fine. About four o'clock. Can you eat with us tonight?" Her voice poised hopefully. "Well, tomorrow then—" She finished and hung up.

Loki beamed.

[53]

"April coming?"

"For a while."

"I glad. I think might-be she not able to get away from the family." Turning the handle of the last door but one in the hall Loki opened it and swept into a large, cool room. A four-poster, with a white canopy and crisply starched mosquito curtains draped behind the head, occupied one wall. A tall *koa* wardrobe filled another. Flowers grouped in splendid masses spilled from a glass bowl. A rocker, rather worn, sat beside a table under windows framing a section of sunlight-flooded garden. Mamo smoothed the quilted bedspread, with the rich breadfruit design stitched in green against a white background, and stepped back to survey the effect of the whole. Loki sighed with pleasure and her eyes approved the room.

"Sure that New York guy knowing us proud-and-happy for have him under our roof," she announced. "Mamo, I got fine idea. Phone Liholiho and tell him to catch one fat wild turkey and bring down quick. Turkey more hot-style from pig for New York peoples, and I think sure Liholiho like fine to come and eat with us—with *you,* tonight. Tell him never mind if us not *kaukau* till eight or nine o'clock."

Mamo looked shy and pleased. Hurrying to the telephone, she rang, got Central and asked for Kahala Ranch. After a brief wait she began talking animatedly, preening herself as if in Liholiho's presence. Loki's eyes smiled. She went back to the veranda and sat down in the rocker which creaked protestingly.

After a little while Mamo joined her. "Liholiho says he will come."

"That fine. Might-be April can *kaukau* first with the family at six, then eat again with us. Nice for Kauka's New York friend to have pretty young girl to talk to whiles you and Liholiho make eyes."

"Mama!" Mamo said, bending down so her cloud of hair hid her hot cheeks.

Loki's laughter filled the bright afternoon.

When the car swooped into the driveway, Thord looked at his surroundings with interest.

"Well, we're home," Kauka gloated. "Fine house, eh, Thord? A bit old, but it's got lots of room."

Loki and Mamo rushed down the steps. Servants hurried out of the house, the yardboy dropped his rake, a few private patients of assorted nationalities, waiting in the garden, swarmed forward. Carlos stopped the car. Kauka bundled out and he and Loki went into each other's arms, kissed, wiped their eyes and laughed. Mamo hugged her father, then decorated him with her lei.

"Aloha, my child, Aloha," he said happily, then signed to Thord to get out of the car. Loki looked him over, then reaching out, took both his hands in hers. "Fine you come our house. Us proud-and-happy," she said warmly.

Thord was curiously touched. Despite her breadth and bulk there was a radiant, childlike quality to Kauka's wife.

"I'm happy to be here," he said.

"This is Mamo." Kauka presented her with fatherly pride and she gazed at Thord with unfeigned interest, mixed with mischievous pleasure.

"Good Lord, what a creature!" Thord thought. He had never seen anyone even remotely like her. She splashed color over life, made a person feel richer by simply being present. She was Hawaii in the flesh.

"Aloha," she said, smiling.

"Aloha," Thord replied.

"What kept you so long, Papa?" Loki asked, finally, when the last person present had been greeted.

Kauka tousled the head of the small Filipino boy standing beside them and explained.

"Oh, poor peoples! Where are the small kids?"

"I left three with Momi. The two for our house are asleep in the car."

Grinning, Carlos opened the door and indicated the front seat where the children were cuddled together like puppies.

Loki picked up one, then the other and embraced them. They looked at her with round astonished eyes then sagged contentedly against her warm body.

"Mitsu, you take care," Loki directed, a little reluctantly. "Plenty kind I got to show Papa."

The Japanese woman came forward. "Opa," she instructed, sliding the smallest child onto her back where it clung like a small contented monkey. Then taking the larger by the hand, she slapped off toward the house, the little Filipino boy following in her wake, watching his new playmates with bright, intrigued eyes.

"Well, better us go eat," Loki said, linking her arm through Kauka's. "Ching mad like hell because breakfast all spoil, and now maybe lunch spoil too." Her eyes darted to the old cook.

"Lunch no spoil!" he said indignantly. "Gar-damn, you velly, velly nice woman, Loki, but talk too damie muchie." And he hurried off.

Thord was astounded, but Kauka chuckled.

"Mamo, show Thord his room," Loki directed over her shoulder. "I go to the office with Papa for a few minutes. One of these kids"— she indicated a Hawaiian woman holding a wee baby—"got a bad sick."

The young woman looked gratefully at her, then started off around the corner of the house.

"Come this way, Thord," Kauka said, hurrying up the steps.

Thord followed. The absolute simplicity and friendliness of these people amazed him.

"You must be tired and hungry," Mamo said as they crossed the veranda and entered the house. "Poor little Takeshi, what an ordeal for an eleven-year-old boy."

"It was, rather," Thord admitted.

Pushing at the door of his room, Mamo looked at him. "If you hear voices, it's only Papa talking to patients in his office. It's next to this room. As well as his plantation practice, he treats people in North, and even South Kona." She gestured toward the open windows framing a distant slope of Mauna Loa. "Papa should have an assistant, but *Haole Hao,*" she laughed lightly, "is tight where the hospital is concerned. Lunch will be in a few minutes—but you'll hear the gong."

After Thord had washed and brushed up, he went to the window.

Body and soul were experiencing a sudden reaction from the semi-detachment from personal affairs which the past thirty-six hours had provided. Who was he to intrude himself into these people's beauty-wrapped lives? He moved, trying to free himself from a net in which he'd become entangled, then folded his arms, marshaling his thoughts and focusing them.

He was completely sober now. During the past hours of action the last trace of his succession of hangovers had been wiped out. At the first opportunity he must talk to Kauka, lay down all his cards, then, if Kauka still wanted him to remain he'd stay on for a while . . .

Through the wall he heard muffled voices and sounds; a baby crying, Kauka soothing it, Loki talking to the mother. The faint smell of medicines and disinfectants crept to his nostrils. Slowly the blood drained out of his face, leaving it the color of chalk. Not so long ago—

The clear notes of the gong floated through the house. Jerking around, he made for the door and walked swiftly down the hall.

"This way, *aikane,*" Kauka called, heading into a spacious room where a big round table of beautifully polished *koa* wood was set with small elaborately woven mats and the center finished with a bowl of cup of gold blossoms which blended into the whole, completing it.

"Here, Thord." Loki patted the chair on her right with a plump tapered hand.

Mamo was already seated, slowly mixing a salad in a colorful Chinese bowl. She glanced at him from under her lashes, smiled, and went on with what she was doing. Mitsu came in with dishes, followed by Ching triumphantly carrying a steaming platter of chicken stew.

"When you have worked hard and not eaten, food is good," Kauka said, piling lavish helpings on plates which the Japanese woman passed around.

Thord nodded.

"Now you try some of this fine *poi.*" Loki indicated a polished wooden calabash filled with a pinkish paste. "Might-be you not like very much at first, but after by-and-by—" She rolled her expressive eyes and patted his hand.

Thord observed that a meal was not just food to these people; it was sociability and enjoyment, to be savored to the fullest. Kauka ate with large relish, praising the cook when he came to refill the platter, admiring the bouquet which Mitsu had arranged.

The dining room was arranged without any particular thought to effect. Well-woven mats covered the floor, polished spears decorated one wall. An old-fashioned, too ornate sideboard, with a glass mirror and out-jutting brackets crowded with cutglass, decorated one end of the room, and on each side tall *kahilis* held their feathered heads together whispering about events which were past and still to come. Wide arched doors opened into a living room filled with wicker furniture, carved teakwood screens, and hung with glass-sided Chinese lamps from which bright silk tassels dangled. A faint hint of incense hung about everything, lending added charm.

The hall telephone rang and Mitsu started to answer it.

"Never mind, Mitsu, it's probably for me," Kauka said, laying down his napkin.

"Sometime I like throw that damn thing out," Loki said. "Always it ring when Kauka eating."

Kauka came back after a few minutes. "I must go—that's Elsbeth."

"Oh, finish your eat and drink your coffee," Loki protested. "That poor *wahine* always think she got a sick. Always she liking doctor around, even if he little fat and old, like you, Papa." She nudged him playfully. "Go ahead, sit down, eat quick. Not take ten minutes to get to *Haole Hao's* house."

"No, I better go," Kauka said. "After I've seen Elsbeth, Hiram wants to talk to me about the hospital—" He paused dramatically. "About fixing it up."

"Funny *Haole Hao* all of a sudden—" Loki interrupted.

"April and I had a talk on the steamer while you slept." Kauka glanced at Thord, making him one of the family. "I explained to

April that if she talked to her father maybe it would shame his eye and—well, you know April."

"Papa, you're a bad rascal," Mamo laughed.

"Sure, but I don't care so long as I can get the equipment to do my work properly." He kissed Loki's glossy hair and laid his hand on Thord's shoulder.

"I'll drive you, Papa. I want to see April," Mamo said.

When they were gone, Loki reached out, took Thord's hand between her plump brown ones and pressed it. "I glad you come and stay with us," she said warmly.

"It's incredible how kind you all are," Thord muttered. "I'm an utter stranger. Why should any of you care?"

"Oh, that Island-style," Loki retorted. "Now, what you like to do this afternoons? Sleep, walk around, or just loaf in the garden and look at that?" She waved at a colorful slope of the island glimpsed through the door.

"The last will do."

"Fine. I send Mitsu with a rug, some books, and might-be you enjoy nice drink of rum and cocoanut milk for let-you-go inside."

Rising, she swept off toward the kitchen and Thord wandered onto the veranda. Presently Mitsu appeared carrying a blanket, some magazines, and a long drink.

"Better put blanket down. Rain last night—ground wet," she said, smiling.

Thord got up and spread the robe. The woman placed the magazines on the grass and handed him his drink.

"Thank you, Mitsu."

She smiled and went off.

After a little, Loki came down the steps and walked serenely among her flowers, snipping them off carefully and dropping them into a basket on her arm. When it was filled with assorted blooms, she went to a young banana tree and tore off some long green strips of bark that hung like semi-transparent ribbons over the brown richness of her arm. When she had sufficient she strolled over and joined Thord.

He started to rise, but signing to him to stay as he was, she sank

[59]

with surprising grace on the grass, placing her flowers beside her. Unlike a white woman, she did not begin talking at once. She sat cross-legged, straight-backed, gazing at the beautiful blueness of the sea, then, taking a few large hairpins out, shook down her hair. A flock of pigeons circled over the house and lighted on the roofs, then began strutting about making their perpetual, characteristic movement of the head, half nod and half bow. Loki watched them, then began deliberately going over the blossoms she had gathered, occasionally discarding one which was not perfect.

Infinitesimal rustlings and whisperings of grass, shrubs, trees, the remote and thrilling echo of the sea, the silent stir of soil which is too fine for human ear to hear—the murmur of growth and the future—spread over the earth.

Thord lay on his elbow while happiness and unhappiness blended inextricably in him. He was too tired mentally and physically from the ordeal of the past months to want to think. He just wanted to be, to let the peace of this place seep into him, to absorb the comfort of this brown woman's presence.

In the cloudless blue of the sky there were magic depths. The day was like a dream, passionate and intense, yet endowed with some unearthly quality. He laid his arm on the cool grass. Strong sunlight walked bravely through the aisles of the gay garden and he felt as if his whole nature was being steadily renewed.

Loki's eyes met his and smiled as if they'd been friends all their lives.

"What kind of flowers you like best for lei?" she asked, her fingers hovering over assorted blossoms piled on the grass.

"Until Kauka gave me some leis two days ago, I didn't even know such things existed," he said.

"Miss lots of fun. Lei makes peoples feel good."

He nodded.

Loki studied him for a moment. "You very pretty," she said simply, as a five-year-old. "Nice nose, very tall, and your hair"—she paused, then finished on an admiring note—"red like the paddles of a warrior's canoe."

Thord flushed.

"No need be *hilahila*—shame. I only speaking true. I think swell you come to Kona. Not got many nice young mans here, *haole* mans. Not very many peoples. Might-be one dozen families. All work for *Haole Hao*. Most Scotch-style peoples. *Haole Hao* liking Scotchmans because no waste money. He like marry-people too, because not making crazy kind things. This no matter for Mamo because she got Liholiho. He come tonight. I like swell when they marry. Liholiho fine. Handsome like hell. Play guitar. Dance hotstyle hula. Liholiho manage Kahala Ranch for *Haole Hao*. If *Haole Hao* knowing Liholiho playing little hooky this afternoon and go after turkey for us to eat tonight, he mad like bull. But April no got any nice young fella for make fun with—" She glanced at Thord from under her lashes, then reaching over ran her fingers through his thick red hair.

"You got some sad-kind thing in your heart," she accused.

Thord made no reply. Loki studied him intently, then said lightly, "Sha, you young. Soon forget. After you stop in Kona with us for some few weeks—" Breaking off, she listened. "Horse coming," she announced, and waited expectantly. "Might-be Liholiho, but little early."

A scamper of fox terriers came around the turn of the driveway and April, mounted on a splendid gray horse, cantered into view. Seeing the two on the lawn she pulled up, spilled off, dropped the reins and, rushing forward, embraced Loki. "Oh, I'm so happy to be with you all!" she said tremulously.

"Sha, silly, I cry too, but my happy too big for me to hold." Loki laughed apologetically, wiping her brimming eyes on a fold of her *holoku*.

Loki and April gazed at each other, spoke briefly of local matters and relapsed into a warm, contented silence which embraced everything about them.

"Isn't Sweet Man beautiful, Thord?" April asked, gesturing at the gray gelding. Rising she went swiftly to her horse and stroked his shoulder. He nosed her gently, looking around with lustrous eyes.

[61]

"He's magnificent," Thord said. "I don't know much about riding, but I like horses."

"I'll ask Liholiho to bring a good one down from the ranch for you," April said.

"How you know Liholiho coming?" Loki asked, looking up from the wreath she had picked up again and was carefully weaving.

"I saw Mamo."

"I tell to Carlos to tie Sweet Man up," Loki announced. "Then I go fix some nice cold drinks and bring out." Placing the wreath of white jasmine about April's neck, she pushed the rest of the flowers off her lap and sent a clear hail across the seemingly empty garden.

"Aloha, Miss April! I glad you come," called Carlos, his teeth flashing, his brown face warm. He led the thoroughbred away, while fox terriers nosed eagerly through flower beds and carefully investigated tree trunks for news of the day.

Just as Loki was starting for the house, sounds of galloping hoofs halted her. A young Hawaiian on a steaming horse reined up, brandishing the limp carcass of a twenty-pound turkey. His hat, freshly covered with red spicy roses twined through ferns, was cocked dashingly over one eye. Like a brown careless god, he sat his mount, with the island behind him. There was an aura of vigorous beauty about him, the beauty that is rough hills and a high sea. His eyes were as black as crusted lava which is still molten and running underneath. His mouth had a triumphant lift to its corners. Superb, unfettered, with a soul as strong and free as his body, he sat smiling down at them.

"Liholiho!" April cried.

"April! Aloha!" he called back. "Fine you're back! I come like hell down the back trail so *Haole Hao* won't see." He slid off his horse, dropped the reins and, with the turkey in one hand, came forward, his teeth flashing like white surf against the bronze of his face.

Loki's laughter filled the garden. "You bad rascal, but I too happy you come. Take horse away, tie up where *Haole Hao* no can see if

he come by." They were all laughing, greeting each other boisterously, then Loki presented Thord.

"Fine, I'm glad you come to Kona," Liholiho said with hearty
friendliness.

"Come and help me make drinks," Loki said. *"After* you hide
your horse," she added with a chuckle. "I take the turkey." And
side by side they went off, like two beings from bigger, happier
worlds who had come to sojourn on the earth.

April seated herself on the grass beside Thord, tossed out her hair,
then clasped her arms about her slim knees.

"Gosh, you can't imagine, not being an Islander, how heavenly
it is to be back where people laugh and have fun all the time," she
remarked.

Thord nodded and plucked a blade of grass. Green gloom
crouched among the trees, sunlight slanted on the lawn, to the west
blue reaches of sky and sea swept into infinity. The air was laden
with fragrance from soil, flowers and trees, spiked by a breath of
salt water.

"Like Kona?" April asked.

"It's incredible," he replied after a moment. He looked at quiet
trees—camphor, breadfruit, Norfolk Island pines, *kukuis,* mangoes,
bananas, flame trees, Monkey Puzzles. Not a breeze stirred, but the
whole garden was mysteriously alive and seemed to be inching up
against him, hedging him in.

"You know," April remarked, "after being home only a few
hours, it seems as though I'd never been in New York. It isn't *real*
any more. School, girls I knew, shows I saw, concerts I went to,
even Dale, are getting thinner and thinner every minute." There
was a wild sweetness to her face as she spoke. Her unfinished
mouth matched her dreamy eyes. "After knowing Kauka, Loki,
Mamo, and Liholiho, and other Hawaiians like them, Americans
make me feel as if they'd all been diluted with water. They're—"
She broke off.

"I understand what you mean," Thord said when she did not go
on. "In the last few hours I've seen more real animation, more real
zest for living, and had more genuine kindness from you all, for

[63]

you're Hawaiian in spirit, than from everyone I've known in my life, added together."

"After you've been here a while you'll realize that Hawaii *is* really a land of friendship, fun, laughter, and happiness," April said.

"What about those poor blasted lepers who were sent to Molokai?"

"A cure for leprosy will be found," April said. "Conditions on Molokai were pretty awful until Father Damien's work there. His death focused the world's attention on the island, and since America annexed Hawaii in 1898 conditions have improved a lot. Doctors are trying out remedies, experimenting with treatments. For a while they were all steamed up over some oil, I can't remember what it was called, but they gave it up because it made lepers sicker than ever."

The bright afternoon was beginning to dim. Shadows commenced stealthily fingering the garden. A few last, slanting rays of sunlight grasped the limbs of trees, dragging them earthwards.

"That's Kauka's dream," April went on, "his hope, that maybe he'll discover a remedy or a cure for leprosy. For years, on the side, he's been working at it secretly. At night, when he should be sleeping, he messes around in the laboratory next his office."

Tiny splitting noises filled Thord's brain.

"You look ill," April exclaimed. "What's the matter?"

"Nothing's the matter," he said, managing his breath with difficulty.

"You look as if you'd seen a ghost."

"I've kept wondering what there was about Kauka that set him apart from other people," Thord answered. "Aside from the fact that he's a doctor"—his voice lingered on the word—"I sensed that there was an extra something about him."

"Don't say anything about this," April warned. "Even Daddy doesn't know. If he and other white people in Kona suspected that Kauka—"

7

"YOU have good time tonight, Thord?" Loki asked concernedly as she escorted him to his room. "You not laugh very much, like us fellas."

"I'm not an Islander. I wish I were," Thord replied. "But I enjoyed the evening immensely. The turkey was wonderful, and I'll never forget Mamo's dancing when Kauka and Liholiho sang that old hula."

"Mamo dance good," Loki agreed. "I proud on her and I happy you had nice time. Listen to the fine rain. That make you sleep good." She patted his shoulder. "Your bed all turn down. No need mosquito net tonight. Mosquito only come when very hot. Aloha." Taking his face between her hands, she kissed his forehead.

"Good night, Loki. Aloha, and thanks for all your kindness."

"Sha, what I make kind?" she demanded as she went off.

Walking to the rocker, Thord sat down. The room echoed with the sound of magnificently falling tropical rain. Its exultant voice filled the night. It raced along gutters, strangling them, spilled over, shattered itself on paved walks, and poured with a hollow sound into a cistern under his window.

For some unknown damnable reason, he felt like crying. His eyes went with little jerks over the room. He felt the love, the pleasure with which it had been prepared for his occupancy, and wondered how many other unfortunates had slept in it. The white plaster walls without pictures to mar them, the tall wardrobe, the *koa* dresser with its low-turned lamp, the spacious four-poster, were restful and homelike.

Through the open windows the scent of drowned soil rose to mingle with the fragrance of clean water rushing recklessly out of the sky. It filled the dark with restless, incessant movement, charged the night with mystery and power. Dragging a package of cigarettes from his pocket, he lighted one.

The evening just past lingered vividly. Happy faces, family music, constant thought and consideration for others, pleasure in tiny things, laughter. It was unlike anything he'd ever known in his twenty-eight years of living. It put to shame the past ambitions he had cherished. Such evenings, he realized, helped one to appreciate that it wasn't what a man possessed, nor what he had done, but what he was, that mattered. He'd met so-called great people who had made a loud noise in the world, but who, in the final analysis had poor, mangy little souls, focused on themselves, on their personal achievements. He'd been one of the breed himself, until life had so abruptly called a different tune for him.

He listened to rain stunning the garden and fancied behind it he could hear the clicking of eternity's machinery working on all sides, that the constantly whirling earth kept winding up. Slashing out of his chair he began undressing, but while he occupied himself with everyday gestures the feeling persisted. He struggled into his bathrobe, rammed his fists deep into its pockets and stood still, as though listening for some message on its way to him which the rain, slamming against the earth, muffled and blurred. Then he headed for the door, halted, opened it, and started down the hall, moving with a sort of passionate reluctance. Arriving at the office door he hesitated, then rapped sharply.

"Come in," Kauka's voice called.

Thord entered. Barefooted, in pajamas, with a cigar in the corner of his mouth, Kauka bent over a glass-topped table, squinting at a slide through a microscope. After an instant he glanced over his shoulder and remarked in surprised, pleased tones, "Just a minute and I'll be with you." He scribbled a note on a pad, then said, "Light the kerosene stove and we'll have coffee. It's fixed and ready in the pot."

Thord looked at the medical equipment like a man in torment,

[66]

then made his way to the double-burner stove. With an unsteady hand he took a match out of a box placed handy, opened the little door, turned up the wick and lighted it. After the blue flame had run around the burner he closed the door carefully. Near-by was a small lacquer tray with cream, sugar, and a cup and saucer covered with a clean napkin.

"Sit here." Without turning, Kauka indicated the swivel chair in front of his desk, then concentrated on his slide again.

Thord watched him. He looked young and miraculously refreshed. Rain drummed on the roof, like galloping hoofs in full stampede, and sloshed down the window panes.

"There." Kauka straightened up. "I'll fetch another cup."

Going to a small sink, he washed his hands and arms carefully in water and a strong disinfectant, then padded off. Thord kept his eyes determinedly off shelves filled with glass-stoppered bottles, glass containers filled with swabs and bandages, cases of shining instruments.

Kauka returned and placed a second cup on the tray, then with swift ease seated himself cross-legged on the floor. Thord rose hurriedly.

"Stay where you are," Kauka laughed. "You forget, I'm half-Polynesian. For centuries my mother's people sat this way. There's a distinct advantage to sitting on the floor." His eyes danced. "You can't fall off it, even if you're drunk."

"Look here, I've got to—talk to you," Thord said.

"*Maikai*—fine," Kauka replied serenely.

"When you know about me, you'll probably not want me under your roof."

"What have you done that other men haven't?" Kauka asked.

Thord hesitated, then said without looking at him, "I might as well let you have both barrels."

"Fire away."

"I'm a—doctor."

"Yes?" Kauka's dark eyes shone with delight.

"Wait. I'm a doctor—but I'm barred from ever practicing medicine again in the State of New York."

Kauka gazed at him compassionately. "Tell me your *pilikea—* trouble," he urged.

The rain seemed to shut them into a world where only the two of them existed, but the stillness of the room was broken by a small, reiterated sound like pain made audible. Thord realized with fury that it was his breathing.

"My boy, is it as bad as that? *Malama—*take it easy."

"When I was ten I decided to be a doctor, like Dad. He died when I was fifteen. I entered Medical when I was seventeen, and graduated with honors. I became an interne at St. Luke's in New York. Richard Barett headed it."

"I've heard of him. Spine specialist, isn't he?"

"Yes, old Barry was a pal of Dad's." Getting up, Thord walked to the window and stared at the streaming dark. "After Dad went, Barry sort of fathered me. After I completed my interneship, he put me on his hospital staff."

"Go on."

Although Thord's back was turned he saw Kauka mentally, gray-haired, wise, seated simply on the floor, less conscious of himself than a child.

"About a year ago, Barry had a breakdown. Besides his work at St. Luke's he had an enormous private practice. As well, we put in at least two nights a week keeping abreast of new discoveries. I was too young to be put in charge of the hospital, some of the finest doctors in the city were on its staff, but Barry turned his private practice over to me." Breaking off, Thord flung around. "Know New York?"

"I've been through. I studied medicine at the Royal College of Physicians and Surgeons in London," Kauka replied.

"Know New York society?"

"Only from hearsay."

"Well, old Barry's private patients were elderly, wealthy dowagers, smart young matrons with not much to do, and overstrung debutantes."

Kauka grunted understandingly.

"One of the debs, Tamara Newell, fancied she was in love with

[68]

me. In lots of ways Tam was a swell person. I beaued her to a few swank affairs, but she was out to make a rich marriage, to retrieve family fortunes which had gone into a tailspin."

Volumes of water crashed through the atmosphere, and wind, created by friction, lashed and shook vines swathing the house.

"I suspected from Tam's behavior with me that she was a bit free but clever enough not to make it obvious and spoil her chances of making a brilliant match. We had a showdown. I made it clear that I didn't have enough of this world's goods, and wouldn't have for years, then signed off."

"Yes?" Kauka's eyes were fathomless.

"Tam had ideas of her own. For some reason I'd got hold of her imagination—"

"Which is more dangerous than love," Kauka suggested.

Thord nodded. "She knew I worked at night, sometimes in Barry's office, and dropped in after late parties—always with some rich young lad in tow, as if she were trying to tantalize me. She pretended a deep interest in medicine. Probably the gamble of life and death did fascinate a girl of her type."

"Probably."

"Usually she and her escorts were swacked. I resented having valuable time wasted by spoiled kids hunting new sensations, and wasn't too cordial. After a bit the visits stopped and Tam dropped out of the picture for several months."

Kauka nodded.

Thord made a sudden gesture of despair. "One night—one morning, rather, for it was after three—I was just about to close up when the door opened. It was Tam. She'd got in a jam and—gone to a cheap butcher. She bled to death in a few minutes, before telling me the name of the doctor she'd been to, or the fellow who had got her into trouble."

"You poor damn kid," Kauka said, getting up.

"The cards were all stacked against me. I'd been seen with her on several occasions, people knew she'd been to my office. After the courts and newspapers got through with me—" He broke off. "When I get to thinking about it I feel as if I'd been rolled in dung!

gs a lot of weight in the medical world, he believed I was
Thanks to him, I got off more lightly than I would have
__wise, but I was barred from ever practicing in New York
State again."

"Smoke a cigarette," Kauka advised. "I'll fix coffee. After we've
drunk up, tell me the rest." Padding over to the stove he dashed the
contents of the boiling pot with cold water, and asked over his
shoulder, "Sugar? Milk?"

"Black, please."

The sustained, stirring roar of rain filled the room. Suddenly
Thord said into the air, "I must appear an ass to take this thing so to
heart, when I know I'm innocent, but the rank injustice of this mess
got me mentally on the run, boiled my mind up—"

"I know. A person doesn't mind, even if he doesn't like paying
for things he's done, but when he has to pay for things wished on
him, it's another matter. You question the justice of life, the right-
ness of things—"

"Exactly."

Kauka turned, and his dark, direct eyes found Thord's blue ones.
"My boy," he said in his kind, slow way, "actually it doesn't matter what happens to a person, *but it matters a lot what they do
about what happens.*" He uttered the words slowly, letting them
sink home.

Thord sat silent, then said, "I get what you mean."

"That's a start," Kauka smiled. "Yesterday is finished, today may
not be so hot, but the future remains yours to shape as you will.
You can do nothing with it, or you can make it an achievement."

Filling the cups, he handed one to Thord and sipped thoughtfully from the one he nursed between his hands.

"I know you're afraid that no matter what you may accomplish,
no matter where you go, this business may crop up in your later
life."

"Exactly. I don't know what to do, where to run."

"Stay here," Kauka advised. "There isn't a chance in a million
that this New York mess will ever trickle to Kona. When the hospital is remodeled and enlarged, I'll need an assistant."

"You mean you believe in me?"

"Completely."

"Thanks," Thord muttered. His eyes hungrily traveled over the shelves of medicines, dropped to rows of test tubes, brushed shining surgical instruments. "But Mr. Wilde may balk at hiring another doctor."

Imps played tag with each other in Kauka's eyes. "I only have to let Mrs. Wilde know you're a doctor, from New York." He stressed the words significantly. "Plus April pulling for what I want—an adequate medical setup—will do the trick."

"They'll expect references."

"When the time comes I can manage that by writing directly to Dr. Barett. In the meantime I'll casually mention you're a doctor incog. here to rest. Think you'd like to remain in Kona with us?"

"Hell, yes."

Kauka began pacing slowly back and forth. "Look, my time's getting short. I'm fifty-six." He stopped before Thord. "I have no son to carry on my real work." He gestured at notebooks stacked in one corner of his desk, then his eyes invaded Thord's as if he were carefully estimating the inner man. "I'm convinced"—he hesitated, then said in tones which sent a tingle along Thord's spine—"that leprosy can be cured."

"April mentioned this afternoon that you've been collecting data about it, on the side. That's what determined me to talk to you tonight, to tell you about myself. I hoped that maybe—"

Kauka smiled, then beckoned to Thord to come to the table on which the microscope stood. "In the work I'm attempting to do, I must have someone I can trust absolutely, as I trusted you instinctively from the moment I saw you. It'll be weeks, possibly months, before the remodeling of the hospital will be completed. In the meantime"—he paused while his eyes looked into the crowded future—"you'll have leisure to acquaint yourself with all, with the very little I know, with the very little I've learned."

"Even if Wilde doesn't hire me, I'm with you all the way," Thord said impulsively. "I have a small income, sufficient enough to keep me here. Until this thing happened in New York, I had

[71]

ambitions of writing my name across the sky in flame, but . . ."

"If we succeed in discovering a cure or a remedy for leprosy, you will."

"The odd part is," Thord interrupted, "that during the short time I've known you, two days, I've realized that that aspect of life isn't what counts."

Kauka gave a grunt and began going through notes and papers.

"My work in this field, of necessity, has been limited," he said. "While I've read every book, medical note, report, and pamphlet that's ever been put out about leprosy, I haven't had a great many opportunities to work with it first hand. On several occasions, when I've had to report cases for deportation to Molokai, I've been able to get samples of blood for analysis and experimentation." He listened to wet darkness lashing down, then his eyes met Thord's. "We may work years, all our lives, without getting anywhere," he warned.

"At least we'll have the excitement of trying."

Kauka nodded in his slow way, then picked up a notebook. A long roll of distant thunder sounded through the rain. Kauka listened to it, then his eyes glowed and he made a slight, expressive gesture with his hand.

"Hawaiians believe if a person tries to do something and the world gives him no recognition, the gods salute him with—Thunder in Heaven!"

8

NO matter how late he worked, Kauka, like most Polynesians, woke early. He felt a mystical union with rhythms of the universe, which is the rich heritage of so-called primitives. For thousands of years his mother's people, living in the scattered islands of the Pacific, had stirred about in the pre-dawn hush, lighting cocoanut-husk fires and starting the daily business of living. The echoes of ancient instincts and activities lived on in his body, and his being automatically roused itself each morning to take part in the never-ending wonder of light welling out of darkness.

Rolling over, he opened his eyes. Familiar objects in the large lofty room were taking shape. He saw the loved mound beside him which was Loki, smelled the fragrance of earth drenched by rain, drifting in through open doors and windows. Sitting up stealthily, he stretched with careful pleasure.

"Oh, sleep some more, Papa," Loki urged. "Little more three o'clock before you come *moemoe*."

"I tried not to wake you." He patted her shoulder. "Today is Sunday. I don't have to go to the hospital till eleven. I'll just walk around a little, smell the garden, maybe make us some coffee." His voice poised hopefully.

"I like that swell," Loki said in lazy, contented tones.

He smiled. On Sundays he always felt as if he'd come into a larger kingdom. There were more hours with his family, more time to enjoy details of living.

He sat staring at the opposite wall. The plaster, white as flour, satin-smooth to the touch, made of coral dust and *kukui* ashes, was a dim, pleasant gray in the changing light. A sense of richness stole through him, increasing the luster of his eyes. Somehow it was appropriate that on a Sunday he should have the knowledge that there was someone eager to work in his own secret field. It went hand-in-hand with the wealth of the day. Peace crept along his bones. It had not been merely compassion for a fellow-human's travail that had pushed him toward Thord. It had been a nudge from God.

Putting his legs over the side of the bed, he tightened the cord of his pajama breeches. He looked at the coat flung over the foot of the bed and decided against it. Despite the night rain, the dawn was velvety and warm. Walking quietly onto the veranda he watched dim whiteness showing behind the slow long shape of Mauna Loa, and looked with placid enjoyment at the morning star burning serenely above its snow-encrusted summit.

On week days the servants were about their duties before daylight. On Sundays they slept until seven. Halfway down the long veranda, surrounding three sides of the house, he stepped into a room with four narrow cots on it, three filled with the sleeping shapes of children. On bare, silent feet he went from one to another. Assured that they were all covered, he went out and headed for the kitchen.

He loitered on his way, allowing the soles of his bare feet to enjoy the feel of cool, smooth mats beneath them. When he reached the kitchen he walked to a table, placed under a long window, and lighted a lamp; then he stoked the range with kindling and firewood placed in a big box beside the roomy old stove. When the fire got under way, with pleasant rustlings and snappings, he closed the door and began assembling coffee.

Putting the pot filled with water where the fire would be hottest, he whipped up an egg, then stirred in a generous amount of coffee and set the bowl aside. Sitting down beside one of the scrubbed tables he smoked placidly while his eyes wandered over the room. Shining rows of pots and pans hung on one wall, dishcloths were strung on a line near the ranges, stacked dishes filled a big set of shelves.

Light was growing outside the windows. He heard cattle calling in the distance and the strident screech of a peacock greeting the dawn. Land smells, tree smells, and the great salt smell of the sea drifted in, mingling with the cozy scents of a lived-in house.

Minute stirrings from behind the stove reached his ears. Going forward he inspected a wooden box, padded with an old blanket, and smiled at a mother cat with a new litter of kittens. She yawned and stretched luxuriously when he stroked her head. A sound made him glance up.

"Aloha, Ching," he said.

"Aloha. What-for you get up so early?" the old man demanded with cross affection. "Today Sunday."

"Nice morning," Kauka explained.

The cook glanced at the garden and nodded. "Velly nice," he agreed.

Kauka went to the stove. Taking the coffee and egg fluff he scooped it into the pot, waited until the mixture foamed up, then dashed it with cold water. Taking two bowls, Kauka filled them with the dark, fragrant coffee. Pouring four heaping tablespoonfuls of brown sugar into the nearest one, he drew out a chair and sat down. Ching sank onto a stool and took the unsweetened bowl. For a while they drank in comradely silence, then the Chinaman remarked, "You tink *Haole Hao* give Takeshi small job? Gar-damn tough Papa get cook."

"I'm going to talk to him tomorrow."

"April got pletty face now. Before, velly thin. No good."

Kauka nodded agreeingly. Ching felt in the breast pocket of his starched coat, drew out a Chinese pipe, with a wee brass bowl halfway up the three-sided stem, and filled it with a thimbleful of tobacco. When it got going he looked at Kauka with narrowed eyes.

"Who this fella you bling home?"

Kauka brightened. "A doctor from New York. Little *pilikea,* so come away," he explained.

"Understan' velly well. Young mans always have troubles. With girl?" Ching's eyes glinted hopefully.

[75]

Kauka nodded, and Ching smiled with evil delight.

"Stop Kona long time?"

"Maybe."

"Look like smart fella."

"Yes." Kauka felt the stubble on his chin with appraising fingers. Ching glanced at the clock. "Now you take coffee to Loki and I fix for other people," he directed, going to the stove.

Filling a clean bowl with coffee, Kauka doused it generously with cream and sugar and started back down the veranda. The sun had sprung up and there was a glorious languor in the air. Multitudes of bees working in the warm shade of the garden, flies buzzing among the sticky leaves of an old fig tree, seemed the full voice of life, discussing the future. He stopped for an instant to drink in the beauty of the new morning, and felt, rather than heard, the sigh and thud of the Pacific against the coastline, fifteen hundred feet below. Turning into the bedroom, he said, "Loki."

She opened her eyes, smiled, sat up, and lifted her hair over her shoulder. "Smell good," she said, reaching out for the steaming bowl Kauka held out.

Seating himself on the edge of the bed, Kauka told her about Thord. Her large eyes narrowed a trifle.

"Be careful, Papa," she warned.

"Thord's okay."

"I know, but might-be you fellas get all steam up and—"

"I have you and Mamo to think of," Kauka interrupted. "We'll work secretly, as I've worked all these years." He kneaded Loki's big knee with his short fingers. "You know what I wish, Loki?"

"No, Papa."

"If we were not always short and always owing back salary to Hiram, I would like to go to Molokai and—"

"Papa, no!" Loki cried.

"But many American doctors are working at Kaulapapa to find a cure for leprosy. I would like to work with them."

"And leave Kona?" Loki said like a horrified child. "Live under *plias* where the sun only shine little while every day—be with only sick, unhappy peoples? Better you stop here. With us. No be downhearted. Who know? Might-be you two finding some medicine for cure *maipake,* here. Then"—her face glowed—"then you make many Hawaiian peoples happy who now got broke the heart." She patted his hand. "Better you get all this-kind stuffs out your head." She sat up briskly. "I pray hard for you and Thord, with only little moneys and not so much time—" Bending forward, she kissed his cheek.

Kauka nodded and walked slowly to an old upright piano standing against one wall. Seating himself he began playing an ancient jingly ballad that spilled notes like gaily colored autumn leaves through the still house. Loki leaned back on her pillows watching his squat figure, lost in music his fingers pulled out of yellowing keys.

"That hot-style, Papa," Loki approved, then glanced expectantly at the door. "Now try one lively hula and sure Mamo and Liholiho wake up. Ah, there Mamo now!"

"Aloha, Mama, Aloha, Papa!" The tall girl, wrapped in a colorful silk kimono, kissed the top of Kauka's head, then, strolling to the generous four-poster, curled up beside her mother.

"Play some more, Papa," she directed, closing her eyes luxuriously.

Loki lifted up a strand of the girl's wavy, unbound hair and passed an approving finger over her eyebrows, silken, slender, curving in perfect arches over the smooth beauty of her eyelids, heritage of her proud, ancient race.

"Sleep good, Mamo?"

The girl made no reply, surrendering herself to the beauty of music pouring from the old piano, but an infinitesimal quivering of the eyelashes signified assent.

"Ah, there, Liholiho!" Loki exclaimed delightedly.

"Aloha, boy," Kauka called over his shoulder.

Liholiho strolled in with large loafing grace which hinted at the strength of muscles barely concealed by blue cotton pajamas.

"Sit down here," Loki urged, indicating the foot of the bed. "Ching bring coffee soon."

Kauka radiated happiness. Beyond everything, he loved Sunday mornings when family and guests congregated in the big bedroom to drink coffee, chat, sing, and listen to a chapter from the Bible.

Liholiho established himself on the spot indicated, with the air of having sat there many times before. Folding his big arms, he settled his back against one of the intricately carved bedposts.

Loki's eyes rested on him contentedly. In a purely impersonal way the woman in her thrilled to the royal man in him. He was of no particular race, or era. He was man, incarnate. His strength, which was the strength of the island under him, drew people to him like a magnet. His skin had the high luster of health and vigorous blood flowing exultantly. He had a conqueror's nose and an imperious mouth.

Though Mamo lay with closed eyes, Loki knew she was acutely aware of his presence. Eagerness mixed with languor wrapped her long, graceful body.

"Hey, Mamo, wake up!"

Reaching over, Liholiho shook her slender, arched foot.

Her eyes opened and smiled at him, then with a slight happy movement she edged her head against the softness of Loki's warm body. "I'm sleepy," she protested. "We stayed up late."

Liholiho gave a laugh like wind in the hills, then said, "Wait, Kauka, I get a guitar."

"Fine," Loki approved. "Tell to Shizu to bring the kids for hear music and wake Thord. Tell to him to have coffee with us. Might-be little lonely and strange this first morning."

"Okay," he called back gaily.

He returned shortly with the guitar. Going to the piano he tuned swiftly, pitching the strings to match the keys.

"Okay, now we go." The men's eyes met and they began singing, of serried headlands with blue seas smoking against them, of spray-dimmed ginger-filled valleys, of jungles steaming under a hot sun, of mornings like crystal and evenings like amber and opals.

Mamo sat up. Loki moved a big loose arm in an expert hula gesture. Ching came with the tray of coffee and hardtack, the

[78]

Japanese house-woman herded the three small children into the room.

"Where other fella?" Ching demanded as the last stirring shout ended with a catch of the heart.

"Coming," Loki replied.

"Good all fellas make family-styles," Ching agreed. "New fella velly nice man." Setting down the tray, he departed with a flourish.

"Hey, Aloha! You sleep good?" Loki asked, as Thord, looking rather bewildered, entered the room.

"Thanks yes, like a top."

"What you think our style Sunday? Music, coffee, fun?"

"It's jolly."

"Sit in that chair." She indicated one by the coffee table and signed to Shizu to lift the three children onto the foot of the bed. "Now give some crackers, Shizu, please," she directed. "Hey, you kids—" Sitting up she placed a big round ship's biscuit in each small pair of hands. Then the children munched like solemn mice, their eyes round and pleased.

Kauka and Liholiho came over, picked up bowls, and everyone began drinking.

"Now, Papa, better you read the Bible and us get dress and eat breakfast," Loki suggested when the last empty coffee bowl was put back on the tray.

Taking up a worn Bible, Kauka read the Twenty-third Psalm.

"That 'Lord is my Shepherd' kind always make peoples feel good inside," Loki commented. "I little *huhu*—mad, inside las' night when I hear you and Kauka talk—talk in office. Doctors smart, but not got very good sense." She watched Thord with merry eyes.

Thord looked at Kauka. Mamo's and Liholiho's large liquid eyes registered amazement.

"Our friend is a *kauka*," Kauka explained, laying his hand on Thord's shoulder.

"Papa will be glad to have you to talk to," Mamo commented. "Maybe after the hospital is bigger, *Haole Hao* will make you his assistant."

[79]

"*Haole Hao*, hell!" Liholiho laughed. "Elsbeth is the one who'll want a fine handsome doctor to hold her hand."

Their laughter blended.

The telephone rang. Kauka went to get it. When he returned he was beaming. "It's all fixed up," he announced. "That was Elsbeth. She is having Reverend Thisbe and his family in for tea and wants us to come too. Maybe they will phone Brewer to come up from his macodamia plantation too. I asked if I could bring my friend, *Doctor Graham*"—he stressed the word waggishly —"*Doctor Graham*, from New York."

Thord looked rather ill-at-ease, and Kauka, noting it, gave his shoulder a playful, affectionate punch.

"I be damn glad when *this* over," Loki remarked to Thord, as the car turned out of the drive and started up the narrow road toward the main body of the plantation. "I like April fine, but *Haole Hao* give me the jim-jams. I sorry for Elsbeth—she have no fun, but sometimes I like push in her face."

Thord chuckled involuntarily. Liholiho and Mamo had gone on ahead, on horseback. Carlos and Kauka, dressed in Sunday best, sat uncomfortably in front. Loki, in a gaily flowered *holoku,* lounged beside Thord.

Kauka talked with his driver, Loki tossed comments into the air, Thord watched the enticing turns of the road winding through groves of *kukui* trees, past small fields of cane. Presently the mill loomed up imposingly, filling the air with vast vibrations. The deadly sweet odor of boiling molasses drifted to his nostrils. In the yards about the mill, straining teams of mules and blue-clad laborers swarmed about flat cars piled with towering loads of cane stalks. Cries, the mighty rumbling of machinery, drifted to his ears. Beyond, on a low rise, the one-storied rambling very shabby hospital backed into trees, as if trying to hide itself.

A minute post office, an austere-looking church, set back in a stone-walled enclosure, and a large smart store, were left behind. The car turned into a graveled driveway, winding through a large formal garden. Two cars were parked beyond the porte cochere.

"Reverend Thisbe here," Loki commented, "and that old rascals Brewer." Her voice had a delighted note. "Brewer run *Haole Hao's* macodamia nut plantation in South Kona, but always on the side he make hell with Hawaiian girls. Reverend Thisbe hate him. Might-be after all us have some little fun."

Carlos brought the car to a stop and they all got out. April flew down the steps to greet them. "Aloha, Thord, Aloha, Kauka, Aloha, Loki!" She embraced them as if they'd been parted years instead of overnight. "Mother's in the back *lanai*. Mamo and Liholiho arrived about fifteen minutes ago."

She led the way through a house with small, high rooms, where various pieces of uncomfortable-looking furniture seemed to be spying on one another quietly.

In a glassed-in veranda at the rear of the house, Mrs. Wilde lay on a couch with a silk wrap thrown over her, eyes fixed expectantly on the door. Her glance leapt over Loki and Kauka and lighted on Thord. Though she made no move, he was conscious of her mind boring hopefully into him. After greeting her, Kauka took Thord's arm and said, with a little formal bow, "Elsbeth, this is my friend, Doctor Graham."

With a faint dry sigh, the woman sat up. Her face was colorless, her straw-colored hair almost invisible, but her eyes were restless, alive, watchful, and demanding. "I'm *so* delighted to meet you," she said. "Strangers are a real pleasure in Kona. Let me present my other guests. Reverend Thisbe"—she indicated a small man who made Thord think of a red ferret—"and this is Mr. Brewer."

A large, loose man with a florid face and small lewd eyes moved forward. "Glad to meet you, Graham, glad indeed. You must come down and spend a week-end with me sometime. I haven't much of a place, but if you take life as it comes, a person can usually manage to scare up fun."

Thord murmured his thanks. The Reverend edged closer.

"I hope we'll, ah, shall see you at church next Sunday. There were no services today. Once a month I go to South Kona to preach. Where"—his small eyes darted around—"is—"

"Prudence is in the garden with Mamo and Liholiho," April put in.

"Sit here," Mrs. Wilde begged, indicating a chair at her side.

Thord sat down. Mrs. Wilde languidly picked up a small silver bell and jingled it.

"Tea will be served shortly, or do you prefer coffee, Doctor Graham?"

"Tea will do nicely, thanks."

"April, will you pour? I don't feel up to it today."

"Of course, Mother."

"Well, you old rascals, what you been doing for make trouble?" Loki asked, establishing herself beside Brewer.

He adjusted a white flower, sitting absurdly above his large purple ear. "You malign me, Loki," he protested. Then he said, in a baiting way, "You've been listening to Rev. Thisbe gossiping!"

"My time is too valuable to discuss, ah, the ways of transgressors," Thisbe snapped, his voice crackling with hostility.

"Rot!" Brewer retorted in a whisky-roughened voice. "The trouble with you, Rev, is you're always poking your snout into other people's business instead of taking on the fun put into the world to enjoy. Now if you'd cut loose and get drunk once a year, you'd feel a damn sight better."

"Drunk!" Thisbe gasped.

"Sure! Don't try to tell me liquor is wrong. I read the Bible once, when I was soused, and remember something about 'Wine that maketh glad the heart of man,'" and he laughed with huge evil glee.

Loki exploded into magnificent laughter. Kauka's eyelashes quivered. April smiled swiftly. Mrs. Wilde appeared not to hear.

"Are you intending to pay Kauka a long visit?" she asked hopefully.

"I have no plans."

"Kona has a charm—for those who are able to get about." Her voice paused. "It's rich in historical interest. In a day or so, if I feel better, I'll arrange with April to see that you get down to see the City of Refuge and Kealakekua Bay, where Captain Cook was killed."

"Please don't bother," Thord said. "Being a doctor, I'll be quite content just making the rounds with Kauka."

Mrs. Wilde waved his remark away, then made a small deprecating gesture. "You should have come a bit later. . . . Our hospital . . . Hiram is going to have it remodeled and brought up to date. . . . A person can't do everything on a plantation at once. New machinery was installed in the mill last fall."

Thord made appropriate replies.

April moved across the room and seated herself beside a small wicker table, as two elderly Japanese women with patient faces came in with tea, sandwiches, and cake. Mrs. Wilde watched them irritably.

"No, not *there,* Otero, put the sandwiches *there.* Iku, turn the pot around so the handle's convenient for Miss April." She gave an exhausted sigh. "You'd think servants, after years—"

"Okay, Iku. That's fine, Otero," Thord heard April saying under her breath. The women flashed grateful, loving looks at her, then waited to hand around the cups.

Mamo and Liholiho came in laughing, accompanied by a girl who, Thord knew instantly, must be Thisbe's daughter. Her plainness was sheer tragedy. She had her father's ferret nose, a colorless mouth, and eyes that cried out in protest that life had been so niggardly with physical lure. But Brewer leapt up to meet her.

"Ah, Prue, my dear! Long time no see. Let me get you a cushion. Graham, have you met Prudence?" And he presented her as if she were some fabulous siren of history.

A faint pleased flush rose in the girl's sallow cheeks and her bleak eyes swam with a sort of fatuous, pathetic gratitude. Reverend Thisbe glared at her, silently commanding her to sit elsewhere. With intense animosity she resisted her father and sank down beside the gross old man who managed to create in her some sense of her feminine heritage. Loki leaned back watching

[83]

from under her eyelashes, while outwardly she joked with Mamo and Liholiho.

Just as cups were being refilled, *Haole Hao* strode in. His watchful yellow eyes swept the group, added it up, as he came forward. While he spoke in brief sentences, Thord analyzed him. There was a terrific repression about him. Every ounce of superfluous flesh had been burned away in grim determination to out-achieve forbears who had preceded him to the virgin fields of Hawaii. He appeared passionless, but Thord suspected him of deep passions. Perhaps that was why Mrs. Wilde had assumed the mantle of invalidism and taken to couches. . . .

The afternoon wore, finally, to its close. Brewer banged Thord on the back. "When you get fed up with things around here, barge down and see me. Well, Prue, my dear—" He pinched her cheek, then turned to take leave of the rest.

"I wonder if you'll have time tomorrow, or next day, to spare a little time for an invalid," Mrs. Wilde said. "Fresh faces, fresh thoughts are stimulating when—" She sighed in a helpless way.

"Of course," Thord said.

"It's good of you." She touched his fingers with the tips of hers, while *Haole Hao* watched with an expressionless face.

April went with them to the door.

"I glad that all finish," Loki said, as they drove off. "But you make big hit with Elsbeth, Thord, so time not all waste."

He grimaced.

There was an almost indecent beauty to the somber and violent sunset burning above the horizon. Dark slopes of the island lunged toward the flat gray sea. The distant mutter of an unusually heavy surf created a feeling of unseen forces marshaling. By the time they got home it was dark, but lamps spilled a cheery orange glow on green lawns, and banked begonias, growing to the eaves, dangled their semi-transparent jewel-like clusters of blossoms in the light.

"Swell to be home," Loki said to Kauka as they went up the steps.

He nodded.

Mamo and Liholiho galloped in and they all went directly to dinner.

"One minute, this Sunday night. Papa say grace." Loki glanced at Mamo and Liholiho, who were laughing, and they became quiet. There was no reproof in Loki's voice, only a loving reminder. Thord bowed his head.

"Give the hand," Loki said, taking his. Looking up, he saw they were all holding hands. He gripped Kauka's and sensed the warm current running around the flower-weighted table. After a short silence, Kauka began speaking:

"Mighty Akua—Creator of Islands, sea and sky,
We thank Thee for the abundance
You have given man.
Our waters teem with fish, our forests with fruit are heavy-laden.
Be with us this day.
Guard our warriors on the lava trails,
Guard our fishermen upon the sea,
Guard the children born trustingly to our loving hearts.
Guard those who stray far from home in anger.
Bless our fishponds, our temples, and our king.
May Laa's warm rays by day
And Mahina's silvery light by night
Cleanse and purify our bodies.
So one day we may walk with Thee
In the strange land of Eternity.
Aloha—our love to you. Amen."

Dinner went its leisurely, pleasant course. When it ended, Liholiho rose to go.

"Maybe some day next week Mamo and April will bring you to Kahala Ranch. I'll find a nice horse for you." He gripped Thord's hand.

"Thanks, Liholiho, I'd enjoy it."

"Swell." He kissed Loki, then threw an affectionate arm about Kauka's heavy shoulders.

"Got fresh lei for Liholiho?" Loki asked.

[85]

Mamo nodded. "It's on the lawn." And they went out together.

"Mama"—Kauka laid his hand on her arm—"we're going to the office for a little while."

"No talk all night," Loki warned. "You got plenty time. Years and years." And she patted him fondly.

Just as Kauka was getting out his notebooks, a tap sounded on the office door leading into the garden. Rather regretfully, he put them away and called out, "Come in."

A tall Hawaiian with intelligent, aquiline features entered slowly. Kauka greeted him warmly. Moku glanced at Thord, looked ill-at-ease, then said, "I want to talk to you alone."

"This *haole* is to be my assistant," Kauka explained. "What is your *pilikea?*"

The man shifted his feet. "Tutu not so well," he began, then switched into Hawaiian. Kauka listened, puffing on his cigar. Moku talked in a hurried, furtive manner, glancing in Thord's direction every so often.

"He no understand Hawaiian," Kauka said.

Moku looked relieved, and when he came to the end of his recital asked in English, "When can you come see Tutu?"

"Tomorrow, when I'm through at the hospital."

"Mahalo, nui loa," Moku murmured; he gripped Kauka's hand and vanished into the dark.

Kauka clasped his hands behind his back and prowled about the office. Thord waited, conscious of the vast night spreading over the island. Multitudes of soft noises came from the dark garden. A leaf drifting down, birds tightening their holds in their sleep, two limbs of an old tree, bent by *kona* gales, groaned faintly as bole wore upon bole, wounding each other every time a breeze moved them. The night seemed filled with arcades and avenues leading to unseen distances. Kauka stopped prowling and stood still. His eyes, like two dark arrows, came to Thord's.

"My boy, Moku's grandmother is not well. He told me she takes no interest even in her grandchildren, which are always the joy of a Polynesian's old age. From what Moku says, I suspect he's afraid

Tutu has leprosy, but didn't even say so in Hawaiian because you were present. I hope I'm wrong."

The telephone began ringing. Kauka went and got it. "Okay, I'll come," he said, sighing a little, and hung up. "Mary Ako is starting to have her baby," he explained.

Thord got up.

"Would you like me—shall I go with you tomorrow?"

"Yes, I would like it," Kauka said simply, as he began gathering what he needed to take in his old black bag.

9

THORD glanced at his watch. They had been driving for over an hour. Kauka sat behind the wheel, deep in thought. Rounding a turn the whole sweep of southern Hawaii showed. Dense forests, slashed by black rivers of frozen lava, spilled to the sea, bluer than the bluest cornflower that ever grew.

The narrow highway ducked through fields of coffee, through forests of *ohia, kukui,* and *koa* trees, across lava flows and into forests again. A line of donkeys passed, soberly following a grizzled Hawaiian, who was riding a dilapidated gray mare. He called out and Kauka waved back. After a while Kauka turned off the round-the-island highway and headed along a dirt road which wound through wastes of guava bushes down to a small blue bay, wedged in between black arms of lava. As they neared the shore, Kauka spoke.

"If Tutu has leprosy, this is going to be a pretty ghastly affair." He straightened his shoulders. "I'll know the instant I see her. There are several types of leprosy and various symptoms to establish it. The most common form in Hawaii begins with an odd beauty. The skin becomes semi-transparent. There's a rosy flush to the cheeks, especially in younger people. When the disease has progressed farther the lobes of the ears swell slightly. A bit later there's a shine under the eyebrows, hairs can be pulled out easily and without pain, and the outer flanges of the nostrils begin to thicken."

He stared into space, then, after a brief silence, he went on. "Moku will resent my bringing you. I'll have to tell him immediately that, to all practical purposes, you're my adopted son, working with me to find a cure for leprosy. Hawaiians are as devoted to children they adopt as they are to their own flesh and blood."

The car bumped on, lurched through ruts, ground over cinders. At times the road was so narrow that guava bushes lashed at the windows. Papaya trees held their heads above the sprawl of lesser growth, like green *kahilis* marching boldly against the sky.

"I've known Tutu years," Kauka said. "She comes of fine stock. She had a good education, and was a court hula dancer during Kalakaua's reign." He swung the car through a rut, gunned it up a short rise, and rattled down a slope which led to a two-story, weather-worn house sitting back inside neatly built stone walls.

Moku came out of the house and, seeing Thord, stopped dead. His face which had been smiling, changed. Resentment and unbelief filled his eyes. Kauka stopped the car, got out, and spoke to him in Hawaiian. He nodded, greeted Thord briefly and started for the house.

Kauka signed to Thord to come, took Moku's arm, and went on talking in a low voice as they started across the garden. In spite of its shabbiness there was a charm to the building. The lower portion was latticed on three sides and open on the one facing the sea. A ruddy gourd hung on a post; shiny black pebbles crunched underfoot. Lacy *kiawes,* and indolent monkey-pod trees leaned over the stone walls, covered with orange and amethyst air-plants. A rangy old sow, followed by half a dozen shoats, grunted and trotted off crossly. In the rear of the building, squatting down in the purple shade of a mango tree, a slim girl was poking wood into a battered-looking stove covered with steaming pots and pans. Recognizing Kauka, she called out that she would be with them presently. An older woman braiding a *lauhala* mat thrust her work aside and hurried to meet them.

"Aloha, Annie, Aloha," Kauka said, taking the woman's face between his hands and kissing it. "Annie, this is my adopted son, Thord Graham. He has come to work with me."

The woman gazed at him with fine dark eyes, then said in a flute-like voice, "I proud-and-happy you come our house."

"Thank you," Thord said.

For an instant Moku, his wife, and Kauka conferred in lowered voices, then Annie said, "Tutu there," waving at a noble old woman seated on a mat in the cool *lanai* fronting on the sea. "I go get *kaukau*—food." And she hurried off.

Moku's arms hung heavily as if he both wanted and did not want to have the next few minutes over with. Kauka felt in his breast pocket and brought out some cigars.

"Have one?" he asked.

Moku shook his head.

"You don't?" he said, his eyes meeting Thord's.

"No, I use cigarettes. Thanks."

Although Kauka gave no sign, Thord sensed the tension of his soul. When he had lighted up, he went forward.

"Aloha, Tutu," he said, and, bending down, kissed the old woman's forehead.

Her kind eyes, etched about with smile-wrinkles, were veiled for an instant, then met his slowly. A muscle inside Thord cramped. Her skin had the transparency Kauka had described; a faint color burned in her cheeks. Even her ear-lobes were puffed, and a faint shine showed under the hairs of her eyebrows.

Kauka presented Thord.

"Aloha," she said, apathetically.

Moku watched Kauka anxiously.

"Smoke, Tutu?" Kauka asked, seating himself cross-legged beside her.

She shook her head. "Eat first." She gestured slightly at Moku's wife and the slender girl who were hurrying out with bowls and calabashes. With gestures of natural hospitality they placed the food on a mat, plucked a few hibiscus blossoms off some bushes and tossed them about.

"Hey, you kids," Annie called, signing to her brood to come in from the beach. "Come, *kaukau!*"

They came scampering up, sturdy little boys and slim little girls, who swooped on Kauka, then sat down eyeing the food expectantly. Everyone except Thord began dipping into the same big calabash of *poi* placed in the center of the mat.

"Eat, eat," Annie urged. "When Moku tell to me Kauka come I stew some fine fat chicken in cocoanut milk. The kids get plenty *opihis.*" She indicated small calabashes of butter-yellow shellfish.

"I'm not hungry. I had lunch," Thord said.

"Might-be you not liking Hawaiian food," Annie said. "Us got bread in the house, nice wild *koa* honeys, and good Kona coffee." She indicated the steaming pot and waited hopefully.

"Thanks, I don't want anything," Thord insisted.

The full golden afternoon lay on the sea. An occasional breath of air stirred the green tops of tall old cocoanuts and a few cattle wandered along the beach. Children and adults ate busily. The gaunt sow came back into the garden. Little waves with crests of jade and azure crisped on the beach.

When the last scrap of food was devoured, the children returned to their play. Annie laid a small baby gently in Tutu's broad lap, glanced at her husband, then assisted her sixteen-year-old daughter to clear away the calabashes and bowls. Kauka lighted a cigar. Tutu rolled a Bull Durham, with wrinkled but beautifully tapered fingers finished by perfect nails. Annie returned and seated herself cross-legged by her husband. Silence enveloped the small group.

Thord glanced at Tutu. In her were all the fine, selected forces of life, mellowed by time into a strange, moving beauty which only the aged have. In spite of her white hair her spine was straight, her gestures perfectly timed.

When she had finished smoking she extinguished the glowing butt on a pebble, turned and looked into Kauka's eyes.

"I have *maipake,* see," she said, indicating her ear-lobes and eyebrows.

Taking her hand, Kauka pressed it between his. Tears began spilling silently down the old woman's cheeks.

"Yes, I see, Tutu," Kauka said gently.

"What can you do for me?" Her eyes met his. "I do not wish to go to Molokai."

"I can do nothing. As you know, for years I've been studying leprosy. The Government doctors on Molokai have been trying and experimenting with different medicines. But to date no cure has been found."

Tutu wiped away her tears with a lock of gray hair and gazed at the horizon. "Many, many years ago, during the reign of Lunalilo, my mother went to Molokai with my father—when he was taken. She lied, she said she had *maipake,* so she could take care of him. After his death she was found to be clean and shipped back to Kona. She—told me about Molokai. I do not wish to go there."

"Things are not as they were in the old days, Tutu," Kauka said compassionately. "There are hospitals now, doctors, nurses. The American Government has spent hundreds of thousands of dollars on the settlement. You will have every kindness, good food, all the skill science possesses."

"That will not make up for being separated from those I love. My son Moku, Annie, my *moopunas.*" She indicated the sleeping baby in her lap and the older children skittering along the beach. "I am old. Over eighty. I have only a small time more to live and wish to be with my loved ones."

Kauka gazed at her. "How long have you known, Tutu?" he asked gently.

"For many months, maybe one year."

"You should have come in. Your presence may spread leprosy among the family."

"People live among lepers years without catching the sickness," Tutu insisted. "Father Damien stayed on Molokai fourteen years before he got it. At most I will not last more than a year. I asked Moku to bring you, hoping that might be by now you had found a medicine to cure *maipake*"—her voice halted, then went on resolutely—"I was afraid to go myself because anyone who sees me, now, would know."

"Tutu"—Kauka patted her hand—"as a doctor working to prevent the spread of this disease which has brought so much unhappiness to Hawaiians, I have to report you. Surely you understand. I will

[92]

do all I can to make it easy as possible, take you to Molokai myself, if you wish me to."

Tutu sat as if she had not heard. Her face was dead wood, with only her eyes living in it. "I have known you, Kauka, since you were small, like that." She looked at the baby in her lap. "Your mother was a relative of my mother's. I know your many kindnesses to all people. As you have no cure for me I shall have to obey the law of the land. But first, I want to ask you one favor." She paused.

"If it is humanly possible."

Tutu gazed into his eyes. "For the deep aloha we have had for each other these many, many years, do not tell my sickness for a month. If anyone comes I will keep out of sight. I wish for just a little more time with my loved ones. I wish to be a while longer in this place where I was born and where my mother lived before me. I wish to watch the morning star rising behind Mauna Loa and to smell gardenias growing in the wet forests of Kona."

Kauka gazed back. A curious expression flitted over their faces. In that instant he was not a man, she was not a woman. He was not a doctor, she not a patient overtaken by a ghastly disease. They were two humans gazing into each other's souls. Below their locked gaze the fat baby slept with the abandoned grace of small things. The blue day leaned over the world. Sunlight rained vitality into the earth.

Finally Kauka, who had been leaning forward, straightened up. Taking Tutu's hands in his, he pressed them. "It is very wrong, Tutu, to ask this of me. And more wrong of me to grant your request. Concealing a leper endangers others; as well it carries a jail sentence." His words hung in the air.

Tutu began crying and embracing him.

"*Mahalo, mahalo*—thank you, thank you. God will bless you for this!" she sobbed.

Kauka wiped his forehead carefully with a clean handkerchief.

"Look here," Thord said hotly as they drove away, "you exposed yourself unnecessarily by touching Tutu and eating from bowls and dishes she and the family used!"

[93]

"As yet it hasn't been proved definitely how leprosy is actually transmitted," Kauka said slowly. "It is only known that clean persons after years of association with lepers are likely to contract it. Yet there are many cases on record where leper parents produce offspring which, if removed before a year, have never showed any symptoms of the disease. I didn't want to hurt old Tutu."

The car ground to the top of a hill and Kauka stopped it.

"Let's get out and sit in the sun for a while," he suggested, rubbing his thick, graying hair. "This is as good an opportunity as any for me to tell you much you must know. At least here"—he looked about him—"we won't be interrupted."

Thord seated himself on a lump of lava, Kauka contemplated the Pacific.

"I'll give you a brief outline of the history of leprosy here in the Islands," Kauka said, after a silence.

"When you know what leads up to this situation you'll understand better—about Tutu." He lighted a cigar and puffed on it for a moment. "As yet, you can't appreciate the terrific tragedy of any disease, much less leprosy, in these Islands where, until white men came, there was no sickness of any sort. Add to that the utter horror and hideousness of leprosy to a people who count bodily beauty the supreme gift of the Creator to mankind."

Kauka looked at Thord.

"While kings and queens and the aristocracy of Europe and other lands went unwashed for years, Polynesians bathed daily, massaged their skins with perfumed oils, and kept their bodies beautiful with exercises and dancing.

"Leprosy, supposedly, was introduced to Hawaii by coolie contract labor imported to the Islands during the reign of Kamehameha III. The name, *maipake,* Chinese sickness, confirms the supposition. At first nothing was done to fight the spread of the disease. Hawaiians are sociable, affectionate, and hospitable. A chance visitor, crossing the threshold of any home, was treated like a loved and intimate member of the family."

"You're telling me!" Thord remarked thoughtfully.

Kauka went on. "As well, never having had any experience

[94]

with disease, the Hawaiians of that day were ignorant of the simplest safeguards against infection. Sick and well mingled freely, eating from the same calabashes, exchanging clothes. As a result, by 1864, during the reign of Kamehameha V, leprosy had increased to such an extent that it caused widespread alarm."

Thord looked at diamond-clear distances. About them was the smell of grass, forests, and the clean perfume of ripe guavas, heated by strong sunlight.

"In 1865 the Hawaiian Government took its first step to prevent further spread of the disease. It was rather late to begin, which gave the move the flavor of sudden, uncalled-for severity. It was decided that the native population living on the isolated peninsula on the north side of the island of Molokai must evacuate, and the spot be set aside for persons infected with leprosy."

Kauka worried the stubble on his chin with his thumb and two fingers while his mind contemplated the past.

"An order was put out stating bluntly, 'All lepers are required to report to the Government Health Office within fourteen days for inspection and final banishment to Molokai."

Thord nodded.

"Unfortunately, this did not mean the lepers would live under normal conditions. No provision was made to house them, no medical aid supplied. Being sent to Molokai meant slow death in desolate surroundings. As a result a new terror was added to the Hawaiians stricken with leprosy. It meant homes would be wrecked, families broken up forever, hundreds sent to a fate more dreadful than the disease itself."

Kauka threw away his cigar and lighted another.

"Many lepers, realizing their condition menaced others, gave themselves up. But more went into hiding, and the order was largely evaded."

He sighed, flicked a guava leaf off the hood of the car, and went on.

"When the Government set Molokai aside for lepers, it imagined it would be a self-supporting colony. With this end in view, horses, cattle, and farm implements were sent over. Not knowing at the

[95]

time that persons afflicted with leprosy are sunk in tragic apathy and unable to cope with hard work, the Government fancied it had done all that was necessary. Of course, the scheme collapsed, so at irregular intervals a sailing vessel was sent to Molokai with supplies. Often, because of high seas, it couldn't land its cargo and sailed on, leaving the unfortunate population practically destitute."

"How ghastly!" Thord exclaimed.

"It was. Things stayed that way until 1873. Then Lunalilo, the new king, decided that sterner measures to isolate everyone afflicted with leprosy must be started. It became a jail offense to hide lepers. Hunts were organized, secret settlements raided and their inmates brought in. Husbands and wives, with the shadow of eternal separation hanging over them, fled into the mountains. Ghastly tragedies took place."

"Go on," Thord urged.

"Conditions on Molokai today are entirely different, but the scar put on the minds of Hawaiians and whites, dating from Tutu's mother's time, has not as yet been entirely erased. The section of Molokai set aside for lepers is cut off from the rest of the island by mighty cliffs two thousand feet high. At the base is a flat peninsula, for the most part arid and bare. The high cliffs shut off the sun, except for a scant few hours during the day. When the royal edict went forth, the handful of Hawaiians living at Kalaupapa left their simple houses of *pili* grass, or branches. At best they were mere shelters against rain and wind and having no foundations were flooded during the rainy season. Inside these foul huts lepers huddled together. Clothing wasn't provided, there was no decent water supply, and food came at irregular intervals. As the number of persons sent to Molokai increased many were unable to find room in the huts and lived as they could in the open. You can see how, under such conditions, the name Molokai grew to be a thing of horror."

"Of course," Thord said.

"At one time there were over two thousand lepers on Molokai. Order and law belonged to the past. They were in the grip of a revolting malady, homeless, half-clothed, half-fed, without the ordinary necessities to give dignity to living."

Kauka drew on his cigar.

"One of the worst evils Father Damien had to fight in 1874, when he went to Molokai, was drunkenness. The lepers managed to make an intoxicating liquor from the root of the *ti* plant which grew abundantly at the foot of the tall cliffs. Life in the squalid huts was a round of drinking, card-playing, dancing, fighting, and funerals. Physical and moral life was reduced to the lowest level."

A skylark flew out of the deep grass, uttered three shining notes, and shot into the sky.

"The more advanced cases," Kauka went on, "crawled about on their hands and knees. There were no doctors, no hospitals. Dying lepers were dragged into a rough shelter, and a hole was scratched in the ground near-by by weakened fellow-sufferers. That was the Molokai that Tutu's mother knew, the image of which Tutu can't get out of her mind. Thanks to Father Damien, conditions improved gradually under later Hawaiian governments. When the United States annexed the Islands, about fifteen hundred persons were living at Kalaupapa. Conditions on Molokai were brought to the attention of Congress in 1905 and appropriations made to improve them, and to establish a Leprosy Investigation Station in Hawaii to study the disease and, possibly, to find a cure for it. Some progress has been made, but—"

"No cure found," Thord put in, quietly.

"Not as yet—" Kauka gazed into blue spaces stretching southward. "For a while doctors thought that Dr. Goto's system of Oriental medicines and hot baths, from which Father Damien got temporary relief, might be a cure. Later the English artist Clifford brought grunjun oil, product of a fir tree growing in the Adaman Islands. It was tried, without results. In 1890 more experimenting was done with chaulmoogra oil, but was abandoned because it produced dangerous nausea."

"As a rule how long does a person who's contracted leprosy live?" Thord asked.

"It varies. A particularly severe case will go fast; again lepers live for years. In Tutu's case, separation from her family and nostalgia for Kona will make short work of her. Why, in God's name, couldn't she have died before she contracted it?"

"You're taking a hell of a risk by not reporting her immediately, Kauka."

"If you were in my shoes, knowing how little is known about how leprosy's spread, realizing the family's already been exposed for months, understanding the passionate devotion of Hawaiians to their families, the utter horror of the disease to a beauty-loving race—" Kauka broke off, then finished. "Tutu is my friend. This is the last thing I can ever do for her. For her little extra happiness I'm willing—"

Thord nodded. "Kauka, in your shoes I'd risk it too."

10

WHEN they got home, long afternoon lights stretched across the island and the earth, soaked by a local shower, sent up a clean fragrance. Loki was rocking on the veranda and waved as they drove in. Kauka parked the car in the driveway for Carlos to take away and came up the steps slowly.

"Hey, Papa, your face got a tired," Loki accused.

"I am a little *pula*," Kauka admitted.

"Sit down and I get *ino*—drinks for you two."

"Fine, we'll wash up while you fix them," Kauka said.

"Never mind wash-up. Drink *kinni*—gin, rest little whiles, then go clean up," Loki called over her shoulder as she started indoors.

Kauka glanced at Thord and they headed for the office. After they had scrubbed with a strong disinfectant, they separated to change into fresh clothes. They had just returned to the palm-filled *lanai* when Mamo appeared.

"Home, Papa," she said in pleased tones, kissing him. "What did you two *kaukas* do today?"

"Hospital in the morning, then to see Mary Ako and her new baby, all the usual things," Kauka replied.

Mamo nodded, sank into a low wicker chair, and gazed with dream-filled eyes through tree trunks at the sea which was slowly dimming to purple. Loki came out with a tray of ice, tall glasses, orange juice, and a bottle of gin. Thord started to rise but she signaled with her head for him to remain in his chair.

"When man's tired, woman's job to fix him ups," she said, her eyes merry. With measured pleasure she began mixing drinks.

The afternoon was moist and sweet. Mynah birds consulted noisily in the trees. A cool little breeze sighed down from Hualalai, hinting that evening was on its way. A car tore by with long banners streaming from it. The driver honked his horn continuously, scattering handbills as he went.

"Picture show tonight, Papa!" Mamo cried, all animation. "I'll phone Liholiho to come down, then call April. We can pick her up as we go by."

"Liholiho was down only last night," Kauka teased. "It's a long ride from Kahala Ranch. Eight miles."

"He can do it in an hour on a good horse." Mamo laughed, flying indoors.

"You like picture show?" Loki asked, turning to Thord.

"Some," he replied.

"Might-be swell Western tonight, better you come with us," she urged.

"I'd like to."

"I'll send Carlos to get Takeshi and his brothers and sisters," Kauka suggested. "We can walk. With the three children we have here the car'll be full."

"Swell, Papa. I hate to think on those poor kids alone up in the coffee. And I like fine walk with my old sweetheart at night." She patted Kauka's hand, rolling her eyes roguishly, while he gave directions to Carlos.

The dinner gong sounded and they went in. When the meal was over, servants hurried about, eager to get duties behind them to be free to go to the picture show. Presently the car which had gone for April and to gather up the children, swept into the driveway. April got out, followed by starry-eyed youngsters.

"*Arrigato*—thank you, Kauka-san," Takeshi said. "We like berry much see show. Mama-san and small brudder good?" he asked hopefully.

"Yes, but I think ten days before Mama-san can go home," Kauka told him.

Takeshi shifted his feet, then asked in a slightly diminishing voice, "*Haole Hao* find small jobs for me yet?"

"Look, Takeshi," Kauka began gently, "you have to go to school."

"Got time after school *pau*," he interrupted. "I no caring what-kind jobs I make, but must help Mama-san. Many kids to feed." He indicated the solemn group behind him.

"You have to walk three miles twice a day, Takeshi."

"Can do. I strong." He edged nearer to Kauka and stood with an air of men who have shared an ordeal together and triumphed over it.

"Okay, we can do with another boy in the garden for a bit. You can work from three to five. I'll pay you ten dollars a month."

"Thank you, thank you, Kauka-san! Ten dollars buy nuff rice and some tea and dry fish for all family every month. Mama-san and Iku"—he indicated his oldest sister with the baby strapped to her back—"can pick coffee when it get ripe in one month, then everykind berry fine. Hey, you kids"—he turned to the smaller members of the family—"I got jobs."

They gazed at him with awed respect.

"Now you all go with Carlos, and Mitsu and Ching give you *kaukau* in the kitchen with other kids. Eat quick, then go to the show." Loki smiled at the brood.

When they vanished with the sturdy Filipino, April walked over and took Kauka's hand. "I'm paying for Takeshi," she announced, kissing the top of his head.

"Good April, kind April," Loki said. "Papa got big heart but always behind with Hiram."

"I know," April laughed. "The allowance Daddy gives me will go to waste. There's nothing to spend money on in Kona."

They heard a horse pounding near.

"Liholiho," Mamo announced, and waited expectantly.

He came into view, dismounted, tied his hot horse to a tree, and strode up the steps.

"You eat already?" Loki asked.

"Yes, I was just *pau* when Mamo rang up. I like to ride at night." He thought of stars, forests, and a strong horse racing down rocky lava trails, winding through tall wet ferns and guava bushes loaded with ripe yellow fruit. "And I got fine news today in the mail. My cousin Homer is coming to stay with me again this summer."

"Swell!" Loki cried, then turned to Thord. "Homer Jordan my sweetheart if I more young." Her laughter pealed out. "Homer handsome like anykind, and smarts. He studying to be lawyer. Next year he going to Yale. I bet you ten years from now Homer big judge in Hawaii. Every summer he come to Kona and have fun with us, but always he study plenty too."

She pushed back her chair and they went out into the scented night. A curious contentment mixed with exhilaration stole through Thord as they walked slowly up the road. He had rarely walked at night except on lighted city streets. Trees seemed to crowd up against the stars. Some extra quality was in the soil and growth about him, and a collective and individual presence was lodged in the tropical undergrowth massed on both sides of the dim, winding road.

He saw the slow shapes of Kauka and Loki moving in the lead, heard Liholiho and Mamo talking in low voices behind him, and felt April's slight figure beside him. She had a gift of friendly silence rare in women, which put her in a pasture of her own.

The road turned and the lighted mill loomed into view, smoke pouring from its tall stack.

"Poor night shift," April said. "They'll be sunk at missing the picture show. It's the great event of the month in Kona."

Thord glanced down at her. In a blue frock that verged on gray, hollowed slightly at the neck and filled with sheer lawn, with full sleeves at the elbow which allowed her slim arms to escape, she looked as alluring as the thin blue light behind a high mountain.

"Well, there's the picture show." She pointed out an old coffee warehouse beside the road. "We must be a little late, everyone's gone in."

As they drew nearer, Thord saw rows of horses and donkeys

and a scattering of shabby cars lining the narrow highway, brooded over by tall still trees. He hurried forward.

"This is on me, Kauka," he announced. "You paid for my steamer ticket."

A lad of thirteen, standing under a solitary electric light bulb said, "Show—quarter."

Thord counted out the money and paid him. Kauka and Loki led the way through the door. The interior of the big shed was flooded with light and Thord saw that the entire audience was seated cross-legged on the floor. The screen was an old piece of sheeting nailed to the wall. The projector was run from the battery of an ancient Packard parked beside the building where a window without panes made it possible to connect wires.

People of half a dozen different nationalities were talking excitedly, drinking pop, and chewing stalks of sugar cane. Dogs wandered about. Mothers suckled babies. Friends called out and joked with each other. Kauka and Loki paused to chat every few moments, but finally found a space and sat down. Liholiho settled Mamo beside them, then streaked off to join some young bloods tuning up guitars and ukuleles. In the rear of the building opposite the screen a Japanese tinkered about the projector, trying to focus the spotlight. It struck the ceiling, swooped over the audience, caught a rafter, and finally settled in the proper spot.

People waited good-naturedly. The volunteer musicians struck up a hula. Strange grindings came from the Packard. The operator worked frenziedly.

"Berry sorry," he called out. "Number One time I making moving picture. Brudder got sick in Hilo but speak better I make show in Kona or lose money."

"Never mind if slow, us wait," someone in the audience called. "What-kind picture tonight? Western?"

"Brill Hart."

Everyone broke into wild cheers. After fifteen unsuccessful minutes dragged by without results of any sort, people began shouting good-natured advice. Finally the machine started and the audience

[103]

settled down to watch. Shadows staggered across the screen, drew down to a focus, and wild bursts of laughter filled the warehouse.

"Why-for all fella on top their heads?" someone called.

The operator stopped the machine, worked frantically, and started again.

"Upside down still!" the audience yelled, rocking with laughter.

"Might-be better all man stand on their heads," a young wag suggested. "Then can see the picture *pololei*—right, anyhow."

A dozen teen age Hawaiian boys attempted it. Children yelled, older folk became speechless with mirth. The long finger of light found the stretched sheet and the picture, right-side up, got underway. Everyone watched in absorbed silence. As the villain appeared about to triumph, people began yelling advice.

"Look out, Bill. . . . Bad-rascal hide behind tree . . . no let him make humbugger on you, Bill. . . . Shoot *wikiwiki*. . . . *Wela-kahao!* Now ride like hell!"

Grandparents, fathers and mothers, children, and all the betweens hung forward breathlessly following the wild ride of the hero over sheer banks, through rivers, across plains, down wild canyons to the final triumph.

When the last reel flickered out everyone relaxed; then with unhurried deliberation they began getting to their feet. No one appeared in a hurry to go home, though work on the plantation started at four. Kauka and Loki visited with friends. Brewer came forward like a big red bull lumbering arrogantly about a lush pasture. He was on vast, noisy good terms with everyone, slyly feeding older women's egos with compliments, peering at babies, ogling young girls of any nationality.

"Aloha, Kauka, Aloha, Loki. Glad to see you ain't too proud to be here, April. Nor you, Thord," he boomed. "Pity Thisbe can't mix with 'his flock.' I tell you those Revs are a bunch of whited sepulchers. Like to stand in pulpits and bleat down at people, where they can't get no back-talk. Now me, I like my fellow-men, especially girls. Young or old. They're all alike in—"

"Shut your face, Brewer," Loki said. "Kids 'round."

"No offense meant, Loki."

[104]

"Say, Tutu no here." Loki glanced through the dispersing crowd. "Second month she missing show. Better you go tomorrow, Papa, and see if might-be someone sick at Moku's house."

Involuntarily Thord and Kauka looked at each other.

"I'll stop by Wednesday when I go to South Kona again," Kauka said, taking her arm and starting for the door.

When they got home April and Mamo went to the kitchen to mix lemonade. Liholiho was eager to be off as he had to get up at three to get round-up steers to ship to Honolulu. Loki was quiet as she rocked on the veranda.

"Papa, I got swell idea," she announced from some depth of thought. "I think good fun if us make picnic and take down to Moku's house Sunday. I no like this business Tutu no coming to moving picture. If nobody sick, us all fish, swim, have fun. If someone got *pilikea,* us jolly up."

"Sunday is church," Kauka reminded.

"Never mind if miss one time. Spose Thisbe little mad I no care. I can go first with Liholiho and the girls in April's car. After you and Thord *pau* at the hospital you can come down."

"Maybe Thord would be more interested in going to the City of Refuge," Kauka suggested.

Loki regarded Kauka intently. "Why-for you not wanting to go Moku's?" she asked. "I have hunch might-be somekind trouble. Not like you, Papa, making this way."

Kauka hesitated, then said, "Thord and I were at Moku's today. Tutu has *maipake.*"

Loki made a smothered sound of horror. "Tutu!"

"Yes."

"Oh, poor Tutu, poor family! Why-for you no tell to me right away? I must go down quick before police mans take her to Molokai." Loki wiped her eyes on a fold of her *holoku.*

"You must not go. We have Mamo to think of."

"You go—"

"I'm a doctor. I have to take risks, but I take precautions too."

"You think I scare on some few germs?" Loki asked hotly. "What

[105]

kind of peoples I be if I no go and see my friend? Tutu and me got big Alohas for each other all our lifes."

"But, Mama—"

"Shut your face, Papa. What today? Monday? I going tomorrow. Not got much time left. Steamer go to Honolulu Friday."

Her voice broke.

Kauka glanced about, assuring himself no one was within earshot. "Loki," he said slowly, "I haven't reported her yet. She begged for one more month with her family."

They all remained perfectly still, as if afraid that if any of them moved the room would explode. Loki gazed at her husband.

"Good Papa, kind Papa," she said—"but bad troubles if anyone finding out you making this kind."

Kauka patted her shoulder in a reassuring way. Loki covered his short expressive fingers with her plump ones, then looked at Thord.

"Guess maybe you thinking Hawaiians got kind hearts but not very much sense." Her eyes waited for his to answer; then, hearing footsteps, she grew watchful. "*Kulikuli*—shut up, about this!" she cautioned. "Better not even the girls, or Liholiho knowing."

11

W ELL, us have to go to church today," Loki sighed, looking regretfully at the sunshine flooding her garden. Then her face brightened. "But after church *pau,* might-be us take picnic down to Honaunau. How that sound to your ear, Papa?"

"Fine," Kauka said, then glanced at his watch. "I have to go to Hiram's office for a little while to talk some more about fixing the hospital."

"Like me to drive you?" Thord asked.

Kauka nodded, pleased. "We'll be back at ten-thirty, Mama." He kissed Loki's hair. "You fellas all be ready." He glanced at Mamo indolently lolling in her chair, peeling a ruddy mango, then at Liholiho busily demolishing his second plateful of ham and eggs.

"I like to sing," Liholiho remarked, "but Thisbe talks too much and doesn't have enough music."

The car was parked at the steps, Carlos smiling beside it.

"Good morning, Kauka," he said brightly. "Nice day."

"Very nice," Kauka agreed. "I got new driver, Carlos. Might-be you like the day off?"

"Like very much," Carlos replied, grinning widely.

"Okay, you're *pau* till tomorrow."

"Thank you, Kauka." He stepped back and Thord slid under the wheel.

They drove off through the cool freshness of the morning.

[107]

"I won't be more than half an hour," Kauka said when they arrived at the plantation office.

Thord looked at the neat building sitting beside the prosperous plantation store where all the hundreds of laborers traded. Behind, on a slight rise, the sugar mill reared up, flaunting its efficiency. Although it was Sunday the place seethed with activity. Machinery rumbled, cane cars, pushed by squeaky little engines, rolled up to the mill, were emptied, then side-tracked to make room for full ones. Laborers of half a dozen nationalities called to each other, smoke poured out of the tall stack, soiling the immaculate blue sky.

From within the office, voices sounded as Hiram Wilde consulted with MacAllister, the head *luna,* about various departments of the vast Wilde estate. "The *makai* lands . . . Seven tons of sugar to the acre . . . not too bad," Hiram's voice said crisply. "As I anticipated, coffee's gone up three cents a pound. Ought to net a tidy dividend this fall. I instructed Liholiho to ship fifty head of steers to Honolulu Wednesday. . . . I'd like to send seventy. Beef's due to drop because of over-importation from New Zealand, but the boat's full and the captain refused to take more."

From where he waited, Thord could see Hiram Wilde, or *Haole Hao*—Iron Whiteman, as all Kona called him, seated at an impressive desk, with carefully arranged papers before him. Slanting rays of sunshine flooded the room, bare as a cell except for the desk, filing cases, a safe and four uncomfortable chairs. While *Haole Hao* talked with the gaunt Scot, who was his foreman, Kauka waited with the patience of his race. After a while MacAllister came out and, seeing Thord, signed briefly with his hand, mounted his horse, and rode off. Thord stared at the lawless land, drunk with its own beauty, then his eyes returned to the open door leading into the office.

Kauka handed *Haole Hao* a paper, which he scanned thoughtfully. After a bit he looked up, and though Thord could not hear what was said, he suspected that Wilde was contesting estimates of costs, necessitated in remodeling the hospital. Kauka talked earnestly. Wilde listened, a detached expression on his gray mask of a face.

Hawaiians in checked *palakas,* clean blue denim breeches, and flower-crowned hats jogged by, laughing and chatting with Liholiho's *paniolos* down from the ranch for the day to see their families. The conference in the office continued and Thord wondered if Wilde was balking at Kauka's pet dream: a playroom in the hospital for convalescent children.

Finally Kauka came down the steps and signaled. Thord got out of the car and hurried over.

"Fetch the family, Thord, and pick me up on your way to church. There are two or three points still to be settled."

"The playroom?" Thord asked in an undertone.

Kauka nodded.

"How much would it cost?"

"Four hundred dollars maybe."

Thord looked at the arrogant mill, the satisfied store, the smug office. "Break him down, the old skinflint," he said under his breath.

Kauka smiled. "You're a rascal."

Thord drove away, collected the family, and returned. Just as they drew up at the office, April appeared in the Wilde roadster, an elegant affair. Jumping out, she hurried over. Her small face, under a wide-brimmed straw hat circled with fresh gardenias, was eager and thoughtful.

"Where's Kauka?" she asked.

Thord pointed toward the office. April gave him a swift glance.

"Is Father balking—"

"At the playroom, I think," Thord said.

April stood in the sunshine. There was something sweet and wild about her that went hand in hand with the green and gold morning.

"I'll fix it," she announced. "I know how to handle Father, but I always wait for the right moment to strike. Kauka has no choice. He has to come when Father tells him to. I'm going to break *that* up." She gestured at the pair seated at opposite ends of the desk. "When Father's in there"—she indicated the cold room—"he feels like Jove on Olympus." She ran up the steps.

Loki watched her. "Never I seeing how such a swell kid come from two old sticks," she remarked. "Seem like might-be they steal her from some real peoples when she small."

After a little all three came out of the office.

"*Wikiwiki*, Papa, or us be late for church," Loki called. "Then Thisbe get a sour face."

Thord smiled, Liholiho chuckled, Mamo's long eyelashes fluttered amusedly. Wilde locked the door, crossed the narrow veranda and came down the steps, his tall angular figure towering over April's. Inclining his head stiffly to the waiting carful, he got into the roadster with April. Kauka settled himself beside Thord and they started off.

Five minutes' running through the amber and jade of forest sunlight and shadow brought them to the church. Breadfruit trees, solid mangoes, and spreading monkey-pods cast a rich, green gloom over the austere little building. A row of Italian cypresses, like exclamation points against the blue sky, stood in a corner of the churchyard, filled with headstones.

Half a dozen cars of varying makes and ages were parked in the narrow lane paralleling the churchyard; carriages and saddle horses were tied to convenient trees, showing that the higher-bracketed personnel of the plantations, and prominent families of North and South Kona, felt it incumbent upon themselves to attend services.

Thisbe's daughter waited at the turnstile leading into the churchyard, greeting her father's congregation as they filed through. Her narrow shoulders hunched stiffly into a starched muslin blouse, finished with an unbecoming neckline. Under an oversized straw hat with three large pink velvet roses sitting on it, her gooseberry eyes gazed morosely at the world.

Studying her, compassion stirred in Thord. Her efforts at friendliness, the tragic hope lurking behind her pupils told that, possibly, she wasn't quite as she appeared in a mirror, told of a soul eternally at strife with itself.

Wilde and April halted to speak to her. Thord guessed the thought in Prudence's mind. She was grateful for April's friendliness, but wished frantically that she would move on, ending the contrast between them.

Loki got out of the car, holding a fold of her *holoku* against the splendid opulence of her breasts. Unlike the other women present, she was bare-headed. A mischievous expression flitted over her face. Plucking a gaudy hibiscus blossom off a bush, she stuck it on top of her high-piled, wavy hair.

"How you fellas like my new hat?" she asked roguishly.

Mamo said, "Mama," under her breath in half-reproving, half-amused tones. Kauka's eyes twinkled, and Liholiho exploded into rich laughter that made people turn startled heads.

By the church steps, Thisbe, tightly buttoned into a black coat finished with a circular white collar, greeted his congregation over the spectacles perched on his thin, questing nose. He stood with fingertips pressed together, exposing hands dusted with sparse ginger-colored hair.

"Ah," he said, as each person went up the steps and paused briefly to address him. "I'm indeed happy to see you this fine Sabbath morning." But all the while he was eyeing new arrivals to see who might have failed to put in an appearance.

The sound of hoofs made Thord glance around. Brewer dashed into view and hurriedly dismounted. His face was the color of an over-ripe tomato, his eyes told of a night of boisterous drinking, but he was dressed in smart riding togs with the usual white flower over his magenta-colored ear. A straw hat, of native weave, circled with red roses which spilled spice into the air, was cocked dashingly over one eye. With his jowls and tight paunch he suggested a lewd Buddha who had gone thoroughly to the dogs and had enjoyed every step of the way.

"Loki, Mamo—Aloha!" he called boisterously. "Aloha, Kauka—old-timer. Didn't suppose you were the church-going sort, Graham," he added, with a monstrous wink.

"As a rule I'm not," Thord replied.

"Fundamentally I'm not, either, as you might suspect from the cut of my jib," Brewer boomed. "But piety has its reward! While Thisbe bleats, I get an eyeful of the fairer sex." He raised his voice,

[111]

projecting the last word across the churchyard where Thisbe was greeting his congregation. Even from a distance the sudden stiffening of Thisbe's thin form showed that he had heard. Brewer's eyes squinched into delighted little slits, then, as if he'd seen Prudence for the first time, he swept forward.

"Ah, Prudence, my dear!" Taking her sallow hand between his highly colored, puffy ones, he pressed it. "You're an eyeful today."

Fiery rose swept up the girl's thin neck and burned in her cheeks.

While Thisbe greeted Kauka and his family, Thord noted, with amusement, that the little man was glaring past them at Prudence coming slowly across the lawn with Brewer. Kauka and Loki led the way to their pew; Mamo, Liholiho, and Thord followed.

The little church was pleasantly full. *Haole Hao* and April occupied the right-hand front pew. The one opposite, also engraved with a W was empty, evidently destined for Wildes who had not materialized during the past two decades, but no one ventured to occupy it.

In rows behind, Scotch overseers with wives and children of plain, sturdy vintage, sat quietly. Half a dozen American and English families, not connected to the network of Wilde holdings, but who lived on the outskirts of Kona, were clustered in a section of the church, obviously reserved for them. They were beings vaguely resembling the Wilde type who, Thord suspected, were the descendants of early, less successful settlers in Hawaii. There was a scattering of Hawaiians and part Hawaiians, *lunas* whom Thord had met with Kauka as they made their daily round of the plantation, lolling at ease, waiting like hopeful children for the singing to begin.

Prudence went to the organ and began playing. Thisbe stepped to the pulpit, adjusted his glasses and peered at the mammoth Bible open on the stand.

From the set of Wilde's head, Thord suspected he was busy computing profits to be realized when the season's cane had been safely ground and sold, and coffee-picking was over. Mamo gazed into space. Liholiho gazed at her. Kauka's eyes were filled with long thoughts. Loki, with an amused expression, watched the little man preaching to them. Brewer eyed Prudence and every so often, ostentatiously, adjusted the gardenia above his fleshy right ear. Children played with hymnals, wiggled, nudged their mothers and were shushed.

When the service finally ended and the blessing was said, Prudence returned to the organ. People replaced hymn books and prayer books in their racks, gathered up purses, children, and gloves, then waited until Hiram Wilde, preceded by April, walked down the aisle toward the square door, framing a bright segment of the garden. Slowly, the rest of the congregation began filing out, collecting on the steps and lawn to chat and gossip before dispersing.

Thord noted, with amusement, that Thisbe, in some miraculous way, had managed to be at the front steps before the church had been emptied of a third of its congregation, determined to enjoy to the full the brief spotlight which was his lot four times a month. He had a word with, or for, everyone.

"Ah, April, my child, it's nice indeed to have you back. Your bright face . . . Yes, Mrs. MacAllister? Prudence is counting on you to pour tea at the Rectory Thursday when the Guild meets to determine Bazaar activities for Foreign Missions. . . . Yes, Hiram?" He quivered to attention.

"Elsbeth told me to ask you and Prudence to dine with us Wednesday."

"We'll be there, I assure you." Thisbe turned to the next person, while an impudent little breeze waved the sparse hair on his head, like the antennae of an uneasy beetle. "Loki! You and yours are here in force, I see. Very commendable, but"—his ferret eyes rested reprovingly on her head, topped by the gaudy hibiscus blossom—"it's, ah, customary for women, ah, to cover their heads in church," he reminded in an undertone.

"You think God care if mans pray with hat, or without hat?" she asked airily. "I can think more good, and pray more good when I *not* wearing hat. Mans and womans just—people, to God. If mans no need wear hat in church, womans no need to wear either. Might-be sometime you waking up, Thisbe," she finished, not unkindly.

Thisbe hunched his scrawny shoulders and glanced around. "It's peculiar," he remarked. "Tutu hasn't attended services for six weeks. She's had a perfect record for twenty years. I must make a point of calling on Moku and his family to see if anything's wrong."

Loki froze, then said lightly, "Kauka go Moku's house last Monday. Moku speak Tutu gone to stay with her cousin-sister in Hilo for one-two months."

"Indeed." Thisbe elevated his sparse red eyebrows. "I've been a bit remiss about South Kona calls, but I will make a point of dropping in sometime next week to see the family." He turned to another member of his congregation.

Sliding her arm through Kauka's Loki clutched him tight to her. "Thord," she directed, "tell to April come our house and make picnic with us."

He made his way to where she stood beside her tall father and delivered Loki's message.

"I'd love to," she said, then glanced up. "Had you other plans for the afternoon, Father?"

"I shall be working. You may do as you please."

"Tell Loki, Thord, after I've driven Father home, I'll come over."

When they were in the car Loki fanned her face with plump, expressive hands. "I glad that all *pau!*" she announced. "Stop at store, Thord, so us can get the Honolulu papers. Sure Hilo mail-truck come with them by now."

When they reached the plantation store, a crowd was gathered, all eager for news of the other Islands; they waited while a perspiring Chinaman unloaded his truck. Laughing Hawaiians, serious Whites, jabbering Filipinos, Koreans, Japanese, and Portuguese were ripping the papers open.

"No open ours now, Papa," Loki begged. "I like go home *wiki-wiki* and take off my damn shoes."

When they got home, she hurried up the steps, sat down in her pet rocking chair, and flipped off her slippers, sighing with pleasure. "Now you kids"—she looked at Mamo and Liholiho—"go to the kitchen and get the nice *kaukau* Ching have put in the baskets for us to take to the beach. Soon as April come us go."

They went off.

"Which paper you want, Mama?" Kauka asked, glancing at the three in his hand. "Friday, Saturday, or Sunday?"

"You read Sunday one, Papa, got plenty nice pictures. I can look tomorrow when you fellas work. Give others to Thord. Might-be he like some outside news. Kona little slow, maybe, for New York guy." Her eyes teased him.

"I'm not in the least concerned with anything happening away from Kona," Thord assured her. "I feel, already, as if I'd always belonged here."

"That sound fine to my ear," Loki said, pleased, then her face became watchful. "What if Thisbe go to South Kona and poke his nose—" She broke off, letting the words hang in the air.

"I must make time and go and see Moku tomorrow and tell him"—Kauka's voice stopped, then went on resolutely—"to hide— Tutu."

Thord moved restively. The Sunday peace which always brooded over the family had somehow become charged with menace. He realized that his past, which had once been so vital, was left behind and unimportant. Nothing mattered except the welfare of these two kind, elderly people whose presence on earth lent dignity to living. He glanced at Loki, marveling at the sumptuous grace of mature Polynesian women; he glanced at Kauka and mentally admired the restfulness of adult Polynesian men. Returning footsteps roused him.

"Where's April?" Mamo asked. "If we wait too long the tide will not be right for fishing."

Loki's eyes brushed her. "Might-be after all April no can come," she suggested. "Maybe Elsbeth throw a sick, or something. Better you and Liholiho go down to the beach on horses. After by-and-by, when April come, Thord drive all us fellas, and the lunch, down to Honaunau."

"Fine," Liholiho and Mamo chorused. They hurried to the rear

[115]

of the house where Kauka's four or five saddle horses roamed a small guava-grown pasture.

Rising, Thord went slowly down the steps into the garden. He saw April's car sweep up the drive, and walked to meet it.

"Liholiho and Mamo have started. We're to follow them with lunch," he told her.

"I'm sorry I'm late," April said. "Mother wanted me to do some phoning. Get in, it's a long walk to the house." Laughing, she opened the door.

They drove the scant two hundred feet to the steps and parked.

"When Papa *pau* reading the paper, us go," Loki announced in her unhurried way.

April and Thord seated themselves on the top step. Loki relaxed in her chair. The garden made little contented rustlings. Slanting rays of sunlight fell on April's delicate, eager face, and for the first time Thord wondered what sort of a man her fiancé might be.

"There's an article about our friend Kieser," Kauka remarked from behind his newspaper. "Kieser"—he explained to Thord—"is a scientist, a botanist actually, but he's interested in everything. He lived with us two years while he was listing the shrubs and trees of Hawaii. He sailed for the Orient three years ago."

"I remember him," April said.

"Kieser little funny-looking, but smart fella," Loki announced. "Read what the newspaper have to say about him, Papa."

Kauka settled himself and began: "Word comes to Hawaii that Arthur Kieser, the prominent Austrian botanist who made Hawaii his home for five years, is in Singapore for a short visit. He will be at the Hotel Imperial for two weeks before returning to Indo-China for further botanical research." Kauka took a fresh breath, and settled himself to continue.

He paused, as his eyes read ahead, then he said, solemnly, "It says Kieser has written about chaulmoogra oil. It was used unsuccessfully in the treatment of leprosy in Hawaii around 1890. Kieser believes it should be given another try." His words fell like stones being dropped into a still pool. "Kieser hopes, when he returns to the Islands to get the Leprosy Investigation Station to ask Congress to make a special appropriation for further study and experimentation of the oil. I'm going to"—he eyed the small group in the *lanai*—"cable Kieser and ask him to send me a few ounces of the oil to try on—Tutu."

"Might-be it not work," Loki protested.

"Has Tutu—leprosy?" April asked in a small voice.

"My child, in my excitement, I forgot you were here," Kauka said.

"Why shouldn't I know?" April asked.

"Because the more peoples who know the more bad-danger for Papa," Loki explained.

"But I don't understand," April began, then a curious expression welled into her gray eyes. "Haven't you reported her?" she asked, as if she couldn't credit it.

Kauka shook his head.

"How long have you known?" April asked.

"For a week, since last Monday," Kauka replied.

April laced her fingers tightly together and sat very still.

"Papa," Loki said, "I am torn between my sorry for my old *aikane* and my scare for you. If you hide Tutu and wait for Kieser to send the oil, might-be it no good and Tutu die. You cannot hide *maipake*. Always our people want to look their dead before bury-time. Tutu got many white friends too, who will go to her funeral. You high respected doctor in Hawaii. I think better you think hard and pray to God and ask Him what-kind *polelei* for you to do."

April gazed at the pair, then she and Thord looked at each other and went silently into the garden.

"Tell me everything," April said, looking at Thord, while a lonely twilight stole across the vast, sprawling island.

He told her.

"I feel as if I were smothering," April said in a small voice, when he finished. "I love Kauka, there's no one like him, but I wish he wouldn't—"

Thord made no reply.

April looked at him, then laid her hand on his arm. "Are you—" she began, then stopped. "You're in on this too," she accused.

"Yes."

[117]

She stared into space. Thord had a curious impression that they were both fading out, dissolving into the universe.

"I feel—cold," she said at last.

Sliding out of his coat, Thord placed it about her shoulders. She gave him a swift, grateful look.

"I feel"—she caught her breath—"as if—" Breaking off, she shivered.

"As if—what?" Thord asked gently.

"As if life were out of control and running away with all of us."

Thord covered her hand with his.

"I feel the same way," he admitted.

They started back for the house. Lights had been turned on. Loki was rocking in her chair. Walking swiftly up the steps, April sank down on the floor and laid her slim arm across Loki's big knees.

"Where is Kauka?" she asked, after a minute.

"Phoning the radio station in Hilo to ask Kieser for some of the oil."

12

TAKING Loki's hand between both of hers, April held it to
her cheek. Thord felt like sweeping both women into his
arms. Differently, they epitomized all the fine, unending
qualities of their sex; April was the shining promise in a cloud,
Loki the deep earth, charged with the secrets of life and growth.

Returning footsteps drew all their eyes to the door. Kauka came
through it. In his face elation wrestled with concern, as though
he were realizing the enormous responsibility which would be his.
Walking to Loki, he laid his hand on her shoulder.

"It's done," he said. "I've radioed Kieser for some chaulmoogra."

"No sound so heavy, Papa," Loki advised. "You have pray. God
have told you what-kind to do. He not making mistakes. Might-be
us have some-few troubles, but that not count against the happy
of peoples who got *maipake,* if the oil cure them. Now I think
better us go eat some supper. When Mamo and Liholiho coming
home they can eat the picnic lunch."

Bending, Kauka kissed her hair.

"Flowers always spring beneath thy perfect feet," he said, in
Hawaiian.

Thord's eyes found April's.

"What did Kauka say?" he asked, as they followed the older
people to the dining room.

She told him, and he was conscious of a curious sense of loss,
wondering if, in his own life, such a miracle of companionship
would ever be. They sat down at the food-laden table. Platters of
cold turkey and pork, salads of Island fruits, fragrant coffee dis-

pensed the magic of normal things, but unrest nibbled at the edges of Thord's being. Halfway through the meal, Kauka glanced across the table.

"I better go down tonight and warn Moku about Thisbe's visit," he said.

"And tell him about the oil?" Loki suggested hopefully.

"I don't want to get their hopes up before I know, for sure, that I can get some," Kauka said. "But I must warn Moku to keep Tutu out of sight."

"Let me go for you," Thord suggested. "You've a full day tomorrow."

"Good Thord, kind Thord," Loki exclaimed. "Papa not sleeping much till he get an answer from Kieser, but he work just the same."

"I'll drive you," April announced, looking at Thord.

"My child, you must keep out of this," Kauka protested.

"I'll wait in the car while Thord talks to Moku. I'm up to the chin with feelings and will burst if I don't do something." She glanced at the marble and gilt clock on the cutglass-littered sideboard. "We'll be back by nine-thirty at the latest."

"I think okay, Papa, if April go," Loki put in. "When fella young they not liking much just to sit. Thord not even need to go inside Moku's house. Call him and talk to him outside. There will be no dangers."

"Very well," Kauka agreed reluctantly.

Jumping up they ran down the steps and got into April's car. She touched a button and the headlights cut the dark. When they reached the highway, April stepped on the accelerator and the engine whispered stealthily, gathering power, as it ate up the dim road. Insects whirled into the light beams, struck the windshield, and died. Trees loomed overhead for an instant then were gone. The lighted mill dropped behind. Canefields gave way to dark, gleaming coffee, then to forests spilling down the flanks of Hualalai. Cold clean wind rushed past. The night smelled rich and damp.

"I can't make up my mind if we're running away from something, or rushing toward it," April said.

"Nor I," Thord confessed.

The car swooped down a hill and tore up the farther side, flinging seemingly fluid roadsides behind it. April's face was like a ghostly white flower in the dim dashboard light.

"It's odd," she remarked. "Life seems to stand still for a time, then begins streaming forward. Last week everything was peaceful and beautiful." She paused thoughtfully, then went on. "It's beautiful still, but scary. I can't even get a full breath." Her laughter was fringed with nervousness. "To be honest, I'm in a panic, Thord. Not only about Kauka." She broke off and Thord wondered what was coming. "I had a letter from Dale today. He's planning to come to Kona in a few weeks."

"Yes?"

"You see, I wanted, fearfully, to be in Kona alone, so I could soak it up, get it safely inside me." She glanced at him to see if he understood.

"Yes, April?"

"When I'm here"—she gestured about her—"I'm not just—me. I'm part of the forests, the ocean, the lava flows."

Thord studied her faintly lighted profile. She was steel and stardust, early morning sunlight and young green leaves.

"Yes," he agreed, "I sense all Kona in you."

"I didn't realize, till I came home, what an awful wrench it's going to be to leave it. Forever." Her voice caught. "I doubt if Dale'll fit in here, as you have." She gave him a quick, approving glance. "Loki and Kauka, everyone who isn't white, will seem like beings from other planets to Dale. If you knew his background you'd appreciate what I mean."

"Having been born in New York, and having grown up there, I know Dale's type."

"But you aren't like a New Yorker," April protested.

"Possibly because my life there was smashed into pieces," Thord said a trifle grimly. "But now, I'm glad it was. I never appreciated what a royal thing living could be until I met Kauka and all of you."

They drove for a while in silence and Thord realized with delight that unlike most women April made no effort to pry into his past. His business was his business, and no concern of hers. They went on in silence through the navy-blue night. Finally April turned.

"I'm going to go sort of hog-wild for the next few weeks, Thord," she announced. "Do everything I love, in a big way. Chase cattle in the forests, swim in the sea, eat and laugh with old Hawaiians." Her face flashed toward his like a bird wheeling in midflight. "That sounds sort of silly, doesn't it—for excitement?"

"Why?" he asked.

"Well"—she hesitated—"why should old people stimulate young ones?"

"Possibly because they know answers to questions that we don't —yet," he replied.

"You're swell!" April cried, then went on impulsively. "Tomorrow Liholiho's getting steers to ship to Honolulu on the Friday boat. Let's go up, you, Mamo, and I. Or do you have to help Kauka?"

"He'll be occupied mostly with hospital plans. I'd like to go, immensely, once anyway. After, if the oil comes—"

"I know how it'll be," April interrupted. "But wouldn't it be marvelous if Kauka did find a cure for leprosy? His hands are so tied, there's so much work on the plantation—"

"But he's managed to collect an astounding amount of data, nevertheless," Thord remarked.

April nodded. "This is the road, isn't it?" She swerved the car off the highway into the narrow, rutted tracks leading down to the sea, lying like hammered silver far below.

"Yes."

The sweetness of fallen guavas rose to mingle with the scent of rain-damp earth. Tires crunched against loose cinders, branches brushed the side of the car.

"I'll only be a minute," Thord said, when they drew up at the stone wall surrounding the old frame house.

"Moku's coming," April announced. "He probably saw our headlights. It isn't often a car comes down here at night."

A shadowy figure was coming at a half-lope toward them.

"Who stop?" Moku called.

April answered in Hawaiian and the tense alertness slid out of his figure. Slowing to a walk, he crossed the garden and halted at the side of the car. In starlight, filtering earthwards, his face showed, glistening with perspiration.

"I think might-be police mans coming for Tutu," he explained.

"Kauka sent us down to tell you to hide Tutu," Thord said. "Reverend Thisbe said he was coming down here to call this week."

"For why?" Moku asked, his voice edged with suspicion.

"Because Tutu hasn't been to church for some time."

"Tell to Kauka, *mahalo nui loa*— After you guys gone I wake Tutu up and hide in some place where *haoles* can't find her." He glanced over his shoulder involuntarily.

"Give Tutu my deep Aloha," April said, a little unsteadily.

"I no forget. That make her happy, even if she no can see you any more." Moku's face twitched and the dull heaviness of his voice was eloquent of his grief.

"It seems wicked," April remarked as they drove away, "that Tutu should get leprosy when her life is almost over. Why couldn't she have died in peace, without the awful knowledge?"

A long pure stream of wind came down from the snow-encrusted summit of Mauna Loa.

"I shouldn't feel as I do," April went on. "I'm only seeing the outside of life. There must be a sound reason for things happening as they do. Feel it"—she tilted up her face—"that wonderful air, pouring out of space. Hawaiians believe wind is God's breath coming to earth."

She shifted into second gear to take the long hill.

"I'm all stirred up," she confessed.

"Perhaps you shouldn't have come."

"No, I'm glad I did. That"—she nodded with her head toward the house they had left behind—"that makes you think! Makes you determine to jam all the joy, fun, and beauty possible into each day as it comes, because no one can tell what may be ahead. I haven't told you everything, Thord." She went on after a pause, "Dale's sister, Sabrina, is coming with him. They plan to stay a month or six weeks. Dale wants me to go back to New York with them, and be married this fall instead of next summer."

"Surely," Thord protested, "if Dale loves you he can wait. A year isn't long."

"I know. It'll be gone in nothing flat," April said in a small voice. "I'm afraid I've let myself in for something. Dale's life has its assets, I'm sane enough to see that, but for an Islander, like me, the dividends I'd have as his wife don't weigh out enough to compensate for all this. I can picture myself at thirty, mistress of a smug, beautiful household, going to the Metropolitan, endless parties, hedged in by people who know nothing of the things I *really* love: stars, forests, oceans, storms, volcanoes, people of different races and colors. Maybe I'm crazy to love Hawaii so much."

"I don't think you're crazy to love this place so deeply," he said. "I've only been here a short while but already I'm conscious of its magic seeping into my bones."

"I'm not going East till my year is up," April announced. "Dale'll have to wait. I won't be cheated, or hustled out of the time I've counted on having here."

Swinging out of the dirt road she squared down the highway, roaring through forests wrapped in a hushed, brooding sleep. Wind tugged at her hair and fluttered the lace collar of her dress against her slim young throat.

"Mind driving so fast?" she asked, after a bit. "I'm running away from my devil. Have you one?"

"Several."

She gave a delighted laugh. "Know how to lay 'em?"

"Probably work's the best way."

"There's a better one, ride after cattle tomorrow morning on Hualalai!"

"I'm not at all sure I could keep up with you all."

"That wouldn't make any difference. When you're up there"—she pointed to the dark shape of the mountain—"you're just part of— splendor!"

"I'd like to try it."

"Okay, we'll leave at three in the morning."

They swept into the garden and stopped. Loki was rocking quietly; Kauka was prowling about the *lanai,* his stocky figure radiating excitement.

"We saw Moku and gave him your message," April said as she and Thord ran up the steps.

"Thanks." Kauka began chewing his cigar. "My boy"—his eyes grew bright and eager as he laid his hand on Thord's shoulder—"will you write to the resident physician on Molokai, and to the Leprosarium on the island of Culion in the Philippines, and to the National Leprosarium of the United States Public Health Service at Carville, Louisiana, for all their most recent data on leprosy? Use the article in today's paper, Dr. Kieser's conviction that chaulmoogra oil should be given another try, as a pretext."

"I'll be glad to."

"While we're waiting for the oil to arrive," Kauka continued, "I'll get specimens of Tutu's blood and try to inoculate rabbits and guinea pigs with the leprosy bacillus. To date, no one has succeeded in transmitting the disease to animals, but—" Breaking off, he gazed into Thord's eyes. "Have you had much laboratory experience?"

"A fair amount."

"Good, good! I'll tell Carlos to build some hutches and runs for small animals in the horse pasture, among the guavas. If only Kieser gets the oil to me quickly."

"Better no get too steam up, Papa," Loki advised. "And I think smarts not telling even Mamo and Liholiho about this kind stuffs. If ever Kona peoples finding out that you and Thord fooling with *maipake*—" Her eyes caught Kauka's and Thord's.

"Secrecy is essential," Kauka agreed. "We will probably have hundreds of failures before we begin to get anywhere."

Silence filled the dimly lighted *lanai* and from far below the grumble of surf against the coast sounded like the muffled language of ancient gods, talking in a long-forgotten language.

April walked over to Kauka. "I want Thord to chase cattle with

[125]

me this morning," she said. "Once the oil gets here you'll both be so lost experimenting with it that nothing else will exist for you."

Kauka took her hand and slowly passed his thumb over the huge diamond on her third finger. "Thord can write those letters now," he said. "Let's go to the office."

"You guys no stay up all night," Loki admonished. "You got wild bad look in your eye, Papa. If these kids go up the mountain at three o'clock they needing little sleep. You too. Big day tomorrow. Hospital going to be fix up."

"We won't be more than an hour," Kauka promised.

"Where are Mamo and Liholiho?" April asked, when the men had gone.

"Liholiho gone to the ranch, Mamo sleeping."

"I'll wake her and tell her we're taking Thord after cattle in the morning," April said.

"That not make her mad." Loki laughed. "Too bad you missing what-kind look she and Liholiho have in the eye when they come home tonight. Bet-you-my-lifes us having big marry in this house *wikiwiki*."

13

AT two-thirty Thord was roused by a tap on his door.

"Coffee will be ready in ten minutes," Mamo called.

"I'll be with you in five." Switching on the light and scrambling out of bed, he hastily began donning his riding outfit—an extra pair of breeches and boots which Liholiho kept at the house, a straw hat, bell spurs.

Outside the open windows, the pre-dawn wind, coming down from Hualalai, sounded like the rushing waters of a mountain stream, keen cold, filled with the sweet dampness of forests. Fragrances rose from the garden, of roses and heliotrope, jasmine and ginger, gardenias, Chinese violets and Japanese musk, but stronger was the smell of grassy uplands and fat cattle over which the wind had blown.

Dressed, he headed for the kitchen. Mamo, busy pouring coffee into three cups, glanced at him as he entered.

"You'll need a sweater," she warned. "It'll be chilly till the sun's up."

A car drove in, stopped, and presently quick, light steps came down the hall.

"Hi!" April called. "Are the horses ready?"

"Carlos is saddling them," Mamo told her.

A sudden air of recklessness enveloped both girls. They drank their coffee standing while wind fingered the corners of the old house. The cups emptied, they hurried out into the indigo night. Stars burned behind dark tree tops, horses snorted and stamped in the circle of lantern light where Carlos waited.

"Nice morning," he announced.

"You bet," Mamo agreed, swinging into her saddle.

"What horse have you got for Thord, Carlos?" April asked.

"*Makule*—old one. I thinking might-be because he *malihini*—he not riding good."

"If you make the grade okay, Thord, on old Auntie," April said, "we'll rustle you a better mount at the ranch."

Thord grinned. "I've ridden a little—academy stuff—but I don't know how much good that'll do me here."

"Stirrups okay?" Mamo asked out of the dark.

"I think so."

Taking up the lantern, Carlos came forward and inspected them.

"Too short," he announced and let them down. "Now try," he directed. Thord put his foot into the stirrup. "There, that's more good?" the Filipino asked, and patted Thord's boot.

As April swung onto a black thoroughbred, Mamo led off. Crossing the highway, they went through a small gate leading into terraced hillsides of coffee. The horses panted as they followed the steep trail up the slope of Hualalai. Branches heavy with dew spilled moisture on Thord's breeches and his nostrils were filled with the faint sweet scent of billions of white blossoms, faintly discernible in the dark, lying with perfect precision on branches radiating from well-cared-for trees.

After a little he noted a new alertness in the girls' figures moving steadily ahead of him.

"*Wanaao!*" Mamo's voice, tinged with delicate anticipation, floated back as she gestured at a pale luminance welling slowly into the sky.

"*Wanaao* is the promise of light, the ghost dawn that precedes the real one," April explained over her shoulder.

Thord had lived twenty-eight years without knowing that there were two dawns. He gazed at the faint, spectral whiteness lying like thin chiffon over a portion of the sky. Behind it, stars blazed with undiminished brilliance, then with a sort of delicate regret the whiteness began dimming. Constellations burned with greater brightness and the "coal sacs" between took on added depth. Then a clear daffodil dawn flooded the sky.

The coffee had long been left behind and they were riding through still, secret forests. Banks of ferns lined the sides of the trail which ever so often threaded its way across a *kipuka*—forest meadow, where the grass was gray with dew.

"Well, here we are," Mamo called out finally.

Thord saw stone corrals, lines of saddled horses fastened to a hitching rail, and a long, low house, banked to the eaves with begonias. Flagged walks, bordered with the flowers of colder lands, ran in terraces across the garden, and tall eucalyptus trees towered against the pure gold-washed sky.

"What a grand place!" Thord exclaimed.

"Isn't it? We've had some fine round-up times here during the summers before I went to school."

Dismounting, they tied up the horses. A delightful shout came from the veranda and Liholiho came charging out.

He gripped Thord's arm, flashed a welcoming smile at April, then caught Mamo's long, rosy-tipped fingers into his own. They gazed at each other, motionless, eyes shining. Then, recollecting themselves, they started for the house.

April fell into step beside Thord, then gave an incredulous, gleeful cry. "Homer!"

A young Hawaiian came dashing along the walk. Thord had never before seen anyone quite like him. In a male way he was as beautiful as the green land of Kona. Actually of medium height, he gave an impression of tallness because of the perfection of his proportions. His features were at once delicate and strong, his eyes lustrous and vital. He moved as the half gods of an older day must have moved, with ease, pride, and assurance.

"April! Mamo!" he cried, embracing first one, then the other.

"But how did you get here?" the girl cried when greetings were over.

"I came from Hilo by stage yesterday, borrowed a horse from Kalani, and rode up here last night."

"Why didn't you come to our house?" Mamo demanded indignantly.

"As usual, I have lots of work to do, but this summer I must be even busier." His face became shy and proud. "Next fall I'm going East to study law."

"Homer, how grand!" the girls exclaimed.

"This is our friend, Thord Graham," Liholiho said, taking his cousin's arm.

"Aloha!" Homer said heartily.

They went into the old, simply furnished ranch house and Liholiho called out to the cook to set three extra places. While he breakfasted, Thord found himself watching Liholiho's young cousin. He estimated him to be about twenty. His happy-go-lucky charm spilled over everything.

"These Islands breed incredible human beings," he remarked to April as they went out to mount.

"Yes," she agreed. "Homer's one of those people I secretly call 'The Anointed.'" She smiled her bright smile. "I've never known anyone whom you love so instinctively, except Kauka. And Homer's going to do big things. You watch."

Thord derived a curious pleasure from her words for they established him as one of them, permanently.

Laughing Hawaiians with jingling spurs at their heels were pouring out of the kitchen and making their way among flower beds to where their horses waited. They called out and brandished strong arms when they saw the two girls.

"Fine you fellas come. Us have swell fun today. Go way up *mauka*—" And they pointed to the tip-tilted, violently colored cones on the crimson and purple summit of Hualalai, visible through a gap in the trees.

"Wouldn't you like a better horse?" April asked.

"This one will do."

"Here, you take Maile," Homer broke in. "She's fine, quick, has a light mouth and is as easy as a rocking chair." Calling to one of the cowboys to fetch another horse, he began unsaddling.

"But I don't want to rob you of your mount," Thord protested.

[130]

Homer threw him a joyous grin. "This is the first time you've ridden with *paniolos*—cowboys, the first time you've been up Hualalai. If you ride a slow old horse, it'll dull the experience. I couldn't be happy if you were behind, alone, when we were all having fun."

Swinging the saddle off Thord's mount, he landed it expertly on the back of the sorrel mare he had been intending to ride.

"There," he said, slapping down the stirrups after the girths had been fastened. "Now you'll have fun." He gave the mare's glossy shoulder an affectionate pat and stepped back.

Thord mounted and discovered, after a few minutes, that the mare under him had winged feet that skimmed over the ground without effort. The mount Homer had taken in her place was an explosive four-year-old who went into spasms of bucking. The young fellow sat him without apparent effort but his high color testified that staying astride the animal necessitated strength as well as skill. Thord suspected that Homer had white blood as well as Hawaiian in his veins. Behind his sun-loved air he sensed the steady fiber of the north fusing with the warmth of Pacific peoples, giving him controlled energy as well as passion.

A breeze loaded with fragrance poured down from the summit of Hualalai. Then Thord saw cattle moving uneasily along a fence that stretched like a cobweb across the wrinkled hide of the volcano. Liholiho instructed his men and they began riding off in pairs.

"You'd better stay with Homer or April, Thord," he directed. "When we head the cattle down, there'll be some pretty fast riding. Come, Mamo," and they went galloping off.

April, Homer, and Thord rode up a long grassy slope and stopped when they came to a stone wall which wound across the undulations of the mountain. Horsemen were stationed along it at intervals; the cattle had vanished in the high shrub and scattered forests. Liholiho and Mamo sat on a hill, leaning on their pommels and scanning the country below. Homer and April sat with their lassos coiled and ready in their right hands. Their eyes were bright, their bodies tense, their horses restless to be off.

Clear of the forests, the whole island spread out before them, girdled by the placid blue sea. Inland the long, slow shape of

[131]

Mauna Loa showed, farther away Mauna Kea lifted its snowy summit, and directly behind, Hualalai held its heights toward the sun.

Suddenly Liholiho gestured slightly with his right hand and the thin line of horsemen began riding down the mountain. Cattle began streaking across swales and pouring down hillsides. The pace grew steadily faster, and presently they were riding at full gallop after fat red steers, romping like overgrown calves down the sides of Hualalai. Horsemen streaked out to head them off when they threatened to break out to right or left. Faint shouts came through the winey air, hoofs thundered, rough wind snatched at hats. Thord realized with pleasure that he was riding stirrup to stirrup with Homer and April. The young fellow gave him a swift approving glance.

"You're okay, *Ulaula*—Red," he shouted, "a real *paniolo*. Sometime I'll show you how to swing a lasso." And he dashed away to turn back a knot of steers trying to head back up the mountain.

"Keep with me, Thord," April cried.

Down, down their horses plunged, racing after cattle pouring with increasing speed toward the dark line of the forests. The sharp sweet whistle of a native bird, winging its way back to Hualalai, sounded overhead. April tore off her hat; wind tugged at her hair and it danced a golden dance with the sun. Galloping beside her, Thord thought of her words of the night before. "I can picture myself at thirty, mistress of a smug, beautiful household, going to the Metropolitan, endless parties, hedged in by people who know nothing of the things I *really* love."

"Isn't this grand?" she squealed like a ten-year-old.

"Glorious!" Thord shouted, then set his teeth as his mare sailed over a fallen log and took off again.

Strings of cattle were converging into a red herd that poured downward with gathering momentum, horsemen racing in on both sides at their heels, urging them toward a long lead-fence that ended in sturdy corrals, just visible at the edge of a clump of tall *koa* trees.

Riders swooped in, steering the cattle in the direction they must go. Faint puffs of dust, jarred out of the earth by running hoofs, floated off and dissipated into the air. Glossy red backs flashed in the light, horses' dark, damp flanks threw off a sharp, clean smell. Flowers wilting about sweat-stained straw hats tossed fragrance into the sunshine. Enormous vitality charged the boundless day and tingled off into space.

Bit by bit, when the fat steers were safely corraled, men flung themselves off their horses, slacked girths and shook saddles to cool their mounts' heated backs. Liholiho rode into the corrals and moved quietly among the stock, mentally marking those which were destined to be shipped to Honolulu. Mamo, her face like a crimson rose from exertion, took off her hat, shook out her black hair, and climbed onto the top rail of the corral. In riding clothes, she looked even taller than she was, and the grace of her long limbs was more apparent.

Homer, standing between April and Thord, grinned. "I scent a wedding in the air," he announced, then thumped his chest. "And I'll be best man and can kiss all the bridesmaids and make their hearts beat faster."

April laughed. "You've set your heart on their marrying—"

"This summer, before I go away," Homer broke in. "Liholiho and I have been like brothers since we were kids. I must stand beside him when he marries, as he must stand beside me when I find my girl."

"You usually manage to have things the way you want," April smiled.

Paniolos began going about the business of getting lunch. A grizzled old fellow, with a face grooved in wrinkles that told of sunlight and laughter, untied a moist bag from his saddle, glanced around, spotted a pool of shade cast by a leaning *koa* tree, and headed for it. A youngster with the eyes of a fawn untied another sack and followed the older man. Homer flung himself down in the green grass luxuriously. April seated herself beside him and Thord dropped down near-by.

"This is great, us all being together again," Homer remarked, his voice making Thord one of them. "When I'm in America, I'll think of you all in Kona." His eyes caressed the green land. "I'm keen to go East, to try new ways of living and thinking, but Hawaii will always have first place here"—he tapped a spot over his heart.

"I don't wonder. For sheer beauty, I'm convinced the Islands outrank anything on earth," Thord said.

"They have more than just beauty to offer," Homer said, sitting up. "Hawaii is the world's finest adventure in friendship. For over a hundred years people of all nationalities have been working and living peacefully side by side. Each brought with him from his own homeland, racial habits of eating, thinking, and worshiping— and borrowed something from other races in return."

Thord watched his eager intelligent eyes and knew he was on a favorite theme.

"The result has been a mellowing and merging of thought processes and a breaking down of racial prejudices. Here there is only one word of greeting, used by all nationalities—Aloha—my love to you. Say anything over and over again"—Homer watched Thord and April from under his long lashes—"and it becomes a reality. Added to that, the tolerance of Hawaiians toward others has broken down old habits of thinking. Result: in Hawaii, internationalism is working one hundred per cent." He gestured about him. "I believe that in our Islands the germ of a seed has sprouted, which will one day spread over the earth. The Land of Aloha has already found the answer to harmonious living, which the rest of the earth is still seeking. Mankind has much to learn from our Islands."

Thord glanced at the other people moving about him, laying out lunch on glossy green *ti* leaves. It was true. They were all part of a life larger and richer than any on the Mainland, moving as if they had eternity to use. They were leisurely without being lazy, and even in repose vitality radiated from their bodies. Consideration and thought of each other was manifest in their every word and movement. Yes, he reflected, here people were more like what God had intended them to be in the beginning.

Lunch over, everyone smoked for a while, commenting on the fine condition of the feed and the cattle, joking, planning for fun when the week-end came again. Then, at a word from Liholiho, grazing horses were caught, girths tightened, the steers to be shipped to Honolulu run into a holding corral, the rest of the herd turned loose to re-seek their mountain pastures.

Guarded by horsemen, the fifty select beeves were headed down the trail leading back to the ranch house. The afternoon was well advanced before ranch houses and corrals came into view. The steers were turned into the holding pasture; men dismounted and began unsaddling tired horses.

A pleasant bustle filled the air. Horses, freed of gear, trotted into their pasture, rolled luxuriously, grinding the feel of sweaty saddle blankets off their backs. Men put away saddles and bridles; the smell of cooking came from the rear of the big house.

"We'll eat dinner here and ride home later," April told Thord, falling into step beside him as they all headed for the house. "There's a baby moon and the forests will be lovely. Did you like your day?"

"I'll never forget it."

"We'll have others—" she began. "Maybe we—won't. If"—she lowered her voice—"the oil comes, Kauka and you will submerge completely."

"Up here"—Thord gestured at green solitudes below them—"all that seems unreal. You feel cut off from—"

"That's why I love coming up. Last night, seeing Moku, knowing about Tutu, seems as if it simply couldn't be true."

Thord nodded. They halted on the walk, the others went on to the house. Blue evening peace lay over the earth.

"Even up here, the feeling of invisible machinery going into action—" April caught her breath.

"Yes. I sense it too."

Their hands locked; then suddenly they went into the house without speaking.

It was late when the girls rose reluctantly to leave. Liholiho turned to his cousin. "Let's ride down part way, Homer," he suggested. "The night is sweet. We are young."

Homer smiled and shook his head. "You four go. I must stay

[135]

here with these." He laid an expressive brown hand on the heavy
books piled at his elbow, as if his spirit were keeping tryst with
some high dream still shrouded by the future.

Thord wondered where all their lives would go to from here.
Through the windows stars looked down, brilliant and uncon-
cerned.

14

TWO weeks went by. Dawns came, swelled into days, and contracted into nights again. Meals were eaten. Work began and progressed on the hospital. Hammers and saws sang their songs. Fresh timber was measured and shaped. Nails driven home. Skeletons of rooms-to-be sprang up, then swiftly became walls. Square apertures were filled with glass oblong ones fitted with doors. Ridge-poles, with herringbone beams, grew into solid roofs.

Between his daily rounds of the plantation sick, Kauka happily supervised the work. Thord took over visiting Mrs. Wilde, and assisted with cases involving minor ailments. Loki occupied herself with the household and garden. Homer studied. Mamo and April rode and swam together. The rollers of the mighty mill transformed juicy cane stalks into sugar. Coffee berries began flushing into rubies. Carlos' work on the laboratory and animal-runs in the horse pasture was completed. Takeshi worked in the garden after school.

"Here's a letter from the Leprosarium in Culion," Thord remarked to Loki one noon when he brought in the mail and handed it to her.

"Fine," Loki said. "That occupy Papa's mind for little whiles." Then she gave a glad cry. "Got letter from Kieser, too! I too glad." She gave a tired sigh. "Papa never saying anything, but he wait and wait until his face gray like old *poi* and his skin all dry up like paper." She started to rip the envelope open, then laid it down. "More fun for Papa to broke his own self."

"Loki, you're a woman in a million," Thord said.

"Go call Papa, *wikiwiki,* and tell to him this fine news."

"Okay." Thord headed for the telephone and called the hospital. "Connect me with Kauka, Sun Moy," he said when one of the Chinese nurses answered.

"He's in the delivery room," she told him, "but I'll send one of the boys to see if he can come."

In a minute or so Kauka's voice answered. Thord told him the news.

"Open it and see what Kieser says," Kauka directed excitedly: "I won't be able to leave here for quite a while."

Thord called to Loki. After a brief wait she came running down the hall. "Tell to Kauka, thank you, God, thank you. Twelve ounces of the oil coming on the next boat. Oh, good Kieser, kind Kieser." She wiped her eyes. "Tell to Papa, Kieser get radio but thinking better make sure he can get some of the most-best oil from his friend Dr. Chung before he tell Papa any-kind—" She was crying like a great child.

Thord put his arm about her big shoulders and relayed the information.

"I go tell Ching to make extra nice lunch for celebrate this fine events," Loki said when Thord had finished talking to Kauka. "Tomorrow Papa can go to Moku's and tell him and Tutu this happy things." Then her eyes got quick and watchful. "Lucky Mamo go to see Momi's new baby today. I not like any kind sad stuffs, like Tutu's sick, spoil her happy when she and Liholiho so in loves. This kind only for us *makules*—older peoples." Her delicious laughter bubbled up. "Sha, you not old, but always I forgetting, because you got such a big smart under your red hair." She gave him a playful push and headed for the kitchen.

Going to the *lanai,* Thord sat down and gazed into the expectant blue of the sky, showing above golden green tree tops. A completely new phase of life was about to begin. He and Kauka would soon be working side by side, with uncounted others, battling the most ancient and dreaded malady of mankind. Their equipment would be sketchy, their time limited, but they had all the available last-minute data regarding leprosy treatments from which to work.

Data gathered in the Philippines, in Hawaii, from Carville in Louisiana by doctors and bacteriologists in the pay of the United States Government.

After dinner, he and Kauka would retire to the office, read the long report from Culion, comparing treatments and remedies being used there, and checking them against those being employed on Molokai and in Carville.

Loki returned with a sewing basket, jerking him back to the present. "Sometimes I try to think how many shirts I fixing like this for Kauka, since us marry," she began, turning a worn collar. "Might-be many fellas thinking us *pupule*—crazy, because us not care very much if we no got swell clothes. Like just now I tell to Ching to go buy one pint of gin for make little celebration, instead of buying a new shirts. What-kind you think, Thord? Better for people have little fun, or only buy hot-style clothes?"

"Your way of living has the other licked to a standstill," Thord said.

"Always I thinking," Loki went on, "not the clothes that matter, only what-kind inside them." She laughed. "When Kauka come, us have some little drink for celebrate the oil coming. Good for Papa to letta-go-his-blouse after all this long wait."

Thord watched her fingers moving and marveled at the peace her presence brought and her ability, on occasion, to sit in a silence that poured out friendship more vivid than words. Sunlight danced among the tree tops, a faint sweet wind came from the sea. He saw Takeshi's small sturdy figure working happily over flower beds and listened to mynah birds jabbering over some object in the driveway that had roused their curiosity. Then a familiar rattle sounded. Laying aside her work, Loki went down the steps.

The old car swept up like a warrior's chariot. Kauka got out, his stocky figure radiating excitement and triumph. Loki held out her arms. They emerged from the embrace with wet eyes.

"My boy—" Kauka began huskily, and could get no further.

"There's Kieser's letter." Thord indicated it. "And here's the data from Culion."

Picking up his friend's letter, Kauka swiftly scanned the closely written pages of Old-World script. "Well," he said, glancing up, "we're really taking off!"

A faint electric tingle ran up Thord's spine.

"This material"—Kauka moved the pages in his hands—"can't be gulped." He laid the letter down reluctantly. "Tonight, at our leisure"—his eyes were restless and eager—"we can compare what Kieser says with the data we have already in our notebooks and segregate what's new. You can go through this Culion report this afternoon. Tomorrow we'll go and see Tutu and read her what Kieser has to say about chaulmoogra."

Loki swept out with a tray holding three tall glasses filled with an opalescent, milky mixture. Handing each man a glass she took up the third. "Here good lucks and warm Alohas to our dear friend Kieser, and happys for Tutu."

Kauka glanced at his watch. "We better eat, Mama. This nice drink and our good news has made me hungry."

"Every-kind ready."

Kauka glanced at the letters on the table and touched them in a regretful way. Noting it, Loki said brightly, "I think hot-style idea if you read what Kieser saying while us eat. Make Ching lunch taste more good if us all share this fine news." She sailed ahead with the white envelope clasped between brown fingers.

Ching was hovering about the table like a high priest officiating at an altar. It was Mitsu's wash day, but she had decorated the table with freshly gathered red hibiscus blossoms, which the polished *koa* wood reflected softly.

Absorbed as he was, Kauka noted that the usually simple noon meal had been made into an occasion. "Peanut-butter soup!" he exclaimed. "Fine, Ching." His eyes caught the old Chinaman's.

"Got fly chicken too—and pineapple flitters," Ching announced loftily, hurrying off.

"Kieser's letter is long," Kauka remarked, glancing at Loki. "I'll read bits of it." He scanned the pages, mentally selecting paragraphs of particular interest.

"This matter of chaulmoogra oil goes back a long time, Mama," he explained. "It has its origin in a legend which goes back for two thousand years, proving that in the Orient chaulmoogra's been identified with the treatment of leprosy for centuries."

"Yes?" Loki said eagerly.

"Listen to what Kieser says." He began reading slowly. " 'While botanizing in Asia I visited Indo-China and saw the jungle-buried towns of Angkor Wat and Angkor Thom. The Khmer Kings date from the first century A.D. Angkor Thom, a place of magnificent palaces, had a million inhabitants. Legend has it, one of its Kings developed leprosy and was banished from the palace—' " Kauka paused to eat a forkful of rice.

"Go on, Papa," Loki urged.

" 'The city is now ruins,' " Kauka read, " 'except for the palace and a few temples which are fairly well preserved. Joining one of the palaces is a terrace known as the Terrace of the Leper King, to which, presumedly, the monarch was banished. It is surrounded by a stone façade, decorated with bas-reliefs of elephants, battle scenes, and the figures of animals. Winding through the figures is a tree, which natives in the vicinity insist is a chaulmoogra tree, symbol of hope for lepers.' "

Kauka attacked his food absent-mindedly while his eyes slid down a few paragraphs. " 'The true chaulmoogra tree grows almost exclusively in Burma. What has been used to date is hydnocarpus, a kind of first cousin to it, which grows in many places. Since receiving your radio, I contacted Dr. Chung, a close friend of mine, and the foremost worker with leprosy in this region. He added more interesting material about chaulmoogra.' "

"Go on, Papa," Loki urged.

Kauka smiled. "I'm skipping technical stuff, which won't interest you," he explained. " 'It seems Japan used to banish lepers to a small outlying island of the group. As in the early days of Molokai, no care was provided for the unfortunates left there. Long intervals elapsed between the arrivals bringing over new victims of the disease and food supplies. In the intervals, the inhabitants of the island, to sustain life, were forced to eat the leaves of a tree growing there. To the amazement of government officials who landed new groups of doomed persons, they discovered that a number of the lepers left

[141]

on previous trips had recovered from the disease, or its progress had been arrested in an amazing way. Needless to say, the trees were a variety of chaulmoogra.'"

Kauka glanced up triumphantly.

"Read some more, *wikiwiki*," Loki begged.

"'Personally,'" Kauka went on, his eyes eagerly following the finely written lines, "'it's the germ, and not the disease, that I'm interested in. As you of course know, but I did not until recently, a Norwegian named Hansen isolated the bacillus originally. Under a microscope it looks something like a germ of tuberculosis, and is known as an acid-fast. Leprosy is a disease, like other diseases, and in time and with sufficient experimentation and work, a cure is bound to be found. I'm convinced the cure will prove to be chaulmoogra. Through the graciousness of my friend Dr. Chung I'm shipping you twelve ounces of the oil, which should be in your hands by the twenty-third, at the latest.'"

Kauka jabbed his fork into a piece of chicken, chewed it, and read on: "'In the meantime, I'll gather all possible information regarding the oil, which may prove of value to you. Your determination to work with it has spurred me to return to Burma for further investigation. Possibly, in time, you'll discover other ways of administering it than by the mouth. If the friend in question can retain it—some can, in others it produces dangerous nausea—it should at least halt the most violent symptoms.'"

"Oh, this sound fine to my ear!" Loki exclaimed. "Kieser got big smarts in his head and no go off at half-cocks."

Kauka smiled, then his eyes went back to the pages still in his hand.

"'In spite of the money the American Government has assigned to Molokai and Culion to find a cure for leprosy, nothing yet has been discovered that holds promise of a real cure. Smallpox, typhoid, scarlet fever, diphtheria, have been brought under control, and eventually leprosy will be—'"

The telephone began ringing.

"Damn on that telephone!" Loki said disgustedly when Kauka

went to answer it. "Always it ring when us eating or having nice time. But that Kauka job, so no sense to get mad."

Kauka came charging back. "There's a big fire in the Chinese section of Kailua. Mama phone Liholiho and Homer to come down, borrow a couple of plantation trucks and join us at Kailua. And phone the hospital to get extra beds ready. Come, Thord."

Kauka and Thord charged down the hall. The old car roared to life and swept off. Loki headed for the telephone, got the messages through, and started back to the dining room. Ching came in and saw the barely touched lunch. "Gar-damn," he exploded. "What-for all fellas no eat my nice fly chicken?"

Loki told him. "I like go help, too. Got plenty flens at Kailua."

"Sure, go," Loki urged. "I take care this." She indicated the littered table.

When it was cleared she went to the *lanai*. April drove in.

"Where's Mamo?" she asked, after kissing Loki.

"She went to Kaawaloa today to see Momi's new baby."

About sunset the telephone rang and April went to answer it.

"Central says the fire is *pau*. All the stores are ashes and Thord and Kauka are taking injured people to the hospital."

A tragic sunset was burning the west, then suddenly twilight came in across the quiet sea.

"I guess Mamo stop at Momi's tonight," Loki remarked. "She be sorry if Liholiho comes for dinner and she miss him."

April smiled.

"With all this fire and things happening today, I forget to tell our big news." Eagerly Loki told her about Kieser's letter.

"How perfectly swell!" April exclaimed. "When Kauka told me he hadn't reported Tutu I was stirred up. Now she may have a chance—"

Hoofs sounded on the driveway.

"Guess Mamo coming back after all," Loki remarked.

The dark shape of a rider loomed up, and when he rode into the light they both exclaimed, "Moku!"

Dismounting, he dropped the bridle reins and came heavily up the steps. "Tutu has vanished," he told them in Hawaiian. "She

[143]

went fishing this morning when the tide was right. When she did not come back around four, after fishing is no good, I went to look for her. . . ." He threw his arm out in an overwrought way.

April's and Loki's eyes met hurriedly.

"Don't get all worked up, Moku," Loki said, speaking in her own tongue. "Tutu is old. Maybe she got tired and went off to sleep for a while."

"No," Moku insisted. "I went back for my wife and children. We have been searching for hours. We found her spear and her net bag for fish. I think she drowned herself."

Loki grabbed Moku's toil-worn hand and held it to her breast. Moku want on talking.

"If she did, it's better than being sent to Molokai—better than being taken from Kona and those she loves. God knows best. Her end is right—but we shall miss her. His voice broke. "Her month was up—tomorrow. She did not want to ask Kauka to let her stay longer, because her sickness was beginning to show too much, and if people found out what he had done—"

"Maybe," Loki interrupted, still speaking in Hawaiian, "she is only hiding as our people do when their Chinese sickness gets too bad. Don't be sad, Moku." She patted his hand. "We will send out search parties to find her."

"If she's found, she'll be sent to Molokai by cursed white people who brought sickness to Hawaii. Before they came our bodies were clean and strong!" His voice was harsh and angry. "No, Tutu is dead. Her footprints in the sand told the story."

"Don't say anything about the oil," April whispered in English. "If Tutu's dead he'll only feel worse, knowing that she might have been saved. When, if she's found—"

"You young, but got a smart head," Loki agreed under her breath.

15

WELL, my boy," Kauka said in pleased tones as they left the hospital, "already the extra cost of that"—he gestured behind him—"has been amply justified. Without the new wing those poor Chinese couldn't have been accommodated properly."

"But technically they aren't Wilde's responsibility, are they?" Thord asked.

"No, but this affair will make headlines in the Honolulu papers," Kauka said with a smile. "Hiram Wilde, Kona Magnate, Turns Over New Wing Of Remodeled Hospital To Kailua Fire Victims, will be the headlines. After details of the disaster and some talk about the need for a Community Hospital, there'll be a write-up about the K. S. C.—focusing spotlight on Hiram and his outstanding work on Hawaii."

"I see." Thord grinned, his steel-blue eyes flickering with amusement.

"And"—Kauka stressed the word slightly—"if I don't miss my guess, there will be a follow-up article announcing that Hiram Wilde has added another doctor to the plantation staff. I saw him watching you in that calculating way of his. It would fit into his picture to add a doctor with a New York background. Of course, Elsbeth's improved health'll have nothing to do with you being taken on!"

"But if Wilde does take me on, he'll want references."

"As I told you the night we first talked in my office, I'll take care of that by writing directly to your friend Dr. Barett. His name is known, even out here. It'll carry more weight than a routine endorsement by a medical board."

"But what logical reason can we trump up for my not remaining with Barry?"

"The best, to satisfy local ego, is 'the lure of Hawaii.'"

"You're a genius!" Thord swung into Kauka's mood. "Gifted Young Doctor Sacrifices New York Career To See Hawaii."

"That's it." Kauka spun the wheel to take a turn. "With you as my assistant, we're set—in all directions. Of course, Kona has long forgotten that I graduated from the Royal College of Physicians and Surgeons in London." He spoke without the least rancor. "But the fact will be revived when you're my teammate. And then when, if, we get somewhere with chaulmoogra, it'll carry weight. In medicine, thank God, there are no prejudices or barriers of race. In six, five days now"—his eyes lighted like a boy's counting off the days till Christmas—"the oil will be here. Between us, we can keep Tutu under constant observation."

Thord nodded.

"Tired?" Kauka inquired.

"Not a bit."

"Nor I. The instant we've had a snack we'll get at the Culion report."

He turned into the driveway and stopped. Loki came down the steps to meet him. When she finished telling of Moku's visit, Kauka pushed weary fingers through his graying hair.

"If Tutu's drowned herself, and it's quite likely she would rather than face being sent to Molokai, it's my fault. I should have told her I'd wired for the oil as soon as I read the write-up about Kieser in the Honolulu paper. I waited only because I wanted to be sure I could get some before raising her hopes."

"Shut your face, Papa," Loki advised gently. "You got a big tired tonight because of all the poor peoples who get burn. You not thinking straight. I sorry for Moku and his family, but Tutu's *pilikeas* all finish!"

"I must notify Sheriff Keoke at once so he can organize search parties," Kauka said, getting out of the car.

"Better you and Thord eat some-kind first," Loki suggested.

"We can't until I've telephoned. We mustn't waste time. How long is it since Moku was here?"

"Might be one hour."

"If Tutu's body is found," Kauka spoke heavily, "with signs of leprosy on it, the fact that Moku came to notify me instead of the sheriff, plus the fact that I told Thisbe a while back that I'd been down there—" His eyes met Loki's.

She made a Hawaiian sign, averting evil, then announced stoutly, "No good steam up about things which might be never happening. Homer and Liholiho coming here for eat some-kind before they go up the mountain?"

"They left directly from the hospital for the ranch. Liholiho has to get shipping steers in the morning, but we must call them again. And phone Hiram, too." As he started up the steps he saw April. "It was good of you, my child, to stay with Loki. Hasn't Mamo come home?"

"Stop Momi's house, I guess," Loki said.

"Don't put away the car, Thord," Kauka directed. "I'll have to go to South Kona."

"Okay."

A tight cold feeling ran around Thord's heart. When he went up the steps, April tried to speak but could not. Reaching out, he caught her hand quickly into his. "Don't feel too upset about Tutu," he advised. "Such things—"

"It isn't only Tutu," she said unsteadily. "It's Kauka. It seems monstrous that just as everything seemed set—"

"I was thinking that too."

She gave a desolate little nod and her fingers worked deeper into his. Thord felt some essence flowing into his hand from hers. There was a force in her slight body, different from his, but related to it. Looking down, he saw her eyes were brimming over, and with a swift instinctive gesture his arm went about her. She dug her forehead against his shoulder. He swallowed, and she clutched his shirt with both hands. For a moment he kept his

[147]

muscles rigid, then buried his face in her flying hair, which smelled like dry hay in fairy meadows.

After a little he said, "April."

Her head fell back on his arm and her face had an expression of waiting on it which sent a sudden want of love running like fire through the nerves and fibers of his body.

"Don't look at me like that," he begged.

Her face went proud and she pressed back from him.

"Don't misunderstand me," he said quickly. "People of our type usually keep their hearts to themselves, but death often jars things loose."

"I'm going to write Dale and tell him I don't love him."

"Don't be hasty. Wait till he comes. You've got to be sure. . . ."

"I am sure," she replied in steady tones. "I'm going to stay here where I belong. His letters about shows and dances and dinner parties"—her lips spurned the words—"are so much deadwood beside what's happening here."

"Steady," Thord cautioned. "All this grim business of this afternoon and tonight has upset you. How damnably young you are—and how lovely!" he added involuntarily. "If I were free—"

"Are you married?" she asked, consternation in her voice, but her eyes did not swerve from his face.

"No, April."

Then, because she did not ask the next question, he told her about himself in a few stark sentences.

"Oh," she gasped, her strong young arms going about him fiercely. "And I—I despised you when I saw you drunk in the bow of the ship when dawn was coming. And I almost hated you when you tore off the lei Kauka gave you and dropped it on the sidewalk. You were only trying to escape from awful things which had happened to you. You didn't know what you were doing."

"I'd give everything on earth to be in a position to say things I want to say to you, April, but—"

"You don't have to," she interrupted. "I'm saying them to you, too. Without speaking."

[148]

So, Thord thought, awed, must the first woman have looked at the first man.

He stood rigid in the circle of her arms. This lovely girl, who had hardly finished with being a child, was laying her love at his feet without shame or hesitation. He must safeguard her.

"Look," he said, almost harshly, "the things that have happened this afternoon and tonight—"

"It began before that," April said.

"Oh, good God!" he burst out. "This moment would come at a time like this. I haven't even time to talk to you. The sheriff, your father, a dozen people—will be here shortly."

She nodded. Hands locked closer, eyes looked deeper.

"Don't think!" April begged in a small voice. "Thinking stops people from doing things they want to." She waited.

Thord felt as if a stealthy, treacherous sea had suddenly washed firm sand from beneath his feet, and in the same instant as if he'd come out of a lifetime of blindness into the glory which is light. This girl dreamed, then rushed fences.

"Please," she whispered, "just once. A long one."

They came out of each other's arms, shaken.

"God knows where we head from here," Thord said when he could manage his voice.

"I'll hold my horses, tight, until we get a chance to really talk. Now you've kissed me, you can go and do whatever you have to."

She looked like a pool filled to the brim.

"April—"

"Yes?"

"There's usually a way out of every jam if people have enough strength of will to hang on, but behind your loveliness I'm afraid you're rather a desperate character. A pirate and a fairy rolled into one."

She did not dispute him. Her eyes met his, steady and strong. The headlights of a car swooped into the garden, and she stopped.

"There's the sheriff," Thord said.

She listened. "No, it's Father's car." And she prepared to wait.

[149]

She's stuff, Thord thought, and won't give ground or run. Then he smiled, despite himself.

"Get that look off your face. Anyone with an ounce of observation—"

"I can't. It's inside me. Besides, Daddy simply doesn't register to inside things. He's only concerned with tangibles."

The car stopped at the steps and Hiram got out.

"You here, April?" he asked.

"I came to be with Loki. Didn't Mother tell you?"

"I didn't see your mother. When I got back from Kailua she'd gone to her room. Pretty ghastly business, this, on top of the afternoon," he added, addressing Thord.

"It is."

"Where's Kauka?"

"Inside."

"Has he phoned the sheriff?"

"Yes. He ought to be here at any moment."

They started indoors, April walking between them.

"Here," Loki called from the dining room.

She had placed cold chicken on the table, bread, cups, and a big pot of coffee.

"Where's Kauka?" Wilde asked again.

"Phoning Liholiho and Homer to come down," Loki replied.

"There's a shipment of steers due to go Wednesday—" Wilde began.

"Daddy!" April said indignantly.

He looked at her, then said, "But of course under the circumstances—" and brushed the rest aside.

"Eat some-kind and drink coffee," Loki ordered, in dignified command of her own house.

April and Thord sat down, Hiram gripped the back of one of the dining-room chairs.

"How come Moku notified you about this before me or the sheriff?" he asked, but his voice was academic.

Silence ruffled down into the room like a big grim bird, and brooded in it. Loki's face was expressionless. She filled two cups, handed them to April and Thord, then looked at Wilde.

"Since I small kid, Tutu and I got warm Alohas for each others. When Mamo born she stay with me—"

"Of course, of course," Hiram cut her off irritably. "I know how Hawaiians are. In times of trouble they invariably go to their own people rather than to those who can help them more efficiently."

Loki watched him from under her eyelashes.

"Surely Sheriff Keoke should be here by now," Hiram snapped.

"Take times to find police mans," Loki told him. Seating herself, she poured out a cup of coffee, added two heaping tablespoonfuls of brown sugar to it. "Better you eat some-kind, Hiram, if you going down tonight with other fellas for help Moku to look his mother."

Wilde did not stir and his face was as frozen as the pillar of salt. But some expression about his eyes showed that somewhere behind the mask he wore he cherished resentment, because of all the people living in Kona, Loki and Kauka were, and had always been, completely unimpressed by his wealth and power. To them he was simply another human being, Hiram—not Hiram Wilde, sugar and coffee magnate.

There's not an atom of warmth to his make-up, Thord thought. He's annoyed rather than upset over the events of the past few hours; over Chinamen injured by a fire, over an old Hawaiian woman getting drowned, over anything that jams the machinery of the plantation, cutting down profits.

Kauka came in. His face was gray and tired. Wilde glanced at him. "You better let Graham go down with the sheriff. He's young and can take it. You're fagged."

"I am tired," Kauka admitted. "But I shall go down. Tutu was dear to me. Moku is my friend and he is in trouble."

"Here your coffee," Loki said, pushing out a chair and placing a steaming cup before it.

Kauka sat down by her. Thord watched them, silently pledged to each other.

He became conscious of April beside him. In her mingled thistle-down and iron. She was Loki and Kauka's breed. She glanced at him in an impersonal way, but her eyes swam behind their long lashes and her pale small face was possessed by memories.

Steps sounded in the hall, coming from the direction of the kitchen.

"What this damn-kind stuff I hear from policemans when I come from hospital just now—about Tutu fall inside sea?" Ching demanded, bursting through the door.

"I'm afraid it's true," Kauka said.

"Sonna-pa-pitch!" the cook exclaimed hotly. "Every-kind happen today. I velly, velly solly. Velly, velly sad when old woman no die inside bed with all family clying."

Thord suppressed a smile. The irascible old man looked comical and heroic as he rallied to Kauka's standard.

April glanced from Kauka to her father, then moved as if her chair were uncomfortable. Yes, Thord thought, to a man of Hiram Wilde's type it must be distasteful to see how in times of stress people rallied to Kauka instead of to him.

A car roared in.

"Keoke and his police mans," Loki remarked.

Kauka rose to meet them. Big men with heavy tramping feet swarmed through the door, their brown faces filled with concern.

"High sea today," the big handsome sheriff said, taking his hat off when he saw Wilde. But he addressed Kauka. "If Tutu fall inside water like Moku thinking, she get all mash up. But us fellas go and look anyhow."

The phone rang and Loki went to answer it. When she returned her face had a mild pleased expression, like a child who has received a gift from a totally unexpected quarter. "That Thisbe," she said. "He hear from Central about Tutu and speak to me to tell you, Kauka, if any-kind he can do tonight to *kokua*—help— just you say. If you need car for taking extra peoples to hunt for Tutu, you can have his. Or he will drive his own selfs, for helping at this sorry time."

Thord glanced involuntarily at Wilde, but his face expressed nothing.

"Ready, Kauka?" the sheriff asked.

[152]

"Yes. When Homer and Liholiho come"—he turned to Loki—"tell them to take my car. Thord and I will go with Keoke and the boys as far as Thisbe's. Then we'll use his car."

"There's no call to do that," Wilde announced. "Thisbe will need it when he goes down in the morning to visit the bereaved family. You'd better come with me, Graham. Keoke can take Kauka. I'm going along too."

The warm atmosphere of the kindly room with its old-fashioned furniture and cutglass-cluttered sideboard fell several notches and froze. Loki stole a glance at Thord, then at her husband, standing heavy and patient by her side. Alarm walked with prayers in the wide pupils of her eyes, but her face gave away nothing.

16

"WELL, Keoke has decided there's no use trying to hunt for Tutu any longer," Kauka informed the family when he and Thord came in to dinner at the end of the fourth day.

Mamo wiped her large, brimming eyes.

Loki nodded. "God knows best," she remarked, making her tone significant for the two men.

Thord glanced at her, his spirit giving hers a swift salute. She had paid prolonged visits to Moku's family and with quick sympathy, gentle jokes, and cookies consoled youngsters who wailed with Polynesian abandon for their lost grandparent. But she had managed to keep her household functioning easily although search parties, coming and going, dropping in at all hours for meals and consultations, had made the old house a miniature hotel. And she had never, by the slightest sign or word, breathed the fear that had eaten at her soul, that Tutu's body might be recovered, with disastrous consequences for Kauka.

"Liholiho and Homer will be here to eat before they go back to the ranch," Kauka said, pulling his soup plate toward him.

Mamo, whose volatile nature had dropped under the shadow which had fallen on Kona, brightened at his words, excused herself and left the room. When her footsteps died away, Loki looked across the table at her husband.

"Papa, the oil has come," she said softly, indicating the sideboard.

Going over to it, Kauka picked up the parcel with reverent hands.

When he heard Mamo returning, he sighed, put the package down and returned to the table. Then, as he glanced up, a remote smile etched itself briefly on his face. Mamo had dried her eyes, combed out her hair and placed a flower above her ear.

Just as the main course was coming in, Homer and Liholiho arrived. Though they had been active in the search, their vigor appeared undiminished. Both strong swimmers, they had dived, searching underwater caves where lava had spilled into the sea, in hope that surges or currents might have lodged Tutu's body in one of them. They had ridden long miles up and down the coast with the sheriff and his men, come in at all hours, eaten, slept briefly, then gone off again.

"Well," Liholiho said, seating himself beside Mamo, "that is *pau*. Tonight I shall have a good sleep."

"I think," Loki said brightly, "swell idea if us all make a big picnic Sunday after church and jolly up after all this sad. Go down to Honaunau swim, fish, eat, make music."

Mamo looked up, fun quivering along her lashes. "We better not go to Honaunau," she said, stressing the word slightly, then began shaking with silent laughter.

"Why?" Loki demanded curiously.

"Because the day I went to see Momi I rode by the City of Refuge and you'll never guess who I saw there, kissing hard behind a stone wall."

"Who?" Homer and Liholiho asked simultaneously.

"Brewer and Prudence."

"What!" everyone exclaimed incredulously.

"I'm not fooling," Mamo insisted. "I saw them but they didn't see me. They were too busy." Her laughter rippled off.

Homer and Liholiho pommeled each other as if they could not endure the joke. Kauka looked completely incredulous; tears streamed down Loki's cheeks, then suddenly she became serious.

"I think fine idea if us ask Prudence and Brewer to go with us Sunday. That poor kid never having fun because she ugly and Thisbe watch her too close. I like swell if that old rascals Brewer marry with her. Better than she never having any mans at all."

Liholiho wiped his eyes, Homer struggled for composure. "But Thisbe would have apoplexy if his Ewe Lamb married that old reprobate," he protested.

"If I were a girl," Liholiho said, chuckling with mirth, "I'd jump out of bed and run like hell if I saw Brewer's red face on my pillow. And if I were Brewer and woke up and found Prudence—"

"Hey, shut up," Loki commanded, but her eyes were merry. "When fellas love, it not only the face."

Liholiho and Homer threw back their heads and their boisterous gaiety filled the room.

"Sha!" Loki cried. "I no meaning what you rascal fellas thinking. Young mans always got a low minds, but that nature." Her voice was tinged with amusement. "But—"

"But what, Mama?" Mamo asked.

"Love is more than only the body, it go beyond that kind of things to God. But I scare Brewer never loving like that. He not that styles. Brewer jolly fun, but always making bad-kind things with Japanese and Hawaiian girls. I little scare for Prudence. When girl no got pretty face or shape, and never any mans making love to her—" She shook her head worriedly.

Kauka signed to Thord that they would go to the office and leave the others to their conjectures and fun. Walking around the table, he kissed Loki's high-piled, wavy hair, said good night to the boys, and placing his hand on Thord's shoulder, took up the package off the sideboard and headed down the hall.

Going to his chair before his desk, Kauka sat down and thoughtfully nursed the package of oil between his hands. Thord perched on the edge of a table and stared through the window as if he expected the night to speak to him. He glanced at Kauka sitting so quietly. As if feeling Thord's mind on him, Kauka looked up.

"My boy," he said in his slow way, "the experience of failure is the most profound as well as the most enriching phenomenon to which man is heir."

The words fell into the quiet room like spaced pebbles being deliberately dropped into a deep pond.

"At the first real failure, life takes on its true colors, for it is only through failure that people begin to understand. It makes you kin to all mankind who've walked the same road at some time in their lives."

A warm, friendly night-rain began rustling across the roof, like a sensitive person, reluctant to intrude. Thord listened to it while he weighed Kauka's words.

"Probably you're right."

"The success or defeat of a life depends, not on what happens to you, *but in what use you make of what happens.*" Kauka repeated.

Thord locked his long arms across his chest.

With the vast patience of a Polynesian, Kauka watched him, waiting for a reply. Since speaking, his whole appearance had altered. From being old, weighed-down, and tired, he now looked resolute and strong again. Thord knew he was gazing through the outer at the inner man. Each gray hair, each wrinkle was a service stripe of living. The joys, sorrows, accomplishments, and defeats of fifty years had contributed their parts toward the building of a soul that looked back without recrimination, remembering only the good, and ahead with faith that ultimately the why and wherefore of living would somehow be proved, and the struggle of living justified.

It drove home the fact to Thord that each man's life was created by himself, for himself, and its full value could never be measured by anyone but himself. Slowly, as if giving each word its full value, he repeated them. "The success or defeat of a life depends, not on what happens to you, *but in what use you make of what happens.*"

"Exactly," Kauka agreed.

Thord sat very still. Behind him lay disaster and defeat. Ahead, seemingly insurmountable obstacles, pitfalls, traps. What use was he going to make of them all?

"That statement of yours is a challenge to anyone."

"*Maikai*—fine, my boy. We've got to begin all over again and plot a new campaign for this." He tapped the parcel he was nursing.

"Now Tutu has gone we are held up as far as immediate experimentation with an individual and animals is concerned."

Thord nodded. "Did you tell Moku about the oil?"

"No, it would only have added to his grief to know there was a chance that his mother might have been cured. We shall have to keep all the members of his family under constant supervision from now on, and if any of them show evidences of leprosy, start treatments immediately."

"Would it be possible," Thord said after a moment of thought, "to write to Molokai and ask for some cultures of leprosy bacillus, explaining that you want to attempt to inoculate small animals with the disease?"

"No. Hawaii is a small place. Word would eventually leak out and Hiram and all Kona would be up in arms."

"But the most outstanding fact I've been able to gather from the data you have on hand is the almost fantastic difficulty of transmitting the germ in spite of tales of getting it from money or Chinese laundries," Thord said. "Why *is* everyone so confoundedly panicked by it?"

"That's something I've never been able to grasp," Kauka answered, lighting a cigar. "The percentage of persons working with lepers who contract the disease can almost be counted on one hand, as medical records of recent years prove. Probably uninformed persons are afraid of it largely because the cause of its transmission is still a mystery. But the universal revulsion toward it is even more mysterious. There are many diseases that look as bad, or worse, than leprosy—an advanced case of syphilis, for instance."

"What do you propose to do about that?" Thord gestured at the package of oil on the desk.

"For the immediate present, nothing. In a week or so we'll see. There are lepers hidden in inaccessible valleys on this island."

Getting to his feet, Kauka walked to the desk, shuffled through papers and brought out the Culion report. "Have you looked at this yet?"

"No."

"I've glanced at it. In the main, it coincides largely with reports from Molokai. In the Philippines, as here, it has been recorded that while leprosy exists all over the world—cases have even been known

[158]

among Esquimaux—the larger incidence is in hot climates. Theories have been advanced that leprosy resulted from certain foods, then those theories were discarded. Others maintain it must be carried by bedbugs, fleas, cockroaches, mosquitoes, but there's no proof. No evidence has been found that any of these insects, even when they were in contact with known open cases, carry the germ."

Thord listened attentively.

"Doctors in the Philippines as well as in Hawaii," Kauka went on, "feel that different areas in different parts of the world should be charted and studied carefully. Both those where leprosy is prevalent and where it is rare. Conditions should be compared, complete clinical examinations and case histories should be kept meticulously. Food, general living conditions, other diseases tending to diminish physical resistance, should all be taken into account, ignoring no factor that could possibly contribute to the transmission of the disease."

"That will take a long time."

"Possibly the lifetime of many men," Kauka agreed. "Suppose it does? If real clues are produced, clues that will lead to an eventual victory, it will be worth it. No disease known to man has caused such heartbreak and misery, not only to the victims, but to the families of those afflicted."

His eyes blazed. "I hope we may both live to see the day when medicine can shout to the world, 'Leprosy is licked!'" So, Thord thought, must have the prophets of old looked when they thundered down laws from Jehovah. Then, suddenly, he was Kauka again, a gentle, lovable, rather untidy figure.

"I wish we were fixed to take on the job—but we've got to make our living at other duties. In that connection Hiram has already approached me about taking you on as my assistant."

Kauka shuffled through the papers littering his desk. "With the new wing, the hospital will accommodate a total of a hundred beds plus outside plantation cases. The work is more than one man can handle adequately. Besides . . ."

"Besides?" Thord asked.

"None of us lives forever. Hiram's policy, and an eminently suc-

[159]

cessful one, is to have men specifically trained to cope with the particular problems of this locality, and under them younger men to fill their boots when their time of usefulness is past."

Thord walked to the window. The rain had stopped but an occasional bright drop fell through the light that reached out from windows and vanished into the dark, like miniature shooting stars.

"Ten days, a week ago," Thord said over his shoulder, "this would have rung bells with me. Now, don't think I'm not keen to work with you, Kauka, but circumstances have come into the picture which makes it distasteful to have Wilde for my employer."

"April?"

Thord started. "How—"

"I brought April into the world. She is as dear to me as Mamo and I know her as well."

"Did she—"

"Not a word, but I saw the handwriting on the wall. I'm glad"— he sighed gently—"for you both. There are many difficulties ahead, and will be for a long time. But a long time is not—forever."

"Her fiancé is due to arrive in a few weeks."

"I know. That is all to the good."

"Why?"

"Like lots of girls of her age, April was in love with love, not with an individual. Her heart is in Kona, and always will be." Pausing, he selected a mango from a plate of food that Ching always left in the office before he retired for the night. "You're her sort," he went on. "Elsbeth is sold on you. By your performance on the plantation you can establish yourself with Hiram. In his cold way he adores April. She's the one person in this world who dares to stand up to him—"

"Except you."

Kauka waved a mango peel. "I don't stand up against Hiram. I merely rate him as another human being, therefore, in his heart he resents me. But that is aside from the matter we're discussing. From a worldly point, April's engagement to Dale Hancock III"— his voice was faintly mocking—"is a feather in the Wilde cap, but any normal parents would prefer to have their only child living near them."

"But my record—" Thord protested.

"There isn't anything that can't be erased with time and effort," Kauka replied calmly.

"God knows I'd give everything to be in a position to—"

"Oust Dale?"

"Yes, but—"

"But you have."

Thord did not contest the statement.

"The end of it's out of your hands already. It rests with you now to steer your ship and April's among the reefs ahead."

"Suppose, just for the sake of argument, that Dale comes and the engagement is broken or peters out. I heave into the picture." Thord's face was white. "Parents are all for our marriage. The step's taken, then from somewhere, before they've had enough time to know me—"

"All hell would break loose," Kauka said.

Thord laughed mirthlessly.

Kauka contemplated the appetizing beauty of the peeled mango between his fingers. "You must act with caution and in the full realization that such an eventuality may turn up at any minute. Actually there isn't a chance in a thousand that it will."

Thord stared out into the dark. "I'll talk to April tomorrow if I get an opportunity. If not, Sunday when we go to Honaunau. I've got to make her see—"

"I know her," Kauka interrupted. "She'll be guided by you to a point. But you can't stem tides, and you can't tell about girls of her type. She'll wait and work a million years to get something she wants. On the other hand, she's liable to go off at half-cock, with both barrels and without warning, and to hell with consequences. That's the danger of missionary stock transplanted to tropical latitudes." Finishing his mango, Kauka went to the sink, washed his hands and dried them. "As well as her own emotions, she's wrestling with the held-up feeling of three generations behind her, transplanted from cold, restrained lands to latitudes throbbing with power and fire. You haven't been here long enough to see the pay-off. I have. I've seen children of the old New England families, the fourth generation, letta-going-their-blouses for themselves, their fathers, grandfathers, and great-grandfathers. I'm not saying April will. She has steel in her make-up—"

Kauka walked over and laid his hand on Thord's shoulder. They stood in silence staring into the drenched night. From far off came a low long roll of tropical thunder, muttering above the dome of Mauna Loa.

"Listen, the *Akuas*—gods are talking," Kauka said.

Thord raised his head.

"Remember?" Kauka asked.

"Yes, Thunder—in Heaven."

Kauka nodded. "When a person tries to be anything, or to do anything—"

"And the world doesn't recognize him—" Thord continued.

Their eyes met, somber and strong, as another giant rumble shook the silence into shining pieces.

17

WHEN they finally went to bed, Thord could not sleep. He lay in the dark, his mind seething. During the past four days he had seen April repeatedly and briefly and always in the presence of others, but she had never been out of his mind. Aside from her loveliness, in her were forces which would take her through anything, provided she considered. the battle worth it. There was a fine sincerity about her, plus a splendid unawareness of self. But Kauka's analysis of the effect of a tropical environment on stock. such as she came from made him feel as if he were walking on crusted lava which was still molten underneath.

If only she were free and he clear of the damnable mess in New York. With a sort of rage he leaped up and turned on the light.

Going to the small bookcase, he glanced at the miscellaneous volumes on the shelves. Novels of no special distinction, a worn dictionary, an out-dated almanac, and Maeterlinck's *Buried Temple*. Taking it up he walked to the rocker and sat down. He turned pages, glancing at their contents, but through wide-flung windows the night sent in the heavy fragrance of belladonna lilies, ylang-ylang, frangipani, and ginger. Kona was potent magic for anyone. He thought for a minute, closed the volume, and got back into bed.

Next morning at breakfast the phone rang. Loki went to get it. When she returned her eyes were shining. "Hiram wants you at the office, before you go to see Elsbeth. I think might-be Kauka have swell assistant tomorrow." She gave Thord's shoulder a fond pat.

"Drop me off at the hospital," Kauka said. "Then take the car."

They went off into the green and blue sparkle of the rain-washed morning. Thord kept his eyes on Mauna Loa, visible beyond the long, green slope of the island. The beauty of the morning filled Thord with restlessness.

"My boy," Kauka said, "don't go into this with misgivings. Accept the seasons of the heart, as you accept the seasons of the year."

"You know, Kauka," Thord replied, "being just with you makes up for all the things that landed me here."

"Youth is always sentimental," Kauka retorted, grinning. "I'm just an old *hapa-haole* doctor. Here we are. Doesn't the hospital look imposing with the new wing and a fresh coat of paint?" He gestured admiringly at the rambling structure on the low green hill. Trees crowded about it, beautiful with sunshine. "Pick me up about noon, and luck to you. With Hiram, and with April."

Putting in the gear, Thord drove around the turn, down the hill, and along the strip of road leading to the cluster of plantation buildings and the rumbling mill. Mighty clouds were holding secret consultations above the Pacific; air like soft hands flowed past his face.

The usual array of cars and horses was in front of the office. Two *lunas* were inside talking to Wilde. Stopping the car, Thord walked up the steps and sat down on the bench outside. Peaceful monkey-pod trees spread their green umbrellas across the road, sunshine rained downward. From within the office came the voices of men. Finally Wilde called out, "Graham."

Thord rose, the two *lunas* filed out, greeted him briefly and headed for their horses. Wilde nodded as he entered, and indicated a chair. The white plaster walls were entirely bare except for two photographs. One of the mill as it had been originally, a small affair, the second of the imposing edifice it now was.

"I presume you've an idea why I've called you here," Wilde remarked.

"Yes."

"I feel, with the continued expansion of the plantation, affairs have reached a point where two doctors instead of one are neces-

[164]

sary. You may not be aware of the fact but in Hawaii medical care among plantation day-laborers is free."

Thord nodded.

"While Kauka has been in my employ for twenty-eight years, and has given excellent service, I feel some of his methods are slightly out-dated. You're fresh from New York."

Thord tensed slightly, watching Wilde's large mask of a face.

"If you're interested, I'd like to put you on as his assistant. When he retires you'll be in full charge and can have some able youngster to assist you."

Thord waited.

"Your salary for the first year will be two hundred a month. After that you'll get two hundred and fifty, as Kauka does."

As if suspecting the thoughts going through Thord's mind, Wilde continued. "After New York our salaries must seem small, but the plantation provides Kauka his house free, gasoline for his car, lights, and firewood.. When, if, you marry a place will be built for you. Of course I'll want references."

"Of course." Thord felt himself getting hot about the ears, then he took the hurdle. "I worked for Dr. Richard Barett for two years," he said.

"Indeed!" Wilde said, looking pleased, then he added cautiously, "How did you happen to give up such a post to come to Hawaii?"

The muscles in front of Thord's ears bulged slightly. "A desire to see Hawaii." There, it was out. Would it suffice?

A faintly satisfied expression flitted over Wilde's face.

"The Islands, mere specks on the map, are actually anything but insignificant," he announced loftily. "Hawaii is the spearpoint of America driven into the middle of the Pacific. We of Hawaii are proud to boast that we pour into the federal treasury more money, annually, in the form of taxes, than fourteen states of the Union. And for sheer science in sugar-growing we lead the world."

"Indeed."

"May I conclude, then, you're interested in working for me? At present your field may seem limited; in time"—he made a sweeping gesture—"when you're in charge—"

"Let's not look too far ahead," Thord suggested a trifle grimly. "I'm satisfied to work with Kauka. He's a graduate of the Royal College of Physicians and Surgeons in London."

Wilde nodded, dismissing it. "You'll be officially on my payroll from tomorrow."

"Very well."

"I'll have arrangements made at the plantation club."

"I prefer remaining where I am, at least for a while longer. For one thing I have no car—"

"The plantation will make the necessary advance."

"I prefer to wait, until I can buy one out of my salary. And I'm very happy where I am. Of course I'll pay Kauka and Loki board."

"I have no jurisdiction over my employees' private lives," Wilde said.

Oh, haven't you, Thord thought.

A fly buzzed frantically against a window-pane, trying to escape from the chilly room, back into the sunshine from which it had come.

Wilde watched Thord, then continued, "I think in the long run, you'll find living at the club preferable. Kauka and Loki's household is typically Hawaiian, a happy-go-lucky affair that's pleasant enough, but hardly conducive to the study necessary to keep abreast with what's new in medicine."

Thord made no answer. He wants to pry me loose from Kauka, he thought, make me entirely his man, like the rest of the help on the plantation. If it weren't for Kauka I wouldn't touch this.

Their eyes met.

"Suppose we let this matter of housing ride for a bit," Thord suggested stiffly. "It's of no consequence, really."

"Very well."

There was a brief acid silence, then Wilde glanced at his watch. "Tell Kapohakimohewa to come in," he said, in dismissal. "Oh, and tell Mrs. Wilde I'm going to South Kona to see how far along the Macadamian crop is and will lunch with Brewer."

"Very well, Mr. Wilde," Thord said, rising and starting for the door.

He spoke to the *luna,* sprawled happily on the bench, and the Hawaiian rose regretfully and went in.

When Thord drove into the Wilde grounds he saw April cutting day-lilies along one of the borders. In a grass-green voile dress with her bright hair, she looked as much a part of the garden as the flowers growing in it. Seeing Thord, she waved. Stopping the car he crossed to where she stood.

"What's happened?" she asked. "You look like a sword."

"I've just come from the plantation office."

"Did you have a run-in with Father?"

"Sort of. He wants me to live at the club and I told him I preferred to remain at Kauka's."

April looked thoughtful.

"After I've seen your mother, I want to talk to you."

"I'll be here. Are you—"

"From tomorrow I'm a cog in the Wilde machine."

"Don't sound so grim. Don't you want to stay here?"

"Of course, but feeling as I do about you, and being in your father's pay, sort of curdles. I don't want to talk to you here." He glanced at formally laid-out walks and austere New England house. "Fake a call from Mamo and let's drive somewhere."

"I'll fix it."

Thord headed for the house. Mrs. Wilde was waiting in her veranda that overlooked the garden where climbing roses spilled perfume from the pillars to which they clung, and irises walked daintily along formal flagged walks.

Thord glanced at the thin, fair woman in her blue kimono. She lay on a wicker chaise-longue, her face expressionless. Behind her Iku and Otero stood in patient attendance, but he saw that Iku had been crying. These Wildes, he thought hotly, then asked in his best professional manner, "How's my patient? Doing nicely, I hope."

"I feel rather better than I did yesterday."

"Splendid." He drew up a chair.

"You may go." She waved Otero and Iku off and they hurried away like children dismissed for a brief recess from a hard school.

[167]

When the slap of their straw sandals died away, Mrs. Wilde turned to Thord. "Have you seen Hiram?"

"Yes."

"Then you're officially—ours?" she asked.

Thord winced. What volumes lay behind that one word!

"Yes."

"That's a comfort. Ever since you came I've been afraid that New York would take you from us, eventually."

"Hawaii's—got me," Thord said, feeling like a child repeating a recently learned verse.

Reaching out, Mrs. Wilde patted his wrist. He beat about in his mind. What, beyond prescribing endless medicines, which she didn't need, could he suggest to keep her interested in day-to-day living? He looked at the garden, panting slightly beneath the terrific down-pouring of light.

"I've been thinking your case over, Mrs. Wilde, and am convinced that sun baths, in the nude, would be highly beneficial to you."

"In the nude!" Mrs. Wilde gasped.

"Yes, there are certain energies which only sun rays can give—"

"But—"

"You can have a walled structure, of bamboo, or some material which will be ornamental as well as useful, put somewhere out here." He indicated the garden in a general way. "At first expose yourself for only five minutes a day, after you've been thoroughly massaged with olive, or cocoanut, oil to protect your skin and nourish your tissues. After a week, increase the time to ten minutes, after another week, to twenty. By the end of a month an hour won't be too much."

"But my husband—" Mrs. Wilde began.

"Mr. Wilde is intelligent, and the results by the end of a month or two will convince him, everyone, of the benefits to be derived from sun bathing."

"But the whites in our pay—"

"Surely your health is more important than a few shocked sensibilities. Anyway, to my way of thinking."

Mrs. Wilde's eyes were absorbed, pleasantly aghast at the spectacle of herself doing such an unheard-of thing. Like all neurotics she had an immense ego, which craved to make itself felt. She'd achieved a measure of spotlight by assuming invalidism, focusing people's sympathies. By this new move she would rouse wholesale interest, command attention, in a district which had a distinctly Old-World flavor, where any innovation was a major upheaval.

"I'll instruct the yardboys," she said.

"Fine. I'll come earlier tomorrow to supervise the building of the solarium. The most beneficial hours for sun bathing are between ten and two, when the ultra-violet rays are most active."

Her eyes, fixed on him, were swimmy with pleasure at the new jargon. Mentally, he watched her thinking . . . solarium . . . when the ultra-violet rays of the sun are most active . . . probably the benefits of sun bathing had not as yet reached Hawaii, a land of sunshine. It would afford spicy flavor to chatter when the Sewing Circle of the plantation met at her house the next Thursday.

April came through one of the French doors leading from the drawing room. Her eyes brushed Thord's as softly and silently as a moth's wings. "Mother, Mamo phoned. Loki's planning a picnic for Sunday, after church, and wants me to plan with them—"

"Perhaps Dr. Graham will drive you over?" Mrs. Wilde interrupted before she could finish. Some inflection in her voice made Thord's nerves go all jumpy. Was she, were they all, trying to crowd him into the Wilde corral? It was satisfying to Hiram to have a doctor with a New York background on his payroll. For a woman of Mrs. Wilde's temperament to have "a doctor in the family" would be the ultimate in delight. His ears burned.

"Of course I'll be glad to drive you, April," he said, resentment at the sham of it all surging through him.

She nodded in a cool, detached way, kissed her mother; and they started across the lawn. When they were out of sight, April caught Thord's little finger with hers.

"Careful," he warned.

"Why?" she asked blithely.

"One of the yardboys might see, and after all—"

"If they did see, they wouldn't say anything."

[169]

"You don't seem to realize the spot I'm in," Thord said, a trifle shortly.

"But I do," April insisted.

"I wonder?"

"Oh, Thord, here we have an hour together, for the first time, since—four days ago and you go all pure and noble."

"You're a wayward chick, hardly out of the shell, wanting to be full-fledged overnight," Thord smiled.

"That's better." Behind her words bells rang faintly and gaily.

"I'm ten years your senior and—"

"I'll adore being an Old Man's Darling," April taunted.

"You're incorrigible."

"I'm in love. I feel full of bubbles inside." Then she added more seriously, "And way down I feel sort of hollow."

He gripped her hand, opened the car door, and they got in.

"Let's drive down to the bluffs above Kealakekua Bay," April suggested. "When I have to think I like to be on a high place that overlooks everything."

They drove down the highway, past the mill and plantation buildings, and turned into a narrow dirt road leading through terraced hillsides of coffee, green and glossy in the sun. After a mile or so, the coffee ended and the road wound across guava-covered bluffs ending abruptly in a thousand-foot cliff overhanging the sweep of the Pacific. Thord stopped the car and glanced at April. Even her hair looked happy.

After an instant she opened the door and got out, facing the faint breeze coming off the blue expanse of water. Around them was the fragrance of ripe guavas and sunshine. From below came the clean, strong smell of seaweed. A long roller, traveling in from the open sea, limitless under the sun, broke at the base of the cliffs.

April gestured at the blue bay below.

"Kealakekua—means the Highway of the Gods." Her voice rang. "You're gorgeous!"

She turned to him. "Kiss me," she commanded.

"I want to. Any man would want to kiss you, to have you, but until Dale has come and—gone, if he does, I'm not free to do the things I'd like to. I'm no hero, but I dislike trespassing on another man's property. When you're in the clear—"

He saw pulses throbbing in her white throat.

"What?" she asked.

"To be honest I don't know exactly what I will do, or ought to do. So many factors enter into our picture."

"Let's forget them—for half an hour." Seating herself on the grass, she clasped her knees with her arms while wind lifted the curls from her forehead.

Thord seated himself beside her. "I'm in hell, April. Your loving me has sort of loosed all the loneliness of my life."

"Yes?"

"You've let me out of a prison I didn't even know I was in."

"Go on," she begged. "I've got to hear it all." She turned her face, rather pale, but eager and alive. "Are your eyes telling me the truth? Do I mean all that to you?"

"You know it."

"Oh," she said under her breath.

Thord had an impression that a great strong hand was pressing them against the earth, warm with the sun. He felt the light wind on his face and heard the echoing of the sea. Reaching out he took hold of her hand and held it against his heart. She turned to him.

"I feel," she said, "as if we were the only two people in the world, as if the earth, sun and stars had been given to us and as if we have no place big enough to put such a gift."

"Yes," said Thord.

A little wind scurried through the guavas, waving their pale green leaves in the sun.

"Not having met Dale," Thord said slowly, "I can't judge him, but I know he must be fine, or you wouldn't have fallen for him. When he comes he mustn't know, or suspect—"

"About us?" April finished.

Thord nodded.

"It's going to take a long while before I feel thoroughly in the

[171]

clear, April. And you must know, if you still feel the way you do, after Dale comes, that no matter what, I love you."

"I do know."

"I want to stay in Kona and work with Kauka—"

"I want you to, too."

Thord looked at the lighted loveliness of her small face.

"Are you strong enough to be my *friend,* as well as the girl I love?"

"Of course. Love isn't only—love," she said. "It's a lot of other things, all the other things, too. Like liking silly things and thrilling to beautiful ones, together."

He nodded.

"Will you kiss me again? Just once?"

"Of course." He drew her to him. She worked tighter into his arms.

18

"SOON as April and Prue come, us go," Loki announced, hovering happily around baskets of food set near the steps. "Some-kind funny, though," she added. "After church when I asking Brewer to come with us his face get all *ulaula*—red, and he said better no. Might-be already he make rascals with Prudence."

Homer exploded into magnificent male laughter. "Shame on you, Loki, she's the parson's daughter."

"No matter if Prue preacher girl or nots," Loki retorted. "She womans and want a man. Here I thinking all the young peoples have someone to have fun with, and Brewer fall out." She sighed regretfully.

"How about me? You've no girl for me," Homer protested.

"You no count because you going to be a lawyer," Loki retorted mischievously.

"Hey! Lawyers are men, too. Look!" Squaring his shoulders, Homer flexed his biceps and spun around.

Thord watched, grinning. Homer hadn't an atom of vanity in him; he was just overflowing with the glee of living and high spirits.

"Okay, as Brewer not coming you make jolly with Prue," Loki ordered.

April and Prudence drove in. Liholiho and Mamo rose from the *puune* where they'd been sitting. Kauka rolled up the Sunday paper and thrust it into his back pocket. Loki stood over the food baskets. Streaking up to the steps, April stopped.

"Here we are, after a million delays," she cried gaily.

"You kids like go to Honaunau on top horses or in cars?" Loki asked.

"Let's ride!" April indicated their breeches.

"Okay, boys, saddle up," Loki ordered. "Papa and I take the *kaukau* in the car and by the time you fellas get down lunch be ready."

"You're my girl—for today," Homer told Prudence, somehow managing to invest her in a cloud of approval.

"Okay," she agreed, flustered and pleased, swinging into the rollicking mood which had taken possession of Homer since he joined the family before breakfast for Sunday coffee.

Liholiho clapped his cousin fondly on the shoulder and they headed for the horse pasture. Thord helped Loki to pack food and guitars into the car.

"Now you kids no waste too much time," Loki admonished. "Already because of church, half this fine day wasted."

"Loki, you're a rascal," Thord grinned.

"Well, I like much not to feel sad anymore. Tutu's *pilikeas* all finish up, now. Us fellas got to live and might as well have jolly fun."

Loki and Kauka drove away. Prudence and Mamo went indoors. A curious little spiral thrill crept up Thord's spine, brewed from strong sunshine and green things moving happily in the sun. He smiled at April, slim and straight in her riding togs.

"You're all this loveliness translated into human form."

She flushed. "You're a darling—*my* darling," she whispered.

Homer and Liholiho led the horses up to the steps, and they all began mounting. Homer darted back into the *lanai,* picked up an extra-large ukulele and swung into his saddle. Liholiho led off, following the steep trail leading down to the sea. Hoofs rang against loose lava fragments littering the trail, larks sang overhead, the Pacific whispered its everlasting secret to the Islands.

When the trail emerged from the coffee it wound down through green slopes of *hilo* grass and groves of silver-barked *kukui* trees. An hour's ride brought them to the coast. Cocoanut groves leaned over a small beach wedged in between low headlands of inky lava.

"This is better," Homer said jauntily. "Now we can ride together, instead of single file like Chinaman going to market." He swung his ukulele jubilantly into position and began singing.

Every so often they passed through small settlements where women, braiding mats under the shade of mango trees or on the narrow verandas of their small homes, called out, "Aloha!" Fishermen, busy with nets and spears at the edge of the water, waved greetings and called out spicy items of local gossip. Homer and Liholiho shouted jokes to graybeards sitting in the shade, who relayed the fun, with lusty rib-nudgings to still older, deafer folk. Girls in wet, clinging dresses, gathering *opihis* off the rocks, offered the shellfish to the passing riders. Naked children splashing in shallow water uttered shrieks of delighted fear when the horses came close.

The last village left behind, they followed a long stretch of sand ending on a lava flat jutting into the sea. Half a mile distant was a similar spit, and between the two, waves rushed shoreward trailing long white manes in the sun.

"That's a rather grim, awesome-looking place," Thord remarked, pointing at walls of black lava rock standing boldly against *kiawe* trees and cocoanut groves.

"You're looking at Honaunau, the City of Refuge," Homer told him. "In ancient times it was the holiest spot in Hawaii. The biggest temple in the Islands was inside those walls. High priests lived there and in the *Hale o Keawe*—Temple of Keawe, the most powerful idols were kept. Human sacrifices were offered to the gods there, and secret ceremonies were performed to assure the success of mighty undertakings."

His eyes glowed, as if he were mentally glorying in the stirring past of his people.

"If," he went on, "a person was falsely accused of a crime, and could escape from his enemies and reach the City of Refuge, no one could molest him. The City was *kapu*—forbidden from the land side. Only priests could enter it from that direction. All other persons must come through the sea. If a man or woman succeeded in swimming safely across that strip of shark-infested water"—he indicated the blue bay between the lava arms—"he was taken in by the priests for a stated time. When he was released, he was inviolate, for having swum the Gauntlet of the Gods, without being destroyed, no man might harm his person."

Thord looked thoughtfully at the tossing stretch of water, at the distant black walls, while they slowly followed, the curving beach.

"Even as mighty a king as Kamehameha, who conquered the eight Islands," Homer went on, sitting his horse with superb carelessness, "dared not enter the City of Refuge proper. Once in a great rage, for he had a violent temper, he threatened to kill his favorite wife, Kaahumanu. She fled to the City of Refuge, swam the Gauntlet successfully, and claimed sanctuary. Kamehameha tried to get the priests to let him in the section of the City set aside for refugees, but was only permitted to talk to Kaahumanu over the wall. She told him, probably to the glee of others present on *her* side of the wall, that her time in sanctuary wasn't up, and she didn't trust his promises not to harm her."

Homer's white teeth flashed.

"Kamehameha swore he would not hurt her, but Kaahumanu refused to trust him. He wept and implored and finally, because she didn't want him to lose face before his subjects, gave in. After that she had powers equal to his in Hawaii." Homer's laughter rang out. "So are men eternally conquered. by women," he announced gleefully, and strumming his ukulele began the most beautiful of all Hawaiian love-songs, *Wahine Ui*—Beautiful Woman.

"For some reason," April said in low tones, turning to Thord, "today seems extra special. I know we'll always remember it. Homer singing, the lot of us together."

"Sad?" Thord asked, spurring closer.

"Not exactly, but it's one of those days when you sense the Angel of Great Happenings"—she laughed rather shyly—"hovering overhead. Something's on its way to one of us, to all of us. I don't know. Island people, even whites, sense such things. Maybe we're crazy, maybe it's because we're all-alive."

"That's better than being frozen assets, like most Mainlanders

[176]

are," said Thord. "When I look at Liholiho and Homer I feel like a log of wood beside leaping flames."

"Inside—you aren't."

Their eyes met, and without speaking Thord said every word a man can say.

"Thanks," April whispered under her breath, "you're the first person I've ever known who I can talk to *without speaking.*"

Their hands locked briefly.

A welcoming hail reached them from the cocoanut groves towering above the black walls of the City of Refuge.

"I think never you kids coming," Loki said as they rode up and began dismounting. "Get into your *malos* and your *mumus.* I like go spear lobsters for make curry tonight."

"Anything you say," Homer agreed cheerfully, unsaddling his horse.. "You're so smart, and so beautiful that when Kauka dies and I grow up, you'll not need to worry about finding another husband."

"Sha, on you!" Loki cried. "You little crazy today. Bet-you-my-lifes you and Liholiho drink *okolehao* last night when you ride down from the ranch. Might-be drink little this morning too. Why-for you no loose up and hand some around?"

"The *okolehao* I've been drinking today, Loki, is in my heart," Homer announced, heaving his saddle to the ground. With an affectionate slap on the quarters, he sped his horse toward the corral in the cocoanut grove.

Liholiho grinned at Loki over his big shoulder, and untied a neatly folded, but slightly bulky, slicker tied behind the cantle of his saddle. "Mama, I brought some *oke.* I thought some drink help to make us all feel good."

"You smart boy, Liholiho," Loki said approvingly. "If Mamo not looking sharps I grab you for my own self. When you boys in your *malos* get some nice young cocoanuts and I fix us drinks before us fish."

"This way, Ulaula—Red," Homer directed, indicating the spot where the men undressed. Thord fell into step with him. The girls went through a break in the outer City wall and disappeared.

[177]

"I feel like a dead white fish beside you all," Thord confessed as Homer showed him how to twist on a *malo*.

"The sun will soon take care of that," Kauka consoled him, deftly securing his own loincloth.

Homer handed Kauka a spear from half a dozen concealed in a lava crevice, then carefully selected another for Thord. "When we see lobsters I'll show you how to spear them."

Retracing their steps to the grove, they eyed the trees, then Homer went shinnying up a trunk, reached among the fronds moving lazily in the sun and tore off a green nut. "Catch, Ulaula!" he cried.

Thord held up his hands and the smooth green nut landed between his palms. When a dozen had been tossed to him, Homer slid down, picked up his spear and asked, "Ever drink *oke*, Ulaula?"

"No, but I drank a hell of a lot of whisky for a bit."

Homer laughed blithely. "*Oke's* dynamite. It makes you try to make love to other men's wives, sass policemen, and bend jail bars as if they were wet macaroni."

"Know that from experience?" Thord joshed.

"*Aole*—no, I've drunk some, but not too much. I want to keep my body fit for the things I want and plan to do."

They joined Loki and the girls. April and Prudence were in bathing suits but Mamo wore a *mumu* and, Island fashion, had shaken down her hair. Its lustrous folds blew softly about her shoulders framing her in beauty.

"How's my girl-for-today?" Homer asked, glancing at Prudence.

"Ready for a drink," Prudence retorted, with the air of an inexperienced rider rushing a horse at a jump.

"*Welakahao!*" Homer applauded.

He began husking nuts with Liholiho. As each one was stripped of its green, outer covering, they handed them to Kauka who, cigar in mouth, beheaded them with a cane knife. Loki and the girls propped them up carefully so as not to spill the fragrant water and poured liberal measures of *okolehao* into each one.

"Now you guys not get *ona* before lunch," Loki warned, when they began drinking. "I want my lobsters."

"Okay, Mama," Liholiho promised.

"*Aloha ka kou*—love to the world!" Kauka uttered the old Hawaiian toast.

"*Aloha ka kou!*" everyone chorused.

"How you like *oke*, Thord?" Loki asked, smacking her lips.

"It's kind of husky."

"Go little easy," she cautioned.

"Homer's already tipped me off."

When the nuts were half empty, they collected the spears and began drifting along the beach which speedily ended in rough lava flats sticking like black fingers into the sea. The tide was out. Pools shimmered in the sun but below the lava ledges the land shelved into deep water, except in an occasional bay where shifting tides and currents had built small, temporary beaches.

Liholiho and Mamo went on ahead, peering into crevices, poking into pools, and every so often their voices and melodious laughter drifted back. Occasionally a long swell traveled stealthily out of the seemingly placid sea and burst against the shore, tossing spray into the air which sunlight transformed into showers of falling diamonds.

"It's so beautiful," Thord exclaimed, "I feel as if I were walking in a dream."

"The dream that's Hawaii," April said softly.

"On a day like this you don't want to think, you just want to—"

"Be?" she suggested.

"Yes."

She linked her little finger through his and they wandered on. A sweet, secret peace lay on everything, and the island, soaked and rich with moisture, stretched out contentedly, generating new growth.

"Let's go in." April signed at the deep blue bay.

"I thought these waters were full of sharks."

"Outside a bit farther, but if we're together there's no danger."

She looked around, and pointed to where Kauka and Loki, Homer and Prudence were swimming.

"Why do you want to end our being alone together?"

"Because"—April caught her breath—"I can't take any more of it. The sun, all this beauty—" She gave him a look hard to fathom. "I—I feel, well, I have a devil as I told you the night we drove down to see Moku. A dunk will do him, my devil, a lot of good." Laughing on a high, unsteady note, she went sprinting away.

Kauka waved a welcoming spear; Loki floating like a large happy child moved her hand. Homer was swimming vigorously, his brown arms making graceful half-arcs as he propelled himself through the water.

Thord dived in after April and the cool water shocked him out of his semi-trance. Homer watched him streaking to join them.

"Ulaula!" he exulted. "You're a born Islander. You ride well, swim well, and are a good all-round fellow. I think we'll keep you!"

After a while Loki and Kauka started back. "Us fix lunch," Loki called.

"We'll be along directly," April promised.

"My girl"—Homer made his voice important—"and I are going to get some lobsters." He linked his arm through Prudence's and headed for a lava spit.

Thord and April stretched out on the warm beach. Little breezes like caressing hands passed over their skin, leaving tingles behind. After a little, April rolled onto her back and gazed into the blue depths of the sky.

"My land," she murmured, placing her hand on the warm sand beneath her. "How could I have ever thought of leaving it!"

Thord looked at her profile and jerked to a sitting position.

"Shouldn't we be going back?" he asked.

"Yes, I think we should."

By the time they got back to the grove Loki and Kauka were dressed and busily unpacking the baskets of food.

"How you think that look?" Loki demanded, pointing at the cloth she had spread on the sand and beautified with leis taken off scattered hats.

[180]

"Beautiful!" April cried.

Thord went off to dress, April remained in her bathing suit. By the time Thord came back Homer was there with a spearful of lobsters.

"There's your curry, Loki," he said, grinning.

"Swell!" Then her eyes went to the empty shoreline. "Damn on those kids! Why Mamo and Liholiho stop so long? I hungry like hell." Then she added, "No use get mad. Young peoples in love always making that style. Better us finish our *oke* and then us no more care if not eating at all."

They sipped and talked while shadows lengthened inland and the changing tide gave the sea a new note. Eventually, Mamo and Liholiho appeared. Something about their figures was different and when they were within a spear's throw of the picnic table Mamo rushed forward and flung herself into her mother's arms.

"Mamo, Liholiho and I are going to be married when the moon is full again," she cried.

Loki began crying happily. Kauka wiped his eyes. Getting up he gripped Liholiho's muscled shoulder. Homer leaped to his feet and when Kauka released Liholiho, he dived at his cousin exultantly.

"At last, you slow old molasses!" he shouted. "Why did you wait so long?"

Liholiho wiped his wrist across his eyes. "I tried to wait till Mamo was eighteen but—"

"Now I shall see you married before I go East! I'll be Best Man at your wedding, Big Chief of Hualalai!" Homer pommeled his cousin joyously.

"Get more cocoanuts," Loki commanded, "and I make fresh drinks for our girl and boy."

When new drinks were in their hands, Kauka lifted his shell solemnly, and put his free arm about Mamo. Loki raised hers and held onto Liholiho.

"May the land sustain you," Kauka said solemnly, "and give you of its fruits. May the sea never harm you. May your years together be long and rich. May your children, after you, enjoy the green ways of the earth." He kissed Mamo's forehead, then, as solemnly, kissed Liholiho's.

Everyone drank the toast with misty eyes, and a happy hubbub filled the grove. Dusk came, cocoanut chalices were emptied, refilled, and emptied again before the meal was eaten. Homer lighted a fire and they gathered around it. A moon, like a huge silver bubble, drifted up from behind Hualalai.

"When you come again"—Loki waved at it—"us having a big marry. *Welakahao!*"

"Mama, you little *ona*," Homer accused.

"Sure! You think my girl catching fine husbands every day. Papa little *ona,* too. Look his eyes."

"I'm *ona* too," Homer shouted. "My head's going round and round. Better us have a little music. If I ride now I'll fall off my horse and spoil my handsome face, then the bridesmaids will scream when I kiss them."

Snatching up a guitar he struck a pose and began singing. Kauka leaned toward the music, his slack, happy figure radiating enjoyment. Mamo leaned against Liholiho, twisting her long, glossy hair about his wrists. Reaching out, Thord took April's hand. Her eyes flashed to his, then gazed into space. He listened to the rich melodious blend of male voices, as Homer, Liholiho, and Kauka chanted words and music handed down from generation to generation.

When the song ended, Homer said, "Let's sing the song April loves." He struck an opening chord and he and Liholiho sang the first verse in Hawaiian. Strange prickles raced along Thord's spine. He did not understand the words, but the music tugged at something in him. Then Homer began singing alone in English:

> *"It is the roads I have not gone*
> *That tempt my restless feet.*
> *It is the flower I have not known*
> *That seems forever sweet!*
>
> *It is the seas I have not sailed*
> *That beat against my breast.*

It is the peaks I have not scaled
That will not let me rest.

It is the lips I have not kissed
That tempt my soul astray.
It is the voice my soul has missed
That calls me night and day!"

Everyone joined in the last verse, sung in Hawaiian. Thord
glanced at April. Just to be near her was like walking on windy
hills.

When the music stopped she said breathlessly, "Oh, thank you."

"Is that a translation from Hawaiian?" Thord asked, finally
breaking the deep silence which followed.

"No, I ran across the verses in a magazine, years ago. I can't
even remember the name of the person who wrote them, and
I'm not even sure if they're correct. They sort of went with the
tune of *Aloha no au,* so I juggled them round till they fitted,"
April explained.

"If I heard that song in Africa, I'd think of you," Homer said.
"You're that way, April. Always hunting and seeking for something—out of reach. You're one of those persons who never comes
to an end."

"How dear of you to say such a lovely thing, Homer!" April
exclaimed.

"I'm a dear person," he retorted, laughing. Getting up he threw
a log onto the fire.

Kauka lay with his head on Loki's knee, Liholiho plucked haunt-
ing chords from his guitar, smiling at Mamo's face, circled by one
arm, while expert fingers worked on the strings that just missed
her chin. April hugged her knees. Thord glanced at Prudence sitting slightly in the background. She was watching Mamo and
Liholiho with curious intentness, unspiked by envy.

He moved restively. The vast island pulsed with the stir of creation. In the forests, in the sea was force, strong, productive, eternally
at work. Hawaii, he thought, a land of wild, clean loves. What better insurance for the future could there be?

[183]

19

"THIS is good business, Liholiho!" Homer asserted as they rode up to the ranch. Flinging back his head, he reveled in the beauty of the star-strewn heavens. "You and Mamo will be married when the moon is full, on the twenty-eighth. I'll sail for the States the sixteenth of August. Why were you so hell-fired slow about asking her to marry you?"

Taking off his hat, Liholiho thrust strong fingers through his black hair and gave an odd laugh. "Hawaiians and part-Hawaiians try to be like *haoles*. As I told you, I felt I should wait until Mamo was of age, but—"

"We have lots to learn from whites"—Homer chuckled—"but they have plenty to learn from us, too. We're natural and recognize love, not only for the body, but also for the experience of the soul. Look at Thord and April. Because he works for her father and because she's engaged to some man in the East, they sit around like volcanoes ripe to erupt. But"—he weighed the thought in his mind—"big blows come to big people. Little blows to little ones."

When they reached the ranch they unsaddled and turned the animals into the home pasture, then headed for the house. Homer lighted the lamp on the living-room table and fondly brushed the piled law books sitting on it. He sighed contentedly, then with the direct simplicity of men leading vigorous physical lives, joined in the business of getting ready for bed.

"Tomorrow we'll brand calves in Waiho pasture," Liholiho announced, pulling off his boots.

"I've got to study, so I won't go out with you to bring them in, but I'll help with the branding," Homer said, stripping off his shirt. Walking to the only mirror in the house, he squared his shoulders and tensed his muscles. "Hawaiians have better shapes than *haoles*," he said in satisfied tones.

"Bet-you-my-life," Liholiho agreed, peeling out of his shirt and standing beside Homer. "I've bigger muscles than you have."

"Mine are better shaped."

"Mine are stronger."

"That's what *you* think!" Homer retorted, giving him a punch. They sparred about the room, then locked into a wrestling hold. Muscles tensed, teeth flashed, eyes contracted.

"Okay, we match in this," Homer conceded. "Let's try *uma*."

Kneeling on the floor facing each other, they clasped their hands and placed their elbows on the floor. At the signal each tried to force the other's wrist downward, so the back of his hand laid on the floor, signifying he was vanquished. Muscles bulged, veins swelled, sweat ran down smooth temples then, slowly, Homer pressed Liholiho's big arm backward until his hand was flat against the rug.

Padding into the kitchen in their bare feet, they lighted the fire and put a pot of water on the heat. While Liholiho ground up coffee berries in the small mill attached to the wall, Homer spun up an egg. When the grounds were ready, he stirred them into the egg-fluff and left them to soak.

They sat down at the scrubbed table.

"I want to get ahead with my work, then I'll tell Hiram I'm going to be married and want a week off." Liholiho lighted a cigarette and exhaled luxuriously. "It would be fun to take Mamo to some of the other islands, Niihau maybe. I have five hundred dollars saved up and can hire a sampan for our honeymoon."

"Name your first son after me."

"You bet, and for Kauka too. How you like this sound in your ears? Homer Kamuela—"

"Liholiho—" Homer put in.

"Okay. Homer Kamuela Liholiho Kalani."

"He'll have to be some man to live up to all those names,"

Homer announced. Rising, he went to the stove. "I hope he can make coffee quicker than I can." Filling the pot, he tested it. "It'll boil in a few minutes."

Wind sighed about the house, then went on about its business. Off in the hills a cow lowed for her calf and a colt gave a questioning nicker.

"When I'm in the East I shall like to think of you and Mamo here, having children, teaching them the ways of our land. It is good."

Getting up, he spread out his hand to test where the stove was hottest and changed the pot a thoughtful six inches. "The fire's slow," he announced.

"It's roaring," Liholiho asserted.

Opening the woodbox, Homer peered in. "Damn, so it is," he said in puzzled tones. "With my right hand the stove felt lukewarm. With my left—" He tested it, then his eyes tore to Liholiho's, terrified. "You don't suppose—"

"What?" Liholiho asked, uneasily.

"That I'm working up for a 'stroke.' I'm too young!"

"You think too much, study too hard. Lay off the books to-morrow and ride and brand with me."

"I guess I will," Homer said, an unaccustomed crease marring his smooth forehead.

The coffee boiled over. Liholiho leaped up and dashed it with cold water, then filled two cups. When they were empty, he rose and stretched. "We better roll in. We'll have to leave for Waiho at three."

Homer nodded then, going to the stove, slowly and thoroughly tested his hands. "I must be *pupule*—" he announced. "Both register now."

Liholiho traced spirals against his temple with a forefinger. "Books are plenty good, maybe, but too much study for Hawaiians—"

"I'm half *haole*," Homer protested, "so my mind ought to be able to take it."

"You've got too much dynamite in you, better find a nice sweetheart."

Homer looked thoughtful, then fun flickered along the edges of his thick lashes. "Umm, I saw a cute Portuguese girl—"

It was after four the next afternoon before the branding was finished. Pleasant weariness, following hours of physical exertion, drugged both men's limbs when they left the corrals and headed for the house. Around them was the scent of clean forests, preparing for night, spiked with the exciting smell of fire, hot irons, scorched flesh, and sweaty horses. The bawling of outraged calves separated for the first time from their mothers, came from the holding pasture back of the house, and men's voices calling out to each other as they wound up the day's work, filled the approaching evening with a pleasant stir.

"That was a fine bunch of calves," Homer commented as he and Liholiho sat down on the front steps and began removing their spurs.

"Butter fat," Liholiho agreed proudly, carefully recoiling his lasso. "When they're two-year-olds they should dress out at about seven hundred. If the price of meat holds, Hiram's pockets will be well lined with extra dollars—as if he needed them." He grinned and laid his rawhide on the step beside him and began scrubbing his dusty face with his bandanna, then gazed at the peaceful green fall of forests seaward. "Mamo's thinking about me," he announced. "Probably she's figuring in a few weeks she'll be here to meet me when I come in from work."

Homer watched his cousin from under his long eyelashes. "Like to ride down and surprise her tonight?" he asked.

Liholiho's eyes blazed. "Swell! How did you know I wanted to?"

"Maybe because I'm a man, too," Homer teased.

"Okay, let's get clean. The moon will be up in an hour."

"Hey, wait a minute. I want to finish my cigarette." He inhaled with sensuous pleasure while he watched a prodigal sunset burning in the west, spilling wild lights and tragic shadows over

[187]

sea and land. Then he turned his head and listened intently. High overhead from the fragile evening sky came a faint, plaintive whistling. "The plover are coming home from Alaska!" he exclaimed, a quick flush of pleasure spreading over his face.

Liholiho listened. "Yes, I hear them. Soon summer will be *pau,* and when fall comes Mamo and I will be here, and when big *kona* gales are building, we'll hear the sea roaring."

The thin whistling of birds, weary from their four-thousand-mile flight, lent an eerie, almost holy, quality to the evening.

"Wonderful," Homer mused, "how they come and go so regularly. Always by the tenth of May they're gone, always before the tenth of August they're back."

"Once"—Liholiho was remembering—"when I was small, my father took me up to the top of Hualalai to see them go. We waited for three days. Flocks of birds, thousands of them, had gathered. They were fat and black-breasted and ready for their long flight. Each night a leader would go up and the other birds followed. They circled and circled, like twisting smoke, then came down again. On the third night they went up and didn't come back. It gave me a queer feeling in my stomach. My father said they leave from the other big mountains in Hawaii the same way, but only a few people have seen them."

Homer gazed into the sky. "You wonder how they know where to go? I guess they're like people. Some know about things, others don't, but they all head in the same direction. I suppose many never reach their nesting places, and others that are hatched in Alaska never get here, but the strong ones come through."

Liholiho nodded, his eyes fixed admiringly on his cousin. There was something about him that made him stand out from others. The red light from the dying sunset, flung across the sea, highlighted his features.

"You look like a dirty little boy," Liholiho announced fondly. "Wipe your face, half the dust of Hawaii is on it."

"That's because I worked on foot, throwing calves and branding, while you rode around on a horse, Big Chief." Pulling a handkerchief from his pocket, Homer rubbed his forehead, then slowly went over his face.

"Better?" he asked.

Liholiho squinted his eyes. "Wipe your forehead some more." Homer polished it, then dug at his eyebrows. "Clean now?" he asked.

"Homer—" Liholiho began, getting to his feet.

"What's wrong?"

Liholiho's jaw muscles bunched into knots. "I can't—tell you. Go and look in the glass!"

Nameless terror enveloping him at the tone of Liholiho's voice, Homer headed indoors and going to the mirror, peered into it. Leaning close, he pushed up the hairs of one eyebrow, then froze as though some invisible enemy had driven a spear through him.

The cook came in, went to the laid fire, touched a match to it, and returned to the kitchen.

Homer's features changed to wood as if all the blood in his veins had ceased to circulate.

Liholiho came in.

"When did you first notice?" Homer asked over his shoulder.

Liholiho made a savage gesture. "Not until—just now. You've always had a fine, high color. When you—wiped the sweat off your face I noticed the shine stayed—under your eyebrows. Then I saw—" He fingered his own ear-lobes, speaking like a man under a spell.

"But if . . . this is so, Kauka must have—seen!"

"We've all been stirred up over Tutu's being drowned, and today Mamo and me—"

A glossy curl fell onto Homer's forehead and he pushed it back with fingers that looked crazed; then like one who has experienced the ultimate in emotion, he turned toward Liholiho, spent and exhausted.

"Say nothing of this to anyone," he said in a voice that did not sound as though it came from a human being.

"But what are you going to *do?*" Liholiho asked, wiping his wet face with the back of his hand.

Homer did not appear to hear the question. "The numbness of my . . . hand . . . ties with this." He shook his head like a horse crazed by an insect in its ear. "Father Damien . . . spilled boiling water . . . on his foot . . . before he *knew!*" His vibrant voice was dead. Striding toward the fire, he kneeled down and thrust his hand into flames.

"Stop it!" Liholiho shouted, dashing his cousin's arm aside.

"I didn't . . . feel. Don't touch me. I'm unclean."

Homer straightened up slowly and heavily. His smooth young face was perfectly wooden. "Liholiho, you must drive me to Kailua in the morning to catch the boat to Honolulu. I'll report at the Kalihi Receiving Station where my blood will be—tested. Then if we're not mad, if we're seeing right, it's—Molokai!"

"Christ!" All the vigor drained out of Liholiho's big body. He flung himself on a couch.

Passing his hand dully over his eyes, Homer began wandering about the room. He trailed his fingers across the table, straightened a picture, and headed for the veranda. He saw the two pairs of spurs and two coiled lassos on the steps where they'd been abandoned and stared at them as if he did not know what they were. Overhead, plover were still streaming in from their migration. In a pasture a horse gave a shrill, joyous neigh. He slapped the sides of his head with the flat of his palms and turned indoors. Going to the big table, he jerked out a chair and sat down.

"I do not want Mamo, April, *anyone,* to know about this . . . ever," he said. "I want people to remember me as I am now." His voice skidded imperceptibly, then plodded on its way. "The names of persons sent to Molokai are never made public. Tell people Central phoned in a radio for me tonight calling me East because a relative of my father's is ill."

"No, no. Couldn't you"—Liholiho jerked to a sitting position—"go to the Orient, or somewhere, the way white men with leprosy did before Hawaii was annexed by America?"

"We're not old-time Hawaiians, we're a new, educated generation. I'd always know what a menace I was to the happiness of others! The thing I can't understand is, how did I contract it? I've

[190]

kept my body sound and clean. To my knowledge, I've never been in the company of a leper!"

Heading for the sideboard, he frowned at a bottle of *okolehao,* picked it up and tried to uncork it. Then, suddenly, he desisted.

"Open the damn thing for me, Liholiho—" He held out the bottle weakly.

Liholiho worked at the cork. Homer laid his bare forearm on the sideboard, his weight sagging on it and the fingers of his sensitive, finely formed hand kept up a wild tattoo. Liholiho jerked the cork out and pushed the liquor toward Homer. He stared at it but did not move.

"It isn't that I don't know I'll have the best of care, kind treatment, what little help science can give—"

"Homer! Homer!"

"Don't talk. I'm trying to think, to *realize*—" Staring at the stacked law books, he straightened up and went over to them. Picking them up one by one, he dropped them to the floor. "I'm trying to face the knowledge that, in time, I'll be revolting to look at. My fine body will become a mass of corruption. I won't be at your wedding, kissing all the bridesmaids. I *feel* the same"—he tensed his biceps—"my muscles are hard, my body full of vigor—"

"Maybe the cure'll be—"

"There's no use fooling myself. I've trained my mind to think in a straight line, to face facts. Doctors have worked for years on Molokai, in the Philippines, and to date no cure has been found. The mark of leprosy is on me. On my face, on my ears, and my hand didn't feel the flames. And I'm only twenty! God! God!" Crossing the room, he peered into the dimming mirror.

20

"WELL," Loki said in a large, happy way, looking about the round table in the *lanai,* "that all *pau!*" She waved at stacked envelopes arranged in an old cardboard shoe box. "Never I writing so much in my whole lifes." She fanned her face with her hands. "How many letters—"

"Invitations." April stressed the word playfully.

"Oh, yes, invitations!" Loki laughed. "Anyway, how many we send out?"

Prudence checked the list. "Over four hundred."

"That sound proud."

"They've got to be sealed still," Mamo said, her eyes shining with happiness.

"I got good idea," Loki announced brightly. "I call Takeshi and tell to him go find some small kids for lick, and I give candy for take the bad taste off the tongue." She sent her voice out in a clear hail and Takeshi scampered across the lawn.

"What-kind I can make for you, Loki-san?" he asked eagerly.

She told him. His face lighted. "You waiting five minutes and I go get the Filipino kids who live down the road." He strode off importantly.

Loki watched him go, then turned with the grace of a big lazy wave swirling into a cove that just fitted it.

"I think fine idea asking every-kind peoples the same kind of way to Mamo's wedding: Japanese, Chinese, Hawaiians, and proud *haoles.*" Her eyes rested on the envelopes. "I like fine to see Takeshi's face when he open his let—invitations." Her eyes sparkled. "And old Pili, when he getting his! Always I have to laugh Monday morning when he drive his big truck to work. His eyes red like tomatoes and his mouth all pull down. I hear Pili and Brewer raise big hell in South Kona last Sunday." She chuckled, then caught herself and stole a remorseful look at Prudence, but the girl's always colorless face disclosed nothing.

Thord drove in and ran up the steps.

"The invitations all *pau!*" Loki informed him.

"Want me to post them? I'm going right back to the hospital and can leave them on the way."

"Envelopes no lick yet."

He smiled, waved to the girls, and went indoors.

"Now better us get the Montgomery Ward book and order some clothes so Mamo have swell—" Her voice halted questioningly.

"Trousseau." April supplied the word.

"Yes, trousseau, just like a white girl. Some shoes and hats and dresses, and might-be one set of dishes."

"That'll cost lots of money," Mamo said, with wistful hesitancy.

"You think Papa and I caring if us go little more in debt to Hiram?" she asked blithely. "Us only got one girl, so can only have one wedding in the family, so us going to letta-go-our-blouses and have big fun. When the order all make out, I tell to Papa to ask Hiram for another advance."

"I'll tell him," April said. "How much will you need?"

Loki hesitated.

"I'll tell Father you'll need at least five hundred dollars. That'll buy Mamo some nice things and take care of food for the wedding *luau.*"

"Sha, you swell kid, April!" Loki cried. "Us can buy"—she calculated hurriedly—"two fat young heifers, ten pigs, plenty chickens, then every family can take some *kaukau* home from the marry *luau* for eat next day. And us can have a big dance!" Picking up the train of her cotton *holoku,* she waltzed roguishly with an invisible partner.

"Mama, you're a rascal!" Mamo gasped, wiping tears of mirth from her eyes.

[193]

Thord came out. "It looks as if Mamo's wedding is going to be a gay affair."

"It will be," April cried. "You should have been at the going-away *luau* Loki and Kauka gave me when I left for school. But this will start a week before the wedding and last for a day or so afterwards."

"Tell Papa no be late for lunch," Loki said. "Ching fix lobster curry for celebrate on all these damn letters finish up. Too bad Homer and Liholiho branding calves this week and no can come down until Saturday."

"I'll see Kauka gets here on the dot of twelve," Thord promised.

Takeshi appeared with six lustrous-eyed Filipino youngsters of assorted sexes and ages.

"Go get candy, Mamo," Loki directed. "Plenty!"

April and Prudence carried the boxes of envelopes to the steps and Loki squatted down and painstakingly showed the youngsters how to lick and seal them. "When tongue taste too bad, eat this nice candy quick." Reaching up, she took the generously filled bowl which Mamo had brought and placed it among the children.

"I got inside my head," Takeshi announced, his eyes bright as a bird's. "Wait, you' kids, I showing you." His pink tongue flashed along the line of glue, then his fingers pressed the flap down.

"Smart boy," Loki said. "Okay, you the school teacher. Watch out sharp these kids make right. Now us look the catalogues."

When Thord and Kauka arrived an hour later, Takeshi and his crew were still licking envelopes and eating candy. Mamo rushed to meet her father. "Come, Papa"—she dragged him toward the big *puune*—"see all the pretty things *Mama* is going to order for me."

Kauka kissed her ear and sank down on the capacious Hawaiian day-bed which could accommodate ten people. He peered eagerly at the pages in the catalogue where crosses marked items ordered.

"That's not enough," he said. "Here, let me pick some stuff too."

Mamo hung breathlessly over the bulky catalogue, as he turned the pages slowly.

[194]

"Which wedding dress did you choose?" he asked, when they came to the section devoted to matters bridal.

"This one." She pointed her finger onto a ruffled white net, marked nine dollars and ninety-five cents.

Kauka appraised it. "You would look beautiful in it, but—" He pursed up his mouth.

"Is it—too much?" Mamo asked, a bit wistfully.

Kauka made no answer, then announced dramatically, "Not enough! I think this one, with a big white carnation lei—" He plunged his pencil at a trailing white satin sprigged with imitation orange blossoms about the neck.

Mamo squealed and butted her head against him. "Oh, Papa, I looked and looked, but it costs twenty-seven dollars!"

"You'll only marry once, Mamo; men like Liholiho don't lose women. So—it's this one!" He made a big cross on the gown, then studied other accessories. "And these white satin shoes and this veil."

"Oh, Papa! Papa!"

"*Welakahao!*" Loki cried. "I try not to spend too much, like a good wifes, then Papa *hemo ka paa'u*—pull off the skirt!" She flung out her arms joyously.

"Mamo, you'll knock the eyes out of everyone," Thord said, peering over their shoulders at the catalogue.

She caught his hand into hers. "You think so?"

"I know so, my little Hawaiian sister will be the most beautiful bride the eight Islands have ever seen."

The telephone rang and Prudence ran to get it. After a minute or two she returned. "It's for you, April," she said, slightly dashed. "Central phoned in a radio for you, and your mother's on the line."

"What is the message?" April asked.

Prudence stole a glance at Thord before answering. "Your fiancé and his sister sailed from San Francisco the day before yesterday and will arrive in Kona the first of next week."

"Swell!" Loki exulted. "They be here for Mamo's wedding!"

April went indoors. When she came back something seemed to

[195]

have been drained from her. "Well, that was a surprise! Dale planned to get here early in September, but he and Sabrina"—she spoke his sister's name in a hesitant fashion—"will see a *real* wedding."

Thord lighted a cigarette. His face was flushed and a little frown sat between his brows.

Sinking down beside Mamo, April studied the items Kauka had chosen. "I'll provide the bridesmaids' frocks, Mamo. What color shall they be?"

"You decide. I'm so happy I can't think."

Ching flounced angrily out of the hall. "What-the-hell?" he demanded. "All you fellas no got ear? I ring lunch bell *five* times."

When the meal was over, Prudence announced she must help her father prepare his sermon, and rode off. Thord and Kauka left to make their afternoon rounds, and Loki, Mamo, and April went back to the *lanai*.

"Need how many bridesmaids for big wedding?" Loki asked, establishing her bulk luxuriously among the pillows on the spacious day-bed.

"Six or eight is the usual number, Loki."

"Okay. Us have you and Prudence, Pua and Maile, Mamo's cousins in Hilo, Hattie and Mary Ako from Honolulu, and Lily and Ruby Spencer from Kauai. They all pretty girls and Homer like much to kiss them."

"Want me to write to them?" April inquired.

"Yes. Mamo no use, she only thinking of Liholiho all the time." Loki gave her daughter a fond nudge. "And always I lazy for write. Might-be Sabrina feel left out unless ask her to be bridesmaid too. Nine okay?"

"Even numbers are better than odd ones," April said, "and Sabrina's been bridesmaid at so many swank weddings in New York, it's an old story to her."

"Any-kind you say." Clasping her hands under her head, Loki gazed happily at sunlight dancing over green tree tops. Mamo stretched out and laid her head in the soft depression of her mother's waist.

[196]

"After I've written to the bridesmaids, I'll have to go home and plan with Mother about Dale and Sabrina."

The afternoon moved peacefully forward. Just as April was finishing the last letter, the phone rang.

"I get," Loki said, sitting up.

When she returned her face wore a worried expression. "That Thisbe. He say for me to tell Prudence go home. Nearly I tell him she no stop, then I think quicks." Her dark eyes grew stern. "Will you drive me to South Kona tomorrow, April? I going to talk to Brewer."

"Of course. What time do you want to go?"

"Best before lunch, then us sure catch that old crooks. But I not knowing what kind to make. I tell to Thisbe, sure, sure, I speak Prudence you want, but"—she gestured hopelessly—"where the hell she stop? Might-be she not going home till late. I no like this kind business."

"Worrying won't get Prudence home, Loki," April said, kissing her.

"You got funny look in your eye. You not glad your sweetheart coming?"

"No," April said honestly, and running down the steps, she drove off.

"Mama," Mamo observed, with the air of wisdom of a young girl in love, "I think that Thord and April—"

"Might-be," Loki cut in. "Damn, I no like any troubles spoil your wedding."

When Thord and Kauka returned, Loki was waiting to meet them. Thord headed for his room and Loki told Kauka of Thisbe's phone call.

"Has Prudence got home yet?" he asked.

"I don't know. If I phoning it look funny—"

"Yes, you'd better not. She must be there, or Thisbe would have called again."

"Always you big comforts, Papa." Linking her arm through his she started indoors. "But damn on Brewer. Tomorrow I going to South Kona and give him hell."

[197]

When dinner was over the four of them adjourned to the *lanai*. The night was still and they listened to landshells singing in the forests and to the faint breathing of the sea against the coast. After a little, Mamo kissed her parents good night and went off. Loki looked after her.

"Seem funny to think that after little whiles our girl not stop with us all the time, but I like swell that she and Liholiho going to marry."

Approaching hoofbeats sounded in the driveway. The three exchanged uneasy glances.

"Prudence?" Loki suggested.

Kauka peered at the approaching silhouette. "It's Moku!" he exclaimed.

Moku dismounted, came up the steps, glanced about cautiously to assure himself that no one else was present, then whispered, "Tutu very bad, she like you to come quick, Kauka."

"Tutu!" everyone gasped.

Moku looked at them puzzled. "I took it for granted," he said in Hawaiian, "that you all knew I'd hidden her and were helping me and my wife to put on a good act."

"Where did you hide her?" Kauka asked.

"In a valley where other lepers are," he replied, still in Hawaiian. "I borrowed my friend Kimmo's car about a week before time to report her, and drove her to Kahala. The day before yesterday I went over to see her—"

"Better you go quick, Papa, and try the new oil," Loki said.

"What oil?" Moku asked.

Kauka told him.

"Why you no tell me before?" Moku demanded, relapsing into English.

Kauka gave his reasons. Then he turned to Thord.

"Tell Hiram I've been called to Honokaa to see a sick friend. You perform the appendectomy scheduled for tomorrow morning. The valley where Tutu's hidden can't be reached by car. I'll drive as far as Kahala, then go in on horseback. I'll be away for three days at least. She'll have to be brought back to Kona for treatments." He paced restlessly. "Moku, go and borrow your friend Kimmo's car. I have to leave mine for Thord to use on plantation work. While you're gone I'll get everything ready."

"Okay. Take one hour to ride back and might-be Kimmo and his *wahine* seeing friends, but I think sure three hour more I get back."

Mounting, he galloped off.

"Big danger to bring Tutu back here," said Loki.

"Everyone thinks she's dead," Kauka answered. "I'll arrange with Moku to take me into"—he whispered the name of the valley with the secret settlement—"and bring me back alone. Then he can fetch Tutu to Kona at night and establish her in the old grass house on their place. No one ever goes there."

Loki moved restively. "I go fix you some coffee and make some sandwiches to take. Long drive to Kahala and you and Moku get hungry."

She headed for the kitchen. Kauka looked at Thord.

"You know," he said after he had pulled silently on his cigar for a while, "we may get results of some sort with Tutu. Her case isn't, or wasn't, when we last saw her, very far advanced. However, frequently in older, less vital persons, leprosy gallops, and from what Moku tells me, I'm afraid it's attacked her respiratory organs. If by some rare break, she's among the few who can take the oil without nausea—" His eyes shone.

Thord turned his head sharply.

"What is it?"

"I thought I heard someone at the door."

They stopped talking. The heavy night pressed down on the sleeping island.

"Just a breeze rustling the shrubbery," Kauka said. "As I was saying, if Tutu can retain the oil, we may see some startling results. And we can get specimens of her blood for inoculation. For Loki's sake I wish this hadn't happened at this time, but it may be for the best."

"It does add a slightly grim touch to a wedding," Thord agreed, "but since none of the younger members of the family know about

[199]

Tutu, it can't taint their fun. I don't see any reason to tell April. Her hands will be full enough as things stand."

"Events sure have piled up during the past weeks. You and April, Hiram hiring you on, Tutu, Mamo and Liholiho's marriage. I wonder what next?"

"In a way, I'd like to clear out until Dale's gone."

"Can't spare you. With Tutu back, it'll take the pair of us to attend to the plantation and watch her."

Thord did not reply, then said explosively, "Dammit, I *know* someone's outside." Striding to the door, he flung it open.

A meager, crumpled female figure leaned against the jamb. Peering closer, he exclaimed, "Prudence!"

Her hand fell slowly from her face disclosing her distorted features. Her eyes were blurred, her mouth twisted.

"I've got to see Kauka." Prudence propelled herself through the door as if one force held her back and a greater one thrust her forward.

"My child, what is it?" Kauka asked, rushing to her.

She grabbed blindly for his arm, clutched it, and buried her face against it.

"Get hold of yourself, my child," he urged. "Then tell me your trouble. Sit in this chair." He guided her gently toward it, his kind arm heavy about her shoulders. "There." He established her in it. "Are you ill?"

"Don't let go of me! Don't let go of me! I want to hold on to someone kind!"

He patted her bent head. "Hold on as tight as you want to. Here, put your head on this shoulder. It's my *family* one. Thousands of people have wept on the other."

"Shall I go?" Thord asked.

Prudence flung up her head. "It's no use. Everyone in Kona will know—after a bit." She gazed bleakly about the office. Lank strings of hair trailed down the lean stalk of her neck, her lips twitched into strange shapes. "I'm—I'm going to have a baby!" She flung the words across the room.

Kauka made a shocked sound which he smothered.

"How long have you known, Prudence?" he asked, patting her hand.

"For—almost two months."

A lonely little breeze sighed down from the summit of Hualalai, prowled briefly about the house, and died of exhaustion. Prudence's pale eyes stared down her nose and every so often she sobbed.

"I can't . . . tell Father. I've got to go . . . somewhere. And I have no money. You . . . you see . . . I want it." Her voice caught dryly in her throat. "It'll love me. It won't care . . . if I'm . . . ugly!"

"*Malama*—easy, Prudence, easy," Kauka urged. "You're a good girl."

"Good," she choked. "I'm bad. But I don't care. I'm glad I did what I did! I'm a woman now, not just a gargoyle! When . . . when Brewer—oh, I didn't *mean* to give him away—"

"*Kulihuli*—you'll wake Mamo, rouse the house," Kauka warned, gently and kindly.

The door opened and Loki entered. Her eyes swept the room, and she opened her arms. "Prudence!" The girl flew to them. "There, there, you poor kids. No need tell any-kind to me. I can guess." Her hand soothed the girl's head, went down her back. "No cry. Kauka and I fix everything up."

"But you don't understand—"

"I hear what you telling Papa, before I come in. Give little brandy, Papa."

Thord leaped to the shelves, poured out an ounce, and took it over.

"Drink this," Loki instructed.

Prudence obeyed, looking around her vaguely.

"I'm so ugly"—she bit down on the word—"that I knew no one would ever marry me. I didn't think, even, that any man would—" Crimson dyed her face and neck, then she went on defiantly, "But one did! Even if he's red and fat and always smells of whisky. I've always felt like a sort of a ghost that's crazy to be human—" Her voice rose on a hysterical note.

"Ssh, ssh," Loki soothed.

"I have to go away. I can't tell Father. When I came in this evening late . . . you see I'd been telling him I was with Mamo and April . . . when I . . . when I . . ." She passed a distracted hand across her face.

"I'll tell Thisbe," Loki said truculently. "Now he got good chance to *be* Christian, not only preach about it on Sundays."

Despite himself, Thord smiled.

"I thought I could stand it . . . till after the wedding." Prudence choked on the word. "But today was . . . too much. I felt as if I had no right to be with girls like April and Mamo—" Her head flopped against Loki's soft, warm side.

"Shut your face, you good girl, too. Only little unlucky. Now, you do just like Papa and I tell and everything get all fix up."

"It's too late."

"Already you tell to Thisbe what-kind *pilikea?*" Loki gasped.

"No. I just told him I'd been riding about because I was unhappy. Because—" She indicated her person with frantic resentment. "And he said—" She gulped.

"Better you countings your blessing or some-kind of hops like that?" Loki asked.

Prudence gave a dreary assenting nod, then snapped her body up. "He said my—my—ugliness—"

"Thisbe not so pretty hisselfs," Loki interrupted dryly.

"That because of my ugliness," Prudence went on, "I must dedicate my life to the Things of the Lord. I told him the Lord wasn't enough when—you were a woman and wanted to be loved. He said I was sacrilegious!"

"You think God make mans and womans if he not intend them to get together?" Loki asked truculently. "Thisbe marry with your mother and have you. Now you no get all boil up, baby. Listen—"

Prudence looked at her in a dead way.

"Already Papa and I got *manau*—hunch, that Brewer like you—"

The blessed tact of her, Thord said to himself. Loki's words magically produced a strange change in Prudence's appearance.

From a cringing huddle amazement, mixed with incredulity, transformed her.

"How—" She could not handle her voice.

"Oh, us old fellas got eyes." Loki tossed her head. "I bet-you-my-lifes, if you making just like Papa and I say, every-kind okay before this week *pau*. Now you go home *wikiwiki,* like a smart girl. If Thisbe find out you no stop in your room—"

"He can't get in. I locked the door and climbed out the window."

"How you get here?"

"I walked."

"All that ways?"

"I had to get to someone kind."

"Might-be us not preachers but us not make damn on peoples if they making some little mistakes. You like make marry with Brewer?"

The girl's face twitched. "Yes."

"That good sense. Always I saying, better girls marry even with rascal fellas than no marry at all. Tomorrow I go see Brewer." Her face grew crafty. "After I *pau* talking with him I think he glad to marry with you quick. If you two fellas try hard to make your marry a go, after by-and-by, when the little baby come, Brewer haul in his horns. Might-be"—her fine laughter poured like sunshine through murk—"who know, he be model husbands after all!"

"But Father would die before he'd let us get married. He loathes Brewer."

"Thisbe not knowing any-kind till you fellas all marry up safe. Then if he raise big hell, it too late. What you thinking, Papa?"

"It's the only way."

"Sure Thisbe, and might-be Hiram mad like any-kind with us for making this-kind, but so what? After little they cool off. How it feel to you to be marry womans at Mamo's wedding?" She tilted her head and smiled brightly.

Prudence's look was answer enough.

"Well, I betting my lifes, this is how it will be. When peoples coming up"—Loki stood in an imaginary receiving line, presenting invisible persons to the draggled girl beside her—"Mr. Whites, Mrs. Whites, I happy you come to my girl Mamo's wedding, and I like you to meet my dear friends, *Mr. and Mrs.* Brewer, from South Kona."

21

APRIL gazed out of her bedroom window at long green slopes culminating in the turbulent summit of Hualalai. The last light from the west gilded tree tops and intensified the purple and scarlet of tip-tilted cinder cones against the delicate pink flush of the sky. Why, she thought rebelliously, had her mother asked Thord to dine with them when she was steeling herself to meet Dale and Sabrina in the morning?

The week-end just behind, despite the increasing tempo of preparations for Mamo's wedding, had seemed hollow. It was unreal that laughing, warm-hearted Homer had gone East without a good-by for anyone. Liholiho, in spite of his happiness at being engaged to Mamo, had moved and spoken like a man whose mind was in a vise. When Kauka had returned from his three-day absence, shortly after lunch, he had looked preoccupied and beset. Tonight, when Reverend Thisbe returned from his monthly visit to South Kona he would find an empty house, and a note from Prudence announcing that she and Brewer were married.

A faint, reminiscent smile lighted the troubled depths of her eyes. She had taken Loki down to see the old reprobate. Loki had swept in on Brewer like a battleship bearing down on an enemy squadron. "You fat, bad old man," Loki had asserted hotly, "but you smarts for Macadamian nuts. When every white peoples in Kona find out you make rascal with preacher's girl, they run you out. Hiram not like to discharge you because he lose money, but sure have to for save his face. Not easy for old mans to find high-pay jobs. Better you marry quick with Prudence. Here you got

good house, not have to work very hard, and if you get kick out—"
She had allowed Brewer to finish the sentence in his own mind.

Loki had gone with him to Hilo for a license, arranged with a
Hawaiian preacher to perform the ceremony, timed to take place
while Thisbe was absent. That afternoon Carlos had driven Loki
and Prudence away. By now Prudence and Brewer were married
and Loki must be on her way home. Around nine Thisbe would
come storming in to her father. . . .

She shivered, and glanced at the small Dresden clock on her
mirror. She was reluctant to leave her cozy, restful room for the
stilted atmosphere of the living room. If only she could have gone
to bed and have her supper sent up on a tray. She was tired, but
must gear herself for the days ahead, entertaining Dale and Sabrina
while she fenced for the right opening to tell Dale she didn't love
him.

She took a last look out of the window. The fierce sunset light
had faded from the mountain top. Drawing the curtain, she
switched on the twin lights flanking the mirror on her dresser.
For an instant the commonplace little act snatched the atmosphere
back to normal.

Going to her desk she took up a photo that Dale had sent recently. It was the work of the foremost photographer in New York,
and artistry of the lens had captured Dale's character as well as
his exterior. Although he was in a polo shirt, with his hair rumpled
as if by wind, he had an air of being immaculately groomed. He
carried the imprint of caste and class.

His eyes were fine, nose and mouth a trifle small in contrast to
a pleasingly angular jaw, but although he was a yachtsman, played
a smashing game of polo and tennis, behind his brawn of shoulder
there was a suggestion of softness, characteristic of people reared
inside safe citadels of wealth. Dale had never had to battle for
anything vital, had never ached to possess anything; everything he
wanted was his for the asking. And I, April thought with a brief
pang, must give you your first jolt!

She heard Kauka's car drive in. Thord! Her body, which had
been chilly, glowed, then her heart gave a slow thud. She wanted

to be with him, but not under her parents' eyes. She wanted to hold his hard hand, to hear him insist that, in time, their way would be clear.

Stifling an impulse to rush down, she waited until she knew he must have greeted her parents. She must not betray how they felt about each other until after Dale had gone. Even then, and for a long time afterwards, they must move cautiously. It went against her nature, as it did Thord's, to act a part, but under the circumstances they had no choice.

When her heart resumed a normal beat she went downstairs, a cool, collected little figure in a frilly evening frock. Everything was just as she knew it would be. Her father was seated in his deep chair, her mother reclining on a couch propped up by muslin and lace-covered cushions whose slips were changed every day. Thord was standing near the unlighted fireplace, his red head doubled in the mirror above the mantel. His eyes met hers, and he went on talking to her father. Seating herself on a blue leather hassock, April tossed out the full skirts of her dress.

"You look tired," Mrs. Wilde remarked.

"Getting ready for Mamo's wedding is a strenuous affair," April said, then gazed at bleak-faced men and women gazing out of heavily framed photographs hanging on the walls. "We Wildes are a forbidding-looking crew," she observed, looking at her father. "Dale may be panicked when he sees the caliber of my ancestors."

Mrs. Wilde made a faint shocked sound. Hiram smiled oddly.

"I'll admit in appearance you hardly look as though you belong to Wilde stock, but underneath I suspect you're a chip off the old block. At any rate I hope so. Softness never got anywhere."

"I wonder? Water's soft, but it wears down rock and gets places," April remarked.

Wilde's slanted yellowish eyes rested on her thoughtfully. The dinner gong sounded, sending discreet flute-like notes through the house.

The meal went its stiff way. Outside, garden and island prepared themselves for sleep. Occasionally April glanced at a chaste clock sitting among the silver and china which had been shipped around

[207]

the Horn from New England in the early eighteen hundreds. In another hour, at most, Reverend Thisbe would burst in, dragging life, raw and undressed, into the proper atmosphere of rooms which had never seen major upheavals, though they crackled with silent animosities bred from the long breach between her father and mother.

When they were all established in the drawing room again, April said, "Read something aloud, Father. I'm edgy. Having a fiancé you've only known a week descending on you unexpectedly is sort of panicking. I don't know how we'll strike Dale and Sabrina. Our ways will seem insular, to put it mildly."

"At any rate there are no skeletons in our family cupboard," Wilde observed dryly. "You can be thankful for that."

"I shall, of course, have a reception for them," Mrs. Wilde said from her pillows.

April winced inwardly. Her mother's tragic efforts at entertaining —dull gatherings that went forward interminably and profitlessly— always left her spent and weak. "Dale and Sabrina are surfeited with social stuff, Mother," she protested. "They'll probably prefer just to—"

"My dear, you're *our* daughter. Everyone in Hawaii will want to meet the man you're marrying. In fairness to our friends, and out of respect for the Hancock family, things must be correct."

"Don't overdo and lose the ground you've gained, Mrs. Wilde," Thord cautioned.

"I'll manage to take my sun baths, no matter what," Mrs. Wilde promised.

April glanced at the clock. Thord was watching it too, bracing himself as was she, for Thisbe's arrival. Wilde picked up a paper and glanced over the pages slowly. "Sugar's due for a rise, I see," he remarked in satisfied tones. "The Cuba crop's short."

"I envy you, Daddy."

"Why?" Wilde asked from behind the paper.

"You just have one drive in life, to make money. It simplifies everything, having a single goal. At times I wish I were like you. Again I'm glad that I'm not."

"Fundamentally, you're a replica of me."

"I'm not at all sure I want to be."

Her father gave her a startled look, as if his tremendous complacent ego had received a jar.

"Why not?" he asked.

"We both fight for things we want," April conceded, "but you trample over people to get them. I don't."

"When you're older you'll find out that people who get places have to drive over anything that gets in their way."

"I don't entirely agree with you, Daddy. Take Kauka, for instance—"

"What has he achieved?" Wilde asked coldly.

"He's the most outstanding personality in Kona and the swellest all-round human being I've ever known."

"What has it netted him?" Wilde asked dryly.

"From a worldly viewpoint, nothing, but when people are in trouble they go to him before anyone."

"I'm fond of Kauka." Wilde's voice was condescending. "He's been in my employ twenty-eight years. But I'm better equipped to act in emergencies than he is."

"I wonder?" April said.

"Don't—don't fight with your father," Mrs. Wilde begged.

"My dear Elsbeth, April and I are too intelligent to fight. We're cut from the same cloth, to a large extent anyway." His voice was tinged with pride. "April's the one person in Kona, aside from Graham, who has a mind."

"Thanks, Daddy. That's a lot from you."

A car drove in. Wilde glanced up and frowned. It was evident he enjoyed talking to his daughter and resented the interruption.

"See who that is, Graham, will you?" Wilde said. "I'm not expecting anyone tonight."

Thord said "Surely," but before he was half across the room Thisbe burst in. His watery blue eyes were half out of focus, red splotches stood out against the chalky whiteness of his face. Even his sparse, gingery hair looked outraged. Mrs. Wilde jerked to a sitting position.

"What on earth—" she gasped.

Thisbe's hands clenched and unclenched. Cords in his thin neck stood out like strings. He tried to speak twice, then plumping down in a chair began crying into his lean freckled hands.

"What in God's name has happened?" Wilde exclaimed, leaping up.

"Prudence—" Thisbe made a furious, ineffectual gesture.

"Is she ill? Dead?" Wilde demanded.

"She—she's married!"

"Married!" Mrs. Wilde gasped.

"To Brewer!" Thisbe hurled the name from him.

"To—*Brewer!*" Wilde shouted.

"To—Brewer?" Mrs. Wilde echoed weakly.

"This—this afternoon!" Thisbe half screamed.

The furniture looked shocked, the room aghast. Bleak women and grim men seemed to freeze in their picture frames. Wilde crunched up the newspaper he still held; a vein swelled on his forehead. "You mean—"

"My daughter's run off with that profligate you hire to grow your damn Macadamian nuts! You've got to discharge him!"

"Reverend Thisbe—you're swearing!" Mrs. Wilde cried hysterically.

"I won't stand for him coming to my church—I'll see him in hell first."

"Thisbe, you're defiling the cloth you wear with such language," Wilde said hotly.

"How'd you feel if your daughter had run off with a man of Brewer's ilk? A drunkard, a seducer of Hawaiian girls—whom you countenance because he makes money for you! He's got to be run out of Kona, and to hell with your Macadamian nuts!" Thisbe shook his skinny fist at Wilde.

Mrs. Wilde began sobbing into her cushions. April hurried to her.

"The marriage's got to be annulled, I tell you!" Thisbe went on.

"Prudence is of age—twenty-two, if I recall rightly," Wilde said icily.

"I don't care a hoot! When I think of her in bed with him—"

"Remember, April is present," Wilde said in a voice as cold and rough-edged as a saw.

"Well, *do* something! You can. We all have to dance to your pipings here. Every last one of us—whether we like it or not!"

"April, leave the room," Wilde said.

"Father, act your age!" she flashed back.

Mrs. Wilde cringed among her pillows. Thord went to her. "Come, Mrs. Wilde," he said gently. "This is bad for you. April, help me to get your mother to bed." Thord picked up Mrs. Wilde, spilling pillows onto the floor, and headed for the stairs.

"I'll get Iku and Otero," April said.

When Mrs. Wilde was in bed and a sedative had been administered, Thord bent over her. "Try and sleep," he urged. "I'll come again in half an hour."

She gave a dreary nod.

"Let's go onto the balcony for a minute," April suggested. "It's awful—worse than I thought it was going to be. Listen."

Voices in high altercation came from the drawing room.

They walked through French doors opening from Mrs. Wilde's room onto the overhanging veranda. April looked at the stars and shivered. Thord put his arm about her.

"Steady," he said.

"I'll be okay in a second, but it's always upsetting to see people letting go all the holds."

"Yes. That helpless little man's gone completely to pieces. All over the place."

"Tonight this." April leaned her forehead against his arm. "Tomorrow—Dale. How—how am I to tell him?"

"Let it ride for a bit. Things are landsliding enough in all directions as it is."

"Yes. Even Kauka, who's usually so serene, looked badgered by something when he came home today."

Thord hesitated, then told her about Tutu.

"I hadn't meant to tell you this, but I feel that if you know you'll realize our jam is nothing to what Kauka's up against."

She nodded, then said in muffled tones, "I wonder what Prue said in her note?"

"Probably plenty. When inhibited persons go off the deep end they usually go all the way."

"Maybe we'd better go downstairs," April suggested.

Thord took her chin between his thumb and forefinger. "I'm kissing you with my mind," he said under his breath.

"I'm doing the same," April whispered.

They walked back into the bedroom. Faithful, patient-faced maids kept watch on each side of the bed.

"Sleep," Iku said.

"Fine." Thord smiled at Iku, then at Otero, and he and April started downstairs.

Thisbe's accusing voice reached them.

"Kauka's had a hand in this! He's been away for three days."

April flashed an alarmed look at Thord. "Father's got him on the run. He's crawfishing!"

"I'll phone Kauka and get to the bottom of this," Wilde said angrily.

"Father—" April ran down the stairs. "Kauka had nothing to do with Prue's marriage. Loki and I—"

"Do you mean to tell me you've known all the time that—"

"Brewer and Prudence intended to get married?" April asked.

"And what preceded it?" Wilde said.

"No one knew anything until three nights ago, when Prudence came to Kauka and Loki for—help."

"What do you mean—help?"

"Didn't Prudence say in her note"—April hesitated, her face pale, then suddenly scarlet—"that she's going to have a—baby?"

"By God, I'll have Brewer on the mat tomorrow! It's unheard of that such things can go on right under my nose, on my own estate, without my hearing a word of it," Wilde raged. "Why didn't you come to me at once, April?"

"What could you do that hasn't been done, Father?"

Wilde looked as if he would explode.

"I won't have that reprobate for a son-in-law, I tell you I won't!"

Thisbe bleated, looking like a half-crushed beetle belligerently dragging itself forward.

"Reverend Thisbe—" Going to him, April took his hand. "When
Prue told Loki about—about herself and Brewer"—she hesitated,
then went on resolutely—"Loki said this—this affair would give
you an opportunity to *be* a Christian, as well as to talk about Christianity from the pulpit."

"The preposterous effrontery of her!" Thisbe spluttered. "I should
have known better than to allow Prudence to come under the de-
moralizing influence of Hawaiian morals!"

April's eyes blazed. "Kauka and Loki are worth all the rest of
Kona put together. If you'd been a real father, Prue would have
gone to you with her trouble, instead of going to them for help.
Aside from being her father, you're a preacher. Put your Christianity to work!" She gulped for breath. "If you and Father blow
up all over the place it'll make things worse. The only sane and
dignified thing to do is to sanction this marriage."

"I'll disown Prudence!"

"Go ahead. I'm going to South Kona to call on her and Brewer
in a few days."

"You will not!" Wilde said.

"But I will," April insisted. "And I'll invite them to the reception
Mother's giving for Dale and Sabrina." She sat down weakly in a
near-by chair. "I—I feel funny—" she finished in a small voice.

Wilde dashed over. "She's fainted! Do something, Graham."

"She'll be all right in a few moments, Mr. Wilde. She's been
through a lot these past few days."

"Did you know about Brewer and Prudence too?" Wilde asked,
his voice edged with cold anger.

"As a member of Kauka's household, it could hardly be otherwise. April's right. If you put a decent face on things this rumpus'll
blow over. If not, it'll afford a fine scandal, which will hardly
reflect to the credit of the plantation." Bending over, Thord hoisted
April into his arms and headed for the stairs. "Where's April's
room?" he called over his shoulder.

"Second door to the right of the stairway. I'll be with you directly."

"I feel like the heroine of an old-fashioned romance," April whispered into Thord's neck. "I 'pulled' the faint, so you would have to hold me."

"You're incorrigible and—adorable," Thord said under his breath. "But I think you've stopped—that." He signaled slightly with his head in the direction of the drawing room, then placed her on her bed.

Wilde came up the stairs. "Has she—"

"She's coming to," Thord assured him.

"I'll send Iku to undress her in a few minutes. Shouldn't you give her something?" Wilde asked, hovering over the bed. "April's entirely right," he added after a moment.

"Entirely," Thord agreed.

April opened her eyes. "Daddy—"

He caught her hand. "I'm here, April."

"I'm tired."

"I'll send Hiro to meet Dale and his sister in the morning."

"No, Daddy, I've got to go. I'll be all right shortly."

"If you insist on going, Graham's going with you."

"Daddy, no! Suppose I was arriving in New York and Dale met my train with some strange girl in tow."

"Graham's our family physician, April. This abominable business has completely upset you. I feel as though I'd been through a wringer myself."

"Would it be all right if I had a little brandy?" April asked. "I feel so—weak."

"How about it, Graham?"

"It would be good for her."

"I'll fetch some." Wilde hurried off.

"I've—I've let you and myself in for something awful," April said, when her father was out of earshot.

"You can't do much about it—now. But you've won a big victory. Brewer won't be discharged and your father's secretly relieved. Don't push your luck. Wilde orders are *orders*. We've just got to

[214]

take this on the chin. I don't relish being present when Dale—greets you."

"My tummy feels as if it were full of unhappy butterflies, just thinking about Dale—kissing me," April said, turning her head and pressing her cheek against Thord's arm.

22

THORD'S fingers tightened on April's elbow as they waited on the wharf, watching the first boatload of passengers putting off from the steamer anchored outside the reef. There was a pearl-like luster to the water. Inland, the domes of volcanoes roared like navy-blue altars against the clear lemon light welling into the east. Hawaiians, Chinese, and Japanese, collected to see who would arrive, laughed and chatted together, but their voices sounded unreal in Thord's ears.

An odd sick feeling stole through April which was an outrage against the peace and beauty around her. She glanced up at Thord. His lips were tight.

"This is a pretty steep assignment," he admitted.

"Yes—and I mustn't muff the deal."

"You won't. You're stuff."

The conviction in his voice injected fresh courage into her.

"Could you sort of beau Sabrina?" she asked. "Then, mostly, it'll be a foursome instead of just two."

"After work hours I will, if it'll make things easier for you."

"It will. Heaps." April's eyes fell to the garlands arranged on her arm. "When I decorate Dale, you give Sabrina her leis."

Separating half a dozen, she handed them to him. Across the long slow swells traveling in from the horizon and uncurling in lead and platinum on the beach, the splash of sweeps sounded faintly in the still air.

"April."

"Yes?"

"Promise me something."

"Anything."

"You're gorgeous!" Thord exclaimed. "Most girls would ask 'What?'" His face tensed. "If, after seeing Dale, you find out that, after all—"

She tore her arm from his hold, then said in a small desolate voice, "I can't blame you. I came home engaged to one man; in a few weeks—"

"You have me all wrong," Thord interrupted. "It's only that your happiness and well-being is of greater importance than my own."

"That goes for me too!"

"Always?"

"Always!"

Their eyes met in a swift up-rush of happiness. Then a little imp of gaiety brushed April. Flashing a smile at Thord, she placed a kiss in the palm of her hand and blew it at him. He pretended to catch it and placed it carefully against his lips. April's face lighted, then all at once she looked young, unsure of herself, as if she were inwardly shrinking from the moment when she would have to introduce Dale and Thord.

The boat, with gathering momentum, was sliding across the water, already streaked with blue. The dark mass of passengers, crowded together on the seats, began to disentangle into definite figures. Suddenly one hand shot up above the others, a long arm waved, a voice shouted:

"April!"

She marshaled her faculties, focused them. "Dale!" she called back, brandishing her free arm. The name floated off and died into silence on the water.

It seemed fantastic that during the time they'd been parted he had not changed at all, while she'd altered completely. For some reason, that morning, instead of wearing a silk sports dress she had put on riding breeches and a blue and white *palaka,* such as Hawaiian *paniolos* wear when they ride after cattle. She was hatless and a gardenia sat in a wave of her hair above the left ear. Perhaps some profound instinct had prodded her to make it clear, by

[217]

her exterior, that she was no longer the girl who had attracted Dale in New York, but a child of the Outside Islands of Hawaii.

He stood among the seated passengers, his tan emphasized by tropic whites. He wore his accustomed air of leisure and nonchalance, reflecting the environment in which he had been reared. Suddenly April realized that he needed the settings of civilization to put himself over to best advantage. To bestride a thousand-dollar polo pony in London-tailored breeches and boots by Maxwell or Peel, to stand at the wheel of a fifty-thousand-dollar yacht, slanting to a stiff breeze, enveloped a person in drama. Dale was accustomed to buying his fun, had spent untold sums acquiring accomplishments that made him outstanding among men and attractive to women. In Kona, money was of little value to purchase laughter or thrills. They sprang out of the earth and from hearts spilling over with zest for living.

She winced at the thought that even if he showed no outward sign of amusement for the people of Kona, because of consideration of her, in private he might laugh at them.

The boat was rushing toward the wharf with the accumulated momentum of strong brown arms pulling lustily. She saw Dale bend to help his sister to her feet. Sabrina's eyes swept the wharf inquiringly, then widened with astonishment. She's seen me, April thought, and is amazed at my—get-up.

Sabrina was fashionably thin and dressed with expensive simplicity that set off her fair blondeness. Her features, while not actually pretty, were distinctive and even the trip across the bay had not disturbed a hair of her coiffure or altered the exactly correct angle of a saucy sport hat.

"Dale's wondering who you are, why you're with me," April said in an edgy voice. "Now Sabrina's seen you; look dynamic and mysterious, Thord."

He laughed curtly. His eyes were so blue they almost looked black, and behind the wide pupils was the satisfaction of a man who has, at last, come up against a long-awaited issue.

The boat bumped the wharf. People crowded forward calling

down to arriving friends, weeping, laughing in the usual Island way.

Dale, standing in the boat, indicated them. "Must I cry too?" he called, then wiped imaginary tears from his eyes.

Sailors began catching up women and children and tossing them into waiting arms. Thord strode forward and a big Hawaiian picked Sabrina up and threw her to him.

Catching her, he set her on her feet. April kissed her.

"Aloha, Sabrina! This is Dr. Graham—he works on Daddy's plantation."

"I'm delighted to meet you," the girl said, then added with a laugh, "I'll never forget you, for I've never been *bodily* thrown at a man before!"

"It's just an old Island custom," Thord assured her as he began decorating her with leis.

She looked pleased, intrigued, excited.

Dale started to vault ashore just as the wave which had lifted the boat sped on, dropping it into the hollow behind. A big Hawaiian jerked him back. *"Malama—take care!"* he warned. *"I speak what-time you can jump."*

Dale looked at him hotly. The man's white teeth flashed in a friendly grin, then he yelled, "Okay—now!" and gave Dale an undignified boost which sent him spinning through the air. But he landed squarely on his feet and recovered his poise instantly.

"Quite an astounding method of making an entrance," he commented; then he bent and kissed April with the tempered warmth of a well-bred person greeting a bride-to-be in the presence of strangers.

When he released her she decorated him with leis.

"There, you look like an Islander now," she told him, then turned. "Dale, I want you to meet Dr. Graham. Father insisted on his coming down this morning, because last night I disgraced myself by fainting."

"Fainting!" Dale exclaimed. "You mid-Victorian!"

"Aren't I? You see, last night, our parson's daughter eloped with a rake thirty years her senior and—"

"But why on earth—"

"If you'd been there, you'd have wanted to pull a blank too," said April, chattering on. "When you meet Reverend Thisbe, and Brewer, whom Prudence ran off with—" She realized Dale wasn't listening.

He and Thord were shaking hands and exchanging cool, measuring glances. Sabrina was also appraising Thord intently, and April was aware of it. She wondered, with a brief rush of panic, why she'd never mentioned Thord in her letters. It might have eased things.

"Where do you hail from, Graham?" Dale asked in a slightly puzzled way.

Thord hesitated, then said, "From New York, originally."

"I thought we'd met before," Dale announced. "Your name and face ring faint bells."

"They do for me, too," Sabrina asserted. "But I can't recollect where we've met, Dr. Graham." Her eyes went to his inquiringly.

April took hold of Dale's arm, while a tiny muscle in the side of her throat fluttered madly. He looked down.

"Let's shove," she suggested. "Breakfast is at seven-thirty. It's past six."

"I could go a good meal," Dale confessed. "You know, April, for a moment I didn't know you." His eyes laughed. "Is this get-up the usual thing in Kona?" He indicated her *palaka*. "Now, if you'd been in a sarong—"

"Sarongs aren't Hawaiian," April said. "South Sea natives still wear *pareus,* but my missionary ancestors ended picturesque garb here. These *palakas*—that means a sort of over-blouse—are a Hawaiian cowboy's regulation riding clothes."

"It's hardly designed to enhance the figure," Dale chuckled, then added, "I'm trying to picture Sabrina and myself wearing them."

"You don't have to. Thord, will you have some of the wharf boys bring Dale and Sabrina's luggage while I take them to the car?"

"I'll attend to it, April."

[220]

"I'll stay with Dr. Graham," Sabrina announced. "I suspect that Dale would appreciate a moment or two alone with you, April."

"Sis, you're wonderful!"

Grasping April's arm, Dale started off. He glanced at her willful, half-wild beauty, and when they were out of earshot, inquired amusedly, "Did my unexpected arrival stymie a budding flirtation with that red-headed Doc?"

April gave him a childlike glare.

"Ouch! If looks could kill, I'd be dead," Dale said. "But Graham's confoundedly good-looking. Sabrina's all set at having someone worthy of her art to use her wiles on during this idyllic interval in the Paradise of the Pacific." He glanced about him, then said in a mild surprised way, "This *is* a thundering sort of island, isn't it?"

"Yes."

"Which of those three mountains is the volcano?"

"They're all volcanoes, but the biggest one, Mauna Loa"—she gestured at the long blue shape in the south—"is the active one."

"When I look at your face, not at your what-you-may-call-it, I see my girl again," Dale said jauntily. "I'd forgotten you were so—well, elusive as well as enticing. I remember the enticing part—"

"You're just the same."

"Meaning you're not?"

"I feel completely strange with you," April confessed. "Being with you in New York and seeing you in Kona is like meeting you for the first time." Her voice caught.

"Not for me. To hell with *where* we are! Young Lochinvar's come out of the East to carry his fair lady away, if not on a white charger, on an excellent steamer—after we get back to Honolulu— and then on an extra-fare train from San Francisco!"

"Let me—get my breath."

"Why?"

"I told you, there was an awful uproar last night and I was in the thick of it. As well, Mamo's to be married in less than three weeks and—"

"Mamo's the lovely half-caste?"

"Yes, my best friend, and my *poi*-bowl sister."

[221]

"What in the name of blazes is a *poi*-bowl sister?"

"When two people eat *poi,* our national food, out of the same calabash, or bowl, it makes them relations. Sort of like the old blood-ceremony."

"I see. Well, to blazes with other people's weddings. I'm only interested in ours."

April did not answer.

"What's eating you?" Dale demanded.

"I was hoping you and Sabrina would get a real kick out of seeing an Island wedding. There are things planned for Mamo's that, usually, outsiders never have an opportunity to see." Her voice fell.

"Of course it'll be interesting." Dale instilled enthusiasm into his voice. "But when a fellow's passed up a cruise in the Mediterranean and come five thousand miles to carry his girl off, a little enthusiasm on her part doesn't seem out of line."

"I'm sorry. Your coming was unexpected, sort of took my breath away. And on top of last night—"

"Skip it," Dale advised. "Probably I'm a bit off center myself. I like life with its clothes on, plus a few extra frills and ruffles. The boat trip yesterday and last night nearly washed Sis and me up. Luckily we're both good sailors, but everything reeked of hogs and molasses and cattle. I can hardly wait for a tub. I feel perfumed with cow!"

They made their way between stacks of sugar bags.

"That your car?" Dale asked, indicating the Wilde limousine.

April nodded.

"Graham drive you down?"

"No, Hiro, our chauffeur. As I told you, Dad sent Thord along because he was afraid I'd pull a faint again."

"Blast Reverend Whoever, and his daughter, and Mamo's wedding, and everything that's taken the stuffing out of you. I'd pictured an enthusiastic meeting—under tropical skies." He flipped the words away.

"I'm sorry, Dale. Probably tomorrow—"

"Do our raptures have to be postponed till then? Get in the car and give me at least one honest-to-God kiss!"

He reached to open the door but Hiro did it, bowing. "Aloha, Mr. Dale. Glad you come!" he said heartily.

Dale did not appear to hear and made no reply. The chauffeur looked at him, puzzled, then the warm friendliness in his eyes seemed to withdraw and fold up inside him.

"Thank you, Hiro," April murmured.

"Send him for the bags. I want to kiss you. Thoroughly!" Dale slid his arm about her. "Why, you mid-Victorian little thing. You look panicked. When we got engaged in New York—"

"This is—Hawaii."

"Somewhere along the line I'd collected the impression that Hawaii was a headlong sort of place. The tropics and all that!"

April looked small and frightened.

"I see I'm going to have to start all over again," Dale said. "Woo you afresh. Maybe I didn't do a thorough enough job of it. How would that suit you, Modest Violet?"

"Oh, Dale—would you?" she asked breathlessly. "Pretend we've just met?"

"It's a confounded waste of time, but if that's what you want it'll be that way. Miss Wilde, I hope that our acquaintance—"

"Dale, you're sweet."

"That's the first flash of real enthusiasm I've seen," he exclaimed, glancing through the rear window. "Oh, hell, here come Sabrina and Graham! I was about to be so bold as to ask if you felt that our acquaintance had progressed to a point where it might be permissible for me to hold your hand."

April looked down. "It—has, but not for too long."

"I'm beginning to think that throwing up the cruise wasn't a bad thing after all. I'm going to have the unbelievable experience of *courting my fiancée*—according to the standards of our grandparents—which is a new experience for Dale Hancock III!"

He glanced out of the rear window again, then frowned. "Confound it, I can't place him. That Doc's face and name keep ringing bells in my mind. Doctor . . . Thord . . . Graham . . . Doctor Thord Graham. . . . If I haven't bumped into him, I've seen his picture or read about him somewhere fairly recently."

[223]

23

APRIL tore up a handful of grass unhappily, and looked at lines of saddled horses tied to trees, at automobiles of varying vintages and makes crowding the driveway of Kauka's garden. Music, laughter, the sound of hurrying feet came from the house.

"Sabrina's fallen for Hawaii hook, line and sinker," she said. "But I'm afraid you've had a dull time, Dale."

He was sprawled on the lawn, waiting with the rest of the bridal party to ride down to the seashore, as soon as Liholiho arrived.

"On the contrary, it's been highly amusing. I'll be able to keep my cronies in stitches for years, impersonating the various personalities and describing the goings-on of Kona. I wouldn't have missed coming for anything."

April embraced her knees fiercely. Dale had a gift for mimicry which had left her spent with laughter in New York, but she winced at the thought of him burlesquing people she loved, and mocking customs of the Islands. No one would be spared, nothing would be sacred. In justice to Dale, she knew there was no venom when he took-off people; it was only a little-boy conception of fun.

"Can't you see old Tops Farley and Piggy Wetherill rolling in the scuppers when I do a Reverend Thisbe for them?" Dale asked. "You remember Tops and Piggy, don't you—the chaps who sail with me? You met them at the week-end you had your brainstorm about coming back to Hawaii."

"Yes, I recall them."

"And when I tell them about that gorgeous Mamo showing her

Montgomery Ward wedding dress as if it were a Worth creation!
I didn't know whether to laugh or cry. It's sheer desecration to
think of a creature so breath-takingly beautiful going to the altar
in a twenty-seven-dollar wedding dress!"

Lighting a cigarette, he exhaled and watched the blue smoke curl
away into the amber sunshine.

"And just get an eyeful of that." He gestured at horses with
flowers in their brow-bands, at rattly old cars with bunches of
glossy *ti* leaves tied to the sides of the windshields. "Damned if
those leaves on top of smooth long stalks don't make me think of
the pompons on hearses." He laughed immoderately. "The only
flaw in this visit is—"

"Me?" April suggested.

"Yes. Confound it, what's got into you? I've tried the Gay Ninety
suitor act, whirlwind attacks, and you stay remote as a cloud. Have
I lost my sex appeal?" He quirked an eyebrow at her.

"It's—Kona," April announced in a small sunk voice. "I—I—can't
leave it, Dale."

He jerked to a sitting position. "What are you trying to get
across?" he demanded.

April moved unhappily. "It isn't possible for a city-born person,
like yourself, to understand how people born in the Islands love the
very earth they're made of. When you're away from Hawaii, you
enjoy new places and people, of course, but part of you is curled up
tight inside, like a hibernating bear, waiting to come out, to be
all-alive again."

"Are you inferring that you love this confounded locality as ordinary people love a human being?" Dale asked.

"Yes."

"Are you telling me, in a roundabout way, that this earth underneath us"—he thumped it with his fist—"means more to you than
I do?"

"Yes, Dale."

He stared at her, outraged into silence.

"You'll never understand that my love for Hawaii goes beyond
mere devotion to the soil, or to the people living on it. For some

reason you haven't fallen for Hawaii, but I've met dozens of people who've visited here, often quite briefly, who love the Islands beyond their own lands, whose one dream is to get back. For good. They don't want to come back just for the beauty and fun here, but for something words can't express."

"You mean," Dale's eyes narrowed, "that for a regular diet you get more out of life here than you would in my setup?"

"Yes."

"Blast it, April, I don't mean to be rude, but you've almost got me on the run. How can a girl of your quality and education cast your vote for what we've had and done these past two weeks, against art galleries, music, theaters, contacts with brilliant minds?"

"I know it must sound insane, but I do get more out of life here than in any place else." She kept her eyes fixed on the vermilion umbrella of a flame tree standing up against the proud bright sea.

"I'll bet my last dollar that after you've lived in New York for six months, Hawaii will be reduced to its proper proportions in the general scheme of things," Dale laughed indulgently.

April made no reply.

"Look." Dale gripped her hand. "I'll make a bargain with you. If, after six months or a year you aren't happier and more stimulated in New York than you've ever been here, you can visit Hawaii for three months out of every year. But I'm betting that before we're halfway across the States you'll have succumbed completely to my Fatal Charm." He brushed her fingers with his lips.

"Oh, Dale, you're fine, sweet, everything a girl could want to have in a husband—"

"That sounds more like it," he said gaily.

"But—" April hesitated.

"But what?" he asked.

"But I'm not going back with you and Sabrina. Ever since you arrived I've been trying to screw up enough courage to tell you. Now I have." Her voice collapsed.

"But, Great Scott—"

She sighed, silencing him. "I was going to write and tell you, but you coming without warning made it impossible. I hate to hurt you—"

"There isn't only me to be considered," Dale broke in. "Mother's ushering in the fall season with flocks of parties in your honor. If you postpone coming until next May, as we planned originally, it'll gum everything up and make me and the family look like idiots!"

"Dale," April swallowed. "Now we've reached this point, it's no use postponing the evil hour any longer. I'd intended to wait until after the wedding to tell you—but I'd die slowly, living the way you do."

"Are you trying to tell me you don't intend to marry me?" Dale asked harshly.

"Yes."

"But you can't do this to me, April. I've known prettier girls, more brilliant ones, but you—ring bells for me. You've got a strangle-hold on my imagination, as well as my heart."

"Oh, Dale—"

"There you are!" Sabrina came streaking across the lawn. "Cut the love scene. Liholiho's here and everyone's ready to start to the Sacred Cove for the Forever-Faithful-Forever-Beautiful Ceremony. When I take the fatal step I'm going to drag Mr. Whoever to Kona to get married."

She adjusted the gardenia over her ear and resettled the seventy-five-cent *palaka* she was wearing over a ten-dollar silk shirt. Then, sensing dynamite in the air, she raised her brows.

"Lovers' quarrel?" she inquired.

Dale told her, his voice savage.

"Oh, act your age," Sabrina said. "Don't take a trifle like a gal getting temporary cold feet so seriously. For some reason, people always get stirred up when a wedding's in the air. Strains of Mendelssohn, the vision of a girl in white walking down a church aisle—"

Dale made an angry retort.

"Oh, act like a civilized being!" Sabrina repeated. "New Yorkers are supposed to be civilized, aren't they? You can't hurl your personal monkey wrench into the machinery of this super-elegant affair and wreck it. I'm lapping it up. Eat, drink, laugh—tomorrow, no, in four days, we go back to New York. Same talk, same clubs, same thoughts, same everything. Shelve the personal equation till the Big Show's over."

"I'm serious, Sabrina, about not marrying Dale," April said.

"I wouldn't give a hoot for an engagement that didn't go on the rocks a few times to add spice to it."

Dale glared at the grass.

"Snap out of it, Dale," Sabrina said. "Get the sweep of this, the color, the fun. It's a sort of Pageant of Nations." She gestured at whites, Hawaiians, Chinese, Filipinos, Japanese, Portuguese—and all the racial crossings resulting from long association—who had been assisting all day with the mammoth preparations, and who were now reluctantly going off until the following morning.

"We'd better go," April suggested, looking toward the house. "Loki's getting ready to start." She got to her feet.

"I'm elated that Mamo added me to her bridesmaids," Sabrina announced. "I'll adore wearing one of those flowing *holoku* affairs you got for them to wear." Linking her arm through April's, Sabrina squeezed it.

"I'm happy you're enjoying yourself so much," April said.

"I've never had such fun in my life. Come, Dale," Sabrina called over her shoulder.

"Presently. I'm doing a think," he retorted curtly.

"Well, think in a straight line," Sabrina advised with sisterly frankness. "Where are my heroes?" She looked at the bridal party assembling on the steps, on the lawn, and in the *lanai*. "I don't know who I've fallen for hardest, April—Thord, or that indecently handsome young half-white who arrived from Kauai this morning. The one who's Mamo's cousin-brother, or something. What's his Hawaiian name—Heavenly Child, or Child of Heaven?"

"*Keike o Lani,*" April said. "Child of Heaven."

"Well, I'm calling him Heavenly!"

"You're grand. I was afraid you mightn't enjoy a time like this."

"You had hardly a chance to get to know me in New York,"

Sabrina laughed. "You know, throwing a scare into Dale is good for him. He's tops, but he has always had his own way—"

"I meant what he told you, Sabrina."

"Well, if you don't marry him, it won't kill him, though I'd have liked you for a sister. Oh, *Heavenly!*" she called, and went rushing off. The young half-white's face lighted.

"Miss New York, see what I made for you." He held up a gardenia lei.

Sabrina ducked her head, and he placed it about her neck with a touching reverence, as though he realized that probably only this once would a blonde girl of Sabrina's breeding and social standing be his to cavalier.

Kauka and Loki were getting into the front seat of their car. The back was completely filled with baskets of five-pointed, honey-colored plumeria blossoms.

"Now you kids no fool too much," Loki ordered. "Every-kind must be *pau* before dark, or bad lucks."

Other cars, taking gray-haired uncles and aunts and small lively children, moved down the driveway. Mamo and Liholiho came out, followed by girls as colorful as peacocks, or suave and finished as gardenias, escorted by brothers and cousins.

"Where's your *haole?*" Liholiho asked, looking at April.

"Coming. I was with him until a moment ago."

Liholiho's eyes narrowed a little, then he untied a snorty young half-thoroughbred which he had recently trained and led him forward for Mamo. Girls and boys were mounting, their laughter ringing through the afternoon. Thord ran down the steps.

"Where's Sabrina?" he asked.

"I'm here, with Heavenly," she called. "You've got a dark-and-dangerous rival, Red."

Liholiho grinned. "That's a swell girl. Too bad her brother—" Breaking off, he assisted Mamo in the saddle, gave her a worshipful look and stepped back.

Thord passed, and Liholiho's hand fell on his shoulder. "Look, Ulaula—" His brilliant black eyes seemed veiled. "Since Homer isn't here, I want you for my Best Man. I like all these kids fine, but

[229]

Homer thought you were—the best there is. He'll be glad to know that you stood where he was going to, beside me, when I'm married."

"Gosh, Liholiho, I'll be proud to!" Thord said.

"Swell." Turning, Liholiho busied himself unnecessarily with the girth of his saddle, swung on, and with Mamo beside him started down the drive.

"Liholiho is hurt about Homer going," April said, looking up at Thord. "I simply can't understand it. It isn't like Homer to let his best friend down, even if some old coot of an uncle who's never seen him did yell for an unknown nephew to rush to his bedside—on the chance of his dying."

"It's got me guessing, too," Thord admitted. "Want me to get your horse?"

"Thanks." She glanced around and added in an undertone, "I've told Dale I'm not going to marry him."

Thord frowned. "I thought you were going to wait until the wedding was over."

"I'd intended to, but the moment came." She hesitated, then added, "He went off the deep end."

Just then Dale came riding up leading Sweet Man.

"Look," he began when he and April were mounted and Thord had left them, "I made rather an ass of myself. Let's call a truce until this shindig's over, then get down to brass tacks."

"We're down to them, Dale."

"Maybe I'll succeed in changing your mind, yet. My vanity, or ego, however you choose to label it, refuses to believe that I can't win you all over again. So on your guard, Gorgeous!"

They fell into the rear of the cavalcade, heading for the sea. Voices, laughter, and the fine sound of hoofs filled the afternoon.

As if the jolt he had received had jarred him loose from himself, Dale presented a changed front that April suspected was not entirely an act.

"You know, every so often a chap takes the wrong turn." He watched the horses and gay riders. "Sabrina's dead right. This wedding *is* something! Look at those fellows and girls, with flowers

[230]

around their necks and hats, playing guitars and ukuleles on horseback. Get an eyeful of that blue wall of water!"

April's eyes lighted.

"Tell me about this ceremony that's to be performed."

"Some ancestor of Loki's blessed a certain cove on the coast and put a *kahuna*—a spell—on it to insure that any pair who swim in it together, before their marriage, will remain forever beautiful in each other's eyes, and forever faithful to the vows they make."

When they reached the Sacred Cove, the sun was dipping toward the horizon. A narrow strip of green forest, which old lava flows had not wiped out, ran down to the lip of a fifteen-foot semi-circular cliff, against the foot of which blue water swelled lazily. Cars and horses jammed the end of the road. Children were tearing about, older folk were carrying baskets of flowers to the brink of the cliff and setting them down.

"See you later, Dale. I've got to be with the bridesmaids," April said, sliding off her horse.

"I'll find Graham and stay with him. He's from my neck of the woods, so I won't feel too completely the fifth wheel on this cart."

Young laughter came from behind luxuriously growing greenery where girls were preparing Mamo for her swim. Pushing through the fragrant tangle, April joined them. In the center of the small grassy glade Mamo stood, wrapped about with a piece of brown and white printed material, to replace the *tapa* cloth of old times. Her bare shoulders were loaded with honey-colored ginger blossoms, and girls were starring her cloud of black hair with the five-pointed yellow plumeria blossoms. Seeing April, Mamo's eyes lighted.

"My heart is beating so fast I can hardly swallow," she confessed. "Till now it seemed as if we were only getting ready for a big *luau*. Now, I know I'm going to be married in two days."

"Better you watch out," one of her cousins, a slim brown dryad of fifteen, advised. "You marry with big handsome brute like Liholiho, and I bet-you-my-lifes you have twins before one year is *pau*."

Shrieks of glee went up. Mamo looked shy and elated.

"If they're girls, I'll name the first for April and the other for

[231]

you, Maile." Then she ducked her head into the crook of her arm, overcome by her own boldness.

"How do *I* look?" Sabrina demanded, when Mamo was complete to the last flower. She pirouetted around.

"You look gorgeous," April said.

"*Pimai*—come!" Loki called.

Escorted by her bridesmaids, Mamo walked slowly toward the cliff. A breeze off the sea rippled her flower-weighted hair. Then the girls, crowding about her, began softly chanting *Wahine Ui*.

"What does *Wahine Ui* mean?" Sabrina asked in a whisper.

"Beautiful Woman," April replied, then her eyes misted as she recalled the last time she had heard it was when Homer sang it on horseback the day Liholiho and Mamo became engaged.

As the girls approached, the thin voices of old women, waiting beside baskets of flowers, joined in the song.

"This—this is getting me," Sabrina confessed. "I'm crying."

"Me, too." April brushed tears from her cheeks.

The mystic loveliness of evening was coming to the Pacific, filming the sky. Slow, golden peace flowed out of the glowing west like a vast benediction. Everyone but Loki and Kauka moved back as the bridesmaids surrounding Mamo came forward. When the procession reached Loki and Kauka, the girls fell back slightly. Mamo stood still, while first her mother and then her father kissed her forehead in silence. Then the bridesmaids closed in again until Mamo stood on the brink of the cliff. Folding her arms, she flung back her head and gazed straight into the west. The bridesmaids formed a half-circle behind her.

"Great God, what a beauty she is!" Dale said in an undertone to Thord. "I can understand why the men of the *Bounty* deserted to stay in the South Seas for sirens like that."

Bridesmaids began strewing blossoms on the sea. When the water was so thick with them that only an occasional streak of blue showed, Liholiho, escorted by his groomsmen, appeared. Their muscled bodies, naked except for scarlet *malos,* suggested a series of bronzes executed by some unknown master's hands.

Walking forward, Liholiho stood beside Mamo with folded arms. Apparently the two were oblivious of each other.

Loki began singing on a high note, Kauka sounded the basses, then one person after another joined in the old chant until it swelled to organ volume, blending into the approaching night and all the tomorrows. In some sharp, strange way the music welded everyone present into a unit, herding them toward shining goals promised mankind in the beginning.

Like an arrow curving toward its mark, Mamo dove outward and downward, her flower-laden hair half concealing her body. With the grace of a falling star she disappeared into the massed flowers, rising and falling with the long slow breathing of the Pacific, receiving one of its children. After an instant she reappeared, tossed back her drenched hair, and held up her arms.

Liholiho poised, then dived down. They both vanished, then, coming up, began calling and signaling for the bridal party to join them. Like a flock of birds taking joyous flight, the girls went in, then the young men—while the sun went down in glory.

24

LOOK, Thisbe—" Placing his hand on the little man's rigid shoulder, Kauka patted it. "Mamo was christened by you, confirmed by you, and in a few hours will be married by you. It will be painful and difficult for Prudence to stand with the rest of the bridal party before the altar in your church, unless—"

"I won't countenance that abomination of a marriage, or forgive you and yours for your hand in it."

Kauka made a regretful sound and gazed out of the window. Thisbe glared at the shabby office.

"No one but Hawaiians would have a woman of Prudence's character as part of a wedding party."

Kauka turned and looked into Thisbe's eyes. "Mamo and Prudence played together as children. Some day their children will play together in turn—"

Thisbe made a small choking sound. "When I realize that in a few months I'll be grandfather to *his* child—" He collapsed into a near-by chair.

"Remember the story of the Prodigal Son," Kauka said gently, and waited.

Through open windows the thud of spades digging earth-ovens, the crackling of fires heating stones for underground cooking, men and women calling happily to each other, laughter, gusts of music, sounded.

"Would you"—Kauka chose his words carefully and thoughtfully—"prefer someone else to marry Mamo and Liholiho? The

[234]

Reverend Stephen Hoapili, my cousin, is coming from Hilo to be with us."

"Of course I shall officiate, and bless Mamo's and Liholiho's union," Thisbe snapped.

"How can you bless—when hate is in your heart?" Kauka asked. Thisbe made no reply.

"Thisbe, in the many years I've worked with people's bodies, as you have worked with their souls, I've learned wise persons do not carry burdens which are behind them, to add to those of a new day. What's done is finished forever. Prudence is married to Brewer; Hiram is keeping Brewer on."

"If that profligate enters my church—"

"He need not," Kauka interrupted. "There is a better way, for all. Mamo shall be married in our garden, where love is."

"But," Thisbe spluttered, "the church is to be decorated this morning."

"Phone your decorating committee. I'll talk to Loki. We will simply say that as so many are present it will be better to have the ceremony outside. Your church only accommodates a hundred and fifty. Over six hundred are invited. This way, the man you hate need not enter your church, so you will be spared and things will be made easier for Prudence. Perhaps under God's sky you will feel kinder toward Brewer and your child."

Thisbe jerked up, then seeing Kauka was not to be budged, said "Very well" in a thin, bitter voice.

"I'll go now and talk to Loki." Kauka started for the door. "You'll find cigars in my desk. Help yourself."

When the latch clicked behind him, Kauka shook himself like a dog coming out of muddy water. A delightful uproar filled the house and garden. Jingling spurs and thudding hoofs sounded as men galloped in with the loot of forests and sea. Mingling with garden fragrances was the sweetness of *maile* vines which women were twisting into leis, and the pungent spicy smell of *palapalai* ferns to cover *luau* tables. The throbbing of guitars and ukuleles, peals of joyous laughter, the gleeful screams of playing children, blended together.

A sense of vast well-being poured through Kauka. This was Mamo's wedding day! Going to the sideboard in the dining room he poured himself a drink of whisky, savored it slowly, and gazed around him with pleased eyes. The room, the house, was overflowing with flowers. Girls were rushing back and forth. One group, returning from decorating the ranch house for the bride and groom, surged down the hall.

"Oh, Uncle Kauka!" Ruby Spencer cried, seeing him, "the house looks beautiful. We put leis everywhere, and laid hundreds of gardenias on Mamo and Liholiho's bed."

"Fine, Ruby, fine," Kauka said.

He was conscious of the glow of good whisky stealing through his body, relaxing him after his visits to Tutu. He waited to let the liquor take further effect, then, feeling eased and fortified for the events ahead, proceeded down the hall.

Loki was at the head of the steps calling out directions to the swarms of volunteer workers. "Put tables more over there." She indicated the shade where indolent monkey-pod and breadfruit trees spread gracious branches. "Not so hot, and all fellas can eat more. Now no forget, but *plenty* of ferns and plenty of flowers on all tables."

Sensing Kauka's presence she turned and smiled. In a *holoku* of beige lace with a yellow feather lei about her stately throat, and another on her high-piled hair, she stood magnificent, serene, dominating operations.

"Papa, I think never you coming from the hospital."

"I've been back almost an hour, talking to Thisbe in my office." He related what had happened.

"Shame his eye," Loki said, giving a lusty Polynesian version of a Bronx cheer. "But I like swell to have the marry in my garden. Then every peoples can see our girl, not only some-few who can catch seats inside church—after all the proud *haoles* have sit down. *Takeshi—*" She sent her voice out in a long clear hail. He came running. "Gets kids and tell to everybodys here Thisbe marry Mamo and Liholiho under the trees. Church too small for big marry like this."

"Okay, Loki-san."

"April—" Loki glanced around.

"I'm here with Sabrina finishing Mamo's bouquet," she called from behind a screen of palms.

Loki told her the change of plans, then said, "Go call Central, please, April, and tell her to phone every peoples who not here."

"Where you think the most-best place for have the marry, Papa?" Loki asked, eyeing the garden.

"You choose the spot," he smiled.

"I think good under the flame tree. Mamo show up fine in her white 'lress with all that *ulaula* behind." Loki slid her arm through Kauka's. "Come, us go look."

They crossed the lawn, pausing to talk with someone every few yards, then proceeded on their way with placid majesty.

"Yes, this good," Loki asserted when they reached the flame tree. She gazed at the glory of color overhead, then at green grass studded with vermilion blossoms which kept drifting down. Then they headed for the slope of the garden where low flower-laden tables were arranged in the cool green gloom of old trees. On a slight rise the bridal table, set cross-wise so as to be visible to everyone, was flanked by red and yellow feather *kahilis*. In their shadow was spread the *Makaloa Mat,* handed down in the family through generations.

"Soon our girl sit here with her *kane.*" Loki gazed thoughtfully at the beautifully woven square of rare grasses.

Making their satisfied, unhurried way back to the house, they headed for the kitchen. On a table pulled into the middle of the room was a four-tiered cake, a yard across. White gardenias, surrounding it, looked like part of the frosting.

"You smart like hell, Ching," Loki told him.

"I work four days." He circled the table, eyeing his handiwork pridefully.

Liholiho and Thord came across the lawn.

"Well, here the happy bridegroom!" Loki held out her arms.

Liholiho embraced her.

"What you think of Ching's cake?" Loki asked, waving at it.

[237]

"Gosh!" Liholiho gasped, surveying it, awed.

"You think 'nuff big?" Ching asked, his eyes crinkling.

"I could eat it all myself," Liholiho asserted.

"If you eat all, you look velly, velly fat—then everybody think you and not Mamo have baby," the cook retorted.

Liholiho's laughter rang out. Then suddenly he grew sober. "Mama, my heart's beating so hard I can't breathe."

"Better drink little whisky. That let-you-go inside," Loki said blithely. "You too, Thord. Your face got tight look. Some-kind *pilikea?*"

"Dale's driving me and himself nuts, trying to remember where he's seen me. In time he'll recall that stink in the papers, the four write-ups, my pictures on the front page."

Loki thought swiftly, then smiled roguishly. "I fix him up, for today anyway. When he come with Hiram and Elsbeth I make a big fuss over him and give him big jolt of *oke.* Then, quick, one more—more strong. Then I tell to Maile and Lehua to make more big fuss over him. They pretty and good fun. Soon he forgetting about you, and might-be, April too." She gave him a gay push. "Now you boys go *wikiwiki,* have your *ino,* and get into the marry clothes. In one more hour you be my son, Liholiho."

He threw his arm about her shoulders, gave her a happy shake and charged off. Kauka looked after him, then laid his hand on Thord's arm. "How's Tutu?"

"The nausea's bad. I told Moku to discontinue giving her the oil until you've seen her tomorrow and checked her symptoms."

"Good boy—*mahalo.*"

While the men dressed, Loki went out for a last survey of everything. The long green tables were covered with layers and layers of ferns thickly dotted with ruffly hibiscus blossoms and fragrant gardenias and ginger *Imus* lined with heated stones covered with banana and *ti* leaves were packed tight with food. Large, kindly Hawaiian women and deliberate noble men moved about, attending to last-minute details. Striplings lounging over guitars supplied unending music. Children played tag. The rambling old house had assumed a greater dignity and the wide driveway, shaded by royal palms, swept from the highway to the steps with a flourish. Grandparents, with bright and eager eyes set in wrinkled faces, looked on.

"April," Mamo confessed as they stood together in her room, "my knees are shaking so hard, I'm afraid I'll fall down on the grass and spoil my wedding dress."

"Take a deep breath, and stand still while I pin your veil." With slightly shaky fingers April slid hairpins home, then stepped back. "Don't look in the mirror till I'm *pau*," she begged.

"I won't."

Darting to the bed, April picked up a coronet of gardenias and set it carefully in place. Then she lifted the huge white carnation lei which older women had made with exquisite skill and dropped it about Mamo's neck, lifting up the long veil to float over it. "Now, your bouquet," she said, placing it on Mamo's arm. For an instant they gazed at each other with wet eyes, then Mamo cried, "Can I look now?"

"Yes."

Turning, she gazed at her reflection. "That isn't—me," she gasped in a voice delirious with pleasure. "I look like a—movie queen. Oh, Mama, come and *look!*" Her voice slid up an octave. "Oh, get Mama, April!" she begged.

April went to the door. Loki was just coming in.

"Mamo! Never in my lifes I see anyone so pretty." She swept forward, then stopped. "No, Liholiho must be the first to kiss you in your wedding dress."

Dashing happy tears from her eyes, Loki rushed to the door. "Papa, Papa, come see our Mamo!"

Kauka came in. "My little girl," he said solemnly. "You're as beautiful as the snow on Mauna Kea."

"Oh, Papa, thank you for the dress and the veil and the shoes." She pointed to each item excitedly.

Bridesmaids were assembled, whispering, arranging flowers about their necks and on their heads. Loki went to look them over.

"Never I seeing so many pretty girls," she exulted. "Prue, you look nice like any-kind." She gave her cheek an approving pat.

The men came out of the dining room. Loki sailed up, gauged

Brewer's eyes, then announced, "No drink too much before the kids marry up safe. After wedding and *luau* start, I no care if you pass out. Remember, this time you marry-guy, Brewer. Okay if you make little rascals, but not big hell like before."

"I'm treading a chalked line, Loki. A fellow's got to make concessions when he's got a wife." He smiled at Prudence.

"Brewer, you okay!" Loki announced.

After several false starts and much milling around, punctuated by cascades of smothered giggles from the bridesmaids, the procession got organized and started across the lawn. Cheers greeted it.

Thisbe waited under the flame tree, a stiff incongruous figure. Sunlight lacquered his almost bald head; his sparse, ginger-colored hair moved about in a disconsolate fashion as light breezes played through it. His hands, holding the prayer book, shook; his eyes slid restlessly along the line of bridesmaids, found his daughter, and dropped.

Thord and Liholiho stood together, red head and black one on a level. Behind them, handsome young groomsmen clustered. Prominent whites occupied positions with unobstructed views. Behind them clustered plantation laborers who had known Kauka's love and kindness for twenty-eight years.

The wedding party arranged itself, red blossoms drifted earthwards, a yellow butterfly sailed past. Then Thisbe began speaking the words of the wedding ceremony. Liholiho and Thord moved forward, Kauka advanced with Mamo.

Some immortal quality wrapped them as they stood tall and straight, repeating the words that united them. The ring was slipped home. Bending, Liholiho kissed it. Mamo bent impulsively and brushed his hair with her lips. Then they straightened up. Their eyes met, and held.

"For better, for worse . . . in sickness and in . . . health . . . for richer, for poorer . . . till death do us part . . ."

The words echoed off into the future.

25

THROUGH the rainbow-glinting prisms of tears, April gazed at Mamo and Liholiho standing together, man and wife. They held themselves with the stance of *aliis*—chiefs, backs flat, heads high. Then they went tightly into each other's arms.

When the tumultuous congratulations were over, bride and groom headed for a grove of mango trees in the rear of the house, where men were beginning to shovel soil off faintly steaming spots on the ground. Kauka took Sabrina's arm, Loki took Dale's.

"Now, Papa and I show to you New York guys how Hawaiians cooking food for *luau*," Loki said in a way that singled them out from everyone else present for the honor.

April's eyes met Thord's, then she fell into step beside Dale. His face, which had been wooden, lighted a little.

"Maid of Honor deserting the Best Man—for me?" he inquired, making his voice flippant.

April nodded. Dale was watching her in an odd, speculative way that filled her with misgiving. For the past two days he had made the gestures demanded of a well-bred man, but she had had the impression that his brain was shuttling back and forth incessantly, trying to find the real motive behind her decision not to marry him. She had a confusing impression that some momentous event was getting closer and closer, like a great pendulum swinging wider and wider, on a vast, steadily increasing arc. When it swung out far enough to contact what it sought . . . She swallowed against the tension of her throat and moisture dampened her skin.

Reaching the grove of mango trees, everyone halted. Young men were shoveling soil aside, then they began peeling back gunnysacks, like layers of wrinkled brown skin, and tossing them aside. Next they removed banana and *ti* leaves, limp from heat. Their work over, the youngsters stepped back, and older men came forward carrying buckets of water.

"Look hard, no miss any-kind," Loki cautioned.

Squatting down, the old men began to snatch hot black rocks out of the pits. After picking up each one deftly and swiftly, they plunged their hands into the water, moving as if engaged in some holy rite. Men and women of all nationalities, who were self-appointed servers, began swarming up with wooden platters.

Hogs, cooked to the last instant of perfection, were slipped onto huge containers shaped to fit them, then flanked with golden sweet potatoes. Breadfruit, bananas, *laulaus* of fish and salt pork, neatly tied up in flat packages of *ti* leaves, were stacked on smaller platters and hurried triumphantly to the long low tables under the trees.

"It smells marvelous," Sabrina cried, sniffing avidly.

"Wait till you eat," Loki said, looking from Sabrina to Dale.

He smiled mechanically, but his eyes were fixed thoughtfully and intently on Thord, standing with Liholiho and Mamo on the opposite side of the still steaming pit. As if aware of Dale's mind upon him, Thord glanced up.

"Blast it!" Dale said violently, "I'll never rest until I can place where I've seen you."

A chill ran over April. Loki raised her long lashes and her eyes swept Dale like a wary animal's sensing danger. Then she adjusted the feather lei on her head and said, "Sha, who care? Come, us all go inside and have marry drink for good lucks for our boy and girl. Then us eat big feast and make plenty fun. Come, Hiram, Elsbeth, Brewer, and all you fellas."

She instructed older Hawaiian women, acting as hostesses, to get the main body of the guests seated, then started for the house. The big round table in the dining room had been massed with gardenias arranged around a nest of sparkling glasses. Carlos and Takeshi, in starched white breeches and shirts, began serving. Carlos poured liberal measures of *okolehao* into the tumblers and Takeshi filled them with cocoanut milk.

Mamo and Liholiho, with locked arms and radiant faces, came forward. Kauka raised his glass.

"May your lives be long and happy, your children many," he said solemnly.

Glasses were raised, the toast drunk. Loki glanced around.

"Where Thisbe?" she demanded. "Why he not drinking with us?"

"He won't drink. He's a Rev, Loki," Brewer boomed. "To the bride and groom. Whoops!"

"Okay, now us eat." Loki smacked her lips.

"Gosh, that *oke's* strong," Dale gasped, replacing his empty glass among the flowers.

"I sign to Carlos make extra-special drink for you, Dale." Loki's eyelashes fluttered. "You my New York sweetheart today." Linking her arm through his, she started down the hall.

Thord glanced at April.

"Where is this day taking us?" she asked under her breath.

"God knows. My one prayer is that Mamo and Liholiho get away before anything happens to spoil it. I've a hunch Dale's instinct tells him there's more to your backing out of your engagement than just leaving Kona."

"He can't suspect—about us. We've hardly spoken a hundred words to each other during the past week."

"Possibly we've overdone that end of it."

"I'll remedy that," April said, taking his arm in a quick, glad way.

They followed the bridal party across the green lawn. With a flourish, Loki waved Liholiho and Mamo toward the head of the table. Awed, they seated themselves on the *Makaloa Mat* and gazed up at the feather *kahilis* set up in a semi-circle about them. Then Mamo lifted her huge white lei and Liholiho ducked his head into it. As they sat, linked together with blossoms, Liholiho's *paniolos* appeared from behind the thickets of bamboo, chanting the family hula, with two new lauding verses added to it for the bride and groom.

Guitars resounded in unison with deep resonant voices. When the hula ended, musical instruments were laid aside and the men went loping down the tables to find places beside friends. April found herself seated between Dale and Thord. Opposite were Loki and Kauka, her father and mother, Thisbe, and other *haoles*.

The table was on a slight rise, dominating the garden. Pungent ferns and flowers strewn about sent up a heady fragrance, mingling with the scent of hot savory food. At intervals down the table, hogs steamed; calabashes of *poi*, faintly lavender and temptingly cool, were set at the right of each guest. Pink crystals of sea-salt, beautifully mixed with sections of tomato, onion, and salmon, filled tiny containers. Garnet-red dried shrimps, butter yellow *opihis*, chickens stewed in cocoanut milk, glossy seaweed, dark rich cubes of *kulolo*— (like sections of plum pudding)—and semi-transparent slices of *haupai*, lavishly heaped mangoes, pineapples, freckled hands of bananas, sent up their perfumes. Musicians who had eaten the first round took up·instruments discarded by hungry *paniolos*, and began singing.

Guests called for favorite songs which were gaily supplied. Platters and bowls were refilled, people made speeches. The afternoon began sliding into evening. When the tempo of feasting began to slack a little, Loki sat up, adjusted the angle of her feather lei, and clapped her hands sharply three times. Silence, sudden and astounding, fell on the garden.

Hidden drums began beating. Steadily, without haste, the sound increased, swelling deliberately toward a sustained crescendo. Behind the sonorous reverberation, men seated cross-legged on the lawn began a monotonous chanting. The drums took on a deeper tone, as if summoning up the life force lodged in the earth. Voices rose to a higher pitch. On and on, faster and louder, the steady pounding continued like an endless procession of marching feet passing invisibly through the garden. Individuals seemed to melt into insignificance beside the solemn sound.

Then through the grove of breadfruit trees a dancer appeared, quickly followed by another and another, until twelve girls with unbound hair and flowers about their throats, wrists, and ankles began swaying in unison on the lawn. The slow undulations of their bodies, the liquid gestures of hands and arms, symbolized the up-welling spirit of a lavishly rich universe.

Mamo and Liholiho watched with shining eyes and rapt faces.

Subtle wrists and proudly moving feet of the dancers spoke of hills and water, clouds and rainbows and the unseen spirits animating them. Behind men's and women's chanting voices, the drums spoke in an older, stronger tongue. Flaming red and orange in the west duplicated the colors of the *kahilis* standing on guard against the tangled green. And still the music pulsed, fiercely, passionately, with a command echoing down the corridors of the ages.

On . . . on . . . on.

April was swept by the sound. The drums seemed to be inside her, shaking her to pieces. On . . . on . . . on. Nothing could halt or interrupt the command.

On . . . on . . . on. The great ultimatum resounded. Twilight died and dark rushed in from the seas. Torches, tied to the flower-wreathed trunks of trees, were lighted. Then gradually the drums lessened, dancers began vanishing like spirits retreating into fastnesses from which they had emerged to counsel and sustain mortals for a while.

April was vividly conscious of Thord sitting beside her. Something strong and clean, lawless and passionate, kin to the great forces imprisoned in the earth, was rising in her nature to clasp a similar force in him, which it answered without shame. After an instant she raised her lashes and gazed into Thord's eyes.

Then, dimly, as though from a vast distance, she was aware of Loki's eyes, commanding her from across the table. "*Malama*—be careful!" they warned.

The last dancer disappeared, the drums stopped.

"That jars a person loose from himself," Dale observed in an odd voice.

"Now us wedding fellas go and dance," Loki announced. "And, Mamo, cut Ching's cake. You"—she faced the long table—"stay all

[245]

night and have jolly fun. Plenty more *kaukau,* plenty music. *Hemo-ka-paa'u!"*

Shouts of agreement answered her.

Mamo and Liholiho rose and waved to the seated hundreds. "Aloha—love to you!" they called.

"Aloha—love to you!" came back like a vast echo.

"Have I your first, April?" Dale asked, when they reached the lighted *lanai* where musicians were tuning up. "Or does it belong to the Best Man?" He stressed the words slightly.

"Of course it's yours, Dale."

"Okay with you, Graham?" he asked unnecessarily.

"Of course, you have prior claim."

Dale took her arm and started toward the house. "I want to talk to you before the evening's over," he said.

"After Liholiho and Mamo have gone."

"There are a couple of points that have got to be cleared up before I go." His words sounded like stones being dropped into icy water.

April gave a quick nod and fled up the steps onto the dance floor. Couples were already out. Loki was waltzing roguishly with Kauka while her eyes followed Mamo and Liholiho moving with tall grace about the floor. Brewer was dancing boisterously with one of the bridesmaids, Prudence with one of the groomsmen. Thisbe's face, from the sidelines, oozed futile condemnation for everything.

Dale led April out. She tried to talk in a vein to match the gaiety of the occasion, but some inner part of her was tense and waiting.

When the dance ended, Loki called out, "Now us go and see Mamo cut the cake and have us another drink."

Mamo and Liholiho led the way down the hall. The cake was in the center of the round table, surrounded by seas of gardenias. Ching hovered near-by, his slanted eyes glittering with pride. Then solemnly he presented Mamo with an immense butcher knife, whose handle was tied with a bow of white ribbon.

April, closely attended by Dale, signed at Carlos and Takeshi, waiting importantly in the background. They smiled and vanished, reappearing with ice-filled buckets cradling quarts of champagne.

"April! Champagne!" everyone chorused.

"That's Dad's and my surprise," she announced, her eyes harriedly finding her father's.

"Oh, *Haole Hao,* how nice of you!" Mamo cried.

"Mahalo nui loa, Hiram," Liholiho said; then crossing to where April stood, he kissed her.

"Cut the cake with the family 'sword,' " Elsbeth directed.

April flashed a pleased smile at her mother, whose face was faintly pink from excitement.

When the cake had been passed around and glasses filled with the pale amber, sparkling wine, Kauka raised his hand.

"To our boy and girl, and to our dear friends—Aloha," he said simply.

"Never I seeing one wedding so swell," Loki exulted. "Come *Hemo ka paa'u*—pull off the skirt! Make big fun. Never minds if some peoples get little *ona*. That wedding styles and okay when fellas make a big marry." Tossing off her champagne, she held out her glass to be refilled.

"Them's my sentiments, Loki!" Brewer bellowed. "Fill 'er up, Carlos!" He brandished his glass. "Hey, where's that father-in-law of mine?" He looked about with bloodshot eyes.

Thisbe, standing at the opposite side of the table, gingerly sipping champagne, went chalk white.

"Come on, Rev," Brewer urged noisily, "down your drink and get that Christianity of yours working. Now's the time to bury the hatchet. On a festive occasion such as this—"

"You're drunk," Thisbe said.

"Yes, and I'm going to get a damn sight drunker before the night's over!"

"Easy, Brewer," Loki cautioned.

"At least I'm no damn hypocrite, looking down at my fellow-men."

Thisbe stalked from the room.

"Go make little talk with him, Papa," Loki begged.

"It's no use," Kauka said, a trifle heavily.

"I'll talk to him," Hiram announced.

"Good on you, *Haole Hao*. No sense for fellas to stay mad in small place like Kona."

Hiram stalked off, his shoulders determined.

The music started and flowed through the house like rich honey.

"My dance," Thord said, coming over to where April stood.

People began pouring down the hall.

Thord led April onto the floor already crowded with young and old. April half closed her eyes. Her lids felt heavy and a curious magic stole through her limbs. Depths in her stirred, filling her brain with swimming sweetness.

Behind the tumult of music and voices, filling the house and garden, she heard the sound of wind pouring through the sky. A hunger to get out of doors swept her. She wanted the stars and moon instead of a roof over her, to get close to the invisible forces peopling the night. Her fingers tightened against Thord's back.

"What is it?" he asked.

"I love you," she murmured. "Dale's indoors with Loki. I wonder if we dare risk making a dash into the garden for a few minutes?"

Thord danced toward the steps. A big mirror on the wall snatched up their reflection as they danced, framing them like a picture. Then they were out of the gilt square, like painted figures impossibly escaping from a canvas.

They reached the steps, ran down into the great beauty of the night. Taking hold of her arm, Thord started off across the lawn. Merrymakers were still seated at the table, eating, laughing, visiting.

He headed for the bottom of the garden. Below, the faint silver sea moved mysteriously in the moonlight. He caught April's hand tightly into his own, pressing his palm against hers fiercely.

"I'm kissing you, April," he said.

"I am too," she answered.

"Instinct tells me hell's ahead," Thord said.

"I feel it too—but I'm not afraid."

Thord looked around him, then down at April. "God," he said, "a few months ago I never dreamed I'd feel like this. I, who was an outcast, stand here with a girl like you, loving me. I have a family, a home, a drive inside me to achieve something big and constructive."

April stood motionless, her eyes fixed on his face.

"Nothing else matters now, does it?" she asked.

"Nothing."

The breeze dropped, and they stood like figures carved out of the night.

"We better go in," Thord said finally.

Dale was waiting at the steps.

"Mamo and Liholiho are getting ready to go," he announced.

"I must help Mamo to change into her riding clothes, and you must go to Liholiho," April said hurriedly, heading for the hall. "Dale's bursting," she whispered when they were out of earshot.

"He looks as if he had enough dynamite in him to blow Kona to pieces," Thord agreed grimly.

"Steer clear of him," April begged.

Thord made no answer, but started for Liholiho's room, which was echoing with hearty male voices. April went to Mamo's.

She was already dressed in riding clothes, with a fresh lei of white carnations about her throat. Bridal finery was strewn across the bed, and her bridesmaids hovered about watching her with a new look in their eyes. She no longer belonged to the company of girlhood; she was a married woman going off with her man. They kissed her, then followed her to the *lanai*. Liholiho was waiting at the steps, his face and eyes highlighted with excitement. Below, *paniolos* waited, holding two horses decked with flowers.

"We must have another drink," Kauka asserted. Benevolence and happiness poured from him.

"Papa, I think you little bit *ona!*" Loki accused in delighted tones.

"Little bit, Mama," he admitted. "But Mamo only married once!"

Loki threw an affectionate arm about his shoulders and shouted, "Carlos! Takeshi!—*ino!*"

"Well, old man," Thord said, grasping Liholiho's shoulder, "all the luck in the world to you and Mamo."

"*Mahalo!*" he said. "We'll come down and see you all next Saturday."

His eyes went to Mamo's, and Thord appreciated that the supreme adventure for man is woman, and for woman, man. Dale moved to where April stood.

"When they're gone—"

"I'm too tired to talk to you tonight," she said in an undertone. "Let's go riding early tomorrow."

"Very well."

The drinks appeared. Kauka took a glass, waited for the guests to be served, then faced Mamo and Liholiho. "May ripe breadfruit load the trees lining the roads you travel, and Lei Alohas always hang over your door!"

Guests drank, surged forward, engulfed the newly married pair. Finally, Loki and Kauka kissed them on their foreheads and they ran down and mounted their horses. *Paniolos* fell back, musicians began to shout a hula, moonlight shone down as the two tall young figures, astride glossy, proudly stepping horses, rode away.

26

APRIL prodded the handle of her riding crop into the moist, hard-packed sand, while she watched iridescent arcs, left by retreating waves, marking the beach. Near-by, their horses waited under some *kiawe* trees.

"Being here with you"—Dale's voice sounded rough and sore—"has changed my slant on myself."

"In what way?" April asked mechanically.

"It's driven home the fact that I'm not much of a fellow."

"Don't go into reverse gear, Dale," she begged. "You're fine and dear and—"

"If I were the sort of chap I imagined myself to be, you'd leave Kona without a backward thought." He ground his heel into the sand.

Light was beginning to spread over the island, edging everything with gold.

"Love can't be commanded," April said.

"Boiled down to essentials, that means I don't stack with you. You want a smashing sort of man, not just an unlimited bank account."

"Oh, Dale, please!" April begged unhappily.

He reminded her of a tall, disconsolate boy suddenly faced with the knowledge of a lack in himself for which Fate, and not he, was responsible. Hurt, smoldering anger, and resentment filled his face, and under his tan he was pale. She stabbed another hole into the sand. The accumulated weariness of the past two weeks weighted her and she wished that the ordeal ahead was safely over.

"In spite of having every material thing a man can want," Dale went on, "I realize my life has missed fire."

"You're only twenty-two. Most is ahead."

"A third's behind me—the part that shaped me, and made me lose you."

April moved unhappily. Growing light fell on her face and figure, emphasizing its soft outlines, its slender delicacy, and the brooding stare in her wide gray eyes.

"During the past three days I've felt as though I've been seized by a ground-swell which I'm not equipped to swim against." Dale paused to light a cigarette impatiently.

"The feeling will pass when you get home to your setup—"

"Dammit, a real fellow doesn't need a specific sort of picture frame," he interrupted. "He stands out in any setting."

April did not contest it. Pushing back her wild, charming hair, she gazed at the green slopes of Kona. "You make me feel as though I'd paid someone who trusted me with counterfeit money," she said finally.

"In a way, haven't you?" Dale asked. "You led me to believe that you loved me. I came out here only to find that you don't." His eyes found hers and held them.

"When I was in New York, I didn't know what love was—" she began, then checked herself abruptly.

"Does that mean that you know—now?" he asked. His fine mood of a few moments before had slipped from him and was replaced by something watchful and crafty.

April sat feeling like a wild creature trapped by a vast, invisible snare. Dale's face had an odd expression on it, as if he too were aware of the undertow of some great tide, resuming itself into the ocean, taking them both with it.

"Why do you ask that?"

She jabbed another hole into the sand.

"Shall I be honest?"

"Yes." Her eyes met his squarely.

"I've a hunch you're gone on Graham," Dale announced bluntly. "Actually I haven't much to substantiate the supposition, but straws show which way the wind blows. I saw you looking at him last night when the drum-hula was ending. Then you both slipped off—"

"You're being perfectly fantastic," April said, while she thought frantically, Why do people have to lie? It makes you feel dingy! Then she went on, "I'm devoted to Thord. He's sort of snapped Mother out of herself, he's been a lifesaver for Kauka, and he fits into Kona as if he'd always been with us."

Dale's lips tightened. "As well, he's damnably handsome and magnetic," he added.

April gazed at the sea. The fierce color seemed to sound a reveille, reaching to the uttermost corners of the earth.

"Yes, he is," she agreed. "But so are lots of other men. I can't begin to tell you how badly I feel about us. But you'll find some other girl who'll fit into your picture better than I ever could have."

"Stop hedging."

"I'm not hedging," she insisted, while her mind wrung its hands. "I'm trying to make you see—"

"Exactly—what?"

"I don't know. I'm all mixed up, tied in knots inside. I hate to hurt people, especially those who love me. I wish you didn't. I wish I'd do something perfectly horrid so you'd hate me."

"Why? So you could feel square with yourself and be free to do as you please—after I've cleared out?"

"Don't be nasty, Dale."

"It's human instinct to strike back when you're hurt. You've cut me to the bone. I could strangle this damn island, or whatever's changed you, *got you*."

His eyes challenged hers.

The instinct for self-preservation, for protecting Thord, clutched her. She must move and speak with caution. The slightest word or incident might throw her into hysterical laughter or tears. Slowly, as if the entire future depended on it, she poked another hole into the sand with her riding crop.

"Time'll prove that it's Hawaii that's holding me," she said.

"We'll see."

"We're getting nowhere—let's go home," she suggested. "Would you prefer to have me wait till you're gone before telling Mother and Dad that we're not going to be married?"

"If they have any observation at all, I should think that that would be self-evident. Your behavior since my arrival, for an engaged girl—" He broke off.

"Oh, Dale, I'm so desperately sorry," she said.

He made no answer. April poked at the sand again. I'm terrified, she thought; I can't stand this. In another minute I'll go all to pieces. And I mustn't. I'm fighting to safeguard Thord's future, and my own. I'll lie, cheat, do almost anything to get over this bump.

"It doesn't actually matter what's robbed me of you, April. The fact remains that I've been robbed. That's burning holes in me. I'd be a poor sort of a man if I didn't want to fight back. Despite your denials, I'm convinced that there's something between you and that red-headed Doc. Blast him!"

April stared at the toe of her riding boot. The hammering of her heart made thinking difficult. Then she saw with icy horror that the holes she'd been punching into the sand had a definite pattern. While she had been talking she'd been automatically stabbing the name of the man she loved into the beach. Thord . . . Thord . . . Thord. With a swift movement of her foot, she passed sand over them. Dale looked down. The deep punctures had not been entirely obliterated. With a slow deliberation he bent over, brushed the sand from each hole, then straightening up, faced her.

"Well," he announced, "you tell me with your lips you don't love him, but your mind branded his name into the sand while you tried to mislead me."

He stared at her in a way that made her feel limp and breathless. She moved as if resisting some mighty force which was sucking her into a whirlpool.

"Why don't you say something?" Dale asked.

"There's no sense in saying anything, now."

"Then you admit that you love Graham?"

"Yes."

"Why did you lie to me about it?"

"I suppose to spare your feelings."

Dale stared at the name prodded into the sand. Suddenly his figure tensed. "Wait—wait a minute!" he commanded. "Don't move, don't speak to me. It's coming! Thord . . . Thord. I haven't met him—*I've seen his name in print!* Thord Graham . . . Doctor . . . Thord . . . Graham." Snatching up the crop, he printed the name in the sand.

April watched like a person under a spell.

"Doctor . . . Thord . . . Graham." Dale pronounced the name slowly, then leaped to his feet. "I remember! There was a foul mess in the New York courts a while back about some doctor who was on trial for illegal practices. The girl died. The case made big headlines in the papers for weeks. Because of pull with some specialist, Graham wasn't convicted of manslaughter, but was barred from ever practicing medicine again in the State of New York. I'll bet everything I have this is the chap!"

Slowly April tore her handkerchief in two. Dale indicated it. "That, and the rest of it adds up," he said hotly. He grasped her by the shoulders. The expression on his face shocked her. "Graham never showed the least eagerness to know where we might have met. Of course, under the circumstances, he wouldn't give me any leads. Look—"

"You're not telling me anything that I don't already know," April said.

"You mean you have the confidence of that mucker?" Dale looked at her, his face a dull crimson. "Of course, a cad like that would try to worm his way into your affections, with doubtless an eye on your father's pocketbook."

"If I were a man, I'd knock you down for that," April said furiously. "Thord didn't worm his way into my affections. It just happened to us—both."

"Does your father know about Graham's past?"

"No, but Kauka does, and—"

"The ethics and morals of tropical races are known to be sketchy," Dale said disgustedly.

"Dale, listen—"

"I know what you're going to ask me—not to give the mucker away." He hurled the words from him.

"Yes. What good will it do you to mess up Thord's life?"

"He messed up mine."

"Not intentionally. You'll go away—you'll get over—me. You have everything; you're safeguarded, as I am, by money."

"So what?"

"Thord was headed for great things in New York; then overnight his career was blasted into bits. He came away, started from the bottom again—"

"Gutter, you mean—"

"No! Surely your sense of sportsmanship—"

"Sportsmanship has nothing to do with a matter of this sort. I love you—"

She gestured, stopping him. "I wonder if you do."

"You know I do. Forget Graham—get him out of your system. Come to New York for a bit, on a visit as a starter. In time—"

"It isn't like that. I can't marry you, now."

"Well, I can prevent your marrying him. Good God—"

"If you blast Thord's chances here, I'll—"

"Look," Dale interrupted. "I'll make a bargain with you. I won't spill the beggar's beans unless you become engaged to him, or marry him. I know your mother's sold on him because he's a Doc. Your father thinks highly of him too. I'd buck my sister marrying a man with his record, and I'm going to buck your doing it too. I'm doing this for your eventual good, April. Some day you'll thank me for it. Steer clear of Graham, and I'll keep mum."

The sea gave a long sigh and flopped a tired wave on the sand. Bending over, April picked up her crop, dropped her torn handkerchief which whirled away toward the water, and started for the horse. Dale strode after her.

"I know you're mentally labeling me a dog-in-the-manger."

"Aren't you?"

"Possibly. But it rests with you entirely whether or not Graham's past remains under cover, and whether he stays in Kona."

27

WITH Dale and Sabrina gone and Mamo and Liholiho married, Kona settled back into its accustomed groove. Summer slid into the thrilling autumn of the sub-tropics. Mountains were saturated with mystery, clouds held spectacular conferences on the foreheads of volcanoes and above the sea, warning each other about Kona storms lurking below the horizon.

The mill, after rumbling continuously for months, became still. Squat, important, little Inter-Island steamers stopped at Kailua once a week to take on brown sugar bags stacking the wharf almost to the roof. Macadamian nuts were harvested, coffee picked, washed of the pulpy berries, and the kernels set out in the sun to dry. From corrugated iron sheds, from wooden trays, from rooftops, the fragrance drifted upward to mingle with the scent of strongly growing forests and the smell of fat cattle.

On week-ends, Mamo and Liholiho rode down from the ranch. April occupied herself with home and district activities, spiked up by frequent visits to Kauka's. Kauka and Thord made the daily round of hospital and outside calls, plus secret expeditions to treat Tutu.

One afternoon, as Loki rocked in the *lanai,* April rode in. Takeshi took her horse.

"Swell you come," Loki said. "I too happy Mamo and Liholiho marry up, but not got enough laughs in this house now. Always Papa and Thord working and thinking hard in the head."

April seated herself beside Loki's big knee and gazed at glimpses of blue sea showing between brown tree trunks.

"This time you more quiet, too. You got some troubles in your heart?"

April moved as if shrugging a distasteful garment from her shoulders. "I've decided not to marry Dale."

"That sound swell to my ears," said Loki delightedly. "Hiram and Elsbeth know yet?"

"I told them today."

"They all burn ups?"

"Mother's delighted." Faint color tinged April's neck. "Dad is too, though he probably winced inside at the thought of me passing up all the Hancock wealth."

"One more fella got big glads in the heart," Loki announced. "Always Thord got deep loves in his eyes for you, April. Thord our boy now. Swell if you two get hitch."

"I can't marry him, Loki." She told of Dale's ultimatum.

"Dale make this-kind?" Loki asked indignantly.

April nodded. "It'll be impossible for Thord and me to marry—ever."

"For why?" Loki demanded.

"Of course, we could go away," April conceded. "But Thord has gone into this chaulmoogra business hook, line, and sinker. He's convinced, in spite of the fact that Tutu's failing, that if she'd had the oil during the early stages of the disease, it might have been arrested."

"Yes," Loki agreed. "Always Kauka and Thord talking this-kind stuff. Papa not so young now, and Thord smart like any-kind for making new mix with the oil."

April's eyes met Loki's. "The blind alley Thord and I are in is nothing compared to the agony leprosy's caused, and will cause until a cure is found. So—" She made a slight eloquent gesture.

"You have tell to Thord the dirty-kind Dale saying?"

April shook her head.

"I guess better not. Only make Thord mad like hell. Sha on Dale! I like to give him big swift kick." She sat lost in thought, then went on in her unhurried way. "Might-be if after by-and-by Papa and Thord finding cure for *maipake,* this business about what-

[258]

kind Dale saying not matter much. Every peoples will have such a big happy in the hearts they not caring for anything else. Papa and Thord be big shots then, and Dale only little—" Uttering a Hawaiian word of complete contempt, she burst into uplifting laughter.

April smiled involuntarily.

"I think best, April, us fellas not thinking too much, just trust God. Plenty times when people no can see a way out of *pilikeas,* God fix them up." She gazed at the sun moving across the sky, at the fruitful island, at the sea forever flowing and ebbing with unvarying rhythm, obeying commands which had set them in motion when the world was assembled. "I only big fat Hawaiians womans, April, but when I look at that"—she gestured about her—"I knowing lifes not just big accident."

"You make me feel ashamed, Loki."

"No sense feel ashamed. Natural kinds when peoples young, they want to love and marry quick. I think good idea if you stop and eat with us tonight. Big hula moon. Might-be you and Thord walk little whiles in my garden."

Reaching out, April held Loki's hand to her hot cheek.

They were still in the *lanai* when Kauka and Thord drove in.

"Some-kind bad happen, Papa?" Loki asked when the two men came up the steps.

"Tutu died this afternoon."

"I too sorry." Loki wiped her eyes. "But that lifes. Young people get marry, love, and have kids. Old people die. Already Tutu bury?"

"Not yet. If we could have got her in the early stages—" He launched into technical details, while Thord possessed himself of April's hand.

"What you going to do, now you not got Tutu for try the oil on?" Loki asked, when Kauka stopped talking.

Kauka chewed his cigar. "There are other lepers hidden in valleys in the Kohala mountains."

"Oh, Papa, please no make fool with them now," Loki begged. "I got hunches Mamo going to have a baby. Might-be when she and Liholiho come down tomorrow they telling us the fine news. Bad shame for Mamo's kid if you get catch and send to jail."

"I won't do anything for a while," Kauka promised.

"You my same old sweetheart," Loki exclaimed.

"Eating with us, April?" Thord asked.

She nodded brightly.

"We've changed, disinfected, before we came home," he said, bending and kissing her temple.

"Are you and Kauka going to bury Tutu tonight?" April asked, catching her breath.

"Yes. No time must be lost."

April gave a violent shiver. "I get all sunk inside when I realize what you're both doing."

Thord tousled her hair. "Many of the world's finest deeds look cockeyed to onlookers."

Next evening when Mamo and Liholiho rode in, the four of them were in the *lanai*. April laid aside the guitar she'd been strumming. Thord threw away his cigarette. Loki and Kauka's eyes leaped together. Some indefinable air of excitement enveloped the tall pair dismounting from warm horses.

"Bet-you-my-lifes I telling you true yesterday, Papa," Loki said under her breath.

Liholiho fastened the horses to a tree, took Mamo's hand, and they ran up the steps.

"Oh, Mama! Papa!" Mamo cried, her voice singing upward. "We're going to have a little baby!"

After the embraces and happy tears, with which Polynesians greet the news of a child-to-be were over, Loki turned to April.

"Tell to Ching and Mitsu our big news," she directed, "so they fix some-kind extra good for dinner."

"Okay," April said, starting off.

When she returned she seated herself on the *puune* beside Thord.

"I think," Mamo glanced up, and her red lips were as fascinating as the voice that came through them, "that our baby will be born in—" Pausing, she did some finger-checking, then finished on a triumphant note, "In—April, so you must be godmother."

"Oh, *Mamo!*" April squealed.

"And you"—Liholiho clapped Thord on the shoulder—"must be godfather."

"With Homer," Mamo put in, an anxious melting tone in her voice. "Just because he had to go away doesn't mean we should forget him. When he comes back from Yale a lawyer, he'll be proud and happy to know that our child will look to him for advice as it grows up."

Liholiho did not answer. There was a heavy brooding silence. Then, straightening his suddenly slumped shoulders, he said, "Of course, I shall write and tell him."

Getting to his feet he walked down the steps, saying over his shoulder, "I must unsaddle the horses. In our great happiness I had forgotten—" Without troubling to finish the sentence, he vanished into the dark.

"I cannot understand. Always when I mention Homer's name, Liholiho looks as if a knife is stuck into him." Mamo's voice was wounded.

"I think Liholiho feel a big sad because Homer going to that old uncle he never see yet, instead of staying for your marry," Loki said. "But after little whiles Liholiho sad be all *pau*."

"I have tried to talk about Homer to him, but he won't talk, and Homer never writes."

"Might-be they have big fight about something, and that why Homer go off so quick. Even best friends get *huhu* with each other sometimes, but good friends not stay *huhu* for always. Better you forget all this things. Not good for womans to be sad when they going to have a little baby."

Mamo nodded, then with deliberate grace unpinned her hair and shook it down, as Polynesian women do when they're at home.

That night after everyone had retired Thord heard Kauka moving restlessly about in the office. For a while he listened to the pad of bare feet, stopping, pacing again. He stifled the impulse to join him, then surrendered to it. The night was heavy and oppressive. Then he heard thunder muttering about the summit of Mauna Loa. Throwing his legs over the side of the bed, he headed for the office.

"Sleepless too, my boy?" Kauka asked when the door opened.

"I'm restless as all get-out."

"Because of Mamo, our hands are temporarily tied," Kauka said, "but we cannot stop." Picking up Tutu's case history he studied it. "I shall do nothing for a bit, for Loki's sake, but I have an idea which must be turned over thoroughly before I take any steps."

He began prowling about the room again. The windows flickered with blue ghostly light, and in the distance thunder sounded like the growl of an inarticulate giant.

"The *Akuas* are talking to us," Kauka said. "If only man's ears were right to understand what they are trying to tell us!"

Thord nodded. Kauka stood lost in thought. The windows flickered again like restless eyes, then blanked out as the thunder swelled to a muffled cannonade. From some recess in Thord's mind, Kauka's words, spoken on the morning they had sailed for Kona, returned, "Man possesses a higher intelligence than mere brain power to guide him under stress. Hawaiians call this force *mana*— spirit essence. When your physical brain is not equal to a situation, your *mana* takes command."

"Out of consideration for my womenfolk," Kauka's gentle voice broke the silence, "I must thoroughly inspect the idea that's come to me. When I've digested it, I'll discuss it with you and Loki."

"I'm with you, whatever it is," Thord said warmly.

"My son"—Kauka's deep eyes filled with towering thoughts probed into Thord's—"you and I no longer belong to ourselves. We belong to this work." He indicated Tutu's case history. "All that's deepest in us is pledged to it. But if people discover what we're doing, before we've accomplished anything concrete, jail and disgrace will be our—harvest."

From the distant summit of Mauna Loa thunder sounded continuously, while pale lightning, in waves of cold fire, flooded and ran off the island in swift succession.

For a while, outwardly, life resumed its tranquil flow; then one day Thord knew from the changed expression in Kauka's eyes that he had made his decision.

"I'm going to talk to Loki tonight and I want you present," Kauka said as they drove home from the hospital.

"Okay."

Loki was waiting in her accustomed place.

"There's a matter I want to discuss with you, Mama," Kauka said after kissing her.

"Now?" she asked in a guarded way.

"Yes." Kauka kept hold of her hand.

"Sit down," she urged. "No, I see you all steam-up inside."

"Suppose, Mama, you were given something precious to deliver to the person it belonged to, would you fool around before getting it to them?" Kauka asked.

"No, I take quick."

"That's the situation I'm in, Mama."

Loki's still eyes watched him. "Go on, Papa, I'm listening." She settled herself with an air of attention.

"As you know, I'm convinced we are on the right track in our work with chaulmoogra oil. As you don't wish us to work in secret any more, I must take other steps. If I don't, people may die who otherwise might be cured."

Loki watched him like a person awakened from a drugged spell. "Not Molokai, Papa—"

"Because of you and those I hold dear, Molokai is out, but I want to go to Honolulu and see people on the Research Staff of the Experimental Laboratory. I'm going to ask to be put on the staff—tell them I have some chaulmoogra that Kieser sent me a while back, and show them the article in the paper where Kieser urges that the oil be tried again."

"If they find a place for you, it means we have to go away from Kona?" Loki's dark eyes lifted to his.

"Yes, Mama. Thord can handle the work here alone, as I did before he came."

"When you like to go, Papa?"

[263]

It was obvious she was stunned by the unexpected turn events had taken, but already love and understanding for her husband was pushing aside her own grief at the thought of leaving the locality she loved, her daughter and grandchild-to-be.

"Next week, when the *Kinau* calls again."

"Okay."

"I shall say nothing to Hiram, merely tell him I've been called to Honolulu to attend to matters of our family."

Loki pushed back her hair, and with her forehead uncovered she looked like a large, careworn child.

"That good idea. Then if they not got a place for you, you can come back and work in Kona—till they getting one."

"Exactly. Only I'm hoping—" His head went up like a thirsty horse unexpectedly scenting water.

"I understand how you feeling, Papa, about this things."

"And where do I come into this picture?" Thord asked, looking at Kauka.

"For the time being, if there's a place for me, you'll hold the fort here. I'll keep you abreast with every development. You can work, experimenting with new formulas—" He gestured comprehensively.

"Whatever you say, Kauka."

The following Wednesday found Kauka gone. The house seemed oddly dead without his presence.

"I am tore," Loki confided to Thord the first evening at dinner, "between my own unhappy if I have to go from Kona, and Mamo —and my more big unhappy if Papa no can get on the staff. This oil more important from Mamo, from me, but that right. Papa doctor, and his job to help mans to get well from sicks. If us go away I like you to stop in this house," she said.

"If you do, I shall want to. Even with your things gone, a flavor of you both will remain."

Loki smiled with quick pleasure, but there was a hint of moisture in her eyes. "I have love it very much," she said simply. "But I love Kauka more, and his happy is my jobs."

A week later Kauka arrived unexpectedly, and without sending word to have anyone meet him. Thord and Loki were at breakfast when he walked in.

"Papa!" Loki exclaimed.

He walked to them wearily.

"You have no lucks?" she asked, catching his hand.

"None," he said, bending to kiss her, one affectionate hand going to Thord's shoulder.

"What-kind this guys speaking to you?" Loki asked, clinging to him.

"I was told that the Research Staff of the Experimental Laboratory had its full quota of competent white doctors, better equipped than I am for such work. Even after I told them that I'd been collecting every bit of authentic data dealing with leprosy for years, and that Kieser had sent me some of the Burma chaulmoogra oil, and that I could get more, they explained that after the correct steps were taken and a new appropriation had been made and passed in Washington, study of the oil would get under way."

There was a somber sound in his voice, as though someone he had loved and trusted had betrayed him, and his whole expression was discouraged and weary.

"Red tape, and the ponderous machinery of state seem of more importance than possibly saving people who are dying, or may die in the meantime, because of delays." Pulling out a chair, Kauka sat down.

Loki took his hand into her plump tapered fingers. Her eyes, deep, observing, kindly, gazed at her husband from under the arches of her courageous brows. Then her free hand stole up slowly to her opulent breast, as if to compress, or make less loud the beating of her heart.

"Papa, the oil is too strong for me," she said slowly. "You two fellas"—her eyes brushed Thord—"make any-kind you thinking best."

28

IKE all Polynesian women, Mamo had the gift of being able to rest men and to make them happy in simple ways. Without altering the arrangement of the Kahala Ranch House, she made it overflow with rich, restful warmth, dashed with fun and gaiety. On fine mornings she was out before dawn to ride with Liholiho and his cowboys; in the afternoons she was home to greet him when he rode in.

To consult with Kimura about dinner, to gather and arrange flowers, to decide what *holoku* would go best with the lei she was planning to wear, to play with puppies and calves, gave her a deep pleasure which mounted steadily when evening lights settled down in valleys and hesitated on the hills.

Liholiho was a great lover, fierce and tender, serious and gay. He always managed to have time to play, but never neglected his work. On fine evenings they sat on the steps after dinner, drinking in the beauty of forests and stars, while he strummed his guitar as only a Polynesian can, with an arm about her neck. When it was rainy they sat before the fire in the living room, filled with contentment.

One afternoon, as Mamo was wandering about the garden selecting flowers for a lei, a cowboy rode in, dismounted, and waved the leather mailbag.

"Honolulu papers, and some-few letters," he called.

"Okay, Keike, take them to the house," Mamo smiled, and continued the more important business of choosing flowers. The afternoon silence was broken occasionally by the silvery maternal nick-

[266]

erings of mares to their colts, by the strident neigh of a stallion rounding up his harem, by the distant bellowing of fighting bulls. Red *iiwis,* black and red *apapanas,* and green *amakihis* called to each other as they flew from tree to tree, sucking honey from *lehua* blossoms.

When the wicker basket hanging on her arm was piled full, Mamo returned to the house. Sitting down on the steps she gazed at the broken line of tree tops merging into solid green masses as the island lunged seaward. Suddenly she listened, and recognizing the sound of Liholiho's horse's hoofs, started for the garden gate.

"You're home early," she called as he rode into view.

"I was *pau,* so came straight home to my sweetheart." Catching her into his arm, he kissed her.

"Fine." She sighed, and in the commonplace little word all the charm of physical intimacy was made vivid.

For an instant Liholiho contemplated her passive loveliness, then began unsaddling his horse. When it trotted off toward the corrals, they started for the house.

"Keike brought the mail," Mamo remarked, pausing to pluck a fresh rose for the right spot above her left ear.

"Good. After dinner we'll read the papers." Taking up a handful of her unbound hair, Liholiho buried his face in it and inhaled its scent rapturously.

Mamo flickered her lashes at him, and snatching her into his arms, Liholiho kissed her parted lips.

"Liholiho," she murmured when he finally released her.

"Mamo," he said on a hard-held breath.

They laughed simultaneously, on a high happy note.

"Always, when I kiss you, it's the first time, Mamo."

"Always for me, too."

When dinner was over, Liholiho took up the mailbag and started for the deep seat on one side of the fire. Mamo sank down beside him with unstudied grace.

"I'm lazy, read the papers to me," she suggested.

Seating himself so the lamp on the table behind the couch shed its light over his shoulder, he unbuckled the bag and shook its con-

[267]

tents onto the floor. Three papers, two bills and a letter slid out. Liholiho picked them up, then his body froze. Aware of the sudden tension, Mamo glanced around and her eyes widened with delight.

"A letter from Homer!" she exclaimed.

Liholiho's hand went up and covered his eyes.

"Liholiho, *what's* the matter? What happened between you two?" Mamo grasped his forearm. "Aren't you happy to hear from him?" She swallowed twice, consciously, to make sure of her throat.

"Wait, wait a minute!" he said heavily.

Mamo stared at him, frightened and bewildered. All the vigor seemed to have ebbed from his body. A sudden languor, like the physical echo of inner struggle, made her own limbs weak; then she leaned forward.

"You must tell me," she insisted, and the emotion in her voice seemed to abandon something of herself to the suddenly charged atmosphere of the kindly old room.

Liholiho pointed at the postmark. Mamo studied it, then a paralysis of horror swept her face.

"*Kalaupapa . . . Molokai!*" The words jammed in her throat.

"Homer made me swear—not to tell anyone." Liholiho sat as though he were hewn of stone.

"Give me the letter, I'll read it," Mamo said, forcing herself for the sake of the man she loved.

Liholiho handed it over. She gazed at the white square of paper like a person under a spell, then turned the envelope over and slid a fingernail under the flap. The tiny sound of tearing filled the room.

Leaning forward she propped her elbows on her knees, putting her weight on them, supporting herself for what was ahead. Then, sliding the letter out of the envelope, her dilated eyes darted from line to line. Twice she tried to speak, but her voice died in her throat. Liholiho sat motionless with his head plunged between his hands.

"Homer wishes us a full, happy life." She managed the words with pain. "For him, it soon will be—*pau.*" The word fell to the floor like a wounded bird.

[268]

Liholiho flung up, *"Pau*—he says—"

Mamo handed him the letter and he read it with savage grief. When he came to the end, he looked across the room to a stack of law books on a small table. Beside them were spurs and a lasso.

"With everything gone from him," Liholiho said, "Homer doesn't want to live."

Mamo's hand fell on his arm. "Perhaps if you went to see him—" Liholiho jerked up. "You mean you would not be afraid for me to go?" he asked incredulously.

"Politicians go to Kalaupapa to make speeches and get votes. If there was any risk, the Government doctors wouldn't permit it. Homer is closer to you than a brother—"

Liholiho seized Mamo's arms. "You're wonderful! Most women in your condition would fight such an idea—" He showered kisses on her wrists.

She sat in the exaltation of love and self-sacrifice, which is woman's sublime experience. The light from the lamp on the table behind them edged her profile in gold, emphasized the modeling of her brow, the straight dignity of her nose, and her mouth's fresh perfection.

"You and I belong to an educated generation of Hawaiians," she said. "If white people are not afraid to go to Molokai, why should we be?"

"More than everything, I've wanted to share this great sorrow with you," Liholiho said, "but because of the promise I made Homer—"

"You must go," Mamo insisted. "At once. You must make him believe that there's always the possibility of a cure being found. Maybe, somewhere in the world at this very minute, some doctor has discovered a medicine."

Liholiho gazed at her. This was a new Mamo. Her face was steady, almost stern. Then she seemed to wake up flushed, and the flush, passing, carried with it the strange, transfiguring mood. With a courageous gesture she pushed back the heavy masses of her hair.

"This is Tuesday," she began thoughtfully. "On Friday the *Kinau* will call at Kailua for sugar and coffee. You must ride down tomorrow and arrange with Hiram to get off for two weeks."

They sat close together, like fellow-conspirators.

"I'll stay here, mostly, while you're gone," Mamo went on, "because I'll feel closer to you." She gazed at the familiar room, at doors leading to other portions of the house, each holding cherished memories of their togetherness.

"You'll be lonely," Liholiho protested. "Two weeks is a long time—when you love."

Mamo's fingers wound tighter into his. "Yes," she sighed faintly. "But there's Homer to think of, as well as our two"—she corrected herself proudly—"three selves. To have you come—"

"I know how I'd feel in his place," Liholiho interrupted, studying her as if he were realizing her for the first time. "If while I'm gone you get lonely, go down and stay with Kauka and Loki."

"I will." The words drifted away, then her voice went on, steady and resolute. "I shall think of you every step my horse takes going down the mountain trail and coming up. Where we've laughed, where we've stopped to make leis—"

Their eyes met and their arms locked about each other.

"Don't tell anyone the reason I've gone away," Liholiho said. "Just say I've been called to Honolulu on business. It would make Homer unhappier than he is, if people thought of him in any way but the way he was. And it would grieve and upset Kauka and Loki to know of this terrible thing. We are young, we can stand the troubles of our generation better than older people."

"Yes," Mamo agreed.

Taking her hand, Liholiho held it against his forehead, in the old gesture of pledging eternal allegiance to a chief. "Mamo, I am doubly yours, now. You have done a great thing for both Homer and for me!"

29

MAMO endured the first few days of Liholiho's absence well enough. The woman who had been born out of the girl on that night of anguish was in command. To create the illusion that Liholiho might appear at any moment, she busied herself with accustomed activities. She arranged flowers, rode down into the sweet secret gloom of the forests, gazed at openings among the trees where they'd raced their horses, contemplated fern banks where they had stopped to make love. In the evenings she sat on the front steps watching sunsets burning themselves out in the west, and basked before the fire after dinner.

This way of living was in no way related to the past, to the separate lives they'd led until their wedding. Together they had created a new life, in which no other person played a major part.

Then one evening, while she watched splendor retreating into the west, a vague sense of depression, mixed with unrest, stole over her. Activities which had sufficed to create the illusion that Liholiho might materialize at any moment, grew unreal. He wasn't here, he wouldn't be here, until—she checked the remaining days on her fingers—six more days, six more nights.

Silly, she thought. I've been happy, content, and now for no reason at all I feel sad. Then an astonished and rather pleased little smile flitted over her face, as she remembered that women with child were prone to vagaries. Deliberately she concentrated on the thought, for it made vivid a fact which, as yet, was unreal. Her young and perfect body had reacted to the most normal of nature's functions without an upset. If anything, she felt more buoyant,

[271]

more vigorous, filled with deeper bodily power. The knowledge that she was to be a mother had been stirring, but unreal. Now it seemed a fact. . . .

Going indoors, she gazed at the lamplighted room, at the fire straining up the chimney, at the table, set for one, finished by a riot of flowers springing from a low blue bowl.

Our home, she thought with a quick little catch in her heart. I'll eat a good dinner, go to bed early and get another night behind me. Tomorrow I'll feel happy, proud, free, as Liholiho's wife should feel.

The cook appeared. "You like eat now, Mamo-san?" he asked.

"Please, Kimura."

"I make chicken stew, *poi,* cocoanut cake. Good for womans to eat plenty when baby coming," he said with Oriental satisfaction.

Dinner over, she sank onto the couch before the fire. But despite her best efforts, she was conscious, again, of an intangible dis-ease which had stolen from somewhere to envelop her. Her thoughts swept backward to the time when the roof and walls about her had sheltered Liholiho and Homer. The house had heard their banter, their laughter, as they went about the business of living.

Summer after summer they had been here together, two strong men whose love for each other was as deep, unending, and colorful as the island beneath them. The old house had given them up to bright mornings, and received them back into its heart at night. Then, suddenly, without warning, one of them had gone from it never to return. Suppose it had been Liholiho, and not Homer!

She sat, perspiration standing on her forehead like dew on the cool white petal of a flower. Then, with a sort of terrific remorse for the instinctive gush of thankfulness which rushed through her, her eyes went to the table where Homer's law books, lasso, and spurs were assembled—like offerings on a deserted shrine. Crossing the room she laid her hand on the piled books. Memory pictures of Homer flickered across the screen of her mind; his flashing smile, his gay eyes, the inner drive and magnetism pouring from him. . . .

What had been said and done between Liholiho and Homer the

night they discovered he had leprosy? She swallowed the pain in her throat. In time, Homer's proud body would become a thing of horror. . . . Innate mental delicacy drew down a shutter in her mind.

Going back to the couch she sat down, trying to compose herself before going to bed, but after a few dismayed minutes she knew that nothing was as it had been. The evening, the house—she, herself, had changed. To date she had been a spectator of tragedy; now she was part of it.

She determined to go down to Kona and stay a day or so, then her mind shied from the thought. It would be tricky explaining to her parents why Liholiho had gone anywhere without taking her with him. Parrying questions of loved ones was always painful. She had talked with her mother several times over the telephone during the past few days, without revealing the fact that she was alone.

She threw a fresh log on the fire and watched flames reaching upward like hands trying to grasp something just out of their reach. She realized her mind was straining to contact some essence of the man she loved. Outside, a little regretful wind kept brushing the corners of the house, as if trying to remove something from it.

It was no use, her weighted mood was not to be shaken off. Always, no matter what, an unobtrusive flavor of Homer would linger in the house. Gay Homer, happy, laughing Homer, who would end his days on—Molokai!

Getting to her feet she turned out the lamp and headed for her bedroom. She undressed slowly, then went to the cupboard for her nightgown. She reached among the garments hanging in it, and her nostrils caught the faint loved scent of Liholiho's clean vigorous body, which clung to garments even after they were washed. A wild rush of hunger for his presence clutched her. Embracing an armful of *palakas* and dungaree breeches, she buried her face in them while her body shook to silent sobs.

Next morning, in clear daylight, she made up her mind to go and spend a day or so with her parents. She could say that Liholiho had feared a steamer trip might make her seasick. . . . Anything would suffice. For her child's sake she must shake off her depression. . . .

The prospect of action brought refreshment and stimulant.

"Ask one of the *paniolos* to saddle my horse, Kimura," she said when she came out to breakfast. "I'm going down to Kona."

"I think berry good, Mamo-san," the cook agreed. "Make time go more-quick till Liholiho come home." He bestowed a faint approving smile on her and bowed out.

After breakfast she went onto the veranda. The garden exhaled a drenched fragrance. Moisture-weighted flowers waited impatiently for the sun to relieve them of their burdens.

Turning indoors, she went to her room and began getting into her riding clothes. The feel and smell of them gave briskness to her movements. Then, in the act of pulling on one of her boots, she felt a strange sharp stir in her body. She caught her breath. Her baby had moved!

How beautiful, what fun to tell her parents, April, Thord! A rush of rapture sent her spirits soaring upwards.

By the time she rode into the garden of her old home, the sunshine, a young horse under her, the healing of the out of doors, had brewed their wholesome magic. She was in complete command of herself. Loki cried out, "My Mamo!" She held out her big arms.

Takeshi darted to take the horse. Mamo slid out of the saddle.

"How the little mother today?" Loki asked, kissing her.

"Fine."

"Your face got funny looks, Mamo."

"Oh, Mama, my little baby moved this morning!" Mamo choked, not realizing that her emotion was magnified by pressure of other things.

"That explain," Loki cried delightedly. "I remember when first I feel you inside my *opu*. Seem like inside I go up in a big smoke."

Mamo's tension snapped, and she threw herself into Loki's arms and wept in the abandoned way of her race. Loki cradled her in her arms, making loving understanding sounds against her bent head. Then Mamo's courage and physical stamina, relieved by the emotional outburst, asserted itself. Wiping tears from her eyes with the back of her wrist, she murmured, "Silly to cry, when—"

[274]

"Always Hawaiian peoples cry when their happy too big for their hearts to hold," Loki said. "When Liholiho coming?"

"He's in Honolulu."

"In Honolulu!" Loki exclaimed. "Why you not go with him?"

Mamo spoke of the seasickness . . .

"Might-be that right," Loki agreed. "Never can tell now when big *kona* come and make the sea rough. Why-for you not come and stay with us soon as Liholiho go?"

Mamo's limpid eyes looked into her mother's in the confident way of a very young child who knows understanding is always its lot.

"Because when I was in our house Liholiho seemed close."

"You two fellas love big," Loki approved. "Sure you have happy marrys all your lifes. I understand, but I glad you come down now. I phone April, and when Papa and Thord come home us all have jolly time."

Mamo spent three days with them, then announced she was going home.

"But day after tomorrow Liholiho come home and all us fellas can go down and meet his steamer at Kailua," Loki protested.

Mamo wavered. Her nature glowed at the thought of a welcoming committee, plus the fact that meeting the steamer would shorten the time of separation by several hours. But how could she and Liholiho, knowing the reason for his trip, behave normally under the eyes of those closest to them, keen to note and record shadings of emotion in features familiar since childhood?

"No, Mama," she insisted. "I want to get the house beautiful and be alone with Liholiho when we meet."

"I understand, Mamo," Loki said. "Long time before, Papa and me feeling the same way. Make any-kind you want."

"We'll ride down and have dinner with you the night *after* he gets home," Mamo promised.

The next morning she rode off, a crimson rose above her left ear and wearing a red carnation lei Loki had made for her.

Reaching the ranch shortly before noon, her heart hastened its beat, as house, corrals, and tall eucalyptus trees swung into view. A few *paniolos,* working the nearer pastures, in for their noon meal, called out, "Aloha!"

"Aloha!" Mamo called back.

Sliding off her horse, Mamo dropped the reins over the pommel, gave the animal a slap on the rump, and it trotted toward the corrals to be unsaddled by the men loafing out their lunch hour.

With buoyant steps she went along the flagged walk and ran into the house.

"Hi-yah, good you come, Mamo-san," the cook remarked. *"Wikiwiki* I fix lunch."

She spent the afternoon robbing the garden of blossoms, while slow sweet contentment stole through her limbs, weighting them pleasantly. Toward evening black clouds, like threatening war-gods, began building up in the west, heralds of a brewing *kona* gale. Mamo watched them. If the storm broke during the night, it meant a delay of Liholiho's arrival by several hours.

She went indoors and began decking the house. When at last the rooms were arranged to her satisfaction, she returned to the veranda and sat down to watch wild savage lights spilling across the sea, bathing it in crimson and burgundy. The edges of furious-looking clouds moved stealthily, and a faint hot draw of air breathed out of the south. It was clear that the *kona* would break before morning. Mamo sighed, then surrendered herself to the awesome beauty of the sunset.

As dark stole the stirring spectacle from her she went indoors. After dinner she lay in bed, listening to the wind lashing across the sky, to thunder crashing.

When rain began falling in silver, smashing sheets, she fell asleep. Rain would beat the wind down, quiet the sea roaring angrily against the coasts of the island. The *Kinau,* due to dock early in the morning, would probably not arrive until noon, which would bring Liholiho to the ranch about sundown.

But it was after dark the next evening before she heard him

returning. Leaping up off the steps where she had been waiting, she ran to meet him.

"Mamo!"

"Liholiho!"

They went into each other's arms. After a little they came out of the embrace and then walked slowly to the house.

For a while after dinner hushed silence held them as they sat together before the fire. Then Mamo, her eyes on the flames, said, "Tell me about Homer."

"As yet, he is not much changed." Liholiho moved uneasily. "But his soul has gone from him. When he saw me—"

Mamo sat still. Outside a rough wind harried the trees.

"We were together four days. But there was nothing to talk about. I told him of our child-to-be." He wiped his forehead. "The things in our hearts were too big for words. . . . I can't get the sights I saw at Kalaupapa out of my mind. The houses for the lepers are good, there are flowers, a fine hospital, kind doctors and nurses, good food, but—" His face worked.

"Tell me everything," Mamo said, her voice trembling. "Then you'll feel better."

"But it's not wise. You're *hapai.*" His voice curved reverently around the word.

"Woman was put into the world to help man," Mamo said.

Liholiho worshiped her with his eyes. "The doctors took me through the hospitals." He gestured as if trying to tear himself free of pictures pursuing him. "Never could anyone dream of such horrors! Some were blind. Others, eyelashes and brows were gone —their foreheads covered with red welts. Some sucked air into their lungs through metal tubes. Others were just hulks of rotting flesh that twitched and jerked."

He dropped his head into Mamo's lap. Her arms went around him, while her heart raced like a mad thing stampeding.

"When I . . . came out I looked at Homer . . . and thought . . ." His muffled voice came out of her lap.

"Don't think of Molokai any more. Perhaps before Homer gets like that a cure will be found. Come to bed with me." Taking his

head between her hands, she lifted it and held it to her heart. Liholiho straightened up.

"You . . . all right?" he asked.

She gave a valiant nod.

Mamo woke, as a pale dawn quivered in the east. Propping herself on her elbow she gazed deeply at Liholiho, his virile hand-
someness emphasized by the abandonment of sleep. As he lay on
his side her eyes passed over his muscled back, lingered on the
bronze barrel of his chest, his flat horseman's back. She ran her
fingers languorously over his shoulder, then began tracing lazy
spirals with her forefinger in his temple.

Clean passion, intensified by separation, which had repeatedly
swept them during the night, had dimmed the events leading up
to it. Never, she resolved, would they be parted again. Leaning
over, she passed her lips lightly over the strong arches of his eyebrows, and smiled. Then she tensed. Drawing back, she parted the
hairs curving blackly above his closed eyes, wiped the skin under
them with her forefinger, then more hurriedly with a fold of the
sheet. Then, from a warm loving woman she was slowly transformed into a thing of stone.

After a time of shaking inaction, she fingered the lobes of his
ears. Then, slowly, as if under a narcotic, she got out of bed and
stood like a young ghost in her white nightgown. Subtly her face,
her whole bearing changed as she came to some great resolution.

Stealthily her eyes fastened on the bed. She changed into riding
clothes and tiptoed into the living room. Her eyes moved with
little jerks from object to object, until finally they came to rest on
Homer's books. Minutes passed, then as if dragged against her
own wishes, she went across the room to the only mirror in the
house, and ripping it off the wall dashed it to the floor.

At the splintering crash of breaking glass, Liholiho charged out.
"What happened?" he demanded. "Why are you up so soon?
Why are you dressed for riding?"

"The mirror fell," Mamo said.

"I see it. *Haoles* would say that's bad luck."

[278]

"We're Hawaiians." Quieted a little by the effort to preserve outward appearances, her mind clung to the fact that she had secured a short period of safety.

"But why are you—dressed?" Liholiho reiterated.

Going to him she placed her hands on his shoulders. "I thought it would be fun if you didn't work today. I was going to make a picnic lunch—"

"Fine," he said. "I'll work more hard tomorrow to make up. Where do you want to go—*kuuipo?*"

She turned her head slightly, as though listening to a guiding voice. "Must you know?" she asked.

He caught the exhaustion in her voice and said remorsefully, "I loved you too much, too often, last night."

"No," she insisted in a voice of penetrating sweetness, tinged with firmness out of proportion to her scant eighteen years.

"Sure?"

"Sure!"

"Okay, I'll get dressed. Order the horses. To go anywhere with you—is heaven!"

30

IF Mamo and Liholiho are much later, I'll have to go and ask Ching for a sandwich," April announced, gazing at the patiently waiting circle in the lighted *lanai*.

Thord glanced at his wrist watch. "Why, it's nine o'clock," he exclaimed in astonishment.

"Might-be the kids stop to make little love in the forest," Loki suggested roguishly.

Kauka's cigar glowed, showing the faint smile in his eyes.

April shifted her position on the floor slightly, drawing up her knees and resting her elbows on them. Solid tree trunks slowly vanished upward into velvety blackness. Warm air stirred through foliage she could not see. Unrest, which had no place in the peaceful anticipated reunion of the six of them, filled her. Her eyes moved in Thord's direction. His hand reached out and met hers and she inched the pillow closer. Loki smiled. Kauka smoked meditatively. Darkness went invisibly on its appointed way, swallowing up seconds and minutes.

Loki, who had sat with the patience of a Buddha for three hours, finally straightened up. "Damn on those kids. Seem like they forgetting got any other peoples in the world." Then she laughed. "But Liholiho got plenty *hanahana*—work to catch up, so Hiram not losing too many dollars. I got make some *inos* for us, to make time go more quick."

"Fine idea," Thord agreed. "I could take a nice long cold one."

"Let's walk to the gate and see if we can hear them coming down the trail," April suggested as Loki went off.

Getting to his feet, Thord drew her up.

"Bothered about something?" he asked when they were out of earshot.

"Yes"—she hesitated—"I feel uneasy about Mamo and Liholiho, though there's no reason to be. Hawaiians have no sense of time."

"You're all stirred up," Thord said, bending to kiss her temple.

"I know I am. Feel." Taking his hand she held it against her thudding heart. "I know it's silly. As Loki pointed out, Liholiho is behind with his work. Besides, he and Mamo are madly in love and probably went up the mountain together." She paused, then went on as if speaking against her will. "But Hualalai is pitted with lava holes. There are cases on record of people being lost in them for days—"

"If a person sends out the wrong kind of thoughts," Thord reminded.

"But it stands to reason that if anything bad had happened Loki and Kauka would sense it first."

"You're more sensitive." Thord's voice was suddenly edgy. "Let's go in. If by the time we've finished our drinks the kids haven't put in an appearance, I'll phone the ranch."

Loki appeared with a tray holding four tall glasses. When everyone had been served, she poised her drink in the air. "To the two *kuuipos*—sweethearts—and to the *moopuna*—grandchild!"

They clicked glasses.

Finally Ching appeared, irritably incarnate. "Gar-damn-to-hell!" he exploded. "Humbugger Mamo and Liholiho make like this. Little more eleben o'clock. If no come soon, dinner all burn up."

Loki's eyes widened. "Eleven o'clock!" she exclaimed.

"Yes, and you speak have dinner leddy eight o'clock!" he snapped.

"Phone the ranch, April, please," Loki said. "Maybe those crazy kids forgetting they say they coming to eat with us tonight."

Thord went indoors with her.

"Like me to make the call?" he asked.

She nodded.

Going to the wall telephone he rang Central and waited for her to make the connection. After what seemed ages of ringing, the bell was answered and Thord began speaking.

"Kimura? When did Liholiho and Mamo leave?" He listened, then exclaimed, "This morning! Do you know if they went up the mountain? No sabe? Ask some of the cowboys if they know where they went. I'll wait."

"There's some very simple explanation, no doubt," Thord remarked to April in encouraging tones; then he waited. The hall was so quiet that April fancied she could hear Time ticking on its way. Then Thord's figure came to attention.

"Kimura? Yes? Nobody knows where they went? What did you say? They took a picnic lunch with them?" A note of relief came to his voice. "Okay. When they come in, tell them to call us."

He hung up. April's eyes met his.

"I guess our young lovers have simply forgotten the rest of the world."

"I feel in my bones something has happened," April insisted in a small dry voice. "If they went off for a good time, they'd end by coming here. Hawaiians are sociable, family-loving people. If Liholiho went out to look stock over, they'd be in long before this."

"I've an unpleasant feeling you may be right."

"Well?" Loki asked as they appeared.

Thord relayed the cook's information, and her big loose figure came to attention. Her eyes, wide with alarm, flew to Kauka's. "Papa—" she began.

"There's no need to be scared, Mama," he said, going to her. "The kids may have gone up Hualalai to look at cattle, or down to the beach for a swim. Probably having food with them they ate, then fell asleep."

"I no like this-kind," Loki insisted. "I got a big uneasy in my hearts. Call Keoke and tell to him speak his policemans to go look every place."

She was on her feet, tense and beset.

"I'll call the ranch again and talk to one of the *paniolos*. If they know nothing, I'll call the sheriff," Kauka said, heading for the telephone. Loki hurried after him.

Thord and April stood close together. Ching came out, a scowl disfiguring his lined saffron-colored face. His scrawny throat jerked nervously.

"Some-kind *pilikea?*" he asked in an offhand Oriental manner. But he was crunching up his clean apron between his thin hands.

Thord told him.

"Sonna-pa-pitch!" he exclaimed. "Me no likee some-kind tonight. All this time I stoppee kitchen, I listen inside my head for some-kind my ears no can hear—"

Returning footsteps coming down the hall made him break off. "I go now, make plenty coffee," he announced in business-like tones.

Loki came out. Her face was quivering. In the very act of vanishing, Ching halted.

"No cly, Loki," he said, taking her plump hand between his skinny ones. "You velly, velly good womans. No need be scare. God not make humbugger kinds for you." He patted her shoulder in a helpless male way.

Loki's chin quivered like a hurt child's. "Papa talk to Kimmo. Nobody knowing any-kind. Just the kids gone. Papa calling Keoke and his policemans now, but no can do much till day comes."

Kauka came out. "I've phoned to Keoke, Mama. He and his men will be here shortly. The trail will be easy to follow when light comes. Kimmo said Liholiho's gray horse is gone. He only wears front shoes."

Loki stared into the garden as if the very force of her anguish could make the darkness and silence yield something to her eyes and ears.

"How many hours till light, Papa?"

Kauka consulted his watch. "Five," he said.

"You speak to Central phoning every peoples the kids get lose?"

"Yes, Mama."

Turning her head in a spent way she listened, then heard the faint ringing of bells for party-line calls. Kauka took her hand.

"Mama, 'In God I have put my trust—'" He let her mind finish the rest.

"I no forget, Papa," she promised, managing a smile. "But—"

Within an hour the house which had been so quiet began filling with people. With incredible swiftness, the sheriff and his policemen appeared. Hiram arrived on their heels, his gray face harassed and indignant. April met him, spoke to him in a low voice, and some of the irritability ebbed. He went to where Loki sat.

"Kind you come, Hiram," she said mechanically.

"Of course I'd come. But this doesn't make sense." He looked around the *lanai* where large regretful policemen waited with apologetic faces. "What on earth could have happened?"

"Only God knows," Loki replied, as if her imagination were dead within her.

"Probably they're asleep somewhere."

"That's what I hoping." Stealthily Loki wiped tears from her eyes.

The telephone kept ringing. Whites, Hawaiians, Chinese, and Japanese arrived on donkeys, on horseback, in cars, eager to be of use. Kauka met them, thanked them, put them all at their ease. Loki roused herself, conscious even under stress of the sacred obligations of hospitality.

"Many peoples to feed before *Wanaao* come, April. Better us go *kokua*, Ching. When guests come in a house, God come in. Us must not forget that-kinds, even when big unhappy with us."

April followed, alarmed by the dead pallor of Loki's cheeks, by something lifeless in her eyes that looked at familiar objects strangely and without recognition.

The kitchen was blazing with lights. Ching, assisted by Mitsu and Takeshi who had remained overnight, was scurrying about marshaling equipment.

"No need *kokua*, Loki," Ching began kindly.

"Plenty mans come, Ching," she replied, staring at cups and plates set out as if for a party.

Heaving a monster pot of coffee off the stove, Ching began pouring it into waiting cups. Takeshi watched Loki from beneath smooth young eyelids, while Mitsu went about her work with

[284]

concerned, compassionate eyes, hiding sorrow behind the uncomplaining front of Japanese women.

Takeshi and Loki went off with trays of coffee. April waited. When Loki was out of earshot, Ching glanced up.

"Me no likes. Me flightened," he announced. "Me velly sick here." He rubbed his stomach.

"I'm scared too, Ching," April said; then taking up a tray with sugar and cream, she went down the hall. Although she had been gone from the *lanai* only a short time, she was astonished by the number of persons who had appeared during her brief absence. Thisbe was there, mincing about and grimacing behind his pincenez. Brewer came boiling out of the dark, his face showing the easy sympathy of the stout. Without so much as a glance at his father-in-law, he went directly to Loki.

"Central phoned, and I thought it might buck you up if I dropped around." His eyes went to Kauka, who was going and coming first to the telephone, then directing search parties that were to cover different sections of Kona. "I'll take charge of operations in my end of the district, old man," he said.

"Mahalo, Brewer."

"To hell with 'thanks' among friends," Brewer said in his noisy way. "You stood by my ship when it was in distress." He gave a lewd, enormous wink which did not dilute the sympathy and concern he showed. "I'll be needing your services shortly." He winked again. "But in the meantime, everything I have is at your disposal. Tell me how you want the search parties handled. We publicans and sinners don't forsake one another when pinches come."

When the first pale light showed in the east, groups began going off. *Paniolos* at the ranch set out to cover Hualalai. The sheriff and his posse roared off to spread the alarm in districts not reached by telephone.

"We"—Kauka's eyes included Hiram, Thord, and Moku—"will take the sea coast between Kealakekua and South Point."

"Sure, me and my cousin-brothers go with you." Moku indicated three young Hawaiians lingering near the steps. "When I got bad troubles—" He broke off.

[285]

"Stay with Mama, April," Kauka said, laying his hand on her slight shoulder.

"I will," she promised.

Bending, he kissed Loki's brow.

Moku led Kauka's old mare forward. Her back sagged slightly as he deposited his weight on it, then she set off in her steady way. Hiram got onto a bay, which Takeshi held for him. Thord swung onto April's gray. Moku and his relatives mounted mules, and followed Kauka's retreating figure down the driveway toward the sea.

"This is fantastic," Hiram remarked to Thord. "It's inconceivable that anything could have happened. Mamo and Liholiho will undoubtedly be found."

"I hope to Christ they are," Thord replied. "If anything's happened to them, it'll half kill Loki."

Hiram gave a noncommittal grunt, holding himself as if he resented the standstill plantation work had come to in one swift swoop.

Thord passed his hand across his eyes. The golden beauty of the morning seemed an outrage. When they reached the towering bluffs above Kealakekua, Kauka halted, instructing two of Moku's relatives to cover the beaches toward Kailua until they met the search party coming from the chief port-of-call. Then he signed to Moku and a younger cousin to follow him.

Slowly they made their way down to the coast. The scent of *kiawes,* the stirring smell of seaweed drying on rocks exposed to the ebbing tide, charged the air. They rode across small sand beaches, made their way through the gloom of cocoanut groves, followed thread-like trails worn into the lava flows. Finally Moku, who had taken the lead again, slid from his saddle to study twin trails cutting a section of the beach ahead.

"Ha!" he cried. "Liholiho's horse."

He pointed at prints, the fore feet shod, the hind feet unshod. Kauka dismounted, studied the hoof-marks and nodded. "That's Liholiho's gray," he agreed. "They're heading for the Sacred Cove."

Anticipation tinged with hope rose in everyone. Remounting,

Kauka took the lead, loping across the beach. Leaping his mare up the low bank onto the next lava flow, he rode on.

As they drew near the narrow strip of forest which the lava had spared, memories of the last time he had been there surged through Thord. Mentally he saw Mamo and Liholiho standing side by side, facing the flaming west, while bridesmaids and groomsmen formed a semi-circle behind them.

"There are the horses!" Kauka called in relieved tones, indicating the animals tied to the trees. "If those kids are sleeping—" He gestured with his fist.

Touching his mount with his spurs, Thord brought it abreast of Kauka's. Then, as if an invisible hand had passed over Kauka's face, wiping hope from it, it changed.

"Those animals haven't had food or water for about twenty-four hours," he announced, indicating their ganted-up condition. Checking his mare, he slid to the ground. Moku and his cousin, Hiram, and Thord, followed suit.

A bag with food in it, two piles of clothes, showed in the peaceful green swale. The horses looked around and nickered in relief. Moku and his cousin began inspecting the grass leading to the brink of the cliff.

"Two fellas go inside water," they announced in charged voices, and began divesting themselves of boots and breeches.

"They couldn't drown—they're both magnificent swimmers!" Hiram said in a harsh overwrought voice. "The sea's been like a millpond since the last *kona*, three days ago—"

Kauka passed his hand slowly across his eyes like a person stunned by a club. Thord went to him.

"Kauka—"

Their eyes locked. Moku and his cousin dived into the water. After a few moments a strangled sound took them all to the brink of the cliff. Both brown faces were horrified and distorted. "Two fella stop down below," they said. "Mamo hair tie to the coral! She have Liholiho in her arms." And they vanished again.

Kauka pulled off his boots and dived in. Thord stood without moving, sweat dampening his red hair.

[287]

"Perhaps there's a note explaining—" Thord said, and began frantically searching through the two heaps of clothes. He recalled his first sight of Mamo, his first reaction to her beauty, that it was sacrilege that she should ever grow old or ever have to end. And vital, life-loving Liholiho. . . . Then his fingers encountered a folded sheet of paper in the back pocket of Mamo's breeches. He straightened up and scanned lines written hurriedly on a leaf torn from the ranch ledger:

"Papa:
I must tell you why I have done this. Homer made Liholiho promise not to tell anyone he had maipake—"

Thord made a smothered sound of horror that brought Hiram back from the cliff.

"What on earth—" he demanded.

Thord struck the sheet of paper. They read it together.

"When Homer wrote from Kalaupapa, I told Liholiho he must go to him. When Liholiho came home, I saw he had maipake *too—"*

"Great God!" Hiram recoiled from the paper, then said in a thick voice, "Read the rest, Graham—"

Thord swallowed.

"I will not have his beautiful body become a thing of horror, like the poor people he told me about on Molokai. When I saw, I made up my mind what I must do. I love you, Papa, and dear Mama, too. Now, and when we're all on the Other Side.

Mamo."

31

BUT doctors, called in from Hilo, confirmed Kauka and Thord's post-mortem diagnosis. Liholiho showed no signs of leprosy. It had been a figment of Mamo's overwrought imagination, fired by the shock of learning about Homer, and exaggerated by pregnancy. Kona, all Hawaii, was stunned by the triple tragedy. Loki moved and spoke as if she were done with time and all the other concerns of the earth.

Life got under way, slowly and painfully. Dawns drew light out of darkness. Mountains swooped downward, the sea upward, to meet in a vast embrace, out of which the fierce vitality of day was born.

A few mornings after the funeral, while Kauka, Thord and Loki were at breakfast, the telephone rang. Kauka went to get it. When he returned there was a line between his eyebrows.

"Hiram wants us both to stop at the office before going to the hospital," he said.

Loki's eyes, which had been unseeing, came slowly to life. Reaching out, Kauka covered her hand lying limply on the table, with his own.

"What is it, Mama?"

"Hiram making some-kind," she announced. "You see." And her spirit went from her again.

Kauka gazed mutely at her like a man trying to decipher writing in an unknown language, which may be big with some revelation. Then, as she said nothing further, he glanced at Thord.

"Done?" he asked.

They went down the hall. Carlos had parked the car at the steps. They got in and drove off.

"Something's in the wind," Kauka remarked, his eyes heavy from sleepless sorrow.

Thord nodded. "Yes. Hiram's been in a blue funk ever since—" He checked himself and gazed solemnly at the glitter of sunlight on the vegetation springing out of rich earth. The morning, the island, seemed to flaunt their vigor, mocking the heaviness of their souls.

When they reached the office, sitting in the shadow of the silent mill, the usual array of horses were tied to the long hitching rail. Three or four Hawaiians, waiting to be summoned, got to their feet when they saw Kauka, compassion on their kind faces.

"Aloha, *aikane,*" they said.

The office door was open, Hiram seated at his desk. Hearing footsteps, he glanced over his shoulder.

"I'll be ready for you in a few minutes," he announced.

Mechanically, Kauka pulled out a cigar and lighted it. Thord touched a match to a cigarette. Their eyes met, then fell apart. One by one the men were called in. Kauka glanced at his watch, frowned, and went to the door.

"I've a tonsillectomy to perform in twenty minutes, Hiram," he announced.

"Call the hospital and postpone it. The matter I want to discuss is of more importance."

Kauka's eyes met Thord's. He elevated his brows questioningly, then went in and began phoning. The last *luna* was instructed and sent on his way.

"Okay, Graham, I'm ready. Come in," Hiram said.

Thord obeyed.

"Sit down."

Kauka finished telephoning and seated himself beside Thord. Silence settled itself on the chairs still vacant. The bookkeeper, Thord noted, was not present. For a while Hiram stared at the green felt on his big desk; then he faced around.

"For the sake of everyone on my plantations, and for that matter for the sake of everyone living in Kona, whether or not they're in my employ, immediate steps must be taken to safeguard, as far as it's possible, the further spread of leprosy here. I've wired to Honolulu asking for one of the doctors attached to the Board of Leprosy Investigation to come over and take blood tests of everyone. You can assist him. As well, every building on my plantations must be fumigated."

Kauka watched him with unfathomable eyes.

"I must confess," Hiram went on in his chilled way, "that I've put in some bad hours, realizing that a leper's been at large in our midst, in our very homes. Of course I have every sympathy for Homer, but—" He broke off.

The room waited.

Picking up a pen, he twiddled it and his eyebrows drew together. "It's inconceivable"—he fixed Kauka with hot, resentful eyes— "that you, a doctor, did not see it. You're Island-born, you should have recognized the symptoms, even in their incipient stages. Negligence in a matter as vital as this is monstrous!"

Thord felt as if the blood in his legs was turning to ice water, then fury filled him, a fury which shocked him. It seemed impossible that a civilized being could feel as he did, like rising up and destroying the man before him.

"Often symptoms appear overnight," Kauka said quietly.

"Homer was on a picnic with you a couple of days before he left."

"I know."

"Were it not for the tragedy which has come to your family recently, and the fact that you've worked for me twenty-eight years, I should feel compelled to dismiss you."

In an effort to control himself, Thord gripped the arms of his chair. Hiram's face looked as if it had been hewn from marble with a brutal ax.

"I think, perhaps," Kauka said, "it will be better for me to be *pau* here." He stared out of the open door.

"You have nothing ahead."

"I know, I'm a Hawaiian."

"If you left, how would you live?"

Kauka sat as if weighing the problem; then a faint remote smile came to his eyes—the first for days, as if he were in possession of some holy mystery entrusted entirely to the keeping of Polynesians.

"Do not worry. I can eat, live," he said simply.

Watching him, Thord envied him the powerful simplicity of faith, of purpose, which made his existence appear almost automatic. Hiram stared at him. Kauka looked back.

"My one regret is that I owe you money, which it is not likely that I'll ever be able to pay back," he said. "In your way, you've been good to us. You were generous in your advance for Mamo's wedding."

Hiram's yellowish eyes looked at nothing.

"As soon as Loki's equal to it, I shall take this matter up with her—"

"But I can't dismiss you from my employ!" Hiram interrupted. "If I did, if you left even, in view of what's recently happened, Kona, all Hawaii, would condemn me."

"Yes," Kauka agreed. "But why should you care what people think, if you feel justified?"

"It's imperative for a man in my position to have the respect and admiration of the community he lives in."

"You are known as a hard man, Hiram, but you are rich, so people will always think well of you." Faint amusement showed in Kauka's eyes. "If, for a while, they feel you've been harsh, they'll forget. Quickly. Easily."

He rose as if, for him, the matter was finished. Thord got up, feeling as if he were standing on wet sand streaming from under his feet.

"Look here—" Hiram uncoiled from his chair, rising upward to his surprising height. "Don't go off half cocked. I was merely being academic. I've been upset realizing that I—that everyone's been exposed!"

His usually masked eyes were dry and brilliant, his face chalk white. Thord saw that, for the first time in his life, Hiram was in the grip of deadly fear—fear which revolted him, which was strange to him. He, like any other person, was menaced by a common danger, in which his millions carried no weight and afforded no protection.

Kauka studied him appraisingly, "In your heart, Hiram, you want me to go."

"Yes, inefficiency is something I can't tolerate, but in this instance, solely for my own protection from censure, I feel compelled to overlook it, anyway—"

"Temporarily?" Kauka suggested.

"Yes."

"Very well. To square what I owe you in money, I will stay until the memory of Mamo and Liholiho's deaths dims a little. When it does—" He gestured.

Hiram writhed his shoulders as if his clothes were uncomfortable. "Very well. Let's get down to the business at hand. Doctor Melville arrives tomorrow."

"Do you want one of us to go down and meet the steamer?" Kauka asked. His eyes met Thord's covertly. So, they said, he's sprung this on us without warning.

"I'm sending my car." Hiram made a pretense of going through some papers. "There's another angle to this affair which I hope you'll believe causes me pain," he said without looking up.

"What is it?" Kauka asked.

"April must not go to your house any more, even after it's been fumigated. Homer was there constantly. Little is known about how leprosy is carried or contracted. She is my only child, she has everything to live for and I can't permit her to be unnecessarily exposed."

"Having had a daughter of my own, I understand perfectly how you feel, Hiram."

Hiram turned slightly, facing his audience, then pressed back in his chair as if to get a better perspective on the situation confronting him. "Elsbeth's been greatly benefitted since Graham came. I wish his daily visits to continue." His eyes left Kauka and went to Thord. "And this will, of course, necessitate your moving to the club."

Strange cold fires began running around Thord's heart. Ruth-

[293]

lessly this frozen image of a man, seated safely behind ramparts of wealth, was stripping Kauka of his last comforts without giving a thought to all he had done for and meant to Kona during the past twenty-eight years.

"Graham!" The cold voice left a rent in the air.

"Yes?"

"Did you hear what I said?"

"Yes."

Silence stretched between them.

"Well?"

"Mr. Wilde, there isn't a thing wrong with your wife as you undoubtedly know. Kauka is my colleague. As well, he is my friend." Thord's eyes bored into Hiram's. "It was through him I came to Kona. If it means forfeiting my position on your payroll, I shall remain where I am."

"My boy—" Kauka began.

"Just a minute, Kauka. I'm doing the talking for a few minutes." Thord's hand fell on Kauka's shoulder. "Mr. Wilde—"

"What is it?"

"To expedite the blood tests and fumigating you've lined up, as well as for appearance' sake, it'll probably be best for us to remain here for a while longer. But when Kauka leaves you, I leave with him."

Hiram, if it were possible for a person so gaunt, looked apoplectic. He went white and then red. His yellow eyes narrowed to slanting slits.

"This—" he began.

"This is final!"

"Possibly," Hiram spoke as if from a lofty pinnacle, "we are all worked up still over the events of the past few days. After Doctor Melville has come, it may be advisable to re-discuss this matter."

"As you please," Thord retorted. "And now, if you're finished, we'll go to the hospital and take care of the operation that's scheduled."

Hiram signed with his head, releasing them.

[294]

"My boy," Kauka said, as they drove away, "April—"

Thord's jaw was grim. "I've got to get out from under. It's galled me to work for him, feeling as I do about his daughter. Damn him! Forbidding her to come to your house when Loki needs her! Telling me I must live at the club!"

He spun the wheel unnecessarily to take an easy corner.

"April will understand," he went on. "We'll get out from under, some way. With this Territorial Doc descending on us at dawn tomorrow, I better hit for home and get the office cleared of all damning evidence of what we've been into."

"Yes," Kauka agreed, looking faintly worried.

"Shall I tell Loki about what's in the offing?"

"Use your own judgment."

"What'll I do with our experimental paraphernalia?"

"Pack it up and I'll figure out something after I've operated on the Gomez kid." He chewed his cigar. "And some way, I've got to approach Melville about Homer. Persuade him, if he has friends at Kalaupapa, to have Homer given chaulmoogra. I've thought and thought about him. The rub is, how to impress, how to drive the fact home, that the oil's beneficial, without giving our hand away."

They stopped at the hospital steps. Kauka contemplated the smart structure with pride and regret. "Anyway, the Kona Sugar Company employees got a decent hospital through our efforts," he remarked, then went up the steps.

Driving home, Thord thought fiercely. It would be best to tell Loki immediately. She was stunned, but not broken. Somewhere inside her body her loyal, valiant heart was waiting to take up its accustomed, sure beat.

He glanced up as he drove into the garden. Loki was in her usual chair. Stopping the car, he ran up the steps.

"Mama," he said, placing his hand on her shoulder.

Her eyes came back from far away, lighting briefly, for he had never called her that before.

"Yes?"

Quickly, he told her everything. Her body, deadened and heavy with grief, became charged with fresh life.

[295]

"Hiram made this-kind to Kauka!" she exclaimed.

"Yes."

"Damn on him!" She heaved to her feet. "I *kokua*—help you to pack all the leprosy-kind things. And I betting you never April stop coming our house. She not that-kind of guys." She paused. "Might-be good if all us fellas clear out." She looked swiftly, lovingly about the house, then her face filled with resolution. "Here, always I thinking of Mamo and Liholiho. In a new place—"

"Mama, you're grand." Thord placed his arms about her shoulders. "But where in hell— Where will we go?"

She laid her hand on his arm. "Wait one minute," she continued, "my *mana* is talking to me because I too tired from my deep sads to think."

A chill prickled Thord's skin. Loki was absolutely still, listening with the depths of her mind. Then she sighed in a relieved way.

"My *mana* has spoken." There was the calmness of eternity in her voice. "Brewer got one house not on Hiram's land. After you and Papa are *pau*, all us fellas move down there. Brewer just like Hawaiian peoples. He no care if us no can pay him money for it. *There*"—she stressed the word—"you and Papa not have much to do and can make big *hanahana* with the oil. If you find cure for *maipake*, Homer and other poor peoples who have the bad sick will have a big happy instead of deep sads in their hearts."

Lifting her hand, Thord kissed it.

"Now better you go pack up every-kinds you and Papa not wanting that Honolulu doctor-guys to see. I go phone Brewer."

"You're the boss, Loki," Thord said, heading for the office.

He moved about the familiar room gathering up all evidence, while a queer sinking sensation stole around his heart. A curtain was coming down announcing the end of an act. His mind swept back, reviewing the time he had spent in Kona, a time so packed with events that it seemed years instead of months. Through windows opening on the sunshine-flooded garden he heard Takeshi singing a queer little Oriental song while he busily raked up the lawn. Mynah birds scolded and argued in the trees and green-scented peace lay upon everything.

After a little Loki came in. "I call Brewer on the phone," she announced. "He all boil up. He speak, 'Come enny time. Us publicans and sinners stick together.' Brewer bad rascals before, might be he still make some hell on the side, but he got big hearts."

"He's all right," Thord agreed, continuing with the packing.

"The most hard things will be when us have to tell Ching and Takeshi, Mitsu and Carlos. Us no can keep them any more. That be big stinks but no can helps. Where I put this-kinds?" She indicated a shelf full of test tubes and bottles.

"I'll take care of them, Loki," Thord replied. "Plantation stuff will stay here for whoever steps into our shoes."

A car roared up the driveway.

"April," Loki said.

Thord went hot and cold. Straightening up, he flashed a look at the peaceful garden, then heard her swift footsteps coming down the hall. The door opened and she was in his arms.

"Thord—" she began, chokily.

"Steady, darling."

"I've just come from the office. Father told me I wasn't to come here any more. I told him I would. He's angry and upset. About everything. About Homer having been among us, because Kauka is leaving. He said he hoped to persuade you to remain. I told him you'd never leave Kauka—"

"I won't. Don't be so upset. After Doctor Melville's gone, we'll be free to give all our time, thought, and energy to this—" He indicated the half-packed boxes on the floor. "The pickings will be lean but my small income will keep us in food. Kieser will supply oil. If, *when*—" He broke off, gazing down long corridors leading to the future.

"But, where'll you go?"' April asked like a horrified child.

Loki told her.

"I'm going with you."

"Better you wait little whiles. If you make this-kind, sure Hiram raising big hell and try to squeeze Papa and Thord off this islands."

"Yes, he would," April agreed, "and I mustn't stand in the way of the work you and Kauka want to do." She gazed around bewildered, trying to orient herself and find her proper niche in the new design of their days.

"When, how soon will you be leaving?" she asked, looking at Loki.

"More quicks, more good. It boil me ups, Hiram making this-kind to Kauka after he work good for so many years. After Kauka gone little whiles, sure Hiram kick his own *okole*. Every peoples got big Alohas for Kauka—"

"I told Father that too," April interrupted. "But he's in a blind rage because Kauka jumped the gun on him. No one has ever walked out on Father before." Her eyes went to Thord. "You're glad to be going," she accused.

"Yes, it stung to work for him when I feel about you as I do. When I'm in the clear, my own man again, I can go after you—" He flung an arm about her and smiled.

32

LOKI looked at the room almost emptied of personal furniture and belongings. "Might-be this old house never see us again," she remarked, turning away to hide the tears in her eyes.

"Houses don't forget people they've loved," April said.

During the two weeks Kauka and Thord had worked with Doctor Melville, April and Loki, assisted by Ching and Takeshi, Mitsu and Carlos, had taken load after load to South Kona. In the way of Orientals, the servants asked no questions, made no comments, but went heavy-heartedly about the business of packing, as if they suspected that shortly, for them, the household, which had afforded them a livelihood and happiness, would be no more.

April looked at walls stripped of the pictures and objects which had given them charm. The long hall, with spears and paddles gone, looked forsaken, and the *lanai,* robbed of hanging baskets, potted palms and wicker furniture, was just a big square veranda. And yet she knew that some essence of Mamo and Liholiho, of Loki and Kauka, would always linger under the roof, making it gracious, kindly, and warm.

"Sit down and rest for some few minutes, April," Loki advised. "Your eyes got big tired. I tired, too." Slowly, she sank into her favorite rocker and contemplated her garden.

April seated herself on the steps. "I am tired," she admitted, "not from all this"—she waved her hand—"but Father's in a silent boil all the time, and Mother—"

"All upset because Thord going with Papa?"

"Yes. She drills into Father every instant he's home."

"And you got deep sads because your *kuuipo*—sweetheart, going to live far away," Loki finished.

"Yes. But Thord thinks that before very long we can be married."

"Better wait little whiles. Plenty dynamite, anyhow, around here when us fellas pull out. If you fellas get marry and Dale write to Hiram about Thord's bad troubles in New York, Hiram blow up and try to run Thord out of Hawaii. Then where Papa be?"

"I know. Father would pull every possible string."

Ching came around the house and, squatting on his heels, began mysteriously inspecting a flower bed. After a bit he went off in a peculiar way which made it seem as if he were vanishing out of existence rather than merely out of sight. After a little he materialized in the rear of the big, almost empty, *lanai*, examining the wall as if for signs, exploring the floor as if for pitfalls. Though he proceeded without haste, the unerring precision of his movements, the absolute soundlessness of each operation, created an impression that he was some conjurer preparing an astounding trick. After a few minutes he disappeared into the house, then shortly appeared on the lawn again and came toward them, his stride truculent. "I tink velly good idea us make talk," he announced, halting at the steps. "Me no likee all this humbugger-kind. What-for all us fellas go stop Brewer house in South Kona?"

"Kauka *pau* here," Loki said.

"Hiram *fire?*" Ching demanded, shocked out of his Oriental reserve.

"No, just go."

"Gar-damn, I think you no speak true, Loki."

"I speak true, Ching."

"How fellas eat if Kauka no get salary?"

"Every month Thord get small money from New York."

"Umm."

"But, Ching, I too sorry, not enough to pay you for cook." Loki's voice was soft with regret.

"You tink only I work for money?" Ching demanded in hostile tones. "You velly good, but always womans velly, velly stupid. If only I cook for money, you tink I stop this house? Always wait, wait, wait! Sometimes seven hours *kaukau* stop on top stove. Make me mad like hell!"

April smiled faintly.

"I got big sads," Loki confessed, "because I must tell to you and Mitsu, Carlos and Takeshi us no can keep any more."

"I stop," Ching announced. "I got money save up for send my old bones to China when I *make*. But if bones no go in velly big style, can use some dollars when us need. Takeshi must help Mother. Mitsu got family in Hilo. Sure Hiram give Carlos job, he velly smart for make everykind." And having arranged his immediate universe to his own satisfaction, he went off.

"Now Takeshi coming," Loki remarked, watching his slow progress across the lawn.

"Loki-san," he began, his round ruddy face solemn.

"Come here," Loki said.

He went to her and she placed her large arm about his taut, muscular shoulders.

"Since you coming here, you have work very good, Takeshi," she said. "Always us got deep Alohas for you, but you the Papan-san for your familys now."

"Yis."

"Us have to go away and us not got enough money for pay peoples to *hanahana* for us, so you must stop here and catch some small work to *kokua* your Mama-san and the small kids."

"Yis. You tink *Haole Hao* give me jobs?" His eyes went to April in a worried way, though his face was composed.

"I'll see he does, Takeshi."

"*Arrigato*, April-san." Then he looked at Loki. "When you fellas —go?" He choked a little on the last word.

"In two, three days, when new doctor come."

His small face worked. "Hard for say *sayonara* to Kauka. He like my Papa-san since my Papa-san got cook in molasses. I tink better I go, *now*."

"Okay, Takeshi. I understanding. Aloha." She kissed his cheek. "Us leave money for this week's *hanahana* with Carlos."

"*Arrigato*. Aloha." And he headed down the driveway, fleeing from memories which might un-man him. April rose and started down the steps.

"Better no," Loki warned. "Sure when us no can see, Takeshi cry, then too much shames. Might-be tomorrow you ride up and see him, after you talking to Hiram about some jobs. That cheer him up."

A car turned into the drive.

"Father," April said.

"This day not so hot," Loki observed, gathering herself together.

Drawing up at the steps, Hiram looked at the *lanai* emptied of everything but half a dozen chairs. His eyebrows slanted toward his nose like two outraged arrows.

"Aloha, Hiram," Loki said, and smiled.

Getting out of the car, he strode up the steps. "I've been intending to see you about this absurd move." He waved at the stripped house.

Loki made no reply.

"Surely, you can appreciate my position, if you all leave!"

"Why you no thinking of that before you sail into Kauka?"

"I—I—was stirred up."

"Hiram, always in your hearts you little *huhu*—mad with Kauka and me because us no kiss your *okole*. Till now, never us having trouble. Better for us to go before our long Aloha get all spoil."

"At least use your influence to make Graham remain—"

Loki gazed into his eyes.

"Yes, I'm thinking of myself," he admitted, "of what people will say and think."

"You rich, Hiram. Soon every peoples forget about this things. Easy for you to get another doctor. Might-be you have to pay little more, that new styles in Hawaii." Loki's voice was tinged with amused malice.

"I'll raise both Kauka's and Graham's salaries if you'll persuade them—"

"Too late, Hiram, our minds all made up, our belongings already stop Brewer house, except for some few little things."

[302]

Hiram ran infuriated fingers through his hair. "You'll live to regret this—"

"Might-be you, not us," Loki suggested.

"If Kauka and Graham are planning to start a private practice they'll find the pickings lean. Three-fourths of all the people living in North and South Kona are in my employ. Naturally, they'll patronize the free plantation doctor."

"We see," Loki said. "For little whiles Papa and Thord take a rest, study, and get catch up on many kind things. After that—" She gestured, committing the future to its place.

Hiram heard the finality in her voice. His face became thoughtful and secretive, as though he were plotting further arguments. April went to him.

"Father, if you're wise, you'll accept this move with the same dignity that it is made."

"I'm not accustomed—"

"There's always a first time," April said.

"I suppose you're remaining here!"

"Yes, I'll be home about nine."

His lips shut into a tight, straight line. Going down the steps, he got into his car and drove off.

A little before sunset Kauka and Thord came home.

"Well, we're through," Kauka said, kissing Loki. "No fresh cases of leprosy have been discovered, so Hiram's relieved on that score. The fumigating's completed, or will be tomorrow."

"Wait, I fix *inos* for us," Loki said, rising.

Thord seated himself on the steps beside April, Kauka sank down on a packing case. The sun was resting its chin on the sea, slanting the last shadows across the lawn. Flowers and shrubs rustled a little, settling themselves for sleep. A curious quiet filled the emptied house. Thord took April's hand. She smiled, then her face became thoughtful.

"Father was here." She looked from Thord to Kauka.

"I know, we saw him just before we came home."

"Did he—"

"Yes, he tried to dissuade us from leaving but I explained that

[303]

when a phase of life ends, you cannot revive it," Kauka remarked quietly. "He's wiring to Honolulu for a doctor."

Loki came out with tall drinks, served them, and sat down.

"I'm sorry, Mama, we've been too busy to help with the moving," Kauka said.

"Nearly all finish up. Tomorrow April and me, Ching and other fellas settle Brewer's place. When finish, it look nice."

Kauka patted her wrist, then studied the contents of his glass. "Melville's a fine chap," he remarked. "While we've been working, we've had opportunities to talk. I showed him Kieser's letter, the first one, about chaulmoogra oil, told him about Homer, and asked him to use his influence to see if the doctors on Molokai will treat him with the oil which I'll supply."

"What he say?"

"He's going to write the doctor in charge at Kalaupapa about it."

"You mean might-be they no can give it to him?" Loki asked indignantly.

"They will, in its crude form, if Homer wants it. If we gave them, now, the improved formula that we've worked out"—he sighed unhappily—"it might rouse suspicion. If this were a story instead of real life, of course we'd manage to smuggle Homer out and save him."

The sun vanished, pulling its light down behind the sea and a lustrous purple twilight filled the garden. Carlos came down the hall, his face working.

"Ching tell to me—"

"That we're all going away?" Kauka asked.

"Yes. Fifteen year now I work for you, Kauka, and me no like *pau*."

Kauka explained the situation. "Hiram's taking you on, Carlos."

"This-kind sad. I got big family, kids eat plenty rice. If I single—"

"I know, Carlos. Maybe when we get on our feet, we can hire you again."

"No forget. Sometimes Sunday I come and *kokua* Ching to feed rabbits and guinea pigs. Ching tell to me he no only cook-mans,

[304]

he house-girl, gardener-boys, every-kinds for you." His voice was envious and wistful.

"Ching all-same *opihi*," Loki laughed. "Stick tights like hell."

"Tomorrow I take rabbits and guinea pigs down. What-kind you two fellas making ennyhow?" he asked, as if his curiosity had at last got the best of him.

"In one or two years, you'll know, Carlos. Till then—"

"I no speaking any fella. I got tight face," Carlos assured him. "But this times got more from one hondred rabbits and guinea pigs. After by-and-by many, many more. Big jobs for Ching to feed and keep little houses all clean."

"If I know Ching, he'll manage."

"I much like rabbits," Carlos sighed. "But I ask *Haole Hao* for truck-jobs, then every Sunday, and might-be one-two time in week after work *pau*, I can drive down and *kokua* Ching to feed." He went off with the air of a person who had successfully navigated a treacherous rapid.

Loki looked at Kauka. "And now, after us stop in South Kona, what you two fellas do?"

"I'm going to Kohala and talk to the lepers there." Kauka glanced over his shoulder involuntarily. "I want to persuade at least half a dozen of them to come to South Kona for treatment!"

Loki tensed, then her face grew resolute. "Where you hide? How you feed?"

"I've decided to use an old village beyond Ka Lae, South Point. It's on a small beach missed by lava flows. I'm going to try to arrange with their families to provide food. Moku's going to Kohala with me to tell them about results of the oil on Tutu—"

"But she *die*"—Loki almost wailed—"and Hawaiian fellas—"

"Some will come, the younger ones who have much of life still before them."

Lifting Thord's hand, April pressed it to her cheek. He felt her lips moving silently against it. Bending over, he asked in a low voice, "What are you doing, darling?"

"Praying," she replied in a whisper.

"Pray your prayer so I can hear it."

April's eyes came up to his. Then he heard her voice, the charm of which he thought he knew so well, saying with a new intonation, "Do you really want to hear it?"

"Yes."

"Oh, God," she said under her breath, "make me brave! Make me strong! Make me believe, no matter what, that life is beautiful, sound, and worth while. And make me take—whatever comes—like a gentleman and soldier!"

Bending, Thord placed his lips to hers.

"Amen," he said against them.

33

THORD glanced up from the table where he was working. Through open windows he could see the turn in the highway which circled the island. It was twelve-forty-five. Ostensibly the mail truck was due to go by at twelve, but knowing the mailman's habits he guessed it would be well after one before Analu passed.

He missed the dense fragrant vegetation of Kona but there was a bold beauty to the lava flows which every few years spilled down from Mauna Loa over the southern end of Hawaii. He studied the awesome shape of the volcano. Might and mystery wrapped it even under a cloudless sky.

In the foreground *kiawe* trees moved lazy, lacy branches above the stone wall enclosing the garden. Two tall old cocoanut trees leaned toward the beach as though they yearned to lay their green heads on the sand and give up the long fight to exist. Ghostly little breezes came off the almost-motionless sea. Sounds seemed unnaturally loud. He felt the rhythm of the Pacific in his bones as it swelled and receded slowly against the shore. Forever and ever . . . Forever and ever . . . it whispered.

He heard Loki and Ching talking in the kitchen as they prepared lunch. He could not distinguish what they were saying but he enjoyed the pleasant rise and fall of voices; it went hand in hand with the hot peace of the day. As he worked carefully and intently with notebooks, case histories, slides and test tubes, he mentally reviewed events which had catapulted Kauka, Loki, and himself out of Kona. His intent face changed expression for an instant,

[307]

then settled into a great resolve. The distant sound of a motor made him glance up and he saw dust smoking from the highway.

"Ching," he called. "Mail truck."

"Okay," the cook sang back. "I got wheelballow."

Thord met him outside and they started down a dusty stretch of road that ended at the highway. Heat rained down from the blue bowl of the sky.

"Gar-damn, velly hot place," Ching commented, deftly guiding the wheelbarrow down the smoothest of the dust-ruts.

"It sure is."

"You see what-kind I make last night?" Ching signed at the galvanized netting runs for rabbits and guinea pigs.

Thord glanced round and noticed that the old man had thatched the runs with cocoanut fronds to provide shade for the small creatures, panting in the heat.

"Ching, you're wonderful."

"I think when Kauka come tonight, he like velly much," Ching agreed, looking important. He managed to discharge his myriad, self-appointed duties without ever appearing to hurry. Hours before anyone else was up he cleaned house silently and had breakfast ready at seven. Between breakfast and noon he fed and cared for the ever-increasing herd of small animals, which stubbornly refused to react to inoculations. Then, miraculously, lunch was ready. The noon meal over he pottered about the garden, and tended a plot of vegetables. Dinner done, he vanished, presumedly to rest, in the small house to the rear of the big one, but frequently sounds of hammering and sawing reached Thord or Kauka's ears as they worked in the laboratory at night, proving that Ching was occupied with mysterious projects of his own.

The mail truck lurched into sight, dust flying out behind it. Analu always drove at top speed, trying to make up the time he lost chatting with friends on the way. Seeing the waiting pair, he brandished his arm and brought the truck to a screeching stop.

"You wait long time?" he asked, pawing through packages of letters stacked on the seat beside him.

"Only one hour," Thord teased.

Analu seemed not to hear. "Plenty letters for Kauka," he announced, grinning, "and plenty of *ukana.*"

Getting out he handed the letters to Thord, then, walking to the rear of the truck which was a sort of combination stage and mail-delivery vehicle, he deposited a fifty-pound moist bag of *poi* into the wheelbarrow. "Here sweet potatoes." He hauled out two gunny-sacks and settled them carefully to leave room for other items. Four rather dilapidated-looking fowls with tied feet were deposited on the sweet potatoes. Analu scratched his head.

"Got bananas too, and one pig." He looked worriedly at the wheelbarrow.

Ching gave an evil smile, rearranged everything, and indicated places for the remaining items.

"Wait, one more kind," Analu panted after settling the white, shaved carcass of a sixty-pound porker. He rescued a carefully wrapped parcel and studied it with perplexed eyes.

"What this-kind always coming to Kauka from—Burma." He pronounced the word slowly and carefully. "You know?" he asked, looking at Thord.

Thord shook his head.

Analu shook the package and listened intently. A roguish expression crept into his eyes. "Might-be some-kind *ino,*" he suggested. "Sometime I drop in and help Kauka to drink!" Laughing, he handed Thord the parcel and climbed back into the truck.

"I no be late tomorrow," he promised cheerfully.

Thord laughed.

"Aloha," Analu gestured with his big, friendly arm and went roaring off to other homes, ranches, and plantations, hidden by the long slopes of Mauna Loa.

Ching watched him until he was out of sight, then started for the house, managing the laden wheelbarrow with the skill of a race accustomed to burdens. Thord wondered how much Ching suspected, or knew of what was going on. In Kona he had been the typical cook, prone to vent his ire at delayed, irregular meals. Since coming to Kau, he had clothed himself with an air of mysterious stolidity, accepting Kauka and Thord's unexplained comings and goings without apparent interest.

Alternately, or together, they paid visits to the eight lepers who had left their hiding place in Kohala to come to Kau for treatment. The beach village which Kauka had first destined for the leprosarium had been discarded in favor of a small, deep valley high on the slope of Mauna Loa. By some whim of the volcano, the lava flows of successive eruptions had circled it, leaving a fertile patch of forest which, from the highway, looked like a small island of verdure in the midst of desolation.

Water had been, and continued to be, a problem. To pack in lumber and corrugated iron for roofs to catch rain would have aroused curiosity and suspicion, so they were obliged to take water in kegs, on donkey-back each trip. The families of the afflicted supplied food.

Thord glanced at the loaded wheelbarrow, then at Ching's narrow back. Surely, he must wonder why, out of the quantities of supplies that poured in, so little was retained for family consumption, so much packed on donkeys and taken up Mauna Loa.

"Lunch leddy," Ching said over his shoulder, as they came into the garden.

"I'll be in soon as I've seen if there's enough water in the trough," Thord said.

Crossing the garden he went toward corrals under the *kiawes* where stolid little donkeys dozed in the semi-shade and his big bay horse luxuriously chewed *kiawe* beans scattered thickly on the ground.

Thord turned on the water, allowing it to run over until the trough was clear, then started for the house. Loki was waiting for him on the wide veranda facing the sea, which she had transformed into a *lanai*.

He handed her the mail and they went into lunch. While he ate, Loki read letters slowly. Sociable and gregarious, mail was a big event in her now isolated life. Except for Sunday visits from Carlos, who had managed to wangle a truck job, and Takeshi who came down with him, they had few callers. Hawaiians living more-or-less

[310]

in the vicinity dropped in occasionally for casual talk. Brewer and Prudence dined with them now and then. April's trips to Kau were unheralded. Because of the nature of Kauka and Thord's work she was careful to leave no trail which other whites might follow.

"Seem like Papa got plenty *aikanes* still, even if he not working for Hiram," Loki commented in pleased tones. "Read some of this letters. They make you feel good." She pushed a couple toward Thord. He took up the nearest. It was scrawled in pencil on lined paper torn from a child's school-pad.

"Aloha, *aikane* Kauka:
    I take my pen in hand for write some few words to my *aikane* of menny years. All us guys on *Haole Hao's* plantation have make big discussions on this matters of you going from Kona. An us all cum to same conclusion and wote the same ticket, like Politick mans say. Big shame on *Haole Hao* to let you go from plantation. New *Kauka* only sit on his fat *okole* and catch pay. He make snort on every peoples who not *haoles*. You never caring if mans Kanaka, Portugee or Japanee. If peoples got a bad sick and live far *mauka* in the coffee where car no can go, you come on top horse. Day-time, night-time all sames to you. This Hookana Doc speak, 'Office hours eight to ten, three to five.' What-the-hell kind *kauka* make like thats? First time I getting right chance I making up my minds to tell *Haole Hao* big shame he no let you keep your old car, after you working for hims twenty-eight year. If you got car you can cum when us fella need you. If *Haole Hao* blow up and I lose my job, I no give damns. Warm Alohas to you three guys. I hope you in good healths like me.
            Your *aikane,*
                Joseph Kapohakimohewa."

Thord laid it down and smiled.

"Seem like plantation peoples not liking Coombs much," Loki observed.

"No one can ever fill Kauka's place in Kona, Loki. The mold was broken after he was cast."

Loki nodded, then her eyes went to Thord. "How long before you fellas telling if the oil work?"

Thord hesitated. "A couple of the cases are progressing splen-didly, but only time will tell whether or not the improvement will be permanent."

"Which two fellas more better?"

"Eole and Kanaloa. We're injecting the ethyl esters of the oil into the fleshy parts of their bodies. Kauka's convinced—"

"What this kind ethyl esters?" Loki asked, puzzled.

He tried to explain the processes of breaking down the oil, and isolating its chemical elements.

"This-kind too deeps for my head," Loki sighed.

The sound of a car approaching stopped him. Loki tilted her head.

"Brewer," she announced in excitement. "Might-be Prue start to *hanao*."

She headed for the *lanai*. Brewer boiled up the steps. "How're the publicans and sinners making out in the wilderness?" he asked.

"Fine, Brewer, fine, this swell house, you swell guy for lending it to us." Loki kissed his mottled, purplish jowl and waited hope-fully.

"Where's Thord?" Brewer asked.

"Finish *kaukau*. You want for Prudence?" Loki's voice poised hopefully.

"No, but it'll be any day now. She's big as a house."

"Might-be she have twins." Loki suggested.

"It's not impossible, I'm virile."

"You rascals," Loki laughed. "What-kind you wanting Thord for?"

"April phoned. Elsbeth's having a bad spell."

"Coombs—"

"She can't stomach him. Hiram suggested she see Thord and sent April down to fetch him."

"What you think on thats!" Loki's voice spilled over with amuse-ment and triumph. "Thord—" she called.

He hurried down the hall.

"Your girl coming to get you." She explained the details.

"How the hell can I go—" He began, then checked himself.

"The King of Kona has issued his ultimatum," Brewer announced with boisterous hilarity. "Better go. Who knows? You may be taken back into the fold. Stranger things have happened. In time even that whited-sepulcher of a father-in-law of mine may discover the Christian virtue of forgiveness. Now I must rattle my stumps. My Macadamian nuts are being fertilized, my wife's in no condition to be left long. If she's still in one piece we'll drop around Sunday. If not, I'll be seeing one, or all of you." And he went lumbering off.

"How can I go, Loki?" Thord said. "It's my night to go *mauka*. Kauka won't be in until after dark and will be dog tired."

"Papa little old, but always when peoples needing help he got enough strong to go again. You leave every-kind for tonight on the desk. When Papa come I give *ino* for make him sleep good one-two hour. Then he eat. Ching and me put water inside barrels and *kaukau* on top donkeys for the poor peoples who got *maipake*."

"Damn women like Elsbeth! But I'll be glad of a chance to spend a few hours with April."

"After all, lucky us no got car now," Loki said brightly. "If Elsbeth keep her sicks for whiles, every week you make same-kinds, April come and get you and bring you home. Elsbeth like you, Hiram too. Might-be soon us have another marry in our family." The lilt in her voice died, as memories marched slowly across the screen of her mind.

Thord placed a comforting hand on her shoulder.

"Sometimes I no can help thinking about Mamo and Liholiho—"

"If you didn't, Mama, you wouldn't be natural."

"But that no right," Loki insisted stoutly. "Us must think of the alive peoples, the *make* ones with God. The alives got *pilikeas,* for work out. Like you and April."

Thord nodded, his eyes deep and thoughtful.

"Your girl coming." Loki indicated the strip of road connecting their place with the highway. "Better you forget every-kind for whiles and have happy time with your *kuuipo.*"

As always, Thord had a moment of surprise, realizing the magic April created by her mere presence. In the most commonplace acts

[313]

she had distinction, beauty, and freshness. She came flying up the steps and went into his arms.

He knew a moment of fierce gratitude that he had come to maturity without falling in love. In most cases early love was an experience for which the soul was not ready and could not appreciate to the full. Looking down into her face he felt he was among the anointed of the earth; when her lips met his, stars, growing green things, seas, and mountains fell into divine order.

"You have eat, April?" Loki asked, when Thord released her.

"Yes, Loki, thanks."

"Might-be if Elsbeth no keep Thord too long you fellas can *kaukau* tonight with us?" Loki suggested hopefully, starved hospitality eager to be assuaged.

"Why not? But we may be late."

"I no care if you no come till ten o'clock."

"It's a date," April promised.

"Come again before the end of the week." Mrs. Wilde gave a dry sigh. "Just seeing you has helped me."

"I'll come up—Sunday," Thord promised. "In the meantime, don't let anything upset you emotionally. Relax. Take your sun baths. And I'm leaving a sedative for you in case you can't sleep." He indicated some small white pills in a glass phial.

"I'll follow instructions." Mrs. Wilde held out a pale, veined hand.

Thord pressed it, then gently laid it under the covers. The two Japanese women came forward and took their accustomed posts on each·side of the bed.

April was waiting for him at the foot of the stairs. They ran down the steps into the garden and headed to where the roadster was parked. Trees gave off green coolness, flowers poured assorted fragrances into the twilight. Inside the house the telephone began ringing.

"One of the houseboys will get it," April said, getting into the car.

They started slowly to circle the driveway and just as they passed under the porte cochere a voice called from within the house. "Miss April, Miss April, terefone."

"Coming," she called back in a slightly exasperated voice.

Thord waited in the car, his eyes on forested slopes climbing toward the violent summit of Hualalai. Liholiho, Homer, Mamo, all gone in a few swift months. Doubling up his fist he pressed it against the steering wheel. We've got to do it, he thought fiercely, we've got to! To save other Mamos, Homers, and Liholihos who bring joy, vitality, beauty, and laughter to the earth.

"Thord." April's voice roused him. "That was Father. He wants to see you before you go home. He's through at the office and will be over in a few minutes."

Their eyes met.

"Any idea why he wants to see me?" Thord enquired.

"I've a hunch he's going to ask you to come back."

Getting out of the car, Thord went silently into the house with April. Despite the hushed silence of formally arranged rooms, the Wilde house was a place of tumult, the silent tumult that has its home in human souls. Suddenly, Thord bent and kissed April. She clung swiftly and silently, then released him. Eyes met, minds fused.

"The way I see it," April said in a small, hushed voice, "is—when life hammers people it isn't to break them, it's to shape them. Everything's been against us—from the start. We're no nearer a solution of our personal problem than before Dale came. At times I feel brittle as glass and ready to fly into a million screaming pieces, but I know that the walls which have been put around us, aren't to shut us in. They're put there for us to break down, burrow under, or climb over."

Thord gripped her hands. "When I look at you, listen to you, April," he said, "I realize that I loved you from the instant I saw you."

The headlights of a car flashed into the garden.

"Father," April said, and waited.

The car stopped at the steps, Hiram got out, glanced at the two in the lighted hallway, and came up the steps.

[315]

"There's a matter I'd like to discuss with you, Graham," he said without preliminary. "Come into my den. April—"

"Yes, Father?"

"Tell the cook that Graham'll be here for dinner."

"Sorry," Thord said. "Loki's expecting us."

Hiram scowled, batted his eyelids, then said, "Very well," and struck off through a hallway leading toward the rear of the house. Thord followed, on guard.

Opening a tall door, Hiram led the way into a large square room arranged for a single person's comfort. Ranked books, a solitary easy-chair with a green reading light behind it, a handy table, expensive rugs were its only appointments. Wrapped cigars, like silver mummies lying side by side, filled a glass-topped box, placed on the polished table. Hiram's tremendous ego vibrated in the room. He glanced at the easy-chair, then decided against sitting down.

"Possibly you've an idea why I want to see you?" he suggested.

"I haven't."

"I'd like you to reconsider your decision to team with Kauka. I need you on the plantation. You get on with all nationalities like an Islander. The present doctor antagonizes people without intending to. He has a secret contempt for anyone who isn't white and my employees sense it."

Thord made no answer.

Hiram selected one of the silver cigars and began slowly removing the wrapper. "Possibly you feel the salary I pay—"

"It had nothing to do with my decision to stay with Kauka."

"What has association with him to offer a man of your background?"

"Plenty," Thord said emphatically.

"What do you hope to accomplish by isolating yourselves in Kau?"

"We're doing some research work—"

"In connection—"

"With tropical diseases."

Hiram bit off the end of his cigar and lighted it.

"Look here," he began, as if realizing the futility of beating

[316]

about the bush. "You know medicine, you're efficient, you fit into Kona as if you'd been made for it—therefore, you're valuable to me." Reaching out, Hiram switched on the reading lamp and the light, coming up through the shade, tinged his face with green.

"I'm afraid, Mr. Wilde—"

"Wait a minute. I'm prepared to pay you a salary commensurate with your worth. I'll provide an assistant, Kauka if you wish, so as to enable you to continue the research work you're engaged in. I'll build an adequate laboratory—"

"I appreciate the generosity, the scope of your offer—"

"Name your conditions," Wilde said, grimly.

"Do you want to know the real reason why I won't work for you?"

"Won't work for me?" Wilde echoed, as if he could not credit his ears.

"Yes—exactly that."

"Name it."

"I love April," Thord said in measured tones.

He burned under Wilde's deliberate scrutiny. The yellow, calculating eyes took stock of his height, noted his broad shoulders, brushed his forehead, lingered on the line of his jaw.

"Why," Wilde asked coolly, "should that be an obstacle? I haven't the least objection to having you for a son-in-law."

Thord's mind spun out of focus, then assembled itself. "You're rich, I'm poor."

"That's easily taken care of," Wilde assured him, smiling as if they shared an obscene secret. "Island families of this, the fourth generation, are constantly coming up against this identical situation. Some upstanding young fellow comes to Hawaii from the Mainland, and falls in love with the daughter of an old, established family. Appreciating the dividend of getting new blood into stock which, in some instances, is getting thin, the family moves over slightly in the nest to make room for the new member. There are numerous instances, among my friends, where daughters have married professional men who, in time, have abandoned their chosen careers to adjust themselves into the particular groove of the families they've married into."

[317]

Thord's skin burned. Behind Wilde's carefully arranged words he saw his real motive. He was not at all adverse to having him marry into the Wilde clan and was, also, paving the way to pry him loose from medicine to become, in time, manager for the Kona Sugar Company.

"I'm afraid, Mr. Wilde, that I don't belong to that—sort of thing. When I took my oath to medicine—"

"I was merely citing instances," Wilde interrupted. "Does April—" Then he laughed. "That's evident. She gave Dale and his millions the gate. At the time I questioned the soundness of her decision. Now, I see she was right. Dale didn't fit into Hawaii. April, after being home a while, couldn't stomach the prospect of living in New York. You"—he stressed the word—"are her kind of man. In addition, Mrs. Wilde's all for you, all Kona's for you and I"—he paused impressively—"have an immense respect for your mind and ability." He waited, then added, "I take it we understand each other, Graham?"

"I'm afraid—we don't!" Thord announced, his skin icy. "As I see it, if I marry April, it would be on *your* terms. Come back here, fall into step—"

"On the contrary," Wilde interrupted. "I appreciate you're a man who can't be swerved from a course you've elected to follow. Nor can I." He injected an intimate, admiring note into his voice. "April's my only child. Her happiness is of prime importance to me." He let the words hang temptingly in the air.

"I'm afraid, Mr. Wilde," Thord said, his voice on edge, "to use a slang term, I can't 'be had.' For instance I simply can't see you agreeing to my marrying April and taking her to live in Kau!"

"That's where you prove you don't know me," Wilde asserted blandly. "Suppose you put that up to—her?"

All the time you're giving in to me, Thord thought ragingly, you're laying traps . . . far ahead. Plotting, eventually, to swing me into line. He looked at the cold, guarded face, with the mask of geniality that could not quite fit over it. I'm as strong, as astute as you are, Thord thought. Shall I risk beating you at your own game?

[318]

34

DRIVING to Kau, Thord observed Hiro's discreet shoulders, silhouetted by the dashboard light, and debated whether or not to tell April of the unexpected turn events had taken. He watched tree trunks melting by as the car tore through fragrant forests and stars wheeled on their age-old orbits. Best, he decided, to discuss the matter with Kauka before saying anything to her.

"Hasn't this afternoon been a dividend?" April said, cuddling his hand under her chin.

"And then some!" he agreed.

"And we've got a couple of more hours together—still," she exulted.

Thord kissed her temple.

"What did Dad want?" April asked as an afterthought.

"To have me back."

"If you weren't working with Kauka to—" She broke off hastily.

"God knows, you're a frightful temptation," Thord confessed.

She brushed the back of his hand with her lips, then held it to her forehead.

"Oh, April—" His voice had a quality she had never heard in it before.

"You know—what that means?" she asked, amazed and delighted.

"How could I fail to—after living all this time in a Hawaiian household?"

"Okay. I pledge eternal allegiance to you—my Chief," April said softly.

"And I," he said, holding her hand to his forehead, "swear forever to uphold you!"

Their arms flew about each other. The car turned off the highway and rocked against the dirt-rutted road leading to the house. Hiro slowed down, and they released each other. Thord peered through the window.

"Kauka hasn't been home very long," he announced, as headlights picked up the shapes of tired donkeys with damp backs, wandering toward the corrals, nipping grass and picking up fallen *kiawe* beans. Pack saddles sat on the ground, blankets were airing on the hitching rail. Empty water kegs, waiting to be filled, food for the next trip, were stacked neatly on a square of clean canvas.

Hiro stopped the car and Thord noticed that his eyes rested on the animals and assembled stores in a puzzled way.

"Somebody come from mounting?" he asked as he opened the door.

Thord nodded casually.

"At last!" Loki called from the *lanai*. Then seeing Hiro she added, "Aloha, Hiro, go kitchen. Ching give you *kaukau*."

Thord headed for the room which was a combined office and laboratory. Kauka was bending intently over the big table. Physical weariness weighted his stocky figure, but his movements were alert as he studied charts and case histories, adding notes and observations.

"How did it come out?" Thord asked eagerly.

"My boy." Kauka gripped Thord's forearms. "They didn't—react. This is the third time!"

"It certainly looks as if you were right at the start, Kauka, when you said that if we could succeed in breaking the oil down to its ethyl esters we'd begin to see results!"

Thord picked up a case history and studied it intently.

"I'm having a few difficulties," Kauka admitted. "The improvement in Eole and Kanaloa is obvious. The rest are all clamoring for the treatment we've been using on them. Keiki almost cried because he's still taking the oil by the mouth, while Kanaloa and Eole get it hypodermically. Lehua was hurt because I'm using hot

[320]

applications on Mele and Hinano's lesions and not on hers. But I believe I have succeeded, finally, in driving home the fact to them that it's only by trying different methods can we discover which is most consistently effective."

"You're tired," Thord said.

"Only bodily." He smiled. "Loki told me Hiram sent for you for Elsbeth, and I suspect for other reasons."

Thord gave details of the interview. Kauka raised his eyebrows.

"I'm tempted to chance marrying April," Thord finished explosively.

"Why not?" said Kauka thoughtfully. "If a man lives fully he must gamble sometimes—as we're gambling with this." He gestured at the table.

"But there's so much at stake." Thord indicated the records of treatments.

"Agreed. Our work's still in the kindergarten stage. It stands to reason that in time someone will get wind of our odd comings and goings up Mauna Loa. In a few more weeks, or months, if our second pair of patients treated with the ethyl esters react as Eole and Kanaloa have, we must turn over our preliminary findings to Molokai. It may mean saving lives which otherwise may be lost.

"If, by some bad luck, what we're up to is uncovered before we have sufficient data to justify what we're doing, we'll have to face the music. But I know you, as well as I, are willing to run the risk. April and Loki are too big to feel disgraced if we're chucked into jail. There'll be a hell of an uproar, but—" Again Kauka took Thord by the shoulders and looked into his eyes, "But if this last treatment stands the 'acid test,' after the flame and smoke of battle dies down, Hiram will be proud that his son-in-law will be numbered among those who have pioneered in this field."

Thord looked plagued.

"It's only a matter of time," Kauka went on, "before the showdown comes, or is forced on us. Why not marry April and—"

"I've no faith that Hiram won't try, the minute I marry her, his shenanigans to get me into his setup."

"He's so keen to get you into the fold"—Kauka's eyes twinkled—

"that I've a hunch he'll give you your head for a while at any rate. By then I hope we'll have enough data that's fool-proof to justify our nefarious activities."

"But suppose we're caught, my record will be traced—that old mess—"

" 'In God I have put my trust. I will not fear what man may do to me,' " Kauka reminded him.

Thord gestured savagely. "Don't say that. The last time you quoted it was to Loki, the night that Mamo and Liholiho—"

"I remember," Kauka said. "I have lost my child, my beloved Mamo, but it hasn't affected my belief that there's a Power behind everything that never stops flowing forward to bigger goals than any mere human ever dreamed of."

"You make me feel ashamed," Thord said.

"Ashamed, my boy? Why?"

"You have shown me that trouble's the real test of an individual," Thord said. "It's easy to be kind, brave, strong, to have faith when things are going smoothly. But when they're tough and you see a person going on, believing when apparently there's nothing to believe in, having fun when there's nothing visible to have fun with, laughing when crying's easier—" He stopped; then he finished with a rush, "I understand why people hurry to share their joys and troubles with you, and with Loki, why they bank on you to go *all the way,* no matter what, why you're a hundred per cent *all the while!*"

"I think, my boy"—Kauka smiled—"frustrated emotions, piling up in you, have made you sentimental. Dinner's waiting. If you're to arrive at your destination before daylight you must leave before eleven."

"Shall I tell April—about Hiram tonight?"

"Why not? She, Loki, you, and I are a *hui*—corporation. If you have joy and share it with others, you double it."

"Elsbeth'll want a big show—"

"She and Hiram are so keen to get you into the tribe they'll take you on your own terms. I've known them twenty-eight years. Their main objective in life is to get things they want, regardless of *how*. Come on, my *opu's* calling for a good meal."

They went down the hall.

"Well, at last you devils *pau* talk!" Loki said.

"Yes," Kauka smiled, pulling out his chair.

Thord seated himself beside April.

Ching came in with a platter of chicken stew and rice. Placing it on the table he waited defiantly.

"Chicken—" Loki elevated her eyebrows.

"Kanaka fellas up mountain got big *poi*—sweet potatoes and bananas for eat," he announced, and went off.

"Ching knows plenty," Kauka observed.

"I still get cold and shivery," April said, "whenever I think about what you two are doing. Everything's been against us."

"It isn't any longer," said Thord. "Your father told me this afternoon—that he has no objections to having me for his son-in-law."

"You're joking—"

"I'm not."

"Father's attitude"—April choked—"doesn't change the fact that we still *can't* get married!" She told him about Dale.

"The"—Thord choked back the word that sprang to his lips and substituted—"swine! I wish I could get my hands— Why didn't you tell me about this before?"

"What would have been the use? There's nothing we can do about it. There's been enough to stand, without adding to this. I love you, I'll always love you, there isn't anyone else for me," she said violently. "But that's all the good it'll do us, unless or until you and Kauka—"

"Don't look like that, April," Thord begged, "as if you hated—"

"I do hate life!" she asserted with the violence of the very young. Now the pallid, mask-like despair in her had broken, she seemed on fire. Her eyes had a wild look in their depths. "Life lays traps for people. Look what it did to Homer! And to Mamo and Liholiho. Look what it's done to us. And it's torn chunks out of Loki and Kauka— I can't sleep. I lie always thinking and thinking. It seems as if God *liked* to hurt people—"

[323]

"My child, hush," Kauka said. "People aren't asked to bear more than they have strength for." Reaching out he laid his hand on her clenched ones. "Remember—big blows for big people, little blows for little people—but in the end, joy in proportion."

April gazed at his steady deep eyes; then, flinging her arms on the table she buried her face. Thord bent over her. Loki glanced at Kauka and, rising, they started out of the room.

"I'm not going under." Flinging up, April began pounding a clenched fist against the open palm of the other hand. "I'll take whatever I have to take, but I don't have to like it!" She suddenly recovered her self-possession.

"None of us do, April," Kauka said gently. "But we have to go on, have faith. Faith is greater than reason—it gets people places that reason tells them are impossible."

"Forgive me for blowing up," April said, looking around the table.

"There's nothing to forgive," Thord said, putting his arm about her shoulders. "I feel as you do, burning up inside—"

April looked into his eyes, then said jerkily, "A car's coming—"

"Who come so late?" Loki's eyes grew wary and watchful.

"I'll go and see," April said, rising.

They all followed.

Lights flashed into the yard, throwing Ching's and Carlos's figures, busily packing donkeys, into relief.

"Brewer!" Loki exhaled with relief. "Guess Prue starting to *hanao*."

Brewer came noisily up the steps. His face was florid and shiny with perspiration. "I need you as fast as possible, Kauka. Prue's started to foal. I got one of the men's wives to stay with her while I fetched you."

"I'll get my bag and instruments."

"You like I come too?" Loki asked.

"It would buck Prue up immensely."

"Okay—I get my coat."

Thord and April stood with locked hands. Brewer mopped his face. "This has got me on the run," he said, lumbering about the *lanai.* "God knows how many girls I've got into trouble, but I haven't been with them during the payoff. God knows Prue is no beauty, but she's my wife. And a damn good one, too. I can't help being fond of her. And now she's in hell—because of me. Blast it, I feel like a crook, all sorts of a rotter—"

Kauka came back.

"Where's Loki? Tell her to hurry," Brewer bellowed.

"Take it easy," Kauka said kindly. "If I know Prue, she'll go through with flying colors. She's that sort. And when her baby comes—well, you'll see. The pain's forgotten."

"Damned if I'd forget it," Brewer shouted; then he shook his head as if trying to locate some thought lost in his mind under pressure of new emotions. "I almost forgot to tell you, thinking about Prue"—he looked at Kauka—"that Central phoned me a radio for you—"

"For me?"

"It's from that Austrian who lived with you—"

"What he say?" Loki asked jerkily as she joined them.

"I wrote it down. Sounded like a bunch of Greek. It was about some oil, and he said he'd be coming to Hawaii shortly. Let's shove. Someone going up Mauna Loa?" He indicated the pack animals as he started down the stairs.

"Thord," Kauka said, grasping Loki's arm and hurrying after Brewer.

Thord gripped April's elbow. Their eyes met.

"I've got to go, darling."

"I know." She gazed at him, then said in a small desolate voice, "I read somewhere, once, that if a person does his work—loving it, as Kauka and you do—he fulfills earth's finest dream."

"But I have another dream, too, April. Know what it is?"

"Yes," she murmured against his lips.

35

BREWER charged for the wall telephone and began ringing Central explosively. "Blast her, she's asleep!" he roared, rolling bloodshot eyes. He began cranking again, tearing at the instrument.

"Easy, Brewer," Loki warned. "If ring too hard, might-be you broke the handle, then you have to go to Kona in the car and that take time. No be scare, Kauka *hemo* plenty babies. He smart like any-kind—"

"Damnation, he's worried. I know from the way he's working—"

"Yes, Prudence having hard time," Loki admitted. "She very narrow in the *opi*—flanks, and baby very big. But after by-and-by—"

Brewer continued ringing, his jowly face livid. Finally the answering ring came. "Central!" he bellowed, "get the Reverend Thisbe! Keep ringing till he answers!"

Loki went off. Brewer waited, listening to footsteps scurrying back and forth, as Hawaiian and Japanese women, called to assist, went about mysterious errands. Every so often he heard Kauka directing them, but he barely recognized Prudence's voice, hoarse with pain, exhausted. Sweat burst out on his skin, waves of weakness swept him.

Loki came back. "Get Thisbe yet?" she inquired.

"No, but Central's still ringing. Curse him, he must sleep like the dead. How are things—"

"Not too good," Loki admitted unhappily, a little worried crease between her eyebrows. "I wish Thord here to help Kauka."

"What in hell is he doing up Mauna Loa, anyway?" Brewer

[326]

shouted. "He knew Prudence was due to foal—" Breaking off, he listened, then roared, "Thisbe? This is Brewer. If you hang up on me I'll come to the parsonage and break your neck! Prudence is having a tough time. . . . Why, you filthy little toad, you're damn well coming down and as fast as you can! Hell-and-damnation, don't you realize that *sometimes women die in childbirth*—"

He listened.

"Graham? No, he isn't here. He went up Mauna Loa. What for? How in hell should I know what for? I don't poke my snout into other people's business like you Revs do. Now, rattle your stumps—"

He listened again.

"Hell, we're all born!" he roared. "Some of us properly, some of us improperly. There's not a dime's worth of difference in the value of the article or the trouble of bringing it into the world. Prudence loves you, God knows why—your attitude toward her marriage—I don't give a goddamn if I'm a reprobate in your estimation. So are you in mine! It's the girl that matters. I'm her husband and I intend to do everything in my power—"

Suddenly his face became choleric.

"He's hung up on me!" Brewer's voice filled the house.

"Kulihuli—hush!" Loki warned. "Not so good for Prudence if she finding out her papa no like to come. Might-be Kauka have to cut her *opu*—"

"You mean it may have to be a Caesarean?" Brewer asked, his loose face ashen.

"If not too late—"

Brewer began attacking the telephone crazily.

"No make like that, Brewer. If you pull off the wall—"

"He's got to come down!"

"Wait, I talk to him." She took the earpiece from him, moving him aside.

Brewer waited explosively, purple hands clenching and unclenching. After a few minutes Loki hung up. "Thisbe not answering," she said, her eyes indignant.

"I'll fetch him—"

"No, you must stay close. Phone Hiram to get—"

"That's the ticket!" Brewer grasped at the suggestion and began ringing madly.

Loki hurried off. Finally the answer came.

"Hiram, grab the dirty little red rat you call a parson and bring him down as fast as you can. My girl's in a bad way. Graham? He went to Mauna Loa. What for? How in hell could I know? Yes? Yes, yes, bring Coombs along. Thanks." He hung up exhaustedly.

Heading for the sideboard he poured out a jolt of whisky, tossed it down, and looked about the living room. The house, once a not too neat bachelor abode, had acquired charm, warmth. Bouquets of flowers, which Prudence had gathered only that morning, breathed sweetness. Carefully arranged books and magazines added color to low tables placed conveniently beside deep reading chairs. Hanging baskets of ferns, well-arranged clusters of potted palms, brought outdoor charm into the room.

"My good Prue—" Brewer muttered thickly, and headed for the bedroom. From it came labored breathing, stifled grunts, smothered moans, followed by desperate strugglings and strainings. Locking his thumbs into his belt, Brewer thrust down on it until it cut into his paunch. A voice hardly human cried out. He stood, crucified between terror and horror. A sickly-sweet, heavy odor filled his nostrils. They were giving her chloroform! Brewer waited, then charged in.

Kauka and Loki were standing on each side of the bed looking compassionately and anxiously down at the white twisted face on the pillow.

"Prue, my good Prue—" Brewer muttered thickly, going forward.

The glazed eyes opened briefly. Picking up her limp white hand, he kneaded it between his puffy, purple ones.

"I'll . . . make . . . the grade," Prudence murmured feebly. "But it hurts . . . like hell. I'm all hurt . . . even my mind." Her eyes roved about until they found Kauka's. "Give me . . . more," she whispered.

"In a few moments, Prue," he said gently.

"You won't . . . let me die? I used to want to. Now I . . . don't. Because I'm . . . loved . . ." Her voice died in exhaustion.

"Damn right you are!" Brewer said.

Prudence looked gratefully at him, then braced against a new pain welling into her body and tearing it to pieces. Brewer glared about wildly. "Give her more chloroform! I can't stand it . . ."

"Is Father—" Prudence gasped.

"Yes."

She made a sign of relief, then began straining. Kauka watched and when she desisted, as if overcome by her inability to get anywhere, he dripped chloroform into the cone and applied it. Her taut body grew limp, relaxed.

"Don't give her too much—"

"Papa know." Loki placed a kind hand on Brewer's fleshy shoulder. "Better you go and rest little time. After little whiles, Prue try again. If us need you, us call."

"Why can't she pop it like Hawaiian and Japanese women do?" Brewer demanded. "Why must she suffer so?"

Kauka took Prudence's pulse carefully, looked at her, then said, "I think you'd better phone to Coombs to come down, Brewer."

"He's coming with Hiram."

"Hiram?" Kauka said.

"He's bringing that scum Thisbe—he hung up on me!" Brewer's voice rose.

"*Pau!*" Kauka warned, indicating the bed.

Brewer leaned down and brushed back a wet strand of hair lying tiredly on Prudence's forehead. "My poor"—he checked the word he'd been about to utter and substituted—"girl." Then he went ponderously out of the room.

He flung himself into a chair. Outside, waves flopped heavily on the sand. Cocoanut fronds rustled faintly. After a little he heaved to his feet and headed for the sideboard. Picking up the whisky bottle he poured out half a tumbler and tossed it off.

From the room sounds began coming again, sounds of a woman in agony fighting without success to bring her child into the world. He hurried to the door.

"How are things coming?" he asked thickly.

"They . . . aren't," Kauka said, glancing up.

"We're not going to lose her?" Brewer choked.

"She's got grit, and fight—"

"Can I—"

"There's nothing you can do. I wish to God Hiram and Coombs would get here."

"Car coming," Loki panted.

Brewer charged off to meet it.

It stopped, and Hiram got out.

"Tell Coombs to hurry!" Brewer yelled.

"I called for him but he had left for Huihui. I told Central to locate him and tell him to come here. How's Prudence?"

"She's fighting." Brewer mopped his red expanse of face. "Did that—"

"Thisbe's with me."

"He better be!"

Thisbe got out, his figure more meager and pinched than ever.

"So you had to be dragged to your daughter's bedside!" Brewer shouted. "I suppose if she dies you'll stand up and read the funeral services in that sanctimonious way of yours—"

"That'll do, Brewer," Hiram said.

Brewer led the way indoors. Thisbe followed. The room was filled with waiting. Presently Loki came to the door. Her eyes were concerned, her face tired and anxious.

"Brewer—"

He hurried to her.

"Prudence want you. Thisbe, better you come too."

Thisbe clasped his hands, swallowed, and moved stiffly across the room. Brewer charged to the side of the bed.

"What is it, old girl?"

"If I die, you won't give our baby—"

"Of course not. But see here, you aren't going to die. What in hell should I do without you? You're a hell of a swell—wife." His voice broke.

"Is Father—"

[330]

"He's here, old girl."

Slow tears began stealing down her chalk-gray cheeks; her eyes looked over Brewer's shoulder. Thisbe stood, his face twitching.

"Blessed be God, which hath not turned away my prayer," Prudence murmured, "nor His mercy from me!" She lay spent, then began tearing at her lower lip with her teeth.

"Better go—" Loki said, her eyes leaping to Kauka's.

Brewer turned. Thisbe followed.

Hiram glanced up. "How are things progressing?" he said.

"Only God knows," Brewer shouted. "I wish to Christ—"

"What?" Hiram demanded edgily.

"That Thord was here!"

"Send one of your men after him," Hiram said shortly.

"But I don't know where he went!"

"Loki or Kauka must know. Ask them."

Brewer ran toward the bedroom. Thisbe walked to the steps and stared into the dark.

"Kauka, where did Thord go?" Brewer asked hoarsely. "Hiram wants me to send a man after him."

There was a moment of silence, broken by the sound of moaning.

"Up Mauna Loa—"

"But where*abouts* up Mauna Loa?" Brewer said in a ragged voice.

A desperate scream tore the night. Brewer recoiled. Kauka and Loki began working frantically. Brewer shut his eyes; then his nostrils were filled with the sickening smell of hot fresh blood. There was a pause, followed by another scream. Brewer clutched his hair, glared about him with the uncomprehending rage of a wounded bull, and bolted.

Hiram strode to him. "What in hell—"

"Oh, Heavenly Father—" Thisbe began in shaking tones.

"Blast you, shut up!" Brewer roared. "He don't listen to people like you. *You only make sounds!*" He glared at the meager, black-suited figure, then began thickly, "Save her, God! You can. Don't take her away from me. I'm an old souse and haven't been a good man, but she don't deserve to die! She's only had a little happiness.

Come on—show that scrub what real prayer can do! Show him up!"

A thin, outraged wail came to his ears.

"The baby's—out!" he gasped, collapsing into a near-by chair. His florid face was drenched with perspiration, his thick gray hair rumpled up. He passed his hand across his forehead, then sank back wearily.

Hiram stood, his hands clasped rigidly behind him. Thisbe moved vaguely about the *lanai*. Loki came to the door.

"Brewer, you got a little son." Her voice soared upward.

"How's—" he desisted.

"Prue okay." She began crying with relief, then vanished.

"Give me a drink, Hiram," Brewer said thickly.

Hiram went stiffly to the sideboard. When the drink was mixed he took it to Brewer. Brewer downed it and got to his feet. "Have one?" he asked. "We must toast my son." Pride rang in his voice.

Hiram nodded abstractedly, his yellow eyes roving over the room. Brewer set out three glasses and poured whisky into them.

"Thisbe, we're toasting your—grandson." His little eyes were filled with merriment.

"I don't drink."

"That's your loss. Well, here's to the small fellow and my good Prue!" Picking up first one, then the other glasses, he downed them.

Loki came out with a wrapped object in her arms.

"Look your fine boy, Brewer," she said exultantly. "Look, Hiram. Thisbe, here your *moopuna*—grandchild." Pride flowed from her portly form.

Brewer inspected the small scarlet face. "Gad, he's got my color, all right. Damned if he hasn't."

Loki blew up into gorgeous mirth. "If that your color, you got plenty kids, Brewer. All baby red when first they come out the mother—"

Brewer raised his brows in astonishment, then chuckled fatly. "Well, I've contributed my part toward populating the world," he admitted.

Thisbe froze inside his dark suit. Hiram contemplated the child.

"What does it weigh?" he asked, searching for something to say.

"No weigh yet, but sure got more from eleven pounds," Loki said. Then her coffee-brown eyes began shining. "See, Thisbe!"

He came as if dragged against his will, stared at the child, swallowed once, then stepped back.

"Well, as everything's over successfully, I'll move on home," Hiram announced. "When Graham returns, Loki, tell him to come to Kona with Hiro and Thisbe at noon."

"Might-be Thord not get back until tomorrow night," Loki said in a guarded voice.

"Where did he go?" Hiram asked in annoyed tones.

"I no hear him tell Kauka."

"When you know, phone me and I'll send one of my men after him—or Brewer can. April went to pieces after she came home last night. I'm concerned about her. Her nerves seem all shot."

Loki made no reply.

"If Graham isn't here by noon and Prudence's condition warrants her being left, tell Kauka to come. There are matters I want settled." And he vanished into the dark.

36

OPENING her eyes, Loki shifted her bulk to a more comfortable position on the sofa, where she'd been cat-napping for the past three hours. She looked across the room to the bed in which Prudence slept with her child, and she felt the deep satisfaction that only women know after the miracle of successful birth.

Prudence had transformed the once barn-like bedroom into a restful affair. Starched white mosquito netting was draped behind the head of the big four-poster. Dotted swiss curtains framed the windows and flounced the bureau and low seat before it. Rag rugs added spots of color to the floor.

Sitting up stealthily, Loki spotted Brewer's portly form, covered with a blanket, stretched on the floor beside Prudence's bed, and her eyes filled with roguish glee.

Outside, day was getting under way. The garden, crowded with blossoming ginger, plumeria, and gardenias, sent up gusts of fragrance and the soft pad of workmen's feet going off to cultivate fields of Macadamian nut trees, added a pleasant stir to the atmosphere.

Better I waking Papa, she thought. Tossing back an armful of hair she sat up, then, on bare silent feet she headed for the *lanai*, unable to resist a brief contact with the morning before duties demanded by the day overtook her.

The house had already been cared for by early-rising servants. Loki's eyes brushed bowls of artfully arranged flowers, appreciated the soft gleam of polished floors broken by lustrous brown *lauhala* mats. Brewer's big desk, set against the wall near the telephone, was heaped with papers and letters which added a pleasant flavor of business to be done.

Thisbe was seated at it, bending over and writing slowly and carefully on a sheet of paper. From time to time he adjusted the spectacles sitting astride his thin, questing nose. He did not hear Loki's footsteps, for despite her bulk she moved with the light sure grace of a cat.

"Good morning, Thisbe," she said.

He jerked up, his hands looking flurried and cautious.

"Good morning," he said stiffly.

"What-kind you making?" Loki asked with mild curiosity.

"I'm making notes—for my sermon next Sunday," Thisbe informed her coldly.

"Bet-you-my-lifes I knowing what-kind stuffs you speaking next Sunday," Loki said. "You *tutu*—grandparents now, so you talking begats."

"Begats?" Thisbe said pompously, his face puzzled.

"You know." Loki's brows drew together with the effort of remembering. "That-kind the Bible speaking . . . And Adam he live many hundred year and begat Seth. And Seth live many hundred more year and begat Enos, and Enos begat Cain." Then the imp which was never dormant long in her bubbled to the surface. "And Thisbe begat Prudence, and Prudence begat— Sha, the small boy no got name yet!" and she exploded in joyous laughter.

Thisbe froze into a white fury. "You're sacrilegious!"

"I not making boob on God, I only making some fun. What the matter? You no sleeping good?"

"Sleep—*in this house!*"

"If you not preacher-mans, I give you slap to your face," Loki announced hotly, her eyes blazing. "You lucky guy. You got daughter, and grandchild."

Going hurriedly into the garden, she let the peace and beauty of the morning soak into her, healing the quick upsurge of grief. In the south, above fields of green trees, the long blue shape of Mauna Loa was etched against the gold-washed early morning sky. She listened to the voice of the land, a great voice compounded out of lesser voices: doves cooing, plover whistling overhead, a cow lowing in the distance for her calf, the sigh and thud of the sea far below, and the tiny rattle of seed pods in the grass disturbed by her angles as she made her slow way across the lawn. Her lost serenity stole back.

Finally she returned to the house and went up the steps leading into the *lanai*. Couches and chairs of uncertain age and origin were gathered comfortably together as if discussing matters of common interest. Sunlight sliced itself into long slender wafers as it filtered through bamboo screens, potted plants nestled their green heads against one another, and a stray bee darted out of the big open-air room like a person caught trespassing.

Loki headed for the spare room where Kauka was sleeping. Crossing to the bed, she laid her hand on his shoulder. "Wake up, Papa. Little-more Hiro coming to take you and Thisbe to Kona."

Heaving to a sitting position, Kauka rubbed sleepy fingers through his hair, shook his head, then asked, "How's Prudence?"

"Weak, but rest good," she chuckled. "Brewer *moemoe* on the floor by her bed. Seem like that old rascals fine husband after all. Eat some coffee and eggs before you go. My old sweetheart got big tired on his face."

"I am tired," Kauka admitted, "and worried. We're walking on thin ice. It's just luck that Thord and I weren't *both* up Mauna!" He gestured at a slope of Mauna Loa visible through the open windows. "We've been planning to spend a couple of days with our patients; then we postponed it till next week. With Coombs not available when Prudence started to *hanao*, you'd have had to send someone to get us." His dark concerned eyes met Loki's.

"Yes," she agreed.

"Have you seen Kieser's message? Brewer said he'd scribbled it down."

"I go find," Loki said cheerfully.

"Mama." Kauka caught her hands. "You're wonderful. You worked as hard as I did last night, but I bet you've been on guard every instant I rested."

"I only making womans jobs," she retorted. "Las' night, and night before, you ride many miles and work all day with poor peoples who like to get cure of *maipake*.. I only wait round at home."

"Which is the most exhausting business of all."

Loki gestured, making it of no consequence. "You go clean up and I find paper with what Kieser's saying."

Going to the *lanai*, she began rummaging through the litter of paper on Brewer's desk, on the side nearest to the telephone.

Finally she found a sheet under a book, scrawled in pencil, glanced at it, saw Kieser's name after several lines of writing. Folding the sheet into a small wad, she gazed at the sunlight-filled garden. Her nature, long accustomed to lush growth, yearned to be outside enjoying tangled greens and bursting flowers. Thisbe was pacing among the beds of blossoms, hands locked behind his back, head thrust forward, like a person plotting some intricate campaign. Her soul condemned and pitied him in the same flash. At such a time, when a man's life cycle had been fulfilled, when the generation he had produced had reproduced itself again to go on, instead of joy and pride, only hate and ashes filled his heart.

She headed for Prudence's bedroom, where she knew Kauka would be. He was just placing the baby to nurse. Prudence looked up, her plain features radiant.

"I feel boundless," she said in a voice as thin and weak as a thread. "There's my husband"—she signed feebly at the floor—"there's my baby."

"You're a good girl." Kauka brushed a limp strand of hair off her forehead. "You had a bad time but all you need now is rest."

"Nothing can touch me." Prudence's voice grew suddenly strong. "I tore what I wanted to from life, and I'll hang onto it. Where's Father?"

"Walk in the garden," Loki said.

Brewer heaved to a sitting position, then to his feet. "How's tricks, old girl?" he asked.

"Tiptop," she assured him.

"That's the only kid we'll ever have," Brewer asserted. "I thought the top of my damn head would blow off when you were fighting to get the little beggar into the world."

"Always man speak this-kind after baby come, but soon forget—and have another kid." Loki's mirth filled the room.

Brewer watched his son nursing. Loki's eyes brushed Kauka's. She handed him the wad of folded paper. He slid it into his pocket. Brewer kissed Prudence's forehead.

"I've got to shower, and see what's afoot for the day. But I'll have breakfast in here and sit beside you."

When the baby had finished nursing, Loki covered them both and slipped out. Kauka was just coming from the kitchen. "This" —he tapped his coat pocket—"is damning stuff."

"I no read," Loki told him.

Drawing the paper from his pocket, Kauka started to hand it to her.

"You tell me what-kind Kieser say, Papa."

Glancing about to assure himself no one was in earshot, Kauka began:

" 'Sending an ample supply of chaulmoogra. Your last four letters were waiting for me at Kin Yang's. Elated to know two of your patients are reacting to the new treatment. This will be a bombshell in the medical world. Keep up the good work. As soon as my affairs here in the Orient are in order, I'll head for Hawaii. Kieser.' "

"Central only Hawaiian girl, Papa. She no pay attention to radio message; only like to catch pay and have good time," Loki reassured him. "And Brewer so scare about Prudence, when he talk with Central he just write down."

"Probably you're right," Kauka agreed. "I wonder what hit April? She was steady enough when she left after dinner. I could wring Dale's neck."

"April, never she making big noise, but she got plenty dynamites inside and all burn up with loves. And always if she not tops Hiram scare like hell. So, better you go. Thord no get back till very late. Might-be seem little funny for you to go back to Kona?"

"Not particularly. I've too many other things on my mind."

The sound of a car coming at high speed shattered the morning quiet. Loki tensed.

"It's probably Hiro," Kauka said, watching the driveway.

April's roadster flashed into view. They hurried to the *lanai*. She was drawing up. Brandishing a wildly happy arm, she piled out of the car, and charging up the steps embraced Loki and Kauka.

"Look—*look!*" she squealed like a ten-year-old, thrusting an expensively engraved piece of paper at them.

Kauka read it at a glance. "My child, I'm happy for you—"

Loki scanned it. "Dale *get* marry!" she cried. "Oh, April, that swell. Now he no care if you and Thord hitch up."

"I feel as if an angel had left millions—to everyone in the world! I'd like to give a *luau* for every living person, a *luau* that would never end!" April cried. Happy tears spilled down her cheeks. "Yesterday I felt licked. Today—" She flung out her arms as if hugging the universe.

"You show to Hiram yet?" Loki asked.

April nodded excitedly. "You don't have to go to Kona today, Kauka. I told Daddy—"

"What-kind Dale say he make if you marry up with Thord?" Loki gasped.

"Of course not, but I faked a bit—said I hadn't wanted to—to hurt Dale's feelings by marrying anyone else too soon."

Loki exhaled a great breath of relief. Thisbe came slowly up the steps.

"Oh, it's you, April." He forced affability into his voice. "I thought it was Hiro. Are you taking me home? I'm ready."

"No, Hiro is coming for you," she said, then turned back to Loki and Kauka. "When'll Thord be down?" she asked breathlessly.

"About ten tonight."

"I'll burst if I have to wait until then to see him. I'll saddle a horse and ride up to meet him—"

"My child"—Kauka cut her off gently, but his voice rang with authority—"you cannot do that. You must not!" Then he glanced over his shoulder instinctively.

Thisbe's small irritable back was just disappearing into the bedroom he had occupied. Kauka and Loki's eyes met; a tiny frown creased April's smooth forehead, then vanished as an upsurge of happiness lifted her.

"If he did overhear," she said in a quick whisper, "it could mean anything—or nothing."

Kauka nodded.

"You like see Prudence's fine boy?" Loki asked.

"Of course," April said.

Hiro drove in. "Thisbe, the car's here," Kauka called.

Thisbe came out of the spare bedroom; Brewer charged out of Prudence's. "Say good-by to your daughter," he ordered in low tones.

Thisbe glared at him.

"Step on it, or, parson or no parson, I'll knock your damned block off! Your brand of Christianity may not demand such a gesture, but us publicans and sinners got the milk-of-human-kindness, as the Bible calls it, in our veins and not just stale vinegar. Now—in you go!" Brewer brandished a big boot in the vicinity of Thisbe's rear.

Thisbe drew himself up, but slid into the bedroom. Brewer mopped his florid neck. "I'd like to kick him from hell to breakfast. He don't deserve a fine grandson, or a daughter like Prudence."

By common unspoken consent, they waited until Thisbe reappeared. His face was chalky, his scrawny neck blotched with scarlet. He passed them as if they did not exist, muttering to himself under his breath.

"Fret not thyself because of evil-doers, neither be thou envious against the workers of iniquity, for they shall soon be cut down like grass, and wither as the green herb."

"Phooey!" Brewer said. "The house'll feel cleaner when you're out of it."

Thisbe did not turn.

When the car drove off, Brewer hitched up his breeches. "Tell my girl I've got to get about the day's work, but I'll have lunch in her room." And he went rolling off.

"I'm going home, Mama, I have plenty to do," Kauka announced. "There's stuff in the laboratory which must be finished up before I go to Mauna Loa tonight. April, will you drive me over and fetch me back here around four this afternoon? I want another look-see of my patients before Thord takes over."

"I'd love to, Kauka."

Loki was seated on the steps making a lei when April returned.

"I like fine to have plenty flowers by me." She gestured at blossoms heaped extravagantly on the steps beside her.

"You miss Kona," April announced, sinking down beside her.

"Little bit, but Kau fine too." Loki's eyes lighted. "Kauka and Thord making big-kinds there, and now, since us come here, seem like you and Thord's troubles, all *pau*."

"It seems like it. I'm going to radio and congratulate Dale." Heading for Brewer's desk, she spent several minutes scribbing on a sheet of paper. Every so often she crossed out a word and rewrote it; then finally she brought the message to Loki.

"You read, April," Loki begged.

April smiled faintly, studied the paper, then began in her low voice:

" 'Your announcement received. I'm happy for you. May Lei Alohas always hang over your door. Now they can hang over mine, too. Please keep mum about what you know. I'll bless you. Reply as fast as possible. April.' "

"That okay," Loki said heartily. "Inside, sure, Dale nice guy. Send quick. After you hearing from him you feel fine."

April headed for the telephone. When the message was given she returned to where Loki sat. Loki went on working. April's lips moved silently.

"What-kind you making, April?"

"I'm not afraid, but I'm praying."

"Good idea." Loki gazed at the land about her holding the house in its green arms. The island flaunted vigor; beauty lay on the sea. Impulsively she kissed April's cheek.

"I feel sure," April said slowly, "that Dale won't spill what he knows—"

At noon, Brewer came in to lunch. About three the telephone rang. April flew to answer it. "It's Kauka. He wants me to fetch him," she said a little disappointedly. "I hoped it was the radio from Dale."

She returned with Kauka within the hour. Afternoon shadows were lengthening across the island. As they came up the steps the telephone began ringing. April scooted to it. When she turned away, her face was aflame.

"What-kind Dale say?" Loki asked.

"Just a second." Dashing to Brewer's desk she began scribbling, then read:

" 'Thanks for your speedy congratulations. Your request goes against the grain, but it's your funeral. Best of luck anyway. Dale.' "

Behind the oddly chosen words there was in her young voice the sound of angels chanting.

"Swell on him," Loki exulted.

"Well, my child," Kauka said, "God is in His heaven—"

"—and all's right with the world!" April finished. "Won't Thord be bowled over? Isn't it swell Daddy's all for us? Now, except for the faint possibility of that old mess coming to light—but I know it won't after this succession of miracles."

Kauka nodded.

"Better you have early supper here," Loki suggested when he rejoined them. "Then after, you can go home and send Thord over here."

"Okay. I'll rest for a while. Wake me about eleven." And he headed silently for the spare room he had occupied the night before.

Loki and April sat watching a blue twilight sifted with platinum slowly blurring the outlines of the island. Brewer rode in. When supper was announced, Loki woke Kauka and they all sat down. Brewer headed the table, the lordly importance of a man newly a father pouring from him. Just as dessert was coming in, hoofs sounded in the driveway.

"Thord," Loki announced.

April hurried to meet him. Several minutes elapsed before they came in, looking as if they had been washed in light. Thord's arm was about April's shoulders, her slim arm circled his lean waist.

"So the wind blows this way, does it?" Brewer shouted with boisterous approval. "Doubtless my noble example inspired you. Nothing like the holy estate of matrimony—nothing. Take it from an old reprobate like me."

"How you home so soon?" Loki asked.

"I figured that Prudence was about due to—"

"It's all over. I have a son!" Brewer boomed.

"So April told me."

They stood side by side like beings freshly descended to earth from some far, shining planet. Kauka's eyes glowed.

"Here are your orders for the next twenty-four hours, Thord. You're off duty until tomorrow night at ten. Loki will stay with Prudence. I'll carry on."

"We're going to tell Father and Mother right away," April said.

"How long does it take to get a marriage license in Hawaii?" Thord asked, his eyes deeply blue under the red flag of his hair.

"With Hiram's weight behind the match, it'll be accomplished in nothing flat," Kauka grinned.

Brewer banged the table delightedly. "I used to sing a song with a hell of a lot of wisdom in it." Leaping to his feet he dominated the room, then, throwing back his head, began singing:

> *"There's a jolly Saxon proverb*
> *That goes very much like this,*
> *That a man first tastes of heaven*
> *When he wins a woman's kiss!*
> *If you want the Golden Apples*
> *You must climb the tree and shake it;*
> *If a thing is worth the having,*
> *You must go right out and take it.*
> *There's danger in delay,*
> *For the sweetness may forsake it,*
> *So go it, bashful lovers—*
> *While you're young!"*

[343]

His big, whisky-roughened voice rang against the ceiling.

"Fine! Fine!" Loki applauded.

"Hell, where are my manners? I must pour a libation to Eros to celebrate this momentous event!"

Heading for the sideboard, Brewer mixed five drinks and handed them around. "May you both be as happy as Prudence and I are, kids!" he shouted. "I know it's senseless to tell you to sit down and eat. Go get spliced, the quicker the better."

"That's just what we intend to do," Thord said.

"Fine! On your way, on your way!" Brewer boomed.

"I hope tomorrow you come back marry peoples," Loki said, reaching out and kissing first April, then Thord.

"If it's legally possible, we will be," Thord asserted.

"Shall we go?" April asked.

Thord caught her hand and his face was answer enough. They walked out of the room, moving as if they were silhouetted against a golden dawn.

"Well, that's a fine bit of business," Brewer said with noisy satisfaction. "The Wilde stock of this present generation is as flat as good whisky polluted with water. It needs new blood. That young red-head will inject dynamite into the next crop of pups."

Having uttered his pronouncement, he settled down to finish the meal, but while he occupied himself with dessert it was evident that his mind was mulling over events, adding them, subtracting them, dividing them.

"Well, I'll have to be on my way," Kauka said.

"Hell, in all the excitement of the past twenty-four hours, I'd clean forgotten to tell you about the wireless Central phoned in. The message is on my desk somewhere," Brewer said. "Don't recall what it said. It was about some oil."

Kauka's and Loki's eyes met. Brewer noted it.

"What in sam-hill are you and Thord up to, anyway?" he demanded. "From cocoanut radio I hear that one or the other of you go up Mauna Loa every night. It's none of my damned business, but it's human nature to be interested in the activities of your friends."

Kauka looked into his eyes. "When you know what we're up to," he said, "you may not want to call us that." He let the words sink in.

Brewer looked bewildered.

"I might as well tell you now, so you can break off connections with us. It's only a question of time before we have to turn over the data we've collected to the Government—or get found out."

Brewer stared at him. "But what in the hell—"

Taking the sheet of paper from his coat pocket, Kauka laid it before Brewer. With the ponderous application of the stout, Brewer read it aloud, thought for a few moments, then shook his head.

"Sounds like a bunch of Greek to me," he muttered, then said slowly, "Chaulmoogra . . . Chaulmoogra . . ." Suddenly his jowls grew ashen. "Isn't—wasn't that the name of some oil that was used in the treatment of leprosy about 1890?"

"Yes."

"You mean—" Perspiration streamed down Brewer's temples.

"We're using it again."

"Great God! Are you telling me that you and Thord have got a bunch of lepers corralled up Mauna Loa and are treating them secretly?"

"Yes."

"I know that concealing lepers is a penitentiary offense," Kauka said, looking into Brewer's frightened eyes. "I've tried, twice, to get on Molokai. Once, some while back, again when Doctor Melville was here taking blood tests, but their quota of doctors was filled."

"But *great God!* All hell will burst loose when—"

"If it comes out that we've had a secret leprosarium up Mauna Loa?" Kauka asked.

"Yes. Even if you turn in what data you've collected, your patients and yourselves, Kona will have hydrophobia!" Reaching out, Brewer drew the scribbled radio message toward him and studied it. Finally he looked up.

"I must have been more roused and upset over Prudence starting

[345]

to pup than I realized, when I took this down. This doesn't look like my handwriting at all."

"Wait—" Loki managed her voice with a supreme effort.

Both men stared at her. Her hand stole to her heart and froze against it.

"This morning when I go look the garden, before waking up Papa, I seeing Thisbe at your desk."

Brewer looked as if he were about to blow up.

"That scum was prying among my papers trying to get something on me! He'd do anything to ruin the lot of us. He hates me for marrying Prudence, and you two for putting over the match." His face was purple. "And—and he found this, or the original of Kieser's message in *my handwriting,* added two and two together, then faked this!" He pounded the sheet. of paper, leaped up and began charging around the room like a wounded bull. "He's—he's got the *original!*"

37

"PAPA," Loki said in a voice of unconcealed despair, "whatkind you going to do?"

Kauka studied the sheet of paper lying on the table.

"There's only one thing I can do now, Mama. Bring in those poor lepers and give them up. And myself, too. Thisbe may act immediately, or delay while he tries to get more on us. That's what I'm hoping. If he's already seen Hiram, Sheriff Keoke may arrive any minute. If he's playing a waiting game, I can make my move first, which will be a lot better than being arrested and dragged in." He stressed the last words.

"Yes," Loki agreed, "but—" Her mournful eyes went to Kauka's.

"I know what you're thinking," Kauka said. "Those men and women came to me trusting that I wouldn't report them. Our agreement was, that if after I'd treated them with chaulmoogra for six months and no noticeable improvement in their condition was evident, they were to return to their hideout. The only redeeming aspect is—"

"If there is one," Brewer interrupted.

Kauka looked at him, silently took a mental hurdle, and asserted quietly, "There is one. Two of the men I've been treating solely with the ethyl esters of the oil haven't reacted for the past two months. It at least suggests we're on the trail of a cure. All outward symptoms of the disease have disappeared and repeated tests show their bloodstreams are remaining clean of the bacillus of leprosy."

Brewer and Loki stared at him, awed.

"When the Medical Board sees Eole's and Kanaloa's case histories, they'll be held at the Kalehi Receiving Station. If they continue not to react, they'll be let out on parole eventually, coming in of course at intervals for further tests and checkups. It's too early in the game to claim we've succeeded in permanently arresting the disease. Only time will prove that. But we'll have some justification for what we've been doing. We can hold out a gleam of hope for Homer, and others who, to date, have had no hope."

"If the two men stay arrested, as you put it," Brewer began, his face crimson with excitement. "Great God—"

"Papa, Papa"—Loki choked, her face quivering—"you speak true? Why-for you fellas no telling me this fine news before?"

"We wanted to be absolutely certain, Mama. If only this hadn't happened—" he indicated the message—"if only we could have had more time. Actually, we're just on the fringe of proving—"

"You ought to thank your stars you have something concrete to turn over to the Medical Board," Brewer said.

"I am, but there are those others to think of. It's grim for them. Molokai." Kauka gave a lonely sigh.

"Might-be better I ride up with you," Loki suggested. "I little scare for you. Might-be every fellas very *huhu*—mad. Might-be—"

"No, Mama, I'll manage. I haven't told the others yet that Eole and Kanaloa are to all purposes cured, that when they go to Molokai the treatment we've used with success on these two will be used on all." Getting to his feet he stood still, a figure of dignity and courage. "If only Thord weren't mixed up in this. Just as his and April's way seems clear—another obstacle. My one hope is they'll be safely married by tomorrow, or at least before Thisbe springs his bolt. Fireworks won't faze April, any more than they will you." He looked at Loki with love in his eyes.

"I no care any-kind, Papa, I so happy for what you and Thord have already make with the oil. If other fellas who have *maipake* get cure, all this *pilikeas* not matter after by-and-by."

Kauka nodded while he pondered the problem before him.

"It's going to be painful to tell the ones who haven't improved, that they must give themselves up. They—trusted me. Then there's no certainty that the ethyl esters of the oil will work in all cases

[348]

and on all types of leprosy. If those I'm compelled to turn in, who have active the bacillus in their blood, don't react, they'll have to remain on Molokai—and on my conscience forever. No matter what may be accomplished in the future, to those unfortunates, I am, and will always be, their—betrayer."

Rising, he started heavily for the door. Loki followed him. They went slowly down the hall, crossed the *lanai* and halted at the steps. To the south, against fields of blazing stars, the dark shape of Mauna Loa loomed.

"Papa—"

"Yes, Loki?"

"When first us marry and got big fire in our hearts, I not loving you so much as now."

"I know." He kissed her forehead, went down the steps and, mounting Thord's horse, rode off toward the dark mass of the volcano.

Loki gazed at stars pouring down their enormous peace while she listened to hoofbeats getting fainter and fainter. When they ceased she returned to the dining room. Brewer was busily drinking.

"Better no get too *ona*," she advised. "Might-be tomorrow everything blow up."

Brewer studied the contents of his almost empty glass. "Kauka gone?" he inquired.

"Yes."

"Last night," he said, "I was praying full blast hoping I'd reform, though I was scared I wouldn't. For long at any rate. Less than twenty-four hours have passed and I'm back at my old tricks. I know I won't go to bed till that bottle's empty, or I pass out." He pointed furiously at the whisky bottle. "And me, a husband—and a father. Bah!"

Next morning, while Brewer and Loki were breakfasting, April and Thord drove in, followed by the Wilde limousine with Hiram and Elsbeth in it. Brewer batted his hot, bloodshot eyes.

"The show's up," he muttered dully.

"Soon as I see their faces I knowing," Loki said.

Brewer followed her to the *lanai*. April and Thord were just getting out of the roadster. There was a sort of indefinable gladness and excitement in their every movement.

"Thisbe not make any-kind yet," Loki said in low tones to Brewer as she waited a welcoming arm.

Rushing up the steps, April embraced her while Thord opened the door of the limousine and assisted Mrs. Wilde out. Hiram followed, his gray face sly and satisfied.

"Thord and I are going to be married today, Loki. Here." She indicated the big *lanai*. "Mother wanted a church wedding, with trimmings, but Daddy—" She laughed on a high happy note.

Loki kissed her. Thord strode up the steps, followed more sedately by Hiram and Elsbeth.

"This is hardly the setting I'd pictured for April's wedding," Elsbeth began, gazing at Thord with fatuous approval, "but our young people"—her voice was possessive—"have taken matters into their own hands."

"And there's nothing to do but fall in step," Hiram added.

"Later," Elsbeth went on brightly, "we'll have a big reception and invite friends from the eight Islands to meet our new—son."

Carlos came in with the suitcases, his eyes gay, even his hair looking happy.

"Which room I put these, Miss April?" he asked, indicating the bags.

"I'll show you in a moment, Carlos," she said excitedly, then laid her hand on her mother's arm. "You better lie down. We can't get married till Kauka comes. When will he—" She hesitated, her eyes flying to Loki's.

Loki computed hurriedly. "Might-be three o'clock, but no can tell for sure."

Thord looked at her with puzzled eyes. "Three?" he said.

Loki nodded.

"Your house is seeing plenty, Brewer," Hiram remarked. "Last night a birth, today a marriage." Satisfaction rang behind the last word.

"Yes, it's seeing *plenty*," Brewer agreed.

[350]

"Who marrying you?" Loki asked.

"Reverend Thisbe. He'll be along any instant," Thord replied.

Loki's and Brewer's eyes met, the same thought in them.

"Thord, show Elsbeth which room she can have. Might-be, April, you like to rest too?" Loki suggested. "Bet-you-my-lifes never you sleeping las' night, just sit up and talk. Brewer . . ."

"Yes?"

"While all fellas look your fine boy, you and me make plan for the marry."

He nodded, realizing that Loki was endeavoring to get them away in order to talk to him alone.

"Look," she began when they had gone; then her eyes, which had been alert, dulled. "Car coming," she said heavily.

"Thisbe," Brewer muttered.

"This hell," Loki said under her breath. "Thord and April not knowing yet what-kind Thisbe have make."

"That's right. They left before I twigged that the message had been copied."

"Oh, what us do?" Loki almost wailed. "I no want April and Thord's marry—"

Thisbe drove in, stopped his car, and sat staring at the hood. Finally he got out, and he was holding the white sheet of paper.

"I catch on," Loki said hotly. "Thisbe waiting till every fella stop one place, then—dynamite, and every-kind blow up."

Thisbe beckoned to them jerkily. Slowly Brewer and Loki went down the steps and walked to where he waited. His eyes came up, then dropped to the paper.

"Already us fellas knowing what-kind you have make," Loki said when she could no longer endure the stifling silence. She indicated the paper.

"Go on, explode your bomb!" Brewer roared.

The Adam's apple in Thisbe's stringy neck jerked. "But—I can't," he mumbled, perspiration beading his skin. "When I got home last night I opened my Bible at random. The first line I saw was 'Even as ye do unto the least of Mine, ye do it unto me.' I got to thinking about what the lot of you have done, are doing. If this means what

[351]

it seems to mean . . . For thousands of years people have been searching to find a cure for leprosy. The only cure on record to date is the one in the Bible, when Christ—" Tears rolled down his dry cheeks.

Folding the paper up, he tore it into fragments with shaking hands, released the pieces and they fluttered slowly to the ground. Brewer watched, then grabbed at the car for support. Loki sat down on the running board.

"Good Thisbe, good Thisbe," she choked. "Wait one minute. When my leg get enough strong, I make big kiss on you. Now you happy, now you walking with God, and all peoples, so always you got big Aloha and peace in your hearts."

38

I THINK," Loki said, addressing Brewer, when the last sumptuous bouquet had been arranged to her satisfaction in the *lanai,* "no need to tell Thord, now, what-kind nearly happening. After he and April come back from honeymoon—"

"I agree with you entirely," Brewer interrupted jauntily. "No shadow must be cast on love's young dream."

Loki nodded and stepped back to survey her handiwork.

"Swell to tell Papa when he bring in the poor peoples with *maipake* they can go back to Mauna Loa."

"Yes, my father-in-law"—Brewer's evil eyes twinkled—"now he's come off his perch, is okay. If I can train him to heft a drink now and then, we'll get on fine." He glanced at the garden where Thisbe was pacing back and forth.

"Better you go wake up all fellas," Loki suggested. "Little more three o'clock. Papa coming any-time now. I go put pretty kimono on Prudence and dress up baby. Then you carry out and put on the *puune* so they can look at the marry. Now I wake April and Thord." She headed for the *puune* in a corner of the *lanai* where she had been arranging flowers. April and Thord lay with clasped hands among gaily colored pillows, like babes in the woods determined not to lose each other even in oblivion.

"Hey, wake up," she said, gently shaking first one then the other. Thord sprang to a sitting position. April opened her eyes.

Loki ran fond fingers through Thord's fiery hair. "Go dress up," she directed. "You, too, April. Papa come soon, then you marry."

"Loki," said Thord, "Hiram and Elsbeth want us to go to their

Keauhou beach place for our honeymoon. But it's putting a heavy load on Kauka."

Loki brushed it aside. "Papa got plenty God, and plenty *mana* inside him, so he plenty strong. He like fine for you and April to stop Keauhou for two-three days. Pretty place, no got telephone, nobody stop, only you two *kuuipos*. After you come back you stay with us at Kau."

"And from there we'll trim sail according to the wind," Thord finished, looking at her meaningly.

"Sure," Loki agreed. "Now dress *wikiwiki*."

"I'd like to have been married in the garden, as Mamo was," April said, "but Prue can't go out, and—" She gazed about the *lanai* with amazed eyes. "Oh, Loki, you've made *this* into a garden!"

"Not too bad," Loki laughed.

"It's beautiful!" April exclaimed, embracing her. Then she grasped Thord's forearm with both hands. "It doesn't seem possible we're going to be married, at last!"

When they disappeared, Loki beckoned to Thisbe and he came in from the garden.

"Look," she said happily, "when Prudence all fix-up pretty, Brewer bring her out here and you carry your *moopuna*. Soon as Prudence enough strong us have more fun, christen the small boy in your church!"

"Have they decided on a name yet?" Thisbe asked in his stiff way.

"I no know, but I think sure name him for you, too!" Her eyes danced.

He nodded in a vaguely pleased manner, like a person who, abandoning an old attitude has not, as yet, adjusted to the new one. Loki laid an approving hand on his thin shoulder. "Now, better you get every-kind ready for the marry."

He nodded and started toward the bedroom assigned to him.

Loki gazed at the sun-drenched garden, then spying Kauka riding in, rushed to meet him. His stocky figure sagged a bit from weariness and his face had a look of waiting upon it. Breathlessly she related the unexpected happy turn events had taken.

He gazed at her, stunned, then his eyes changed slowly. Expressions difficult to analyze flitted over his face as if he were thinking furiously; then the thoughts crystallized into decision.

"Fine, Mama, that's fine! Let's get the kids married and off on their honeymoon. Keauhou's just what they need."

"You bring in the poor peoples?" Loki asked as they started toward the house.

He nodded.

"They happy like any-kinds when you telling to them they can go back to Mauna Loa for you try out the new-kind"—she hesitated, then leaped joyfully on the elusive word—"*formula!*"

For half an hour the house echoed to hurrying feet. Prudence, and the fat, round-faced baby, were established on the *puune,* the men of the party assembled for drinks, looking superfluous as men do at baptisms, weddings, and funerals. Servants hastened about, setting out refreshments. Finally Loki waved from the hall.

"Little bride all dress up and ready," she called. "Better you guys line up."

Thisbe took his place before the improvised altar, fashioned out of a table solidly covered with gardenias. Kauka, Thord, and Brewer went to their assigned positions. Hiram waited for his daughter. Elsbeth came out crying softly, but her eyes leapt across the *lanai* to where Thord stood. Moving forward, she sat down on the *puune* where Prudence and her child were nested among piled cushions.

"Weddings," she murmured, dabbing at her eyes, "always—"

As she spoke, Hawaiian voices rose from the garden, filling the afternoon, blending into the sunshine. Softly at first, then louder as instruments and throats throbbed in unison.

Loki and April came down the hall. In a short white dress with a white carnation lei like fluffy snowflakes about her throat, and one gardenia sitting in a wave of her honey-colored hair, April looked hardly twelve years old. But her face, dewy and tremulous, radiant and resolute, was a woman's.

[355]

Taking her father's arm, she headed across the *lanai*. Her eyes saw nothing but Thord, his saw only her. Loki followed like a ship in full sail, moving triumphantly forward toward a long-waited landfall, at last safely in sight.

Thisbe began the marriage service, the old deeply moving words falling slowly from his lips. . . . Then, suddenly, it was done. Thord took April in his arms.

"Sha, I feel so happy I all weak," Loki said, and began joyously embracing everyone about her.

"*Welakahao!*" Brewer shouted. "Now for libations in honor of the bride and groom. Getting married is an exhausting business, but worth it, isn't it, old girl?" His eyes went to his wife and child.

Servants and musicians swarmed in to wish Thord and April happiness. The *lanai* echoed to voices, laughter, and fun. Hiram and Elsbeth stood about stiffly, but satisfaction enveloped them.

"My boy"—Kauka placed his hand on Thord's shoulder—"from the depths of my heart I wish you and April happiness, the lasting happiness that grows out of taking bumps and glory, defeats and victories—together."

"It'll be ours," Thord said, catching April's hand deeper into his.

She looked up. All the beauty of love and passion, the forgetfulness of self, which creates a greater self, was framed in the ivory oval of her face.

Bending, Thord kissed her; then he straightened up and gazed down at her. In the depths of both their eyes were strongholds of security to which they could retreat when they felt the need: old thoughts and ideals strengthened, new ones discovered, new understandings, new goals, which would forever put them beyond the reach of other people's confusions and anxieties.

"You kids better shove off," Kauka advised, "if you're not going to waste your three-day honeymoon. I'll expect you back," he hesitated, then continued resolutely, "Wednesday."

"Okay," April almost sang, "I'll get my coat."

"And I'll fetch the suitcases," Thord said.

They went off, hand in hand.

[356]

"That's a sound piece of business," Kauka commented, looking after them.

"It is," Hiram agreed. "Elsbeth, we'd better start."

"Yes, the children are dining with us before going down to Keauhou," she brightly informed those around her.

Loki looked at Kauka, and said under her breath, while amusement quivered on her long lashes, "Hiram and Elsbeth no can wait to show those old peoples in the big pictures what-kind new son they catching in the family."

Thord and April came out. Rice and flowers flew through the air. Laughing and ducking, they raced across the room and dashed for the roadster. Carlos held the door open triumphantly.

"Aloha! Aloha!" everyone called, crowding to the steps.

"Aloha!" they called back, waving happy arms, then streaked off into the plum-colored dusk.

"I so happy and so tired I have to sit down," Loki confessed, when Thisbe and the Wildes had gone. "Never in my lifes so many-kind things happening so quick. Now, after you telling the poor peoples waiting at our house they can go back to Mauna Loa—"

"I can't tell them—that," Kauka said.

"For why not?" Loki demanded.

"Because, Mama, before I came here I phoned Sheriff Keoke to come and get us, at eight o'clock."

Loki gave a low cry. "You have told him—"

"Everything."

She began to cry.

"Listen, Mama," Kauka said in his quiet, steady way, "this is best, for all concerned. Thord and I have worked under handicaps, with inadequate equipment. Speedier and more accurate results will be made when expert chemists of the Leprosy Investigation Board in Honolulu take off from where we've started. When I told my patients that Eole and Kanaloa's cases were arrested, they were not only eager to come in, but want word sent to other lepers hiding out to give themselves up and go to Molokai."

"But, Papa, you fellas have to go to jail and Thord and April just get marry!"

[357]

"No steamer sails for Honolulu until Friday. Hiram will put up bail for his son-in-law." Kauka smiled faintly. "Even if he blows up when he learns of this, as he will in a few hours, the kids will have their three days and a lifetime together—afterwards."

Walking up the steps he gazed across the dark shape of the island. Loki wiped her eyes, went to where he stood, and slid her arm through his.

"Papa, if all fella who got *maipake* no get cure—what?" she asked from some depth of thought.

Kauka gazed into her eyes. "Mama, for those who must suffer, others will some day profit. For those who profit from this new treatment, all those whose sufferings led up to it will not have died in vain."

Loki gave an understanding nod.

"By giving ourselves up, the ethyl esters of the oil will be used immediately in cases where delay might prove fatal. When a person gets a long enough perspective on events, he sees that everything falls eventually, into a divine pattern. Even Mamo's and Liho-liho's deaths"—his voice did not falter—"worked toward that end. Through them we learned about Homer. Because of their deaths, Thord's and my work with chaulmoogra was speeded up. And somewhere, maybe years hidden away, hidden in the future, the ultimate triumph, the complete victory, waits."

"I seeing," Loki said quietly.

Kauka glanced at his watch. "I have to go, Mama, I must be with them—when Sheriff Keoke comes."

"Might-be for whiles every peoples in Hawaii very *huhu*—mad with you—"

"I'm counting on the people of Hawaii to uphold me. From the tiny seed we've started, a great tree will some day grow."

Loki nodded, her face solemn. Kauka kissed her, then went down the steps toward his horse. Fresh cold wind poured down from forests, like a slow breath expelled from mighty lungs, whispering that the deeper the sorrow carved into a person's being, the more joy it could contain. Bulking high over Mauna Loa, piled clouds like splendid silver gods marched against the stars, their triumphant heads held high.

[358]

GLOSSARY

Aikane: friend.
Allis: chiefs.
Akuas: gods.
Aloha ka kow: love to the world.
Aloha no au: I have love for you.
Amakihis: a mountain bird.
Aole: no.
Apapanas: a mountain bird.
Arrigato: thank you.
Euris: cucumbers.
Haole: white man.
Hanao: to give birth.
Hapa-haole: half-breed.
Haupia: arrow-root and coconut pudding.
Hawaii no ka oe: Hawaii is "tops"; the best.
Hemo: take off.
Hemo ka paa'u!: pull off the skirt!
Hilo: a kind of grass.
Hilahila: shame.
Holuku: Hawaiian version of Mother Hubbard introduced by missionaries.
Huhu: mad or angry.
Hui: corporation.
Iiwis: a mountain bird.
Ino: drink.
Kahilis: ceremonial emblem.
Kahuna: spell.
Kane: man.
Kauka: doctor.

Kona: southerly gale.
Kapu: forbidden.
Kaukau: food or eat.
Kealakekua: Highway of the Gods.
Keiki: child.
Keiki o lani: child of heaven.
Kiawe: a kind of tree.
Kinni: gin.
Kipuka: forest meadow; opening in the forest.
Koa: a kind of tree.
Kokua: help.
Kuhui: a kind of tree.
Kukui: candlenut tree.
Kulihuli: shut up or be quiet.
Kulolo: coconut and sweet potato pudding.
Kuuipo: sweetheart.
Lanai: open-air sitting room.
Lauhala: leaf used in weaving mats.
Laulaus: meat, fish, and pork wrapped in *ti* leaves and steamed underground.
Luau: native feast.
Lehua: a kind of tree.
Maiki: good.
Maipake: leprosy.
Maile: vine.
Mahalo: thanks.
Mahalo nui loa: thanks a lot.
Makaloa mat: sacred mat for chiefs to sit on.
Malama: easy, or take it easy.
Malihini: stranger.
Malo: breech-clout.
Mana: spirit essence.
Manau: hunch.
Moemoe: sleep.
Moopuna: grandchild.
Mumus: short, loose garment for swimming or sleeping.

Ohia: a kind of tree.

Oke: okolehao.

Okole: rear end.

Okolehao: intoxicating native drink made from the root of the *ti* or *ki* plant.

Ona: drunk.

Opu: stomach.

Opihis: edible limpet.

Palaka: Hawaiian blouse worn by cowboys.

Palapalai: fern used in making leis and covering *luau* tables.

Paniolo: cowboy.

Pau: finished.

Pili grass: used for thatching huts.

Pilikea: wrong.

Pimai: Come!

Poi: native food used in place of bread.

Polelei: right.

Pula: exhausted.

Pupule: crazy.

Puune: corner bed common to Hawaiian houses.

Shoyu: soy sauce.

Tabu: forbidden.

Tapa: paper-like cloth made in Polynesia.

Ti: tuberous root from which *okolehao* is made.

Tutu: grandparent.

Ukana: package or bundle.

Ulaula: red.

Uma: wrestling with hands.

Wahine: woman.

Wahine u'i: beautiful woman.

Wanaao: ghost dawn.

Welakahao: hurrah!

Wikiwiki: quick or quickly.